KU-062-249

'A fresh, original love story beautifully told'
Rugh Hogan, author of *The Keeper of Lost Things*

'Warm, thought-provoking and unexpected – *Bonnie and Stan* is an uplifting reminder of the enduring power of true love'
Isabel Ashdown, author of *Lake Child*

'It's a total charmer, so sad but sweet and uplifting, staying with me long after I'd read it. I really enjoyed the sentiment that love stays with you after someone has gone, the feeling of reading it and it ending was the same'
Laura Kemp, author of *Bring Me Sunshine*

'Sweet, funny, heartbreaking and uplifting'
Rachael Lucas, author of *Finding Hope at Hillside Farm*

'I sobbed my way through this read. Heartbreaking yet funny, clever and life-affirming too'
Caroline Smailes, author of *The Drowning of Arthur Braxton*

'Full of heart, wit and rock and roll *Bonnie and Stan* is an uplifting joy to read. I highly recommend it'
Katie Marsh, author of *The Rest of Me*

Anna Stuart has wanted to be a writer ever since she sat up in her cot with a book. For years she wrote short stories and serials for women's magazines before being published by Pan Macmillan as a historical novelist under the pseudonym Joanna Courtney. Her *Queens of the Conquest* series, set in the pre-1066 years, has been published to acclaim in all formats including audiobook and been translated for European markets but she is delighted to return to the contemporary world for *Bonnie and Stan*.

BONNIE AND STAN

Anna Stuart

TRAPEZE

This edition first published in 2019 by Trapeze.

First published in Great Britain in 2019 by Trapeze,
an imprint of The Orion Publishing Group Ltd
Carmelite House, 50 Victoria Embankment,
London EC4Y 0DZ

An Hachette UK company

1 3 5 7 9 10 8 6 4 2

A CIP catalogue record for this book is
available from the British Library.

ISBN 978 1 4091 7763 0

Typeset by Born Group

Printed and bound in Great Britain by Clays Ltd, Elcograf S.p.A.

www.orionbooks.co.uk

For Brenda and Jamie
in friendship, real ale, and garlic golf ...

Chapter One

Stan stepped out of the hospital doors with the scrap of paper clutched so hard between his fingers it was starting to disintegrate against his sweaty skin. He forced himself to loosen his grip. Let the wind take the wretched thing – the words wouldn't change, however high they rose into the stark spring sky.

The lingering March chill stung his eyes, making them water. He rubbed them and glanced to his left. A concrete path led along the front of the hospital to a fenced-off area, optimistically called a 'Garden'. He could just make out the jaunty blue sign, fixed onto a plastic trellis threaded with shivering rose plants, inviting him to 'come in and relax'. Fat chance! Bonnie was waiting for him through there, pacing up and down, telling herself over and over that it was going to be good news and he would have to be the one to savage her gorgeous optimism with the sharp cut of his piece of paper.

'I'm so sorry, Bonnie,' Stan whispered.

He looked out across the car park to the sprawl of Liverpool beyond. He didn't come to the city much, but he was strangely glad of it today. It seemed right to get the news that his life was ending here, in the city where he'd first met Bonnie and it had felt as if it was truly starting. He glanced to the garden again and forced himself to move towards it.

Bonnie had not been happy to be sent out, he knew that. He wasn't even sure why he'd done it. He'd intended her to be with him to see the consultant, but when Dr Mirabi had asked, 'And will your wife be coming in with you?' he'd panicked and said that maybe it was best if she waited outside. She'd objected, of course, but his illness – possible illness, as it had still been back then – had given him a strange, calm certainty and he'd insisted.

'You can wait in the garden if you like,' Dr Mirabi had said to her kindly, and Stan had been glad the doctor was there to share the force of Bonnie's glare.

It had been the right decision, though. He wouldn't have wanted Bonnie in that blank room, wouldn't have been able to keep calm in the face of her distress. At least this way he could compose himself a little before he broke it to her.

Stan took three more steps towards the garden. A young woman was sitting on a bench ahead of him, wrapped so tightly in a blanket that only her head was visible. Her face, however, was turned up to the thin sun and her eyes were shut in quiet bliss. Stan guessed she hadn't felt fresh air for some time, and his eyes slid to the tired-looking older lady at the girl's side. Her mother, it had to be. She was angled towards the girl and watching her with the sort of terrified love that she must have felt since the day she was put in her arms as a newborn. He offered her a smile and she returned it.

'Spring's coming,' she said.

'I hope so.'

Her eyes pulled back to her daughter and Stan moved on. A sudden wind whipped across the car park, sending a Styrofoam cup scuttling across the pathway like a scared creature and tugging again at the letter in his hand. Once again, he considered letting it go, just sending it up into the clouds and forgetting about it, but Stan wasn't a man to turn his back on trouble. Forty years as a plumber and builder had taught him that ignoring even the smallest niggle only gave it licence to grow. Issues had to be faced head-on to stand a chance of being dealt with properly. More's the pity.

'It's liver cancer, I'm afraid,' Dr Mirabi had said as Stan sat there, mute and alone. 'Stage four.'

'Stage four?' Stan had asked blankly, and the doctor had stalled.

'Would you like to fetch your wife back in before we go through all this?'

'No! That is, no thank you. I can manage.'

'You're very calm.'

A little bit of Stan had been proud at that. Proud! How stupid was he? *Look at me, facing the news of my own mortality with a nice stiff upper lip.* Idiot! This wasn't the 1920s. He was allowed to rage and scream and even cry if he wanted – not that he did.

'Should I not be calm?' he'd asked instead.

'Oh no, no. That is, yes. Absolutely. It's the best way.'

The best way for what? Stan wondered now. He turned his eyes back to the city, letting them drift through the Liverpool bustle, over the Mersey and to the fields of the Wirral beyond. Home. In his mind's eye he could see the stakes he and Bonnie had planted in the ground two weeks ago, marking out the footprint of their dream house.

It had taken them years to get planning permission. Their twins had been bolshy teenagers when they'd bought up the land on the edge of the village, and now they were approaching middle age. But Bonnie had refused to give up and at last they'd done it. Regulations had changed, she'd said, though he suspected it was more that her name as an award-winning local architect had finally swayed the council.

It didn't matter. *That* piece of paper, with permission to build their dream home, had been so very welcome. They'd drunk champagne the day it had arrived – proper stuff they'd been saving from his seventieth – and Bonnie had posted her designs all over Facebook with words as bubbly as their drinks. *Dream house on the cards at last! So excited!! Now Stan and I can enjoy our twilight years in style!!!* She wasn't normally one for exclamation marks, his Bonnie, but that day they'd burst from her. And now his stupid slip of paper was going to crush them all into flat little full stops.

He pushed on towards the garden, stepping sideways to let a man on a mobility scooter move past. A tiny terrier sat in the basket at the front wagging its tail and the man's eyes were fixed upon his pet as he took it for a walk in the only way he was now able. What condition did he have, Stan wondered, and instantly hated the fact that he was now in a world in which everyone had something wrong with them.

He shoved his hands into his pockets as the man sailed round the corner of the hospital, accompanied by the dim whine of an electric engine and a small yap from the dog. Stan had been aware he'd lost weight recently, of course he had, but he'd just been quietly pleased with himself for not getting thickset. Fool. A bit of podge would have been far preferable to what was actually going on in his gut.

His fingers closed around his car keys. He drew them out slowly and looked into the face of Terry, the tiny troll key ring Bonnie had bought him years ago because his screwed-up face had reminded her of Stan on a bad morning. He wasn't sure when he'd started talking to Terry. On the whole, he was as grumpy as he looked but the chap was a good listener and right now that was exactly what Stan needed.

'If I hadn't bothered going to the doctor, Terry, I wouldn't be here now, would I? That would be better, wouldn't it?'

Terry shook his little head in the wind.

'You're right,' Stan groaned. 'I needed to know. At least this way I get to cherish my last, my last . . .'

4

The words did dangerous, bubbly things in Stan's throat and he swallowed madly. This couldn't be happening. He had things to do, so many things. There was a list. Bonnie had written it and pinned it to the fridge, as she had all the way through their marriage. In the old days it had featured jobs like 'paint over the damp patch' and 'find cheap sofa' and 'try not to kill your dad – you know he means well'. Later it had been 'buy Lisa ballet shoes' or 'find Rachael a new piano teacher' or 'take the girls to the theatre – they need some sort of culture'.

Now, alongside 'build dream house' were a thousand other treats. 'It's all fun from here,' Bonnie had scrawled at the bottom but nowhere on the list did it say 'fight off terminal disease'. Then again, that wasn't possible anyway, was it? Stan glanced back to the hospital. The young woman had got up from the bench now and was shuffling towards the doors into Oncology, her mother hovering after. Presumably she'd got cancer too, poor lass. Could Dr Mirabi treat hers? He did hope so.

'Have you got any questions?' the doctor had asked Stan.

'Can I be cured?'

Dr Mirabi had dressed the answer up in several 'so sorries' and various 'there are things we can do to ease matters', but in essence it had boiled down to one word: 'No.' Stan's illness – an illness he had not known he had until thirty minutes ago – was terminal. Dr Mirabi had been reluctant to give specifics but had eventually conceded that it was unlikely to be more than twelve months, and that had been more than specific enough for Stan.

Barring a miracle, this time next year he would be gone. His life was now finite, not in a 'we'll all die one day' way, or even in a 'we best enjoy our last years' way, but with the months and days and even hours nailed to the wall to be used with the utmost care.

Stan was close enough to the garden now to see the start of tiny buds on the thin roses. They were getting ready to burst into life, whereas he . . .

'Goodness, Stan,' he heard Terry admonishing. 'Get a grip. You're hardly the first and you certainly won't be the last. What makes your life so very special?'

There was, of course, only one answer to that: Bonnie. It had always been Bonnie. He'd known from the very first moment he'd seen her, right here in the heart of Liverpool, in a club bursting with music and chatter and exuberant, excitable hope, that he'd been put on this earth to be there for her, and now it seemed that was coming to an end.

'No!' he said out loud. 'No way. I'm not leaving her alone.'

The roses shook and he heard a little gasp in the garden and then footsteps coming towards him.

'Stan?'

And then there she was, Bonnie, stood beneath the trellis looking even more beautiful than the first day he'd seen her. She laughed at him when he told her how gorgeous she was, pointing into the mirror and scoffing at whatever imperfections she saw there, but for him their fifty-four shared years were written like a poem into the lines of her face, making it even more special with every day.

'Bonnie,' he stuttered.

'Stan, you chump. What on earth are you doing lurking out here?'

He almost smiled. Then he forced himself to draw in a deep breath, stepped up to her and held out the paper bearing his life sentence. She looked down at it and then back to his face and, to his shame, he felt tears well up as she opened her arms and he stepped into them.

'I'm sorry,' he gasped out. 'I'm so, so sorry, Bonnie. I've let you down.'

6

'Never.' She pulled him fiercely against her, crushing herself into the folds of his coat so it was almost as if they were both wearing it. 'You have never once let me down, Stanley Walker, and you aren't letting me down now. We'll fight this. We'll fight it together, and one way or another we'll win.'

Stan drew in a deep breath and let his tears soak into her white-blonde hair, and when he looked up he could see clearly again. He remembered the love in the eyes of the mother on the bench as her daughter had drawn the sun into her skin, and the joy in the scooter-man's face as he'd watched his dog wag its tail at the world, and he smiled. The roses were budding and Liverpool was as bright in the spring sunshine as it had been back when he'd first met his wife. And she was right, she must be right because they were Bonnie and Stan and they had to stay that way.

Chapter Two

February 1963

Bonnie Jessop closed the door of her tiny attic room and flung her book-bag into the corner. She was home, thank heavens, or at least what passed for home these days. She'd spent her first term in Liverpool living in university halls but had found them cold and unfriendly and after Christmas she'd snatched at the chance to move in with Susie-Ann, the one girl who'd been truly welcoming.

Bonnie loved it in the rough and tumble of Susie-Ann's house, and the Cobden family's warm welcome was a blissful contrast to the snotty reception she'd had from the other students on her architecture course, who treated her with suspicion and disdain because she was the only girl. It was stupid. There were plenty of girls in art and design and interior decoration, but the minute you wanted to draw houses rather than cushions or pretty pictures everything seemed to change.

'I'll show them,' Bonnie muttered, retrieving her book-bag and looking for something to wipe off the muck from where a gaggle of art students had 'accidentally' knocked it into a puddle. They'd been girls, all of them; surely they should be on her side? But Bonnie had learned quickly enough that the girls were often the worst. All except Susie-Ann, of course. Susie-Ann was different.

Her friend and new housemate had a broad Scouse accent, eye-catchingly short skirts and an irreverent attitude, and she stuck out even more than Bonnie around campus. It appeared that she was the white sheep of a contentedly black flock – her three older brothers spent their days moving goods off the back of the city's lorries faster than the police could keep up. As a result they had an endless supply of up-to-date clothes and, most importantly to Bonnie, records hot off the American ships down the docks.

'Hey there! Bonnie? You up here?' There was a clatter of high-heeled shoes on the stairs and Susie-Ann burst into the room, her long dark hair in big rollers and a green face pack slathered over her pretty face. 'You *are* here! Thought I heard you.' Susie-Ann took in the sight of Bonnie's muddy bag and stuck her hands on her miniskirted hips. 'Those bastards been at your books again? It's too bad, Bon, really it is. I'll let our kids loose on them, shall I? They can be dead scary when they want, so they can.'

Bonnie didn't doubt it. Setting the three Cobden boys on Bonnie's tormentors would certainly do the trick, but her Aunt Nancy had brought her up to stand on her own two feet and she wasn't about to stop doing that just because she was miles away from her sleepy Cheshire village.

'It's fine, really. I just dropped it.'

Susie-Ann raised a perfectly plucked eyebrow but then shrugged.

'Have it your own way. Who cares any road – it's the Jac tonight!'

She grabbed Bonnie's arm, squealing, and Bonnie couldn't help but squeal with her. She'd loved music ever since she was tiny and the famous Jacaranda club had the best bands in town. Her earliest – and only – memories of her long-gone parents were of them dancing. They'd been solid, hard-working people, her father an accountant and her mother a maths teacher, and Bonnie remembered her young life as a largely serious business, save in the evenings when they'd let Charlie Parker and Ella Fitzgerald creep up through the needle of the gramophone and spark them into life.

Bonnie remembered waking to the sound of jazz and creeping down to sneak a peek at her parents dancing in each other's arms just like Ginger Rogers and Fred Astaire. She'd got Aunt Nancy to play their favourite records endlessly after their deaths, as if it might make them dance on in her memory, and she still treasured those songs now.

As she'd got older, though, she'd moved on from jazz, discovering Buddy Holly, Eddie Cochran and the heart-melting glory that was Elvis, and her Aunt Nancy had insisted that Liverpool was the place Bonnie had to be. There were musicians doing amazing things there, she'd assured Bonnie, and Bonnie had only been at the university for a week or two when a group of local lads called the Beatles had exploded into the big time with 'Love Me Do'.

Bonnie had longed for friends to go to the buzzing clubs with, but the girls in her hall had spent all their time in the library and the boys on her course had taken delight in excluding her. Many was the night she'd lurked outside the entrances to the Jacaranda and the Cavern, longing for the courage to go in alone, but it wasn't until Susie-Ann had swept her under her wing that she'd ever had the chance. But now, tonight, Bonnie was actually going to a gig at the Jacaranda and not just going there, but going there on a blind date with the lead singer of tonight's band, the Best Boys.

'Spike,' Bonnie said out loud, hugging her bag tight, not even noticing the mud as she tried to imagine what on earth it would be like to be that close to a real musician.

He sounded so young and cool and glamorous, a world away from the staid Tonys and Nigels who'd asked her out back home, and she was in equal measures thrilled and terrified about the night ahead.

'Don't get too hung up on the wretched boy,' Susie-Ann said, pulling her from her reverie, 'or you'll make him even more big-headed than he is now. But come on – we've got to get ready.'

She grabbed the bag from Bonnie and flung it aside, edging her towards the door.

'Where are we going?'

'Front room. Iron's on.'

'What?'

But Susie-Ann was tugging her down the stairs, and if she didn't want to tumble down all three flights she had little choice but to acquiesce. They burst into the front room to find the rest of the Cobden family gathered around the little TV set the boys had procured from who-knows-where two weeks ago. The three boys, John, Mark and Kevin, were lounging on the lime-green settee, another new acquisition that sat incongruously in the otherwise beige room. Mr Cobden was in his saggy old armchair, wreathed in smoke, and Mrs Cobden was stood at the ironing board behind him.

'Mam!' Susie-Ann said indignantly. 'Get off – that's for Bonnie's hair.'

'What?!' Bonnie and Mrs Cobden demanded at the same time, but Susie-Ann just hustled Bonnie forward, sweeping her mother out of the way.

'It needs to be straight,' she announced, bending Bonnie over so that her shoulder-length hair was spread out on the board.

'Straight?' Bonnie gasped, trying to put a hand to the careful waves she always styled into her blonde hair.

'Yep. You look very sweet and all, queen, but it's just not the in thing any more. You ever see Jean Shrimpton with a wave?'

Bonnie shook her head – or as much as she could with her hair pinned to the board.

'Good. Now, stay still and let me sort you out.'

Susie-Ann lifted the iron like a weapon. The boys all looked curiously over and even Mr Cobden waved smoke away to watch.

'Susie, no!' Mrs Cobden gasped as her daughter brought the iron down and ran it smoothly over Bonnie's blonde hair.

There was a soft crackle and out of the corner of her eye Bonnie saw strands rising on the static as her friend lifted the iron again but her wavy hair, miraculously, was straight. Everyone stared.

'Well I never,' Mrs Cobden said. 'Will you look at that. It's silky-smooth, lass.'

Bonnie tried to stand but Susie-Ann was already turning her to do the other side and all she could manage was a grateful smile to her host. When she'd first arrived at the Cobdens she'd feared that she'd never fit into their anarchic household, despite their warm welcome to a friend of Susie-Ann's. She'd noticed Mr and Mrs Cobden peering at her over supper and thought that they were taking in her conventional clothes, middle-class manners and polished speech and wondering if Susie-Ann would end up like her.

She'd liked to think they hoped so, but feared it was actually an outcome they dreaded and had felt awkward around them until she'd found out that every one of the Cobdens loved music. From the moment they'd plugged in the gramophone and pulled out their collection of mostly bootleg singles, Bonnie had slotted right in. After just a few weeks, she felt far more comfortable around the rough-and-tumble family.

Not that she was exactly used to the quiet life, she reflected as Susie-Ann contorted her over the board to do the back of her hair, the boys still watching on. Her father's younger sister,

Nancy, had moved in to care for her when her parents had been killed, but at twenty-two she'd been barely more than a child herself and it had never been a conventional upbringing. Nancy was a tiny woman, barely five foot tall and with rather jumbled features, but she radiated an energy that drew people to her from far and wide and the house had always been full of fun.

She was an inventive cook at best, and apt to forget about eating altogether if she had friends round – which she often did – so Bonnie had learned to put meals together as quickly as she'd learned to mix the perfect vodka martini. Having left the Wrens to care for Bonnie, Nancy had a work ethic every bit as strong as her nose for a party, and had been fiercely adamant that Bonnie do well at school and push herself in life. It was she who had championed Bonnie's right to study architecture and helped her secure the place at Liverpool.

Bonnie knew Nancy had been disappointed when she'd finally admitted at Christmas that she wasn't enjoying university life but, being an arch-fixer, she'd soon found the solution. The Cobdens had been delighted to have the extra money for their attic room and if Bonnie had to sometimes share it with cratefuls of unusual goods, it was a small price to pay. The studying was still hard but at least at the end of a day of lectures she could escape and breathe again.

'Perfect!' Susie-Ann announced now, finally letting her stand up. 'Isn't it perfect, Mam?'

'Perfect,' Mrs Cobden agreed dutifully, before adding, 'Can I iron the kecks now?'

'Do what you want,' Susie-Ann laughed. 'Bonnie and I have got make-up to be getting on with. Come on, Bon.'

And with that she swept Bonnie back up the stairs, pausing only to retrieve a large make-up case from her own room. Bonnie felt as if she were at the centre of a small whirlwind.

With her stomach already churning with nerves, she gave herself up to Susie-Ann's ministrations.

'Tell me about Spike,' she said as her friend pushed her down at the little desk beneath the window, sweeping her books to one side to make room.

'I've told you a million times! He's tall and dark and his hair is all quiffed up, just like Elvis. He's a plumber down the docks by day, but by night – which is more important, let's face it – he's a singer. He's got a voice like melted chocolate and deep brown eyes and the tightest little arse in Liverpool.'

'Susie-Ann!'

'What? It's important.' Susie-Ann was fixing big heated rollers around the bottom of Bonnie's hair and bent down in front of her to add, 'Don't let Sticks hear me say that, though. He's a right jealous one, Lord love him.'

Sticks was the drummer in Spike's band and Susie-Ann's boyfriend of almost two years. Bonnie hadn't actually met him yet but she'd heard him throwing stones at her friend's window just below her own and then climbing up the drainpipe to join her. She'd heard other noises too but had buried her head beneath her pillow and tried not to listen.

Aunt Nancy had been frighteningly forthright about sex.

'They'll all want to do it with you,' she'd told Bonnie shortly before she'd first left for Liverpool. 'Boys that age are panting for sex with practically anyone and especially a pretty girl like you, so you'll need to stand up for yourself.'

'To stop them?' Bonnie had asked, terrified.

'If you want to.' Nancy had laughed and taken her hands. 'But if you fancy it, then why not? It's rather fun, honestly, as long as you're careful and you only do it if *you* want to. OK?'

'OK,' Bonnie had squeaked, not convinced she'd ever want to.

One or two of the lads down the youth club had let their hands wander when they'd kissed her, but she'd found it more ticklish than sexy. Maybe with Spike it would be different, though. Maybe with Spike she'd feel the tingles that everyone seemed to feel in the films.

'Do you do it?' she'd dared to ask Nancy.

'Me?' For a moment Bonnie had thought she'd gone too far, but Nancy was almost impossible to offend. 'Course I do, sometimes – if I want to.'

'But who with? I've never seen a man stay the night.'

At that, though, Nancy had just winked and said, 'It doesn't have to be with a man, sweetheart,' and Bonnie's head had spun with the sudden realisation of just how much she had to learn about the world.

In the event, though, the boys at university hadn't seemed to want to do anything but sneer at her, and so she'd been able to avoid the thorny issue of sex all term. Susie-Ann's world, however, felt like a very much more grown-up place and she was already worried what her gorgeous date might expect of her.

'Is Spike very cool?' she asked Susie-Ann as the other girl layered mascara onto her eyelashes with careful concentration.

'Spike? Don't make me laugh! He's just a kid from down the road and don't you forget that, whatever act he tries to pull on you. He can be bit of a knob if you're not on to him quick, but he's a handsome one all right. And a dead good singer. He's going to be famous – as famous as bloody Paul. They all are.'

'Paul McCartney?' Bonnie breathed, though she already knew the answer.

She'd quizzed Susie-Ann endlessly about the Best Boys and knew full well that it was their avowed intent to be the next big Merseybeat band, and she felt her stomach fizzing with joy that she was soon going to meet them.

'I've had my new dress hanging up all day,' she said, indicating the alcove below the dormer window.

She'd bought it last week with Aunt Nancy's Christmas money. It had cost more than she'd ever usually spend but Nancy's new friend Astrid, an Amazonian Swedish woman with a huge laugh and a doting way of looking at Nancy that made Bonnie's head spin, had added to the pot and with Spike to impress, she'd decided to splash out. It was red and white gingham – just like Brigitte Bardot, or so Susie-Ann said – and it was short, a good inch above the knee. It had a pleated skirt and a bow at the neck and she felt both playground-small and backstreet-grown-up in it. It was quite the most risqué thing she'd ever worn, but she was going to be with the band so she had to fit in, right?

'*Head up, Sweet Bonnie,*' she could imagine Nancy saying in her crisp voice. 'Wear it like you mean it!'

Automatically she stuck her head up and Susie-Ann squeaked in protest as the super-pale lipstick she was applying smudged with the movement.

'Hold still, idiot, or we'll never get you beautiful in time.' She pulled back and then grinned. 'What am I banging on about? You'd be beautiful in a bloody coal sack, Bonnie Jessop. Spike is going to do his nut when he sees you.'

'Really?'

'You better believe it, queen. Right, dress on and you can have a look at yourself.'

She whipped out the rollers and then stood back to pass Bonnie her dress. Bonnie stepped into it and let her friend zip it up at the back. The nerves were fizzing stronger than a sherbet dib-dab in her stomach and she hardly dared look in the mirror as Susie-Ann held it up. When she finally did open her eyes, she stared in astonishment. Was that really her?

Her fringe was flat against her forehead and the ends of her now straight hair were curled out instead of under. Her super-dark eyes and pale lips made her look like a negative of the girl she'd been before and she stared and stared, wondering how on earth she'd find the nerve to inhabit this glamorous creature.

'Beautiful,' Susie-Ann pronounced. 'You look like something off the cover of *Cosmopolitan*. Spike will die for you!'

She beamed proudly and Bonnie drew in a deep breath and nodded.

Wear it like you mean it! Nancy's voice said in her head again, and she was determined to do just that.

'Bonnie! Charmed to meet you.'

Spike took her hand and planted an extravagant kiss on it before raking his fingers through his dark quiff.

'You too,' Bonnie managed.

Spike was every bit as cool as Susie-Ann had described. He was wearing a dark suit with a tight cut that showed his toned legs and a high-collared shirt that framed his handsome face. He was tall but not so tall she had to strain to look up to him, and muscled without being too showy about it. And his eyes! His eyes were the deepest chocolate brown, and Bonnie was sure she could melt right into them. She felt heat radiate out from the spot his lips had touched and put her hand to her burning cheek as he drew her into the Jacaranda coffee house. She'd stood outside so often that it was unbelievable to finally be heading inside, and it was every bit as fantastic as she'd imagined.

The Jacaranda was a tiny little place with a chrome-trimmed bar running the length of the thin room, and people were crammed into every bit of space. In the far corner a jukebox held court, coquettishly flashing its lights and pouring out Elvis's syrupy voice for a penny. Bonnie could feel the pulse of the music beating time against her skin and the air buzzed with conversation as if someone had wired up all the words to the electricity.

'I've heard so much about the Best Boys,' she gushed to Spike once he'd wormed them into a space at the bar but it sounded horribly naive, so she quickly added, 'Are you ready to play?'

'Born ready, honey!' Spike gave her a broad wink that seemed to instantly dry her throat and she could do little more than giggle in reply. He leaned in closer. 'Susie-Ann said you were a stunner, Bonnie, and she was right, too. Let me get you a drink.'

She nodded dumbly and was grateful when Spike turned to the bar. She glanced round for Susie-Ann but her friend had disappeared into the pulsing crowd; it was up to her from here on in.

Head up, Sweet Bonnie, she told herself in Nancy's voice and looked around the bar as Spike ordered coffee. She almost gave herself away again by gasping in astonishment at the space-age machine behind the counter and had to turn it into a discreet cough. The barman was turning knobs and handles and the machine gurgled and hissed and threw steam over the heads of the staff, wreathing them in bitter-scented magic.

'Here!' Spike turned back to her, proffering a tiny cup, like something out of her old doll's house. Dark liquid steamed within and Bonnie stared at it. 'Espresso. You like it, right?'

'Oh. Sorry. Yeah. Course I do. Thanks.'

Nervously she took the cup, trying to hook her fingers securely through the dainty handle. Spike lifted his own.

'Cheers, hey? Oh, but hold up!'

He held aloft a shiny pair of miniature tongs and something plopped into the drink, sending a hot splash onto Bonnie's skin. She flinched.

'What's that?' she asked nervously.

Aunt Nancy had told her over and over that drugs were evil and so, more convincingly, had Susie-Ann's tough brothers. Spike blinked.

'It's sugar. You do want sugar?'

'Oh, yes. Yes, please.'

Did she? Bonnie barely knew more about coffee than she did about drugs. The first she'd heard of the racy new drink was when Astrid had brought a pot of Lyons Instant to the house at Christmas, but she wasn't about to say that now.

'Lovely,' she said, peering up at Spike through her eyelashes and seeing his handsome face between clots of Susie-Ann's mascara. 'Thank you.'

Spike beamed, slicked his fingers through his hair and, in one practised motion, threw back half his coffee and rolled his eyes comically at her.

'That's cracker!'

She nodded, smiled, brought her own cup to her lips and braced herself. The 'espresso' – some sort of coffee concentrate – hit her tongue like a right hook. She reeled but then steadied herself as it swirled across her taste buds, first bitter then sweet. Bonnie took another sip, bigger this time, and felt tendrils of sensation curl around her mouth and straight up into her brain.

'Nice,' she breathed, drinking the last of it and putting the little cup down, relieved to have passed this first test.

Glancing surreptitiously around at the other girls, she was pleased to see that Susie-Ann had made her look just the part for this funky bar, but she still had to act it. Thankfully at that moment someone put 'Please Please Me' on the jukebox and the place went wild. Bonnie felt the beat of the music pull at her hips and began jumping along with everyone else.

'I love this!' she said to Spike, but to her horror he frowned. She stopped jumping instantly. 'Don't you?'

'I do,' he said, so quietly she had to lean in to hear. 'It's nearly as good as it was when I wrote it in school.'

'What? But surely Paul Mc . . .'

'Always had light fingers, did Paul.' She had no idea what to say and he must have seen it because he dropped a kiss on her cheek. 'Just messing with you, lass. It's a boss song. Really. I just need to get downstairs and set up with the rest of the band.'

'Course. Right.'

Her stomach twisted. Was he going to leave her up here all alone? She'd look like a total wallflower.

'You wanna meet them?'

Oh, thank the lord!

'I'd love to, Spike. Is that OK?'

'Yep. You're with me, remember?'

He grabbed her hand and she felt the touch of it like the headiest coffee ever. She was with Spike, she was with 'the band'! She was actually doing this! A tiny part of her couldn't wait to get down to the phone box tomorrow and tell Nancy all about it but she mustn't wish the night away, not when she'd been dreaming of this for so long.

Spike pulled her to the back of the bar and through a slim door. A bouncer was keeping punters out but he gave Spike a respectful nod and, with a thrill, Bonnie ducked through in his wake and found herself in a tight stairwell. Instantly the noise was muted, as if someone had thrown a cloth over the place. She could make out random chords and lines of chat drifting from below, but the door at the bottom of the stairs was shut, so, for the moment, they were alone. She followed Spike closely down, keen to see what was beyond the lower door and when he stopped suddenly, just before the bottom, Bonnie tumbled into his back. He turned, his face barely an inch from hers.

'Did I say you look proper stunning, Bonnie?' he murmured.

'You did. Thank you.'

She patted self-consciously at her straight hair. It didn't feel like hers at all but Spike seemed to like it. He leaned in closer and when she bit at her lip, uncertain what to do next, she heard him groan.

'You're doing me head in, Bonnie Jessop.'

Then suddenly his lips were on hers, pressing the crease from them, and she had to grab at his neck to stop herself staggering back. For a moment the length of him was against her and their shared heat seemed to flare in her lungs, robbing her of breath. So this was kissing! She'd tried it before, of course, but that had been with the Tonys and Nigels at the stiff little dances in the youth club in Congleton, and had been nothing like this. She gave herself up to the rush of sensation until, eventually, Spike pulled away.

'You're pure hot, Bonnie.'

He put a hand to her knee, his touch soft, almost reverent, and she felt it glow through her thin tights. She was definitely tingling inside and with her make-up and her dress she felt almost like she was in a film, but she had no idea what he was going to do next. Would he want to have sex right here? Right now? She wasn't ready, no way.

'Spike,' she stuttered and he visibly shivered but then, thankfully, stepped back and, with a startled cry, fell down the last three stairs, knocking the basement door wide and tumbling through on his back.

'Oh my goodness! Are you all right?'

Bonnie scrambled after him but he was up already, twitching at his jacket and raking at his sculpted hair. And there, in a tumble of jeers and laughter, were the band, and the tension of the moment on the stairs dissipated instantly.

'Fallen for her, hey Spikey lad?'

'You've knocked him off his webs, queen!'

Bonnie looked at the three young men stepping down from a low stage and coming towards them. They were immaculately styled to match Spike in dark, high-collared suits and rock-solid pompadour hairstyles and Bonnie drank in every detail of her first sighting of the Best Boys in case she needed to remember it in years to come.

Sticks she picked out from the fact that he had Susie-Ann wrapped all around him. He was a wiry lad with long limbs, prominent ears and the brightest ginger quiff Bonnie had ever seen. He was far from conventionally handsome, but his grin ran from ear to ear and Bonnie could tell instantly what her friend saw in him.

The other two were both nice-looking boys – though not as heart-meltingly handsome as Spike – and they both had guitars, but there the similarities ended. One was tall and broad with a shock of floppy blond curls fighting the Brylcreem attempting to hold it straight, and the other was thin and dark with aquiline features and almost jet-black hair. They looked intimidatingly cool but then Sticks said, 'Welcome to the stage, lass,' and it all felt a lot easier.

'Thank you,' Bonnie replied, attempting to pout her no doubt smudged lips and smiling round at them. They all beamed back. These were not like the university lads, demanding to know her A-level results and her aspirations and whether she was entitled to be here in Liverpool. Bonnie felt herself relax just a little. 'You must be the Best Boys.'

'That's us,' agreed Spike, shaking the last of the stair-dust from his trousers. 'This here is Danny – bass guitar and manager.' The tall blond lad stepped forward and shook Bonnie's hand firmly. 'Danny's a posh lad. Went to some poncy school out on the Wirral. He's meant to be helping his da run his business empire these days, but he prefers hanging around with us lot.'

'I'm your manager,' Danny said in a surprisingly cut-glass accent. 'Who else gets you lot gigs? Being one of the Best Boys is a full-time job.'

'Wish it were,' muttered Sticks, unwrapping himself from Susie-Ann to give Bonnie a wave. 'Hi, I'm Sticks. We've not quite met, but you may have heard me once or twice.' He grinned broadly, clearly untroubled by any noises that might have come up through her floor. Bonnie thought of Spike kissing her in the stairwell and flushed with a dark heat, but Sticks was still chatting away and didn't notice. 'I'm the drummer and the one all the girls fancy.'

'Oi!' Susie-Ann objected but he silenced her with a hard, deep kiss.

'Got eyes for no one but you, queen,' Sticks said when he surfaced. 'But I can't stop them looking – they're only human.'

The others groaned.

'You're a tosser, Mickey,' Susie-Ann told him fondly.

'Oi! I've told you only to call me Sticks.'

'Except when . . .'

'Oh, yeah. Except then.' He grinned wickedly and turned back to Bonnie. 'Mickey's my real name but only my da uses it these days. And even he calls me Micks now.'

'Why? What's wrong with Mickey?'

'You wanna be named after a mouse?'

'I guess not.'

'No one uses their real name,' Danny said, grabbing his guitar and striking a pose. 'It's cooler to have a stage name – a persona, if you will.'

'But Danny's a real name, isn't it?'

'You could say that. It's my middle name – same as Paul is McCartney's middle name.'

Bonnie looked at the big lad curiously.

'What's your first name?'

Danny, however, just flushed all the way up into his sandy curls and didn't reply.

'It's –' Spike started, but a glare from Danny silenced him.

'I wouldn't start that, "Spike", mate. I'm sure your fans would love to know *your* real name.'

'Wouldn't put them off. They'd all want to sleep with me anyway.'

Bonnie blinked at her date, then told herself not to be so silly. Of course he slept with people; he was gorgeous. He could have anyone he wanted, and he wanted her! She felt herself grow warm again and turned to see the last of the four band members step forward and nudge Spike.

'Oh yeah, this here's Lee. Lead guitarist and techie. Lee's the auld fella of the group.'

'Yeah,' Sticks agreed. 'Lee's ancient. He was off at high school when we were still chasing hoops round the playground.'

'I'm twenty,' Lee objected.

'Exactly – ancient.'

Bonnie looked at Lee more closely. He did look a little older, actually, not wrinkled or anything but thinner-faced and more serious. It gave his sharp features definition and she could imagine he would look great in photos. Though not as great as Spike, obviously.

'I may be old but I'm cooler than the rest of you lot put together,' Lee said.

'Think you'll find that's me, Lee lad,' Spike shot back, slicking back his already slicked hair.

Bonnie looked from one to the other, revelling in their easy banter and desperately hoping she could be a part of it.

'And together you make the Best Boys,' she said, with a smile.

'Too right, my sweet Bonnie,' Spike agreed, pulling her close and kissing her full on the lips so that her head spun. 'We're the *very* best boys. We're going to be famous, and if you're lucky we'll take you along for the ride.'

Bonnie giggled and tried to think of something appropriately grand to say but the boys were already turning to their instruments and muttering important-sounding things about 'tuning up'. Behind them the bouncer had opened the lower door and people were straining to get in and she was grateful when Susie-Ann linked arms and pulled her over to perch on a table to one side of the room.

The boys were strumming and humming and fiddling with the knobs on the sound system and Bonnie watched, rapt. There was a lot of complaining about how basic it was, but to her it looked like something out of the Americans' fancy space missile test centre, and she loved it.

'Earth to Bonnie!' Spike was back before her, waving his hand in front of her face. 'You in there, queen? You look miles away.'

'Oh goodness, Spike, I'm so sorry. I was thinking about space travel.'

Spike looked a little stunned, but rallied.

'She's clever, is our Bonnie,' he told the lads. 'She's at the university.'

'Like Susie-Ann,' Sticks said, sounding suddenly cross. 'Dunno what you wanna bother with all that for. Even posh boy here in't going to university.'

'That doesn't mean it's a bad thing to do,' Danny said stiffly.

'What's the point, though?' Sticks demanded, jabbing a drumstick in Bonnie's direction.

She flinched back, horrified. Had she done something wrong already? She looked to Susie-Ann for help, but her friend just scowled.

'Sticks don't approve of girls going to uni.'

'Sticks don't approve of *anyone* going to "uni",' Sticks corrected her fiercely. 'Waste of money. What's wrong with getting a job like everyone else?'

Bonnie swallowed.

'But I can't be an architect without a degree.'

25

'An architect?!' Sticks' eyebrows pinged up into his ginger quiff. 'Get a load of you, lass.'

Bonnie felt her skin flare beneath Susie-Ann's careful make-up and fought back tears. She'd known she wouldn't fit in. Hadn't she known it? What on earth was she doing in Liverpool? No one at the university thought she was up to it, and it seemed no one here did either. She bit at her pale lips and glanced longingly towards the door, but a huge crowd was straining to get in and there'd be no escape that way. Then Lee stepped forward.

'Let the girl alone, hey, Sticks. She can do what she wants with her life, it's none of your business.' He turned to Bonnie. 'Don't worry, lass. Sticks here just isn't used to people with dreams.'

'Bollocks, Lee. Shut your grid or I'll break your guitar.'

'You will not.'

Lee's slim hands went protectively around his guitar. Sticks squared up but big Danny inserted his strong shoulders between them.

'Sticks has dreams, don't you lad? Dirty ones!'

Danny gave Sticks a nudge. For a moment the red-haired drummer bristled and Bonnie felt a dark tension pulse through the band, but then he looked to the growing crowd on the stairs and gave way.

'Sure do. And Susie-Ann here is in every single one of them.'

He grabbed his girlfriend, sliding a hand right up her skirt as he kissed her again. Susie-Ann squirmed but didn't push him off and Bonnie edged away, doing her best to look cool. She turned nervously to Spike, but he just gave her an easy grin and threw an arm around her shoulders.

'Put her down, hey, Sticks,' he said. 'The punters are arriving and we've got to get ready. We're the Best Boys, remember, and we need to play well tonight, all right?' Bonnie felt Spike's strong body rippling with a new intensity and it thrilled right through her. 'Listen, lads – I heard Epstein was on the prowl again, so we nail this and it could be us playing the boss venues – the Tower Pavilion and the Litherland Town Hall and the like. But not if you lot are messing, OK?'

The other three gave a mumbled chorus of agreement. Sticks slid behind his drums and played a riff on his cymbal. Spike sprang onto the stage, Danny and Lee took up positions either side of him and as people began to come clattering down the stairs, Bonnie saw all four boys throw back their shoulders and pull their microphones closer.

They had become, before her eyes, not just four lads from Liverpool, but a *band* and Bonnie was reminded that, above all else, she'd come here to hear the music. She closed her eyes and for a moment she saw her parents dancing to Ella Fitzgerald in each other's arms, and instantly she knew she could do this; she could belong here.

She opened her eyes again to see Spike staring straight at her. He winked and, noticing several girls looking enviously her way, Bonnie flicked back her turned-out hair just as Susie-Ann was doing and went to perch on the little stage. Her gingham skirt rode up her thighs and as Spike's eyes widened appreciatively she fought the urge to tug the fabric down to a more modest level. Tomorrow she would call Aunt Nancy and describe every single little thing about this amazing place, but for now she was here in the Jacaranda Coffee House and she was with the band and she was going to make the most of every crazy minute.

Chapter Three

'What time are they arriving?' Stan asked, turning away from the half-hearted rain dribbling down the kitchen windows.

Bonnie looked up from chopping carrots and brushed a curl of white-blonde hair from her eyes.

'Lisa said she'd be here at one, so any time now.'

Stan glanced at the clock. Gone ten-to – their daughters would soon be upon them.

'I still don't see why you invited them,' he grumbled.

'I didn't invite them, Stan. If you remember, they invited themselves. Well, Lisa did. She seemed very keen and she's bringing Greya. It'll be nice to see her after her gap year travels, won't it?'

'It will,' Stan agreed reluctantly, 'we never see enough of her compared to the other grandkids, but it's not like Chamonix's in darkest Africa. Next week would have done just as well.'

'Grumpy,' she teased, putting down the knife and coming over to kiss him.

'I'm sorry. I'm just not sure I'm ready.'

'I should have put them off, I suppose, but Lisa was so insistent and she sounded . . .'

'She sounded what, Bonnie?'

'Nervy. On edge. She said something about work. I hope they're not pushing her too hard.'

Stan reached out to tuck the stray curl back behind her ear.

'They're always pushing her too hard. It's tough at the coalface of the justice system, you know.'

'Certainly seems that way. Lord knows why she's so keen for Greya to do law too. But we'll find out more when they get here, and we don't have to tell anyone about . . . you know . . . if you don't want to.'

Stan sighed.

'That won't work, Bon. Our daughters can sniff out a secret at a hundred paces.'

'True.'

She wrapped her arms around his waist and he drew her close, feeling her body slot into place against his as if finding the grooves so many years of marriage had carved into them both. He sighed.

'It just sort of feels like if it's only us who know, we can contain it. Once we tell other people, it'll be out in the world. It'll be . . . *true*. Stupid, hey?'

'Not stupid,' she said. 'But sweetheart, I'm afraid it's true whoever knows.'

She stood on tiptoe to plant a kiss on his nose, and he tried to smile at her though his gut was still twisting painfully.

'We've just not had much time. We only found out a few days ago and we've barely done any research. They'll all want to know what we can do about it and I'm just not sure what to say.'

Bonnie put her hands either side of his head and looked deep into Stan's eyes.

'We say we're going to find a cure.'

'But . . .'

She shushed him.

'We've been round and round this, Stan, and there has to be a way. I know Dr Mirabi doesn't believe there's much he can do but although he might understand cancer, he doesn't understand *you*. And fair enough, why should he when he sees hundreds of cancer patients a week? It's up to us to find a miracle cure and we will, Stan. We *will*. No negativity allowed.'

Her hands tightened against his temples and he placed his own over them.

'You're right. We have money, don't we? And we're not stupid – well, you're not.'

'Or you either, Stanley Walker. You're not playing the "thickie builder" card on me here, OK?'

Now Stan had to smile. The "thickie builder" card had been his way to avoid all sorts of admin tasks he hated over the years, but this was more than just holiday arrangements and ticket bookings. This was his life.

'OK, Bon. You're right, of course you are.'

'Of course I am. It was in the marriage vows, wasn't it?'

'If it wasn't, it should have been.'

'Exactly. No negativity. Now, fetch the gravy granules for me, will you?'

She stepped away and Stan felt the cold of her absence, but she'd already turned back to the carrots so he made obediently for the pantry at the rear of the kitchen.

When they'd bought this house, just before the girls were born, it had been a small, if very pretty, cottage. It had not, however, taken Bonnie long to work her architectural magic on it, creating a large timber-clad extension to the rear that had proved the perfect place to bring up the girls – a vast, light space where homework jumbled in with meal preparation, craft projects and work plans.

Stan loved it but he had to admit that the pantry, tucked under the stairs at the back of the kitchen, was still his favourite bit. It had the wonderfully musty smell of past lives lived, and now he stood drawing in the mingled scents of herbs and soily vegetables and the delicious, malty musk of home brew. Automatically, he lifted a bottle to the light to check for clarity.

He'd been attempting to perfect the art of brewing for the last few years, with his best mate and long-standing colleague Dave as a willing taster, and was confident that this latest brew would be the best yet. Now, though, as he watched the light from the tiny window winking through the brown glass, the impossible enormity of his situation seemed to coalesce into a single, horribly easy-to-grasp idea. Dr Mirabi had given him a year at best, so when his beer was ready to drink in three months' time he might not be here to take the first sip. He staggered and the bottle slipped from his fingers and fell to the ground, smashing on the tiles.

'Stan? Stan, what is it? What's wrong?'

Bonnie burst in and he blinked back to reality.

'Nothing,' he said hastily. 'That is, nothing more. Just, you know . . . It.'

He fumbled for the gravy granules above his head as if normality could somehow be found in the Bisto but his hand was shaking and they too were dropped to the floor where they spread through the brown rivulets of beer like dirt.

Dust to dust, a voice intoned in his head and Stan pressed his hands to his eyes to block the sight of his own grave at his feet. No negativity, he tried to tell himself, but it was so much easier said than done. He heard Bonnie draw a deep breath and knew she would be counting to seven. It's what she always did when she needed time. Ten was too much, she always said, and five too little and besides, she didn't like such 'obvious' numbers. Seven was apparently underrated – though not by her.

'Stan . . .' Her voice was so, so gentle. She'd reached seven then. He felt her fingers on his and let her draw his hands away. 'Stan, we're going to sort this, I know we are.'

'How do you know?'

'Because I'm good at sorting things, you always say so. And you don't have to do it alone, Stan.'

'No,' he shot back, 'but if I die *you'll* have to.'

That was it! That was what he'd been trying to explain, that was the picture that had haunted him these last sleepless nights – not death and whatever supposed horrors it might bring, but the stark image of Bonnie sat on her own once the funeral was done and the mourners had gone back to their happy lives. His hell was the thought of Bonnie without him to hold her hand, or bring her a cup of tea, or suggest that they were too tired to cook and would be better popping down the chippie. His grip tightened on her hands, but at that moment a cheery voice echoed out from the hall behind them.

'Hellooo!'

They both froze.

'Rachael!' Bonnie gasped. 'And the grandkids. They'll be in here in . . .'

'Grandpa! What are you doing?'

Bonnie and Stan turned, still locked together, and saw ten-year-old Jamie standing before them, his brown eyes wide. His little sister, Marleigh, came skittering in behind him, paused a moment and then dipped a toe in one of the brown rivers oozing into the kitchen.

'You've made a bit of a mess,' she commented, scrunching up her face in disapproval.

'It stinks!' Jamie added, holding his nose.

'It does a bit,' Stan agreed, reluctantly letting go of his wife. 'Could you find the brush, mate?'

'Sure.'

Jamie grabbed the broom and set about chasing the granules down the streams of beer just as Rachael strode into the kitchen.

'What on earth is going on here?' she demanded, hands on broad hips.

Their younger twin (by twenty-three minutes) was strongly built and, dressed today in a dark red jumper dress was an assertive presence. Stan avoided her eye as he went forward for a hearty hug.

'Just your old dad getting clumsy, lass.'

'You, Dad? You're Mr Careful. Had your eyes tested recently? You're meant to, you know, once you're as ancient as you are.' She grinned at him but for once he struggled to rise to her teasing and when he made the mistake of meeting her dark eyes, she read him instantly. 'Dad? What is it? What's wrong?'

'Nothing, nothing.' He ducked away. 'Come on, let's get you a drink, shall we? What'll it be? G and T? Wine, beer? I've still got some home brew from . . .'

'Dad! Don't avoid the question. This is me, remember?'

'I remember – I'm not *that* old.'

But it was too little, too late. Rachael knew him inside out, having worked with him every day since she was nineteen. Not that she'd wanted to at first. She'd gone off to study geography in Manchester but had hated it.

She'd stuck it out until the middle of the Easter term when she'd turned up at home saying she couldn't take it any more. She didn't like city life, she'd sobbed, and she didn't like the course and she missed home too much. This last had been flung at them as if it was their fault, but they'd both had a suspicion it was more to do with her 'best friend' Andrew from down the road, a quiet artist and the only boy in the area with shoulders wider than her own.

Sure enough, barely three weeks had passed before Stan had gone to sort the rubbish one night and found them locked together in a passionate embrace on the doorstep. He'd been very calm about it, as he'd recounted many times since, simply asking them to put the bins out when they were done. It was a good story. In fact, it had been the centrepiece of his speech at their wedding two years later.

Whatever the reason for Rachael's return, she'd joined Stan and Dave as an apprentice plumber and when they'd branched out into house renovations, she'd proved herself a key part of the team. These days she more or less ran the show, including the building of Bonnie and Stan's dream house. The one he now might never see. Stan blinked furiously and, as Rachael fixed him with a dark gaze, he crumbled.

'OK, Rae, I do have a little bit of an, er, issue I need to talk to you about, but can we wait til Lisa gets here?'

'That could be hours.'

'No, she promised she'd be here for one.'

'She always promises and she's always late.'

'Well, that's true, but getting out of London can be tricky.'

'Does she know then?'

'Know what?'

'This thing of yours, this "issue" – does she know what it is? Have you told her already?'

'No! Of course not. I want to tell you together. How are the house foundations coming on?'

'Fine. Why? Is the house the issue?'

'No! No, of course not.'

'Is it too much for you?'

'Why would it be?'

'I don't know. You're being weird. And it's a big project.'

'Nothing we haven't done before.'

She leaned back with a sigh.

'I know. I know that. Sorry. It's me, really. I've got . . . That is, my back's been a bit dicky recently.'

'Your back?' Stan peered at his youngest. He'd not noticed her having problems, but now he looked closely, her broad shoulders were a little hunched beneath her dress and the skin around her eyes was as dark as coal holes. 'Are you ill, Rae?'

'No, Dad. Just getting on a bit. All downhill once you've kissed goodbye to forty-five, hey? Ah, Andrew!' She turned to her husband as he ambled in, a bottle of wine in each hand. 'Where've you been?'

'I got stuck helping Lisa in.'

'Lisa's here?'

'Yep.' Andrew put down the wine bottles on the island and reached over to grab Stan's hand in his usual crushing grip. 'Afternoon, Stan. Hope you're feeling brave.'

'Why?'

Stan looked uncertainly up at his son-in-law. Andrew was a giant of a man who looked as if he'd be most at home working on one of Stan's building sites, but he was actually a talented artist who made a very decent living painting delicate watercolour portraits of people and pets. He had a little studio in the back garden of their pretty house in the next village, and he and Rachael flexed their working hours to take care of their kids.

Having known Andrew since he was a grubby-kneed schoolboy, Stan often thought of him as the son he'd never had and would trust him with anything, but why was he saying Stan had to be brave? *Please don't let Rachael be ill too*, he thought in a sudden panic. He'd take double cancer like a shot if he could spare her that. Rachael, though, looked as bemused as he did.

'It's just that she's got a lot of suitcases,' continued Andrew.

'Suitcases?' Stan repeated like an idiot, but then heels tip-tapped across the hall tiles and in came Lisa, sleek in designer clothes with Greya in tow, the eighteen-year-old's once-hazel hair now shot through with lilac and silver.

'Suitcases,' Lisa agreed with a smile. 'We've come to stay for a week or two. Isn't that great?'

Chapter Four

As Lisa stared expectantly at them both from the wide doorway, Stan felt Bonnie's hand slide into his and clutched at it.

'A week or two?' he asked, his voice faint.

'If that's OK?' Lisa shot back, her tone daring them to say otherwise.

Lisa was Rachael's polar opposite. So self-consciously slim she would almost fit twice into her just-younger sister, she'd left home the moment she could and thrown herself into a high-powered London career. She'd chosen to have just one child to 'maximise resources', and her husband Simon, then a fast-living merchant banker, had backed the decision all the way.

Things had changed a little when Simon had suddenly volunteered to take a career break to be at home for Greya. He'd loved the house-husband role more than anyone had expected, and had begged Lisa for more children but her reply had been that if he could grow himself a womb, he was welcome to them. As this had not been an option for the poor man, he'd settled for retraining as an accountant and volunteering on every kids' sports team and PTA event going. Stan had rather admired him for it but he'd always suspected that Lisa had not.

Bonnie had tried to talk their daughter into having another child, but once Lisa's mind was made up nothing could change it. Rachael often grumbled that she must have been a terrible sister to make Lisa so convinced a second child was such a bad thing, but Bonnie said that the messiness of motherhood had terrified Lisa too much to try again. Knowing his perfectionist elder daughter, Stan suspected his wife had the truth of it.

'Of course you can stay,' Bonnie agreed now, hurrying forward to hug Lisa. 'Of course. Lovely. Is Simon with you?'

'No.'

Bonnie glanced at Stan. They'd been worried for a while that, with Greya leaving home, there wouldn't be much to hold Lisa to her husband, but perhaps he was just busy.

'OK then,' Bonnie said lightly. 'What about you, Greya, will you be staying too?'

'She will,' Lisa confirmed before her daughter could open her mouth. 'She's come back from skiing with all sorts of mad ideas and could do with a bit of guidance from her wise old grandparents.'

'We're not old,' Bonnie said indignantly.

'Or wise,' Stan added, giving Greya a wink. Greya smiled gratefully at him and sidled round the island as he turned back to Lisa. 'Any particular reason for the long visit?'

'Reason? Does there need to be a reason?'

'No,' Stan said carefully. He'd forgotten how damn prickly Lisa could be when challenged. 'But haven't you got work?'

'Oh! Yes. Yes, exactly. I've got a trial on in Manchester and thought it would be easier to base myself here.'

She beamed, clearly on more certain ground, but now Rachael pounced.

'Not because you wanted to see more of Mum and Dad, then, Lise? Or spend a bit of time with your niece and nephew?'

Lisa looked at her twin and laughed.

'Nope. Not that.'

Rachael rolled her eyes.

'Silly me. Work first, I remember.'

37

Stan flinched but Lisa just eased past Rachael and came over to him. She was immaculate in beautifully cut trousers and a simple pale blue jumper with a discreet logo he should no doubt recognise, and as he bent to kiss her, she air-smacked both his cheeks, confusing him. He'd never get used to these southern ways.

'How's things, Dad?'

He flinched. How were 'things'? Terrible, miserable, terminal . . . He looked round for Bonnie, but she was preparing starters and didn't see.

'Fine,' he managed. Such a silly little word, so often wrongly used. 'It's lovely to see you,' he added hastily but Lisa didn't seem to notice his evasion.

'Well good, because it took ages to get here. I let Greya drive and she's so steady.'

She flicked a manicured hand towards her daughter as everyone gathered around the island.

'People don't normally fret about their teenagers driving too slowly, Lisa,' Bonnie said, putting down a big plate of Italian nibbles.

'She does it all the time,' Greya told them, taking a bruschetta and lifting it like an imaginary steering wheel. '"Can't you put your foot down, darling? It doesn't do to be dull".'

It was an inch-perfect imitation of Lisa's voice, and Stan laughed. It sounded alien after the last few days. Is that what cancer did to you – ate away your sense of humour along with your vital organs? He laughed again, just to check he could, but everyone else had stopped and the sound clunked into the silence. Bonnie put a quiet hand on his back and he drew in a breath.

'Drink, Lisa?' he asked, putting his own hand back to touch Bonnie's and feeling their shared secret burn between them.

'Yes please. G and T would be marvellous. Oh, but we should perhaps get our suitcases upstairs first. Andrew, could you . . .?'

'Andrew is not a bloody porter, Lisa,' Rachael objected and Stan glanced ruefully down at Bonnie.

All their lives the twins had been at each other, as if they resented being so closely joined. They'd chosen different hobbies – Rachael going for football and kick-boxing, and Lisa for horses. They'd insisted on different hairstyles, as if Rachael's dark curls had not already been distinguishable enough from Lisa's straight blonde locks. And if Bonnie had ever dared to try and dress them in matching clothes – even just in the same colours – they'd both thrown fits, united, at least, in their desire not to be so.

'Dinner's nearly ready, Lisa sweetheart,' Bonnie said, 'so it would be better if we could sort the rooms out later, if that's OK? Have you got much stuff?'

'She's got loads,' Greya said. 'Mostly shoes – useless material objects.'

'Like iPhones and laptops and ski boots?' Lisa shot back at her daughter.

'Exactly. We all need to purge our lives, but it can be very hard as an individual to break through cultural barriers.'

Greya bit loudly into her bruschetta and Lisa tossed her head.

'Hear that?' she asked. 'That's the sort of thing she says all the time now. She met some hippies on the slopes and has come back all "save the polar bears" and herbal teas.'

'What on earth is wrong with herbal teas?' Greya demanded, and Stan was interested to see that the once-biddable public schoolgirl was learning to stand up for herself.

'They're all smell and no actual taste – like a lot of your fancy ideas. Give me an honest gin and tonic every time. Talking of which – where's that gin, Dad? It's been a hell of a week.'

Stan reluctantly let go of Bonnie to fetch the gin. He poured a generous measure and added ice from the dispenser, but as he came back to the group at the island, Greya caught his arm, making the ice cubes in the glass chink.

'Do you know a big freezer like yours emits around three hundred kilograms of CO_2 every month?'

'It does?' Stan paused, struck, then asked, 'Is that a lot?'

'Not especially, but it's twice what it would be without the ice-maker.'

'Right . . . Oh dear.' He looked helplessly at the four fat ice cubes bobbing in the glass. 'G and T wouldn't be the same warm, though, would it?'

'Priorities!' Greya sang, flicking her hair in a futuristic shine of colour. 'Do you want mine and Jamie and Marleigh's kids to still have electricity?'

She gestured to her young cousins, picking flecks of spring onion off their bruschetta.

'Erm . . .'

'Or heating?'

'Well, of course I do, but a few little ice cubes . . .'

'Could make all the difference, Grandpa.' She winked, surprising him. 'Just something to think about, that's all.'

Stan looked at the ice again but Lisa whisked it away and added tonic, though not, he noted, very much of it.

'I told you, she's spouting a lot of that sort of stuff, Dad. She's met some crowd in France who've turned her head with it all.'

'They have not "turned my head", Mum. Or if they have, it's in the right direction. Do you know what we're doing to the planet? We have to act – now! I'm going to do Ecological Studies at Sheffield next year.'

'You are not!' Lisa said. 'You've got a place for law.'

'But I can change. I've asked them. Ecology is vital, Mum – far more vital than bloody law.'

'*Bloody* law?' Lisa choked, looking genuinely panicked.

Stan knew Lisa had always had big plans for the daughter whose resources she had so carefully 'maximised' and looked for words to smooth things over, but now Rachael came up next to her niece.

'Good point, Grey,' she said. 'If we don't keep the planet viable the lawyers will die with the rest, won't they?'

'Exactly! This is the most important degree there is right now. Dad agrees.'

Lisa tossed her head.

'Your dad would. He's got no idea about how to get on in the world.'

Greya's eyes clouded briefly and Stan looked between his granddaughter and daughter in concern. He and Bonnie had often said they should get more involved in Greya's childhood but with that part of their family living in London it had been hard, and now it seemed their chance was gone – Greya was all but a woman. And one with every bit as much spirit as her mother.

'What about hair dye?' he asked Greya.

'Sorry?'

'What's the environmental impact of hair dye?'

Greya's eyes widened and Stan heard Lisa laugh but then the girl just said, 'Very good point, Grandpa. I'll have to look into it. I might be a walking future-stealer.'

'Goodness, I wouldn't go that far! I just wondered, that's all.'

'And you're right to wonder. It's good you're so engaged at your age. Other adults could take a leaf out of your book.'

She shot a look at Lisa, who took a studious drink of her gin. Stan felt his head spin, wondering how on earth he was going to slot his dreadful news into all these other problems, but now Rachael was nudging her niece.

'So, you're going to be here for a couple of weeks, Greya?'

'Looks like it. I'm joining this amazing new project on eco bikes, so I've got a few people to see but that'll just be at weekends.'

'So you'll be kicking around in the week?'

Greya looked suspiciously at her aunt.

'I guess, for a bit. Why?'

'Fancy a job?'

'Paid?'

'Of course.'

'I might. Doing what?'

'Building. On Granny and Grandpa's new house. It's an eco design, you know.'

Lisa finally looked up but it was too late. Greya's eyes were shining.

'Cool! Did you design it, Granny?'

'Of course,' Bonnie agreed. 'I love all the new technologies. It'll have a ground source heat pump, solar panels and a state-of-the-art heat recovery system. It will be made almost entirely of sustainable materials, and we're even using lime mortar.'

Greya's mouth fell open and she looked at her grandmother with open respect.

'That's sick, Granny. I didn't know you . . .'

'Were so up to date? You have to move with the times in my business, sweetheart.'

'Great. I'd love to be involved then. Can I, Rachael?'

'You'd be very welcome.' She glanced at Lisa and must have felt a pang of conscience as she added, 'if your Mum's OK with it?'

Lisa shrugged.

'Be good for her to be busy, I guess,' she said, the closest she'd come to a thank you.

Stan, glad of the momentary truce, reached for a slice of parma ham but then spotted poor Andrew still mopping the pantry floor and dived over.

'You shouldn't be doing that, Andrew. Sorry.'

'Not at all. It's safer than being over there.'

The two men exchanged conspiratorial grins.

'You might be right there,' Stan agreed. 'But you need a drink at least. Home brew, or something decent?'

Andrew hesitated only a second before valiantly opting for the home brew. Stan made a big fuss of choosing a bottle and poured, pleased to see the ale was clear. Andrew took a tentative sip, then another.

'Hey, Stan, you're getting good. This is the best yet, for sure.'

'You're very kind, but let me tell you, the next lot will be . . .' Words ran out on him, as they seemed suddenly to be doing all too often – as if he had cancer not of the liver but of the vocabulary. 'Thanks,' he forced out instead. 'Now, look – you'd better get some of the starters before that greedy lot nick them all.'

Andrew looked at him with concern and Stan ducked away, moving to the French windows to look out into the back garden and compose himself. Neither he nor Bonnie had green fingers so they'd kept the outdoor space simple – a lawn for badminton and French cricket, a big patio for barbecues and a lot of hardy shrubs and perennials in the borders all around. A cherry tree in the centre of the lawn gave welcome colour in spring, but that was about as sophisticated as it got. Stan didn't care; he preferred the colour of bikes and swings and paddling pools to fancy roses anyway.

Today, though, the rain was dribbling against the glass and all the lights were on, casting a second, blurry family across the window's misty surface. Andrew had gone to join the girls and Stan watched the pair of them, slim blue shoulder to broad red one, listening to something he was saying. Greya had bent down to talk to a rapt Marleigh, and Jamie was sneaking slice after slice of ham, as if he hadn't eaten in days. It was an easy, happy scene at last – one he really didn't want to upset.

Then he saw Bonnie bending to the oven, all alone, and his heart almost broke. He turned from the blurred mirror of his family and rushed to help.

'OK?' he asked, bending down at her side.

She nodded, though her eyes were damp.

'You're crying.'

She shook her head, her mouth set in a determined line. 'It's the steam. What about you, Stan – you OK?'

He kissed her.

'I am now. Shall I lift the meat out?'

'Can you? That is, I didn't mean *can* you. I know you can. I just . . .'

'Bonnie, it's fine.'

He kissed her again. She looked stricken and he hated to see her unsure amongst her family for perhaps the first time ever. Again the hellish picture flashed before his eyes of Bonnie sat in this great big room, all alone once he was gone, but what could he do? Save fight this with all he had.

He reached for the oven gloves and lifted the big joint out. The fat sizzled and popped in the open air and there was an appreciative murmur as he set the pan down on the side.

'That looks well tasty,' Greya said, rubbing her hands.

'You've not turned veggie then, Grey?' Stan asked lightly.

'Nah. I've thought about it. I mean, I should, but meat just tastes so nice.'

'Priorities?' Lisa suggested, and Greya stuck her tongue out at her.

'Well, it looks absolutely delicious to me,' Andrew said. 'Shall we get everyone sat down, Bonnie?'

Bonnie nodded, composed again now, and Stan watched as he and Rachael drew everyone across to the table. Children had been slow to come for their younger daughter, and Stan was relieved to see them so content. Rachael still looked pale, but perhaps she was just tired. She had a lot to juggle with the kids and work, and he hated the fact that he was about to add to her worries just when she needed it least.

He watched Jamie take his seat, smoothing down his ever-present, if slightly tight, Everton shirt and made a mental note

44

to buy the lad a bigger one. If he was anything like his 6' 3" dad, Stan thought, he'd got a lot of growing ahead of him, and then he realised with a deep growl of pain that he was unlikely to ever see that happen. Still, he couldn't start thinking that way, so, shaking himself, he carried the beef platter to the table and lifted his carving knife with a flourish.

The meal was pleasant, Stan was pretty sure of that, though he felt as if he were watching it from the sidelines. All the moves were right. He carved the beef as he always did and everyone handed it round and fought for their preferred level of pink. The veggies steamed in big bowls in the centre and the kids squealed 'Not that much!' as they were ladled onto their plates, sneaking extra roasties as compensation. The Yorkshire puds came fresh from the oven, puffed up with their own glory, and Bonnie handed them round to cries of delight that the poor carrots would never receive.

Gravy, perfect despite the mess earlier, was poured and the air filled with the chink of knife on plate and sighs of appreciation. The bickering of earlier was gone as the twins settled back into each other and began to joke and tease warmly, and Jamie and Marleigh buzzed with Greya's attention. Wine glugged into grown-up glasses, Coke into kiddies' ones and, as always, Jamie poured too much and it fizzed up and onto Bonnie's white tablecloth and Rachael tutted and apologised and Bonnie said it didn't matter. And it didn't. It really, really didn't, because they were all here and all smiling and if Stan had known that was a precious thing before, it felt doubly so now.

And he was going to wreck it.

'Coffee?' Bonnie suggested when the last of the pudding had finally been scraped from their bowls.

Stan noticed her fingers gripping the edge of the table and knew she, like him, was holding on through all this easy joy. It was time.

'Maybe shortly,' he said.

He felt he should stand up but couldn't bear to. Something in his voice, though, must have signalled a 'speech' was about to happen as his ever-voluble family shut up as one and looked his way. Stan noted Rachael clutch for Andrew's hand under the table and saw Greya glance to Lisa with a look more ten-years-old than eighteen, and he hated himself all over again.

He glanced around the kitchen and caught sight of Terry lolling in the key bowl on the side. Lying at a jaunty angle, the troll seemed to be suggesting he was making an awful fuss and, thus admonished, Stan drew in a deep breath and faced his family.

'It's bad news, I'm afraid.' It was a blunt way to start but there was no better. Everyone leaned forward and he forced himself to continue. 'I've been diagnosed with liver cancer.'

There, he'd said it. He waited for the usual hullabaloo of questions and opinions but none came. They all just stared, their reflections eerily still in the windows beyond. Someone, maybe Rachael, gave a sob, quickly smothered, and everyone looked down at the remains of their lunch.

It was Lisa who recovered first.

'That's terrible, Dad. I'm so sorry. *We're* so sorry.' Everyone nodded. 'What can we do?'

'We're not sure yet. It's early days.' He looked to Bonnie and she nodded him on. 'We're exploring the options.'

It sounded so trite, so empty – so basically untrue – but it seemed to satisfy. His daughters, like his wife, had always been ones for action and they leaped into life at the idea of 'options'. There was talk of holistic cures from Greya, and of America from Lisa. Andrew knew an excellent doctor, Rachael had heard an amazing story . . . The table thrummed with the determination that this family would be the one to beat cancer.

Stan drank wine and waited. He had not spent this many years in a household full of women without knowing when to sit back. They would all know best and it was easiest to let them get on with it. He glanced to Terry again and saw him reclining on his bed of keys as if this was all in a day's work. His indifference was a strange comfort.

'I'm doing lots of research,' Bonnie said eventually, drawing the conversation to a close. 'But anything anyone else can find out would be very helpful. Then we can pool our resources and take it from there, yes?'

There was a chorus of agreement then Marleigh jumped up and ran to Stan, flinging her little arms around his neck and everyone else followed, clustering round him.

'I'm so lucky,' he gasped out, clutching at them all. 'So very lucky to have you and I . . . I'm sorry.'

They told him not to be, of course. They told him they were the sorry ones, but he knew their burden was the greater. His would end. When they sat down to a dinner like this after he was tucked up in the peaceful oblivion of eternity, it would be them still feeling the pain.

Who would carve, he wondered, and the simple question undid him. Who would lift the meat out of the oven for Bonnie? Who would slice it up? And who would sit with her when everyone else had gone and laugh over the vagaries of the day? He looked down the table to where she was sitting, folding her napkin around her fingers. Already she looked lost, alone – the nightmare of his imaginings.

But he wasn't gone, not yet. He reached out a hand towards her and she released her fingers and lifted her own back, offering him a sweet smile, even if it wobbled a little at the edges. He had to believe in a cure for her sake. Everything he'd read told him such a thing would be impossible, but so what? Finding Bonnie had been a miracle and all these lovely family members who'd followed had been a miracle too, so why not one more? At the very least, he had to try.

Chapter Five

Stan pushed on the door of The Crown and was hit by a waft of floorboards, beer and vinegar. He paused a moment to take in the blissful normality of the scene. Their local was a 'proper' pub – not a wine bar or a gastropub or a chain but a basic little tavern that put more time into keeping its ale nice than painting its walls. Plus, it had the best range of pork scratchings on the Wirral and he was hoping to sneak a pack after an all-too-healthy week.

Part of Bonnie's determined research had thrown up a list of 'superfoods' that Google assured her would fight cancer and, in the absence of anything more concrete, she'd thrown herself into cooking them. Stan had nothing against beetroot or kale per se but they hadn't the satisfying, cholesterol-laden crunch of a pork scratching, and he approached the bar with his mouth watering.

Dave was already there, his back solid with the muscle that comes with spending weekdays as a builder and weekends on the squash court and the golf course. Stan's friend was nearly ten years younger than him and had become his apprentice just after Stan had taken over the business from his father. Stan had been in desperate need of help and he'd certainly found it in Dave. The man had an energy matched only by his strength, and had shown a flair for the hardest of manual work.

His only fault had been an impatience that, in his early days, had translated into an unfortunate lack of attention to detail. After the unpleasant incident with the village hall flooding (Stan still shuddered to remember all those furious WI members), it had seemed best to keep Dave away from the trickier jobs, but once Stan had started on his and Bonnie's extension he'd found his colleague's true talent – Dave had turned out to be a genius with brickwork. He loved the speed of the work and the visible achievement and was far more precise at positioning bricks than he'd ever been with pipework.

Once the extension had been done it had seemed logical to find similar work, and so Foundation Stone Builders had been born. Dave and Stan were the perfect partnership: Dave did the big, heavy, showy jobs and Stan did the hidden, finicky ones. Once they'd added in Rachael's organisational genius they'd been unstoppable, and Stan considered himself very blessed in his workmates.

'Evening,' he said to Dave's back.

Dave looked over his shoulder and grinned. He was a ruggedly handsome man with a twinkle in his eye that had the ladies constantly falling over each other to be let down by him. He'd never let Stan down once, though.

'Evening, Stan lad,' he said, shaking his hand and pulling him in to the bar. 'I'm honoured. Thought you'd given up drinking with me.'

'It's only been a week, Dave.'

'Only?! What you having?'

Stan shifted. This wasn't going to be easy, but he'd promised Bonnie.

'Lime and soda, please.'

'Lime and . . .? What the . . .?'

'I'm cutting back.'

'So have a mild.'

49

Stan laughed.

'I don't think that counts, Dave.' He turned to Frank, the landlord, who was already reaching for a pint glass. 'Lime and soda, please.' Frank's eyes widened but, after just a moment's hesitation, he complied. 'And a packet of pork scratchings.'

Stan looked nervously around the few drinkers but Bonnie and her friends tended to steer clear of this place, preferring the more architecturally stylish Three Feathers at the other end of the village, so he could indulge unnoticed. He turned back to Dave.

'Good weekend?'

'The best,' Dave agreed, always easy to distract. 'New woman – Gail. Gorgeous.'

'Gorgeous Gail?'

'Exactly. Insatiable Gail, too. I'm knackered.'

'Lucky you.'

Frank placed the lime and soda down on the bar and all three men looked at it. It was quite a pretty green, Stan supposed, if you liked that sort of thing, but it just didn't have the appeal of a real ale. Stan pulled it towards him but didn't take a drink. Dave frowned.

'Everything OK, mate?'

Stan sighed.

'It's not been the best week,' he admitted.

'Surely not trouble at home?'

'No. No, nothing like that. Just . . .' He took a sip of his drink. Nope, definitely not the appeal of a real ale. 'Just medical stuff.'

'You're ill?' Dave looked him up and down. 'You don't look it. If anything I'd say you've lost weight again.'

'Maybe.'

'Is it Bonnie? Is she ill?'

'No, no. Bonnie's great. Top form.'

'Wearing you out then, is she?'

'Not so much her, no. More, well . . .' He reached into his pocket for Terry but the little chap just gave an annoyed squeak – troll for 'get on with it', no doubt. He had a point. 'More – liver cancer.'

'What?'

Dave blanched paler than a weissbier.

'Liver cancer. Or so the doc says.'

'Liver c . . . Shit. You sure?'

'Yep.'

'Oh, mate. That's crap.'

'It is a bit.'

'Is it . . .?'

'Terminal? Yes.'

'I was going to say curable.'

'Right. In that case, no.'

'Oh. That's *really* crap. You sure?'

'Not one hundred per cent. Bonnie is busy looking at different therapies, and yesterday the doc prescribed palliative chemo.'

'Chemo?' Dave snatched at this. 'That's good, isn't it? I mean, not good. Bit yucky in fact. I dated a girl who was going through it a year or two back. She lost all her hair. Not that that'd bother you, yours is pretty much all gone anyway.'

'Cheers, Dave.'

'Any time. Point is, it cured her. She's still going strong I hear – though not with me, obviously.'

'Obviously.'

Dave hadn't dated anyone for longer than three months in the last thirty years. He'd tried marriage once in the mid-eighties but had strayed within a month and been out on his ear before his first anniversary. Ever since then he'd worked to keep things casual and even now, in his mid-sixties, he showed no sign of settling down.

'But it could cure you too, couldn't it?'

Dave was looking at him intently, just as Bonnie had done all week. Stan forced a nod.

'It could do.'

He and Bonnie had been back to see Dr Mirabi yesterday morning and he'd explained that Stan's liver was riddled with a 'hepatocellular carcinoma'. It had already spread to his lymph nodes, which were likely to send it chasing all around his body. They'd both wobbled a little when he'd said that, and the doctor had rushed on to discuss palliative chemotherapy, designed to stem the spread of the disease to offer Stan a little more time before it took complete hold.

'But won't the chemo itself make me ill?' Stan had asked, and Dr Mirabi had nodded and agreed that was possible.

'But it might also kill the cancer?' Bonnie had insisted.

'Some of it.'

'Maybe all?'

'Unlikely.'

'But possible?'

'In very, very rare cases. Maybe one in ten thousand. You really shouldn't pin your hopes on a miracle, Mrs Walker. What we are trying to do here is prolong Stan's life. Give him a few extra months. You see . . .'

But Bonnie had already tuned out and Stan knew her hopes were very much pinned on a miracle. She'd convinced herself they were going to find a cure and when, in the car on the way home, he'd tried to suggest it might not be possible, she'd reacted with rare fury.

'That's just you all over,' she'd raged, banging her hand on the steering wheel as he'd sat there, stunned. 'You always see the worst case scenario. It's the bloody plumber in you – everything's always a flood about to happen, isn't it?'

'I suppose so,' he'd stuttered, 'though I've only ever had

one flood in all my years as a plumber and that was actually Dave's fault.'

'Exactly! So just look on the positive side for once, will you? Just believe. It's got to count for something, hasn't it? *Hasn't it?*'

He'd agreed, of course he had, but he couldn't help the way he was made. He was the detail man, the fixer, but it seemed the practical stuff had run out on him and all they had left were ephemerals – dreams, hopes, belief. Well, that and being wired up to a poison drip once a week for a month, starting tomorrow.

'I guess all we can do is give it a try,' he said to Dave now.

'Absolutely. You're a fit bloke, so why shouldn't it work?'

'That's what Bonnie says.'

'You don't agree?'

Dave had finished his pint in record time. It was the only visible sign of how much Stan's news had shaken his old friend.

'I just think it would be wise to be prepared for if it doesn't.'

'Right. God, Stan.' Dave lifted his pint automatically then, finding it empty, put it back down. 'So if you don't, like, sort it, how long have you got?'

Stan fingered his still unopened pork scratchings.

'He wouldn't say exactly. Different in all cases, blah blah blah . . .'

'OK. So it could be ages, then. It could be, like, years even.'

'He said max one year.'

'Oh.'

'Though the chemo might get me a few more months.'

'Right. Great. I bet it gives you loads more than that. It's not like you're an old knacker or anything.'

'Thanks, Dave.'

'It's true, though. Anyway, what I'm trying to say is that you must have plenty of time to do the things you want to do. Right?'

53

Stan nodded. This was the sort of approach he could cope with. Indeed, he had a 'to do' list already.

'What do you suggest then, Dave? I mean, what would you do?'

Dave raised a suggestive eyebrow.

'What do you think, mate – sleep with as many women as I could! Preferably all at once. I bet you could get away with anything if you were . . . That is . . . Sorry.' He swallowed then added hastily, 'What about you, Stan? You ever slept with anyone other than Bonnie?'

Stan flushed and looked around the little pub. There were two lads playing snooker on the far side, a travelling businessman catching up with the sport on his phone and a couple who were far more interested in each other than him. No one was listening.

'No,' he admitted.

'Not even before you met her?'

'No. I was pretty young.'

Dave smirked.

'I thought you pair met in the sixties? Summer of love and all that. Weren't people at it all the time back then?'

Stan laughed.

'That was later. We talked about it more than we did it, to be honest. It was the early sixties, remember – things were only just getting going. The Beatles hadn't even released *Sergeant Pepper*. The sexual revolution was in its opening moments for sure, but we certainly weren't all at it all the time. Well, I wasn't.'

'Oh. Shame. But you've really only done it with one woman? That's mad. Oh, but what about since? Any little indiscretions? You can tell me. I'd understand, you know I would.'

That much Stan did know. Pretty much Dave's whole adult life had been an indiscretion, but he himself had nothing to tell.

'I've had no indiscretions of any sort, Dave.'

'Really? Weird. Don't you wonder what it would be like with someone else?'

'Not really. I mean, I suppose I'm a bit curious, but as for actually doing it – nah!'

Dave looked intrigued but all he said was, 'You're not after a little dalliance, then?'

This was accompanied by a wink and a nudge to the ribs, causing Stan to snort into his lime.

'No dalliance needed, thanks all the same.'

'Right. OK. Fair enough.' He glugged down the last of his beer. 'Another?'

Stan looked into his pale green drink and shook his head.

'I'm all right, thanks.'

'Mind if I have one?'

'Course not.'

Dave motioned Frank over and Stan looked across to the snooker table as he poured the pint. The lads were down to the black ball but judging by the sighs of frustration, neither of them were having any luck with it. Stan watched, wondering morosely when his own ball would fall into the eternal pocket. *No negativity*, he reminded himself fiercely and ripped open his pork scratchings, but now they were in his grasp he didn't really fancy one.

'It's Bonnie,' he said.

Dave froze, his fresh beer halfway to his lips.

'Sorry?'

'Bonnie!' Her name came out too loud and Stan put a hand to his mouth. 'Sorry. It's Bonnie – that's what worries me, leaving her alone.'

'She won't be alone, mate. She's got the twins.'

'I know, but they've got their own lives, their own families. It's not the same. I just keep picturing her sat all alone in an empty house and I can't bear it.'

'What about her Aunt Nancy?'

'She lives in Sweden with her wife.'

'Course. The Swedish lesbians!'

Dave's eyes lit up automatically and Stan groaned.

'Nancy's ninety, Dave. She's always been something of a wild child, I grant you, but these days she's probably only any use to you if you're into zimmer frames.'

'Ah. Not really. Thanks all the same.'

'Anyway, I'm sure Nancy would come over to see Bonnie, but she's got way too good a life in Sweden to move back in with her. Nope. If I die I'll be leaving her alone and I can't do that.'

He remembered her sitting at the end of the dining room table last Sunday, already looking alone, and his heart ached as if Dave had his electric sander grinding across it.

'I'm not sure you're going to have much choice.'

'No.' Stan set his glass down with an angry thunk. 'No, you're right, Dave, but there must be something I can do about it.'

Dave considered.

'You could have a hologram of yourself made.'

'A hologram? Wouldn't that be a bit creepy?'

'A bit, maybe.' Behind them one of the lads finally potted the black with a cry of triumph. 'What about a recording, then?' Dave suggested. 'You could record messages – like, one for every month or whatever.'

'I guess. It wouldn't be me with her though, would it?'

'Well, no.'

Dave looked into his pint, considering, then said, 'Tickets!'

'What?'

'If you want to make Bonnie feel better you should buy her tickets – one for a different concert or play or gig each month.'

Stan looked at Dave.

'That's quite clever.'

'I'm not just a pretty face!'

They drank, Stan thinking.

'But who would she go with?'

'I don't know, whoever she wanted. Friends, the twins, her new . . .'

Dave stopped and glugged at his beer, his face red.

'Her new . . .?'

'Nothing. Her new nothing.'

'New man – that's what you were going to say, isn't it?'

'No.'

'Yes it is.'

'Well, OK, yes, I was going to say that but it was stupid. It was me thinking as me, not as you, or as Bonnie. Of course she won't want a new man.'

'She might.'

Even as he said it Stan felt a sting of long-forgotten jealousy. When he'd first taken Bonnie out as his girlfriend, he'd spent half the time fretting about who else was talking to her and what she thought of them. If she caught him she'd shout at him, insisting it was ridiculous and he should trust to her love for him and eventually, year by happy year, he'd learned to do so. But this sudden sting seemed written deep into his body, a wound he'd learned to live with but that had never actually healed, thought it was, at least, a cleaner, brighter pain than the unbearable grind of picturing her alone.

'Maybe she should,' he said.

'Should what? Stan, mate, you're not making any sense.'

'I am. If *I* can't be there for Bonnie, I need to make sure someone else will be, don't I?'

It seemed so obvious now. It was piercingly painful, but that almost made it better – if she was going to hurt, then it was only right that he should too. Dave, however, did not look so convinced. His eyes widened and he shuffled his stool back a little.

'Stan, I couldn't do that. There's Gail, you see. And even if there wasn't . . .'

'Not you.'

'It's not that Bonnie isn't gorgeous,' Dave continued. 'She is, for her age. Actually not just for her age. She's a good-looking woman any which way you consider it. Not that I do. I mean, I would, obviously, if I didn't know you and all, but I do and . . .'

Stan put a hand on his arm.

'Not you, Dave. Lord, I wouldn't wish you on anyone, least of all my Bonnie.'

'Oh. Right. Thanks for that.'

'You know what I mean. You'd break her heart and I can't have that. It's very fragile is Bonnie's heart, more so than you'd think. I don't want her with some git who'll move on to the next woman in three months' time. She needs a keeper.'

'Fair enough, mate, but here's the thing – I don't want to put it too bluntly or that, but you won't be around to decide. It'll kind of be up to her.'

'It can't be.'

'Why?'

'She's got terrible taste in men.'

'Fair point.'

'Not me. Well, actually, I was a pretty terrible choice at first, but I came good. That is, I've done OK by her.'

'More than OK, Stan. Oh Lord, do we have to do mushy stuff now?'

'No! God, no. No mushy stuff, quite the opposite. We have to be practical. There's no way Bonnie will go out and look for a new man. She'll think it's disloyal, that she's betraying me, but if I, you know, start the ball rolling maybe she'll pick it up.'

'Ball?'

Dave frowned, but to Stan it now felt like an obvious solution. If he couldn't be there for Bonnie then he had to try and find someone who could. It was like plugging a leaky pipe – no point in sitting around bemoaning the fact the pipe had burst, you just had to get on and deal with it.

Stan had a horrible feeling that he was avoiding the real issues here, but so what? Dave had said he should focus on what he could do with the months he had left, and this was one such thing. The only question was *how*.

'Where do you go about finding men?' he asked. The lads at the pool table looked up and he flushed. 'For women,' he said quickly. 'Where do women go about finding men these days?'

The lads nudged each other and Stan shoved a pork scratching into his mouth. It tasted claggy and far too rich.

'Yates's is still a good pick-up joint,' Dave said.

'Dave! I am not going to Yates's to "pick up" a new husband for my seventy-three-year-old wife.'

'Right. Good point. Well, there's only one way then – online. It's all the rage these days. There's loads of apps.'

Stan felt a little faint. He knew about apps. Jamie had put a messaging one on his phone so he could send him pictures of his football team and things he wanted for his birthday and random animals that he seemed to find very funny. To be fair, most of them were. He also had the BBC Sport app and the Everton app and a weather app. A dating app, though – that was a whole new kettle of fish. And how on earth would he know what to look for?

'Any you'd recommend?' he asked nervously.

'Loads. I met Gail on one called *Good in the Sack*. It's great for . . .' He hesitated and drank the last of his pint. 'Probably not the sort of thing you're looking for.'

'Not really, Dave.'

'No. Sorry. Look, Stan, are you sure about this? It seems a bit . . .'

'Wrong?'

'Weird.'

'Maybe you're right. I'll think about it.'

'You should. Really. You're probably in shock, like. Or maybe it's that green drink making you go funny.'

They both looked at Stan's barely touched lime and soda.

'Maybe.'

The couple in the corner rose and made for the door, clutching at each other, and Stan felt suddenly deflated. It was madness, all of it. He glanced at his watch.

'I'd better get going, Dave. Chemo tomorrow.'

'Right. Lovely. Me too. Not chemo, obviously. Getting going. Got to be on site early to get ready to start digging the foundations.'

Stan swallowed. The foundations. He wouldn't leave Bonnie in their cosy farmhouse kitchen but in the new house, the dream house. And if he found her a new man, she would be there with him instead. For a moment that idea felt impossible to bear but better that, surely, than her being all alone. He'd have to think about it further but, at the end of the day, if you truly loved someone you had to want the best for them, whatever it cost you.

Chapter Six

February 1963

It was the smell that hit Bonnie first – a potent cocktail of sweat, damp and something like rotting veg. She recoiled and glanced to Spike, but his eyes were glowing with excitement and he tugged her towards the steep stone stairs that led down to the Cavern Club.

They'd been dating for two weeks now. Bonnie had been to another Best Boys' gig in a backstreet hall, and she and Spike had been to the cinema and out to a new American diner with Susie-Ann and Sticks. Her boyfriend was as meltingly gorgeous as ever but she'd also got to know him better, and every so often a flash of the boy from down the docks came through the smart clothes and the slicked-back hair and Bonnie liked him more for it.

Plus, he was shyer than he'd seemed in the Jacaranda, and although they'd kissed plenty – Bonnie flushed happily at the heady memories – he'd not yet tried anything more on. Bonnie felt both relieved and somehow disappointed, but their one shared passion was music and a few days ago he'd surprised her with tickets to the Cavern.

'We're only playing lunchtimes so far – but there's some half-decent bands on and you never know who you might meet.'

'I can't wait,' she'd assured him and she'd meant it, but as she took the steps downwards she felt more as if she were descending into hell than Liverpool's most happening venue. The Cavern was right in the heart of the city, just a few streets back from the great Mersey, and she'd been thrilled to be a part of the excited young crowd queuing to get in. Now, though, a jumble of heat and noise rose from the pit below and when she put her hand to the wall to steady herself, she found it sticky and damp.

'Ugh!'

She jerked away, looking at the brickwork for fungus or slime and Spike laughed.

'It does get a bit damp down here, even when it's baltic out.'

'A *bit*, Spike?'

'Be worse later,' he said cheerfully. 'Sometimes it fair runs down the walls.'

Bonnie glanced fearfully at the exposed brick, as if slime might ooze from it as she watched.

'What's the smell, Spike? It's like vegetables or something.'

'Oh that!' he laughed. 'It *is* vegetables. There's a market above and it never gets cleared away very well. Don't fret, though, you soon get used to it and it's worth it. Look!'

They turned into the Cavern itself and were hit by a crush of people. Music pulsed off the low ceiling and laughter and chatter buzzed in the air every bit as much as it had at the Jacaranda. Bonnie felt her heart pick up a beat as she looked around. She was in a brick cellar whose tri-arched ceiling curved not far above the heads of those within. Big pillars divided the room into three sections. There were chairs laid out in the central one for those wanting to listen to the band on the low stage at the far end in comfort. To the right, people milled about around a small bar, trying to chat over the pounding music, and to the left, the whole section seemed to be moving up and down as a packed crowd danced like mad things.

The band were playing 'The Hippy Hippy Shake' and Bonnie's feet began to tap. Spike swung an arm around her waist and pulled her close to speak into her ear, and she saw a couple of girls look jealously over and felt proud to be with the most gorgeous man in the club. Tonight he was in a wide-collared shirt and white jacket, and with his dark hair slicked back he looked just like Elvis Presley in *Jailhouse Rock*.

She saw him pulling his 'lead singer' persona into place, as if the atmosphere in the packed basement was snaking under his skin, and she flicked back her hair and tried to match him. If he was Elvis, she would have to be Judy Tyler. She and Nancy had been to the flicks to see that film three times and the thought of having her very own rocker felt unbelievably thrilling. She wished she'd been able to afford another new dress but she'd had to buy books instead, so she was in an old one that Susie-Ann had altered. It didn't feel anywhere near as glamorous as her gingham outfit, but – *head up* – it would have to do.

'We can dance over there.' Spike guided her towards the heaving left-hand section where a mass of people were not so much dancing as jumping up and down. 'The Cavern Stomp,' he explained. 'There's no space for jiving, see.'

Bonnie stared, astonished, but now the band were striking up with their version of 'Love Me Do' and everyone was going wild. Tugging off their thick coats and scarves and throwing them to one side, they somehow crammed themselves into the crowd. Bonnie felt the music whizz through her blood and jumped with the rest, her self-consciousness turning to raw excitement.

Susie-Ann and Sticks scrambled in at their side with Danny in their wake, although he seemed too distracted to dance. Bonnie had had a chance to get to know the big lad a bit better at the Best Boys' second gig and had found him quietly charming and definitely the calmest of the quartet. She supposed that was why he was their manager.

'OK, Danny?' she called over the music.

'Good, thank you,' he agreed in his plummy voice. 'Just looking for Bob Wooler, the manager. I had some cards printed, thought it might help us get noticed – look, they're colour and everything.'

He reached into his pocket and pulled out a wad of small, shiny white cards. Reluctantly, Bonnie stopped jumping to look at them but then smiled to see 'The Best Boys' written across the middle in a curving red script.

'These are amazing, Danny,' she said, taking one and stroking it. The lettering was glossy beneath her touch.

'Thanks,' he said diffidently. 'Important to catch the eye, my father always says.'

'Your "father"?' Sticks teased in a drawn-out accent, but he was quick to pocket some of the new cards.

Even Spike looked impressed. He turned one of the cards over and over in his hands before slipping it into his jacket.

'These must have cost a bit.'

'Yes, well, you have to invest at the outset.'

'Or, rather, your "father" does.' Sticks bent down. 'Think this fell out too, lad.'

He handed Danny what looked to Bonnie like a rubber glove. Danny flushed – as he seemed to do very easily – then snatched at it, shoving it into his pocket with the rest of the cards. Bonnie couldn't begin to imagine what he needed rubber gloves for and wasn't sure she wanted to ask, but thankfully Spike was keener on talking about Wooler.

'You gonna talk him into giving the Best Boys a chance on stage, then, Dan?'

'That's the plan,' Danny agreed, turning to him with evident relief at the change of subject.

'We've done lunchtimes here,' Sticks explained to Bonnie, 'but not as often as we'd like.'

'Cos Lee's always bloody working,' Danny said.

Sticks shook his ginger head.

'So? It's OK for you, Danny. Your da's minted. You don't understand about actually earning a living.'

'That's not true,' Danny protested. 'I work for my father too. You just have to be flexible if you want to succeed. *You* are, Sticks.'

'Cos Da lets me do evenings instead. Lee works in a café – how's he meant to swerve lunchtimes?'

'But doesn't Lee work *here*?' Bonnie asked, confused.

Spike had told her Lee ran the Cavern cloakroom and as she looked over the gyrating bodies towards it she could just about see the dark-haired older lad battling with a long queue.

'He does both,' Danny groaned. 'He's always working.'

'Cos he has rent to pay, you blert.' Sticks leaned in to Bonnie again. 'Lee has his own pad. Not like us soft lads still hanging around with Mam and Da.'

'That's cos he's ancient,' Spike said. 'We'll all have our own places when we're in our sodding twenties, and mine's gonna be a proper mansion.'

'When the Best Boys make it big?' Bonnie asked him.

'Exactly! I want this, Bonnie lass – fame, fortune, the lot!'

He kissed her and she felt giddy at his touch. The band switched down into 'Save the Last Dance' for the end of their set and Spike slid his hands around her waist and pulled her close, as if they truly were in a film.

His shirt was nearly as damp as the wall had been, but his toned chest was warm and as she ran her own hands over it, she felt his heart beating against them. His hands dropped lower, creeping below the hem of her skirt to touch the top of her thigh. It sent strange, exciting sensations between her legs and when she didn't pull away his hand moved higher.

'Spike,' she gasped. 'Should we?'

'Course we should. Don't you like it, Bon? Doesn't it make you feel goooood?'

He drew the last word out, crooning it against her lips like the star he was trying to be and it did – it did make her feel good. *If you fancy it, why not?* Aunt Nancy had said, so Bonnie dared to press herself a little closer. But then Spike hardened against her and, shocked, she pulled back. He frowned, lines creasing his handsome brow, and at that moment two heavily made-up girls descended on them.

'Spike! It's Spike, isn't it? Spike from the Best Boys? Oh, I just adore you. Don't you adore him, Violet? We *adore* you!'

Spike let go of Bonnie's waist to run his hands through his perfect hair and she staggered back. Instantly Violet, a dark-haired minx in a beret and barely-there skirt, stepped calculatedly across her and batted her eyelashes up at Spike.

'You're such a super singer. Can I have your autograph?'

Spike preened.

'Course you can. You got paper?'

The girls pouted.

'No. Silly bints. We didn't know we'd be meeting a star, see. Bet they'll have some at the bar, though. Can we get you a Coke? Please? Lord, wait til the others hear we had a Coke with Spike from the Best Boys!'

Spike looked uncertainly to Bonnie but one of Aunt Nancy's other bits of advice had been never to be clingy so she nodded him on.

'I'll be straight back,' he assured her with a kiss, then moved away to collar the fresh-faced barman for a pen.

Bonnie looked uncertainly round the buzzing club. Not being clingy was all very well for Nancy as people seemed to fall over themselves to talk to her, but Bonnie didn't want Spike seeing her standing at the edge like a wallflower. She looked for Susie-Ann but she was being all but swallowed by Sticks and, with Danny gone off after Mr Wooler, she had no one to talk to. Then she remembered Lee.

Hastily she gathered up their coats and made for the cloak-room. The 'auld fella' of the Best Boys was alone too and with the queue growing all the time panic was shading his angular face. Bonnie thought once more how cool he'd look in a photo, but this was no studio and the poor lad needed help.

'Want a hand?' she offered.

'Really? Oh Bonnie, that'd be great. There's another girl meant to be working but she's off chasing bands like usual.'

'It's fine.'

Out of the corner of her eye Bonnie could see Spike with at least five or six girls gathered adoringly around him. So much for coming straight back, she thought, stung, and dived into the little cloakroom.

'If I sort the tickets can you hang the stuff up?' Lee asked.

'Course.'

It wasn't hard. In fact, Bonnie enjoyed herself hanging up the range of jackets and coats. Some of them were outrageous – bright reds and yellows and swirling patterns. Surely not coats to be worn all the time?

'How do people afford these?' she whispered to Lee as he handed over a particularly striking purple velvet jacket.

'Snidey fabrics,' he whispered back. 'Only meant to be worn for a season.'

Bonnie was shocked. A coat should last ten years at least! Aunt Nancy had drummed that into her, always making her hang hers up by the radiator if it got damp, or brush off any mud so it didn't 'taint the fibres'. For a moment, stood amongst a hundred jackets in the back of the pulsing club, Bonnie felt horribly far from home.

When she'd phoned her aunt last week, Nancy had told her she was off on a trip to Sweden to see Astrid's home town.

She'd been very excited about it, so Bonnie had done her best to sound pleased, but the thought of Nancy so far away had made her feel very small inside. It was fair enough, Bonnie knew. Nancy had given so much of her life to looking after her that she deserved to go and be happy. And, after all, Bonnie was off having adventures, so why should Nancy not do so too?

From across the club she heard Spike laugh and leaned out of the cloakroom to see him strutting about with a gaggle of fans. The barely-there skirt girl was all over him and Bonnie wished now that she'd let Susie-Ann cut her own hemline higher. Not that it would have mattered, anyway, as Spike had clearly forgotten she was even here. Miserably, she pictured her five-year-old self peering down at her film-dream parents dancing romantically. Real adult life seemed so much harder and messier than she'd imagined it would be from that brief glimpse – was she crazy to even imagine she could fit in?

'Oi! Who are you? And worra you doing in my cloakroom?'

Bonnie was jolted back to the present moment to see an auburn-haired girl glaring at her. She glared back.

'I'm Bonnie and I'm helping Lee.'

'Sweet on him, are you?'

'No!' Bonnie ducked round the bristling girl. 'I'm with Spike, actually.'

She gestured to where Spike was now signing beer mats for his acolytes.

'Looks like it.'

'Well he can hardly dance with me when I'm in here, can he?' Bonnie shot back.

'In here doing *your* job, Cilla,' Lee said, coming over. 'Don't be so catty, lass. You know Wooler won't let you sing if you don't work proper.'

The girl – Cilla – sighed but then nodded and stuck out a slim hand to Bonnie.

'Fair play. I can be a right cow. Ta, Bonnie.' Bonnie blinked but took Cilla's hand. She pumped it surprisingly hard for such a little thing, then shoved the purple coat back at her and said, 'Here, then – you might as well hang this up.'

'No,' Lee said firmly, taking it from Bonnie and handing it back. 'It's your turn, Cil. Bonnie and I are taking a break.' Cilla did as she was bid and Lee ushered Bonnie to one side and handed her a Coke from a stash below the counter. 'You've been a big help. Cheers.'

'Cheers, Lee.'

She drank her Coke and snuck a peep across the dance floor to see if Spike was looking for her yet. He wasn't. She felt anger start to build inside her; how dare he treat her like this? She'd drink this Coke and then she'd go and find him. She might not be clingy but she wasn't a pushover either. At her side, Lee stood watching the band, absorbed by the music. Bonnie saw the lights flickering across the angles of his face and wondered how he'd got into all this.

'Do you like working here?' she asked him.

'Not the job, no, but I love the place. It's cool.'

'It's smelly,' Bonnie said and he laughed.

'S'pose it is. It's the market upstairs, but you get used to the . . . earthiness. And I don't care. To me it smells of excitement and change and . . . and *promise*.'

'Promise?'

'Promise of a new way. Liverpool's a top place to be, and this joint is top of the top and we're here. That's amazing, don't you think?'

Put that way, and with Lee's dark eyes shining so intensely she supposed it *was* pretty amazing.

'You want to make it big, Lee?'

'I do.' He said it softly but with real purpose. 'I proper do, Bonnie. I know Spike's the star, like, but he needs the Best

69

Boys to make it. Everyone loves bands – look.' He pointed to a poster on the wall which announced a 'Good Friday R&B Marathon'. Topping the bill was Liverpool's biggest band.

'The Beatles are playing here?' Bonnie gasped.

'Sure are. Tickets go on sale soon and it's gonna be mad. I want that to be the Best Boys one day. I want folks to go mad for *us*. I've left my da's business to play music and it has to work out. They think I'm soft, my folks. Irresponsible, reckless, all that.'

Bonnie smiled. Quiet, hard-working Lee seemed the very opposite of reckless.

'My aunt says it's important to follow a dream if you're lucky enough to have one.'

'Does she? That's cool. What's your dream then, Bonnie?'

'I want to design beautiful houses.'

'Course. You're studying architecture, right?'

'That's right. I love it, even if it is a long course for a girl.'

'Does it matter if you're a girl?'

Bonnie stared at him.

'Did you really say that?'

'What?'

She shook herself.

'Nothing. Sorry. That's what I think too, but not many seem to agree.'

'Barm pots, the lot of them. Surely being good enough is what counts?'

Bonnie looked at Lee with new eyes. Around university, some people were buying into the idea of equality, or at least saying they did, but the cold shoulder she routinely got from the supposedly enlightened students said otherwise. Out in the 'real world' people were usually astonished that she was doing such a 'difficult' degree. Except Aunt Nancy, of course.

Nancy had backed her all the way here, making sure Bonnie had the best education they could manage and slaving over her homework with her, even once it had become clear Bonnie understood it far better. She'd marched into school when the headmistress had suggested architecture was too difficult for a girl and demanded to know how any self-respecting female teacher could say such a thing. Then she'd paid for extra tutoring and driven Bonnie to the interview herself. She couldn't let Nancy down by giving up. She *wouldn't* let her down.

'You all right, Bonnie?'

She shook herself.

'Course. I'm fine. Great.' She suddenly remembered Spike calling Lee the 'auld fella' of the group and could see why, but she'd done without a father for most of her life and she certainly didn't need one now. 'I better find Spike,' she said. 'He'll be looking for me. See you, Lee.'

He nodded and she ducked out of the cloakroom and plunged into the crowd. The band was playing a rasping rendition of 'Some Other Guy' and Spike was dancing, to cries of delight from his fans. Bonnie wriggled through the crowd towards him.

'Spike,' she called but he didn't hear her. No wonder – it was hard to hear anything over the music. 'Spike!'

She made a grab for his hand and to her relief he clasped it tight and spun her round and into his arms. Her heart lifted, but when he looked down he blinked and said, 'Oh Bonnie, it's you,' and it dropped straight to the rough brick floor.

'Who did you think it was, Spike?'

The fans were jostling like hyenas round their prey but Bonnie fixed her eyes on Spike and ignored them. He shifted and glanced around.

'I knew it were you, queen, course I did.'

'Really? Because it seems to me that you'd forgotten I was even here.'

'How could I forget you, gorgeous Bonnie?'

He was turning on the charm but his eyes were darting around his followers and she felt stupid again. So much for being Judy Tyler to his Elvis. Well, fine, this was real life, not the movies.

'You tell me,' she said, her hands on her hips.

He flushed.

'Lord, Bonnie, don't give me down the banks. It's embarrassing.'

'So is being left alone on the dance floor.'

He grimaced.

'You did say it was OK for me to go.'

'And you did say you'd be straight back.'

He rubbed self-consciously at his neck.

'Can I help it if so many people want to talk to me? Didn't have you down as the clingy type.'

The word stung and she drew herself up tall.

'I'm not a "type" at all, Spike, I'm just me. You asked me here and then you ditched me. I call that downright rude, don't you?'

'Don't be so old-fashioned. This is the Cavern, not a tea dance.'

He rolled his eyes at Violet, who batted her mascara-laden eyelashes back. Bonnie drew in a slow breath and counted to seven in her head – something she always did to buy herself time to think. She might be a country girl, new to Liverpool and rotten-veg music cellars and stomp dancing, but she wasn't taking this. Aunt Nancy had raised her to stand up for herself and she damned well would.

'It'll never be fashionable to be rude,' she said loudly, but to her horror Spike just burst out laughing. She dug her nails into her palms. 'Fine, Spike, if that's how it is, we're finished.'

Panic flitted across Spike's dark eyes but then he remembered his audience and clasped his hands to his chest in a pantomime of grief.

'Eee, my poor heart,' he cried and, sensing blood, the hyenas pushed past Bonnie and she was out of the circle.

Well *good*. He wasn't worth it if he treated her that way, and if she hurt inside it was only pride. Pride, as Aunt Nancy had often told her, did no one any good, so she shoved her head up high and stalked away. The movement felt strong but even before she'd reached the arches, her anger had lost steam. She thought she and Spike had been getting on so well and she'd had such hopes for tonight, but now it was all spoiled. She put a hand to the brick pillar to steady herself and was thankful when Susie-Ann came bouncing over.

'Spike being a bastard? He's getting a bigger head than bloody Napoleon Bonaparte, that one, won't fit up the stairs out of 'ere if he's not careful.'

Bonnie gave her a small smile.

'It's over.'

'Between you and Spike? Blimey, that was quick. He's a thick blert, mind, to be throwing you over.'

'I finished it, actually.'

'Oh. Right. Nice one.'

Susie-Ann grinned at Bonnie and she felt a little better.

'Fancy a Coke?' she asked her friend, but at that Susie-Ann's smile slipped a little.

'Er, we was just getting off actually.'

'Leaving? This early?'

'Yeah, well . . .'

Sticks popped up behind Susie-Ann and put his hands around her slim waist before, right in front of Bonnie, running them up to clasp her breasts.

'Susie-Ann and I got things to do to each other,' he said lewdly.

Susie-Ann gave her a cheeky smile and Bonnie tried not to feel hurt that her friend was ditching her just when she needed her most but she supposed she just had to grow up. And fast. She forced a smile onto her face.

'Right. Course. Fine. See you, then.'

Up on stage the band were waving at Cilla to join them and all eyes were thankfully turning that way. Bonnie watched Susie-Ann and Sticks make for the exit and leaned back against the wall, only to feel the damp and sweat of the bricks soak into her dress. She leaped away, disgusted. She wasn't ready for any of this. She was just a small-town girl missing her home and . . .

'Bonnie? Oh Bonnie, are you all right? Oh, your pretty dress. Poor you. Here.'

Bonnie felt a soft wool jacket go round her damp shoulders and saw a laundered hanky before her face and looked up to see Danny looking down on her, concern in his blue eyes.

'Oh, Danny, thank you.'

'My pleasure. Spike really shouldn't leave the prettiest girl in the Cavern alone like this. It's not gentlemanly.'

Bonnie tried to scoff at his old-fashioned assertion but actually felt soothed by it. There was something very reassuring about Danny's big shoulders, floppy hair and bright eyes. He was nowhere near as edgy as Spike, but right now that felt like a very good thing.

'Thank you, Danny,' she murmured.

'No need to thank me, it's true. You ask me, he doesn't deserve you as his girl.'

Bonnie glanced over to Spike. For a moment he caught her eye and she thought she saw apology in his gaze but then Violet slid her hands round onto his bum and he looked away again.

'I'm not his girl,' she said firmly, and felt Danny step a little closer.

'Really? I'd treat you right, you know, Bonnie, if you were mine. I'd treat you like a princess, I swear it.'

Bonnie looked up at him, trying to process what he was saying. Was he asking her out? Was Spike watching?

Danny slid an arm around her shoulder and Bonnie leaned against him. Out of the corner of her eye she saw Spike openly staring, his chocolate eyes as dark as Bournville, and she turned her face up to Danny.

'I think you're the most beautiful woman I've ever seen,' he told her, his cut-glass voice rich with emotion, and she felt it like a balm to her jangled-up body.

Danny was kind and educated and intelligent. Maybe she'd been with the wrong Best Boy. And maybe tonight, far from being a disaster, was actually the start of the rest of her life.

Chapter Seven

'Hiya, I'm back!'

Greya's voice bounced through the house just as Bonnie and Stan were settling down to a quick omelette for lunch. Lisa and Greya had been staying for two weeks now. They'd been back to London the first weekend but Lisa had returned early, muttering about allotments. Simon, it emerged, had managed to secure one near the house and he and Greya were gleefully digging it out – not an activity of which Lisa approved.

Lisa was working such long hours on her Manchester trial that they barely saw her, but Greya had joined the build team and was around every evening quizzing Bonnie, chatting about all sorts of current issues and eating her way through enough food to feed a small nation. She had, however, been at an eco camp all weekend and the house had felt very quiet without her. Now it seemed the peace was over.

'Through here!' Bonnie called.

She was in a happy mood, mainly because Stan's chemo seemed to be going rather well. It wasn't much fun, though. He had to spend every Wednesday rigged up to a drip sending poison through his bloodstream and, for at least two days after that, creep around the house sleeping most of his precious hours away, drinking endless water and avoiding germs. Marleigh and Jamie had been banned in case they brought kiddie bugs in, and he missed them popping by with Rachael or Andrew as they'd often used to do.

It seemed as if at least half his time was being poured into the nasty treatment, but at his check-up yesterday the nurses had insisted it was going really well and that had pleased Bonnie so much that it was worth it all. Even so, he was bored stiff stuck in the house and got up delightedly as Greya bounded into the kitchen, purple hair flying and hazel eyes shining.

'Hi Gramps, Granny.' She hugged Bonnie and dropped a kiss on Stan's head. 'Wow, omelette! Fab. I'm starving.'

'Have mine,' Stan said, pushing the plate towards her.

'No! Oh no, I couldn't do that.'

'Go on. I can make another.'

'Really? Fantastic.'

She threw herself into a seat and began attacking the food with vigour.

'Didn't they feed you at the camp?' Stan asked, standing up to reach for new eggs.

'Oh, they did, but it was all beans and that. I'm trying to get into vegan cooking as it's definitely better for the planet, but honestly, Gramps, this tastes *so* much nicer.'

Stan noted that her plate was all but empty and cracked more eggs into the bowl.

'So was the camp good?' Bonnie asked, sitting down next to her. 'Apart from the beans, of course.'

'Oh Granny, it was fantastic. Inspirational. I am *so* doing Eco Studies, whatever Mum says. I met the guys working on this power-bike and they were amazing. It's such a cool idea – really. You'd love it.'

'I would?'

'Totally. It's going to be the future for all modern homes.'

'A power-bike? Like a motorbike?'

'No! A bike for generating power. You keep it somewhere easy and then when you want to, say, boil a kettle, you take the bike over, plug it in and pedal til the kettle boils.'

'How long does it take?'

'A while,' Greya conceded, 'but it's, like, developing technology. The dynamos are getting better all the time.'

'Dynamos?' Stan asked, intrigued. 'Your mother had dynamo lights on her bike when she was a kid. Rachael, too – though they had to be a different colour, of course. All the rage they were, in the eighties, then they sort of went out of fashion. I'm not sure why.'

'LEDs,' Greya said wisely. 'Small and efficient but not as good for the world as generating your own energy.'

'It's a good idea, Greya,' Bonnie said, 'but what if you're ill or old? How do you get a cuppa if you can't physically pedal?'

'There'd have to be backups,' Greya agreed. 'And there could be community schemes where fitter people provided power for the less fit. Conversion of kinetic energy is improving all the time, so it has to be a viable way forward, don't you think?'

'I do,' Bonnie agreed, 'and I know someone else who might as well.'

'Who?'

'A friend of mine from way back. She's high up in the Department for Energy with specific responsibility for future-proofing. I've done a few things with her over the last year or two.'

'You know the Energy Minister?'

It was clear Bonnie was going up in Greya's estimation all the time.

'She was a friend of mine at uni. Suzanne Cobden – or Susie-Ann as she was back then. She read history, in theory, but if I remember correctly she spent most of her time partying, didn't she, Stan?'

'She wasn't the only one.'

'Oi! She led me astray.'

He laughed and kissed Bonnie.

'And thank heavens for that.' He turned to Greya. 'Granny's Aunt Nancy arranged for her to board with another student's family and picked a girl with her finger on the pulse of all that was going on in Liverpool.'

Bonnie laughed.

'Not everyone's guardian would deliberately pick someone wild for them to live with, but then Nancy wasn't your average guardian.'

'She certainly was not. I must thank her again for sending you my way next time I see her. That is . . .' He stalled at the thought that he might never again see Bonnie's lively aunt, but Greya was looking at him with such concern that he couldn't give in to misery. 'That is, you and Susie-Ann both turned out OK, Bon, and it's a great idea to get in touch with her about this bike thing. Right, Grey?'

'Absolutely. Totally. It would help us one hundred million per cent. And it's such a worthwhile project, really it is. Just think – no one will waste energy if they have to generate it themselves, and if they do, it doesn't matter as we're not ruining the planet for it. And what's more, it will solve the obesity crisis too. Perfect!'

'It certainly sounds it,' Stan agreed, impressed. 'Why aren't we doing it already, hey?'

At that, Greya sobered.

'It's the bikes, Grandpa. They're not very good.'

She turned her beautiful eyes up to Stan as he brought the new omelettes to the table and he froze. He vividly remembered that sort of look from when the twins had been young – it had always brought trouble.

'What?' he asked.

'I've got one of the prototypes outside. The lads said I could have it on loan because I know someone who's bound to be able to improve it.'

'You do? Who?'

She smiled angelically at him.

'You.'

'Me?'

'Yeah. I bet you can. You're brilliant at all that sort of stuff.' She hesitated and then added, 'If you're, like, well enough, that is?'

Stan sucked in a breath.

'I'm quite well enough, thank you, Greya. It's days since I had the second chemo, and Dr Mirabi says I'm reacting very well to it.'

'*Very* well,' Bonnie repeated, the hope raw in her voice.

It made her sound vulnerable and that scared Stan, but even he had to admit that the nurses' encouragement was starting to make him feel hopeful. At the very least it meant he could get on with life for now.

'I'd love to help if I can,' he said firmly.

Greya beamed.

'Great. I'll do it with you, Gramps. I know loads these days, and I'm dead patient. Actually I'm not patient at all, but I'll try. For you, I'll try.'

'For *me*?'

Stan looked at Bonnie, bemused, but she was too busy laughing at Greya's ruthless manipulation to save him.

'Can I eat my lunch first?' he asked, indicating his omelette.

Greya nodded, her second one disappearing as fast as the first.

'Course you can, Gramps – hurry up though, hey? You're going to love this.'

*

She was right about the bike, Stan reflected as they all stood looking down at it lying on the drive. It was very ugly – dark and spiky with big clumpy feet, presumably to stop it falling over as its poor rider tried to summon up enough power for a cup of tea.

'It would look better in a paler colour,' Bonnie offered. 'I have a lovely aqua-white eggshell that would do it.'

'See!' Greya cried, delighted. 'I knew you two would help.'

'It won't change the functionality though, sweetie.'

'That's what Grandpa's for,' Greya said confidently, and Stan couldn't deny the sheer thrill of usefulness it sent through him.

He crouched down, peering at the cog system.

'Talk me through it, then,' he said, and within a millisecond his granddaughter was doing just that.

The next thing he knew they'd dragged it into the big garage-cum-workshop to the right of the house, and his afternoon spiralled away in a whirl of chains and wires and pedal-power. Greya did, indeed, know loads, but loads turned out to not be enough and she had to fetch her laptop to call up fact sheets and technical specs from the project files. Stan's brain ached trying to figure them out but it beat the more usual pain in his digestive organs, and Greya greeted his every suggestion with enthusiasm.

'So you really are keen on doing Eco Studies, then?' he asked her as he considered the tension on the bike's chain.

'I really, really am, Gramps. Dad's totally on board with it. He's really thrown himself into his allotment and he's started cycling to work, and he's looking into getting solar panels and everything. Problem is, the more he does, the more Mum resists. I swear she's going to stop eating veggies the minute he actually grows one, just to make a point.'

Stan sighed. That certainly sounded like something his stubborn daughter would do, but it seemed such a shame.

'I get why she wants me to do law,' Greya went on, 'but it's sooo dull. This, though, this I feel passionately about and that's important, isn't it?'

'It is.'

'Were you always passionate about building?'

Stan laughed.

'Not always, no. Truth be told I wanted to be a musician.'

'A musician? Like a pianist or something?'

'No! A guitarist. And a singer. I was in a band.'

'A band? That's so cool. When?'

'Oh, when I was young and idealistic and, frankly, mad. We'd never have made it but everyone was doing it at the time and it seemed like a good idea.'

'Did you do gigs?'

'Oh yes. The Jacaranda, the Cavern, the . . .'

'But those are proper venues, Gramps! I've heard of them.'

'Must be proper then.'

'The Beatles played there!'

'Certainly did. I was at their big Good Friday gig. Granny, too.'

'You were together?'

Stan felt himself flush and tugged harder on the bike chain.

'You know, if we took a link out I think it would really help. This feels a bit slack to me.'

'It does?' Greya peered at the chain. 'OK then.'

'It might not work, though. Are you sure we're all right to tinker?'

'Absolutely sure. That's why they lent it to me.'

'OK, but we should take lots of photos so we can get it back to this state if it goes wrong.'

'Good plan. I'll do it.' She whipped out her phone and started snapping away. Peace descended, but not for long. 'So you'll, er, talk to Mum then, Gramps?'

'About what?'

'About me doing Eco Studies. Bet you can convince her.'

'Convince Lisa? What do you think I am, a magician?'

Lisa had always been certain her own way was the right way, and the years did not seem to have mellowed her. She did her best to be polite when she came in from work and always made an effort to see how Stan was doing, but ask her about herself and she clammed up straight away. Stan looked more closely at his granddaughter.

'Is everything OK with your Mum, Grey?'

'Mum? Course. Apart from the degree thing. And . . . and she does seem to be arguing with Dad quite a lot.'

Her head sank into her chin so that her sparkly hair covered her face and Stan stood up.

'Arguing, sweetie?'

'Quite a lot, yeah. Even more than usual, though maybe I was just so busy with my A-levels I didn't pay much attention before. It was when I came back from skiing that I noticed it – snide remarks at each other, hissed criticisms, that sort of thing.'

'Right,' Stan said, wishing Bonnie was here; she was so much better at this stuff than him. 'Like what?'

'Oh, all sorts of crap.' Greya tossed back her hair and coughed. 'Classic modern marriage issues if you ask me. We did it at school in personal development classes. Dad's supposedly dead proud of Mum's success and A-OK with her being the higher wage earner, but underneath it hurts his pride and he secretly yearns for a wife in a pinny and fresh lipstick to have his meat and two veg ready when he comes in from his own day.'

Stan blinked. Where did kids these days learn all this stuff? The internet?

'Greya, maybe . . .'

'And Mum's just as bad. She says she likes that Dad's cool with her having such a big career and proud he knows which end of the hoover sucks, but really she'd like him to sweep home in a Jag bringing diamonds and carry her caveman-style up to . . . Well, you know.'

She suddenly looked shy again and all the fancy words seemed to drain out of her.

'I'm sorry,' Stan said awkwardly, feeling for both his daughter and his granddaughter. 'We'll talk to Lisa, I promise. But what about you?'

'Me?' Greya asked. 'Oh, I'm OK. I'm pretty much grown up now, right?' Stan wasn't so sure about that, but she was staring at him so appealingly that he nodded. 'And you'll tell her it's a good idea for me to do Eco Studies?'

'I'll try, but I'm not making any promises. Have you done those photos?'

'Yep. Is this OK?'

She turned the screen to him and flicked through myriad photos at lightning speed until the phone came to a stop on a shot of her face, smiling straight into the camera, purple hair glowing from a light somewhere behind.

'What a lovely photo,' Stan said.

'Do you think so?'

She was blushing, he was sure of it.

'Is it for something special?'

'Oh, no. Not really.'

'Greya?'

'Honestly, Gramps! If you must know it's for my profile on this dating app. It's not one of those stupid mainstream ones, though. It's for quirkier people. People with something proper to say for themselves.'

'Is it now?' Stan sidled up to her. 'Can I see?'

'I guess.'

With a flick of her nails, Greya pulled up the app. The logo said 'Cherry Creek' and the picture below it was of a tumbling set of rapids with the slogan 'Love Out of the Mainstream'. Stan's heart started to beat faster. He'd ventured on to the computer a couple of times to look into dating sites, but the wealth of information was daunting.

He'd looked at one called 'Second Time Round' but it had seemed to be mainly for younger people looking to 'blend families'. Then he'd found one for 'Golden Years Together' and read a number of touching accounts of people finding partners to ease their loneliness. The talk had all been of companionship and support and care, and had convinced him it would be a good idea for Bonnie if the treatment didn't deliver the miracle they were hoping for. But not one person had been advertising in anticipation of widowhood so he'd lost his nerve. Could this more alternative app of Greya's be the one he needed?

'Can you advertise for any sort of partner on here?'

'I'm not sure "advertise" is quite the word, Grandpa, but you can post a profile, yes.'

'For men and women and . . .'

'And anything in between. Totally. Why?'

Stan leaned back on his workbench and picked up a spanner, running his finger around the reassuringly perfect hexagonal head and feeling its edges bump soothingly against an old scar.

'It's just an idea I had. You'll probably think it's mad.'

'I like mad things.'

'OK. I just . . . I just wanted to see if I could post something looking for a new husband for Bonnie for when – *if* – I'm gone.'

Greya seemed to stare at him for an eternity and Stan looked out of the window, shifting under her gaze. In the house he could see Bonnie poring over some plans at the big dining table. He watched a white curl flop over her face before, finally, his granddaughter spoke.

'Is there no hope then, Grandpa?'

He felt a lump form instantly in his throat and shot across to grab her in a hug.

'No, Grey. That is, of course there's hope. The chemo is going well, all the nurses say so. I just want, you know, a backup plan. In case. I hate the idea of Bonnie being left alone, and thought maybe I could help a little.'

'That's so sweet, Grandpa.'

'Is it?'

Stan looked back to her, relieved.

'It is, yes, but wouldn't she be better finding someone herself when – if – she wants to? Isn't it a bit, you know, patriarchal to do it for her?'

Stan smiled.

'A bit, maybe. But I know Bonnie. She's not good alone, but she doesn't realise that. She thinks she's brave and strong and capable and she is, up to a point, but after that . . . I'm not planning on setting up some bloke to stand at the funeral and claim her, don't worry. I just thought that if I found someone nice I could introduce to her as a friend then she might have an, an option.'

'An option?'

Stan's heart seemed to fill up as he looked at Greya, stood there staring up at him, so innocent despite the purple hair and the grown-up ideas for the planet. There was something of the Bonnie he'd first known in her eyes and it took him all the way back to the start, to the essence of them and the reason why he had to do this. He grabbed Greya's hands.

'She's been such a wonderful wife to me, Greya, and we had such plans for more. If I can't give her that, maybe someone else can. I don't want her to suffer my cancer too. I want her to live, to be happy.'

Greya's big eyes were moist.

'That's so sweet,' she said again. 'So generous and kind and . . . and sweet.'

Stan scuffed his shoes along the rough garage floor.

'You'll help me then?'

Greya smiled.

'I'll help you, Grandpa. Here.' She pulled up a stool, whisking two pieces of drainpipe off it. 'Take a seat and let's begin. Now, name . . .'

It didn't take long. With Greya's technical know-how and unabashed media creativity, Stan had a profile within twenty minutes – a profile that stated clearly that he was looking to meet a 'kind, warm, caring' man to offer friendship and maybe more to his wife once he was no longer able to do so himself.

'Do you want to specify anything?' Greya asked. 'Ethnicity? Hobbies? Job? Economic status?'

Stan crinkled his nose.

'Why would I want to do that? "Kind, warm and caring" says it all I reckon, don't you?'

'Totally. Oh, people are going to love this, Gramps. You'll go viral.'

Stan wasn't sure he wanted anything viral but this, at least, was something he could do to help Bonnie. There was no way he could tell her about it, not so much because he was 'dating' as because it might suggest to her that he was giving up, but he surely owed it to her to ensure there was a Plan B?

'Submit?' Greya asked, her finger hovering over the button.

'Submit,' Stan agreed and with a flourish, she did so.

Chapter Eight

Stan stared at the building site from the safety of his car, scared to get out and join the others. For so many years he'd driven past this field at the edge of the village, imagining what it might be like if they could one day secure the planning permission they craved; so why, now that they'd done so, was he avoiding it? Sometimes he even went the long way into Brecksby so as not to go past, but today the lorry was coming to lay the foundations and he'd never missed that on any of their projects.

He had to be here, he knew, but a nagging part of him shied away from seeing his dream house sink its feet into the ground without knowing if he'd still be here to see the roof stuck on top. Besides, blinking Dr Mirabi had said he shouldn't have 'too much exertion', so Bonnie had banned him from doing anything on site until the treatment was over, and he hated being a spare part.

On the other hand, the third batch of chemo had gone even better than the second and he was starting to believe his wife's fierce assertions that it could be more than palliative. Doctors made mistakes. Bodies were all very different. Stan had rarely had a day's illness in all his life, so maybe his immune system was supercharged. It was possible, especially with all Bonnie's beetroot coursing around it. Stan pulled the keys out of the ignition and looked down at Terry.

'The doctor says that my treatment is very encouraging,' he told him. 'That's good, isn't it?' Terry did not look convinced, but then he never did. It's what Stan usually liked about him but he was starting to think maybe the troll had life all wrong. 'Very encouraging,' he repeated more loudly, then shoved Terry into his pocket, pushed open the car door and stepped out.

He headed past the squat concrete lorry towards the others, smiling to see Rachael marching around the trench with her laser-measure, making final checks. Greya had been muttering all week about how bad concrete was for the environment but as Stan came past the lorry, he noted that the dark eyes and pronounced muscles of the driver's young assistant seemed to be overcoming her principles.

'All set, folks?' he called.

Everyone looked up.

'Stan!' Bonnie set a brick on the plans she'd been checking with Dave and came rushing over. 'I'm so glad you're here.'

'So am I,' he said and, seeing the light in her eyes, he truly meant it. 'Ready for action, Greya?'

'Course.'

Greya detached herself from the young man and came across, brandishing her spade like a medieval weapon. Stan grinned at her. With Lisa's trial coming to a head this week, she was working all the hours God sent, but Greya had become quite part of the family and he was loving the chance to get to know her in these final moments of her childhood. Plus, Rachael looked tired again, so the extra pair of hands was very welcome.

Andrew had been round the other day to ask them to make sure Rachael wasn't doing too much on site. He'd seemed his usual self, in a paint-spattered jumper and with the kids springing around him, but he usually left Rachael to fight her own battles and Stan had urged Bonnie to keep a close eye on her.

'And you, Dave?' he asked, turning to his old friend. 'Gail not weakened you too much this weekend?'

'On the contrary, mate, she's rejuvenating me.'

'Still together? That must be some sort of record.'

'Rubbish. It's only been three weeks. I swear I've done at least four before now. Mind you, I did have a very interesting Facebook message this weekend. From an ex, Emma. Remember her?'

'I lose track.'

'Oh come on, it was a long while back but I went out with her for ages. Three months at least. She came camping with us all when Greya was a kid.'

'Camping?'

'Yeah, in Wales I think it was. Emma loved it.'

Greya considered.

'Did she have really long hair?' she asked.

Dave nodded.

'Almost down to her knees.'

'I remember her! She was great fun.'

Something sparked in Stan's memory.

'Emma who liked to do naked star jumps in the morning?'

Dave smirked.

'That's the one. Surprised the hell out of that bloke next door, didn't she?'

'It must have taken him hours to pluck up the courage to come and talk to you.'

'He was so pompous, remember? "This is a family campsite and standards of decency should be maintained." Arsehole.'

'And you,' Bonnie laughed, 'said, "Come on, mate, you saw her – my standards are well above plain old decent".'

Stan could picture the scene now – the man puce in the face and not sure where to look as Dave proudly put his arm around a giggling Emma – and he smiled at the sudden clarity of the memory.

'And Greya went on and on about how she wanted to do naked star jumps too,' he said, chuckling.

'Did I get to?' Greya asked.

'As I recall, you did. The man left that day.'

'Stupid fool,' she said happily. 'Some people are so uptight. Did Mum do naked star jumps too?'

'I think so, yes.'

Greya squinted into the low sun.

'I don't think Mum would do that now,' she said sadly.

'You never know,' Bonnie told her, squeezing her shoulders. 'She might just surprise you.'

'She might just,' Stan agreed, pointing to the site entrance where, as if she'd heard them talking about her, Lisa's powder-blue convertible was driving onto the site.

'What's she doing here?' Rachael demanded, as Lisa slid out and walked towards them, incongruously elegant in a cream suit.

'Maybe she's interested in the house,' Bonnie suggested.

'That'd be a first,' came the curt reply.

It was a fair point but, in her defence, Lisa had been very busy. Stan put out an arm to hold Rachael back but he was too late and she was already marching up to her twin.

'Hi, Rae,' Lisa called, sounding unusually bubbly. 'The trial finished early so I thought I'd come and say hello. We won,' she added.

If she'd been expecting praise, she didn't get it.

'You can't come on site in those,' Rachael said, pointing at Lisa's designer heels.

Lisa jumped but recovered her poise instantly. Taking a cool step back, she looked her sister up and down, openly assessing her black combat trousers, sturdy work boots and high-vis jacket.

'OK. Where does the site start?'

Rachael blinked.

'Sorry?'

'What's the boundary, Rae? Am I OK here? Or here? Or what about here?'

Lisa bounced around like a grasshopper and Rachael's eyes narrowed.

'No further,' she said.

'What about sideways, then? Can I go sideways, or is that part of your precious domain too?'

Rachael huffed and squared her shoulders, which were considerably wider than her sister's.

'I'm only saying it for your protection, Lisa, but if you think you know better, go ahead. Why not? Step into that trench there if you're so clever, and you can literally be a part of the project.'

Lisa flinched.

'OK, sis. No need to be like that. I only came to have a look at what great work you're doing here.'

'That's nice, sweetheart,' Bonnie said, but Rachael cut her off.

'You'll need boots then. There's some in the office.'

'Thank you.'

Lisa spun on her pretty heels and made for the caravan at the side of the site.

'Very welcoming, Rae,' Bonnie said and Rachael groaned.

'Sorry, Mum. She's just so irritating.'

Bonnie grinned.

'I know, love, but surely you're too old for all this bickering? At least she's showing an interest. And she's having a hard time at the moment.'

'Is she? How?'

'She's having a few problems with Simon,' Stan said.

'Why? What's he doing to her?'

'Nothing. It's just . . .'

'I bet he's been criticising her again, hasn't he? He's always criticising her. Says she works too hard, but when they got married they were both high-flyers. It's not her fault if he got scared of the clouds, is it?'

'Erm . . .'

As ever, Stan was stunned by how swiftly his twins could switch from fierce criticism of each other to even fiercer criticism of anyone who dared to try the same. But now Lisa was coming back out, clad in too-big boots and an old coat of Dave's that drowned her slight figure, and Rachael was spinning back to her.

'What's going on with Simon, Lise? Has he been getting at you again?' Lisa looked stunned. 'Is that why you're up here? Is it all getting too much?'

Lisa seemed to crumple.

'Rachael,' Stan warned, but there was no stopping his younger daughter once she was on a roll.

'It is, isn't it?' she insisted, marching up to Lisa. 'Oh, poor you.'

And at that, to Stan's astonishment, Lisa burst into tears and flung herself into Rachael's arms.

'Oh lord,' he heard Greya mutter. 'Looks like the dam's finally burst.'

Dam? Stan pictured Lisa as a great wall and found the image fitted perfectly. She'd been building herself up brick by tight, neat brick ever since she'd pinned down her GCSE choices aged thirteen and set her sights on being a lawyer, and she'd never allowed cracks to form in that vision. Or so it had seemed – until now. She was sobbing in Rachael's arms, and as Stan reached out to rub tentatively at her back he could feel her ribs. She'd always been thin but now she felt tiny and so very fragile.

'Lisa, darling, don't cry.'

'It's her fault for starting me off,' she gasped out over Rachael's shoulder, adding in a tiny flash of the usual Lisa, 'Pathetic, isn't it?'

'We can't say until you tell us what's wrong, sweetheart. *Is* it Simon?'

Lisa looked at him with red eyes and detached herself from her twin.

'We've tried, Dad,' she said wearily. 'At least, *I've* tried.'

'I'm sure you have.'

'It's just got so hard. We seem to want very different things out of life at the moment. I think, if that's OK with you two, I might need to stay a few more weeks? And anyway, it would be good to be around to, you know, look after you a bit, Dad.'

'Of course,' Stan agreed. He wasn't sure "looking after" people was Lisa's strength, but it was sweet of her all the same. 'You're welcome for as long as you wish. Greya too.'

'Sorry, Greya.'

Lisa reached for her daughter's hand and Greya let her take it.

'It's fine, Mum. I can go home whenever I want, and I like it here.'

'That's good to hear, but I'm sorry about me and your dad. It's just that everything I do seems to irritate him and then he gets all cross and that irritates *me* and we just argue more. He wants me to work less and spend time grubbing around on his bloody allotment, but how can I do that? I want to make a success of my career like Mum and Dad have.'

'What's it to do with us?' Stan asked.

Lisa turned on him.

'Everything! I want you to think I'm doing well, Dad.'

'But I do, Lise. I think you're amazing. I always have. Why on earth would you imagine otherwise?'

Lisa sat down on a nearby wheelbarrow and waved her arm around the site.

'Cos I went away and Rachael came back and worked with you and you're like this team and you're here together, on the Wirral and not in stupid London and I don't want you thinking that I'm some, some idiot who got her life all wrong.'

'What on earth?' Stan stared at Lisa open-mouthed as she sobbed again. He'd always known girls were hard to understand but this took the biscuit. 'Lisa, darling, I'm fiercely proud of you.'

'But you and Mum, you're so good at what you do. And you're so good at being married, too. Bloody perfect at it, in fact. I can't do it as well, Dad. I'm sorry, I . . .'

'Lisa, hush! You're being ridiculous. For a start, we're far from perfect.'

'That's not true. You never argue. When we were kids all our friends' parents argued.'

'And that was a good thing?'

'No! But at least it gave them something to improve on.'

'Right. Sorry?'

'It's OK. You're the ones who've got it right. Rachael too. She and Andrew are fab together. Never a cross word.'

'That's not true,' Rachael laughed. 'You should hear me swearing at him and the kids about tidying up, especially recently. I had a right hissy fit over a load of messy paint-brushes the other day.'

'Rubbish,' Lisa said before Stan could ask Rachael more. Was she on edge because of him? Was that what Andrew had actually meant when he'd come round? Was Stan's illness making both his precious daughters pick away at their own lives? He hated that idea.

'I'm the one who went away and got it all wrong,' Lisa was saying, and he grabbed furiously at her hands.

'But that's just not true, Lise. It doesn't matter that you did something different – in fact, I admire you for it. I wanted to do that too when I was young.'

'You did?'

'Absolutely. I kicked against my dad. Insisted I wanted to be a musician and get away from family stuff.'

Now it was Lisa staring at him.

'Really?'

'Yep. Mad, hey? I got myself in a band and everything.'

'The Best Boys,' Greya supplied perkily.

She'd been plying him with questions over the last few days and had clearly been paying attention to the answers. Both of the twins looked curiously to her, then back to Stan, who nodded.

'That was us and I was determined to make it work, to be a star. We all were. We'd track Brian Epstein around Liverpool hoping that one day we'd get to play for him and he'd sign us and we'd be the next Beatles. Told you it was mad.'

'Not necessarily, Dad. What happened?'

Stan shrugged.

'Things changed.'

'What he means is that *I* changed things.'

It was Bonnie. Both girls were now looking from one parent to the other.

'Because you don't like music?' Lisa asked, and Stan saw Bonnie stiffen and rushed to defend her.

'Because it wasn't the right thing to do with my life,' he said firmly. 'But that's not the point here. The point is, Lisa, that I gave up and moved to the Wirral because I was too scared to stay in the city.'

'Same as me,' Rachael said. 'That's exactly what happened to me. We're not as brave as you, Lise, that's all.'

Stan nodded and squeezed his older daughter's hands tight. She'd stopped crying but she still looked unconvinced.

'We'll sort this out, Lisa, I promise.'

'But how, Dad? And more to the point, how soon? You're ill. You might . . . you might be dying. I don't want that. I haven't seen enough of you or Mum these last years and now it feels like it might be too late. I don't want you to die, and I especially don't want you to die whilst I'm being an idiot.'

Stan clasped her close, feeling inappropriate laughter building up inside him.

'Whatever happens to me, Lisa, I will never, ever think you're an idiot. You're fantastic, sweetheart – bold and strong and good at what you do and I love you for that.'

'And I love you, Dad, way too much. Please don't die.'

'I won't. Not yet, anyway. Not even soon. The chemo's going well, isn't it, Bonnie?'

'Very well,' she agreed, coming up at his side. 'You really mustn't fret, Lisa.'

Lisa wiped tears furiously from her face.

'No. Quite right. Stupid. I always get a bit emotional when a trial ends.'

'But you won. That's great.'

'It's good, yes. Pays the wages and all that.' She stood up, brushing herself down and pulling her usual composure back into place. 'But I'm interrupting and it looks like you're rather busy here.'

'We're about to pour the concrete to lay the foundations,' Bonnie told her. 'You can help if you want.'

'Can I?'

'*Can* she?' Rachael repeated.

'Course she can,' Bonnie said firmly. 'Here – take Greya's spade.'

She held out her hand and Greya handed it over. Lisa took it, turned it around in her hand a few times and then stuck it into the ground and stood on it like a conquering hero.

'I'm ready. Now come on – are we going to get this concrete poured, or what?'

They all snapped into action and Stan was pleased, if a little astonished, to see Lisa stepping up to her task, standing with

97

Dave ready to help smooth the flow. It felt even better with her here too, and he thanked the heavens that he'd resisted his urge to stay away. He might not be working physically, but he was still a part of this and the warmth of that coursed through his body as effectively as any chemotherapy. He watched contentedly as the concrete began pouring into the perfect trench, but then he became aware of Greya hissing at him.

'Grandpa!' She moved closer, nodding her head strangely in his direction. 'Grandpa, over here!'

'Everything OK, Grey? Are you upset about your mum?'

She gave a self-conscious shrug.

'A bit, I guess. I mean, it's so nice to see you and Granny still happy together, and Mum and Dad'll never have that and that's a bit sad. But there's no point in them being miserable, right?'

Stan gave her a hug.

'Right, Grey.'

He dropped a kiss on her forehead but then she pulled back and said, 'Which reminds me, you old romantic – you've had some replies.'

She pulled back and took out her phone and his heart jerked. He looked around but everyone else was absorbed in the concrete so he grabbed her arm, pulling her behind the lorry.

'You mean on Cherry Creek?'

'Yes! People are loving it. There's been all sorts of chat about how romantic it is.'

'What use is that?'

'None, but there've been some proper replies too.'

Stan shifted and peered round the edge of the lorry to see Bonnie hunched over the rapidly filling trench with Rachael. Nice as it was to have Greya on his side, he hated deceiving his wife and had nearly told her all about his plan several times as they sat in bed together late at night. Throughout their marriage, bedtime had always been when they'd chewed over life's problems together, and he felt his secret lying like a stone between them.

'There's a bloke called Jack who seems very nice,' Greya was telling him earnestly. 'An ex-detective inspector.'

'That's impressive.'

'That's what I said. Well . . .' She blushed. 'You did.'

'You answered as me?'

'Should I not? It's not like you can put it on your phone, is it, and I didn't think you'd want me bothering you with it all the time.'

'No.' Stan snuck another look around the lorry but Bonnie was still engrossed. 'No, I guess not. OK, so "I" said that was impressive, and what did he say?'

'He said thanks. He enjoyed his job but it wasn't great for his love life and now he's retired, he's lonely. He wants someone to care for.'

'That's what we specified, right?'

'Right. So . . .?'

'So?'

'Do you want to meet him? He suggested some pub called The Salty Dog out on the coast.'

Stan's breath caught. That was one of his favourite pubs. Was it a sign?

'I know it,' he admitted. 'Nice place. They brew their own beer.'

'Great. You'd like that then?'

'I would if I could drink it.'

'Course. Yes. Sorry.'

Greya looked crestfallen. Even her purple hair seemed suddenly to have lost its sheen in the shadow of the concrete lorry and Stan felt bad.

'Don't be sorry, Grey. It's not your fault. You're doing a great job, really. I'm just nervous, I guess.'

'Course you are. But you know what, Grandpa, you *should* do things that make you nervous – it means you're stretching yourself. Pushing your boundaries.'

'It might be a bit late for that, Greya.'

She put her hands on her slim hips.

'But it isn't, is it? That's the whole point of what you're doing here.'

She was right, he supposed, however little he wanted her to be, and he reached out a hand for her phone, but at that moment a voice said 'Stan?' and Bonnie marched round the side of the lorry. She sized them up in a moment. 'What on earth are you pair up to?'

Stan froze but Greya was far quicker off the mark.

'Sorry, Granny. Just a stupid cat video one of my mates sent me. Grandpa looked a bit sad so I thought it might cheer him up.'

'Sad?' Bonnie turned her piercing violet eyes on Stan, who glared at Greya. His granddaughter, however, was pocketing her phone and strolling away as easily as if she had, indeed, been showing him cats falling off curtain rails. 'Why are you sad, Stan?'

'I'm not, sweetheart. Really. Well, only cause I couldn't help out.'

She softened instantly.

'I know. I'm sorry but it's for the best, really it is. And you'll be back working as soon as the chemo is done.'

'You're right.' He took her hand, feeling guilty for ever doubting it and, worse, for conspiring with their granddaughter to put someone else in his place, just in case. 'Sorry, Bon. I'm fine, honestly.'

She searched his face, but was apparently satisfied.

'Good. Come and see, then – it's all done. Save one important task that I need you for.'

'Me?'

'Absolutely. Come on!'

He let her draw him to the filled trench that marked the footprint of the building, now standing a bright, determined grey against the brown earth. Dave was sorting things out with the lorry driver and Lisa and Rachael were chatting away together, flushed with their shared task. It was a wonderful sight.

'Looks like the dream house is going to be a reality,' he said. 'That's brilliant. You've done it, Bonnie – you've really done it.'

'*We've* done it,' she corrected him. 'Now come on – your job.' They were stood where the foundations bent outwards to form what would one day be the front porch. Bonnie pointed down at the concrete. 'I need your print.'

'Of course.'

Stan smiled at her and knelt down, trying not to show the effort it cost him. He and Bonnie had put their handprints in the damp foundations of the extension on their cottage, and continued the practice when they'd started up in business together. These days there had to be some fifty-odd homes in the area with their mark buried in their foundations, and this one would be the best of them all – if possibly the last.

Stan swallowed and reached forward, silently begging his hand not to shake as he hovered it over the wet concrete. The chemo had made his hands and feet tingle as he remembered them doing when coming in from sledging as a kid, but he didn't want its poison intruding on this special moment. He looked to Bonnie, who'd knelt at his side.

'Here?' he asked.

'Here is good, but I thought as this one is our very own we might make the mark a little special.'

She placed her hand over his so that, as they pressed down together, their interlinked fingers dipped into the foundations as if they were from one hand. For a moment they knelt there together, suspended in this little moment of creation, but then Dave bounced over waving the obligatory bottle of bubbly and they both drew back.

'Time to celebrate,' Dave said. 'Look, mate – it's non-alcoholic stuff, just for you. Well, its five per cent, but that's much the same, right?'

Stan heard Bonnie tut but he was touched. And relieved, too, to be taken out of the intense moment of making their mark on their house.

'Let her fly, Dave!' he instructed, clambering to his feet and helping Bonnie up with him.

He looked to the bright line of the foundations and to his and Bonnie's assertive mark at the very front of them, then across to his dear little team of workers as they came over to share the moment, and felt proud. But then, masked by the pop of the champagne cork, he heard Greya whisper, 'Date's all sorted, Gramps,' and suddenly the foundations seemed as wobbly as if they'd been laid in jelly. It looked as if, after fifty-four happy years of marriage, Stan was going dating again.

Chapter Nine

Stan might be a mature, experienced man of seventy-five, but as he headed out to the coast his stomach felt utterly teenage. The nerves were so bad that he almost stopped the car and turned round, but it seemed a bit rude to his 'date'.

'This Jack must be even more nervous than me, right?' he asked Terry, dangling stoically from the ignition.

Terry nodded his ugly little head and Stan turned resolutely towards the pub. He felt his foot ease off the accelerator and pushed it fiercely back down. The engine growled, as teenage as his stomach, but then there was The Salty Dog, a big white building gleaming in the lunchtime sun. Stan could see a terraced beer garden at the back looking over the beach, and a handful of people sat at bleached wooden tables. Was one of them him – Jack?

'Jack Robinson', he'd been called on the app. A solid name, Stan had thought, and the little photo had showed an appropriately solid bloke. He was six foot, his profile said, with 'remnants of darkish hair and a little bit of a gut'. So, pretty much like any bloke in a pub then.

'I'll wear a green T-shirt,' he'd offered when Stan had dared to reply to his messages.

'I'll wear . . .' Stan had typed back, mentally scanning his wardrobe and coming up with little but checked shirts. 'I'll wear a checked shirt.'

'And a carnation,' Jack had sent back.

'A carnation, yeah, right.'

Jack had sent a smiley-face emoji, but as Stan pulled into the car park he wondered if he'd actually meant it. It was the start of the Easter holidays and the beer garden was filling up fast. How on earth would he find him? He looked to Terry as he took the keys out of the ignition but the troll had spun round and seemed to be looking at the pub as if urging him to get on in there. Stan sighed.

'All right, all right,' he said, checking for his wallet. 'But if I don't like him I'm not hanging around.'

Terry spun back and seemed for one bonkers moment to wink at him. Well, at least the troll approved – that was something. Stan tucked him into his pocket, got out of the car and drew in a deep breath of sea air, catching a tantalising undertone of pale ale on the gentle breeze. He was planning on allowing himself a half-pint and that, if nothing else, was worth coming to his favourite pub for.

The garden was awash with families keen to make the most of the gift of spring sun. The wooden climbing frame in the far corner swarmed with kids, and grateful parents were gathered in pairs and fours at all the tables – all bar one. Over by the fence, determinedly guarding a whole table with outspread arms, was a man in a green T-shirt. He looked ill at ease amongst the chattering groups and without a further moment's thought, Stan headed towards him.

'Jack Robinson?'

The man leaped up but his legs were tucked into the fixed bench seat and he almost toppled over. Recovering, he stuck out a big hand.

'That's me. Stan Walker?'

'Yep.'

'Great. Good to meet you. Drink?'

He gestured down and Stan saw a bottle of white wine chilling in a Perspex cooler and two glasses, one half-full. He looked to the pub then back to Jack's bottle.

'That's very kind, Jack, but I'd rather have a beer.'

Jack's face fell.

'Of course. I should have thought. I'd prefer that myself to be honest, but I've found that on dates it eases things in if you've got a drink ready. That's with women, though, I guess. And this isn't a date anyway, is it, not really?'

'No, not really,' Stan agreed hastily, glancing around to check no one was listening. 'I'll go to the bar. Do you want a beer then, Jack?'

'I've got this now,' he said, jerking his head at the wine.

'It'll keep.'

'It will, won't it? Go on then, cheers.'

With the wine pushed to one side and two beers in front of them, things felt a little easier. They skirted around the weather, football and the England cricketers' chances at the World Cup until eventually Jack said, 'So you're ill, then?'

'Fraid so.'

'Only you don't . . .'

'Look it? I know.'

Stan had thought the same thing himself that morning. This bloke's never going to believe I'm dying, he'd told the mirror and had deliberately chosen a short-sleeved shirt that made his arms look thin and more than usually yellow. Absurd, really.

'My doctor says I'm dying and I can't believe he'd lie.'

'No. Of course not. I'm sorry.'

'Not as sorry as me, especially not if . . . . You've never married, Jack?'

'No. Not for want of trying. It's my job, see. I am – I was – a policeman. A detective inspector in the end.'

'So you said on the app. That's impressive.'

'So *you* said on the app.'

'Oh, yes. I did, didn't I?'

He fiddled with his beer but Jack didn't seem to mind being called impressive twice.

'It's not all Morse and Taggart and that, though,' he went on. 'Murders are pretty few and far between, thank God. For the rest, it's hit and runs and petty thieving and gangs. Especially bloody gangs. Sorry. Shouldn't swear.'

'I can take it.'

'I guess so. I'm used to being on my best behaviour on . . .'

'Dates?'

Jack grinned ruefully.

'Exactly.'

'You date a lot then?'

'Not really. I've been trying to recently because, well because I'm lonely, to be honest. Why else would you? It's not easy, though, not at this age. Back when I was first in the force I had several long-term girlfriends but police work is very time-consuming. And cases niggle at you.'

'I can imagine.'

'Sorry. Don't mean to moan. It's dull, isn't it, to hear other people's work gripes. I just meant that in the end, every time, the girls got fed up. One asked me to leave the force – them or her, she said. I said "them". She wasn't best pleased.' He chuckled at the memory, then remembered Stan was sat in front of him. 'She cut up my uniform,' he explained. 'Very imaginative, she was – a big slit all the way round the crotch and two nipple holes in the jacket.'

'Nice,' Stan said, trying to imagine Bonnie doing something similar and failing.

Jack nodded.

'Super wasn't best pleased. Threatened to make me wear

it out on the beat but decided in the end that it wouldn't be "good for the public image of the police force".'

Stan laughed.

'So you got away with it?'

'Nope. I had to wear it for a whole week at my damned desk – double punishment. I patched it up best I could but needless to say the lads had a field day. I was Sergeant Bumcrack all the way until I made detective and even then if they thought I wasn't listening. I kind of gave up on dating for a while after that.'

'I can see why.'

'I was on track for promotion by then and I decided that was more important. And it worked. I did well. I was happy for ages, but in the end it grinds you down a bit. I guess all work does, right?'

Stan shrugged.

'Maybe I've been lucky. I build houses and I've always loved it.'

'You *are* lucky, then. You still at it?'

'Yes. That is, I'm doing my best.'

Stan's thoughts shot to the new house and his and Bonnie's joined mark shining in the concrete. He looked at Jack. What if it was this big, solid policeman who carried Bonnie's shopping over that mark, who ushered her over it after a night out and who locked the door over it when they went up to . . . The beer garden swam suddenly. It was all very well imagining a hazy figure keeping Bonnie company, but to have a flesh-and-blood man in front of him felt all too real.

Stan looked hastily out to sea. It was a calm day and the waves were less breakers than floppers, tipping lazily onto the sand as little kids jumped over them, squealing. Further out a clutch of sailing boats were tacking around to catch what breeze they could and a young man battled with one of those stand-up paddle boards Stan could never see the point of. Is that what he was doing here – paddle-boating along, more effort than effect?

'We're building a new home,' he told Jack, 'but it's not easy.'

'I can imagine. You're very brave.'

'Building a house I might never live in?'

'No, not that. That makes sense – you should keep going, keep building. I meant this, meeting me. Not many blokes would. Does she know, your wife?'

'Bonnie? No. Not yet. She wouldn't get it.'

'You setting her up with someone else? I can see why.'

Stan gave a rueful smile.

'Me too.'

'So, what's your plan?'

Stan grimaced.

'It's nothing as concrete as a plan. I just thought I might find someone I could, maybe, introduce quietly to Bonnie as a friend, who might then be there if . . . if she needed him. And he her, of course. It's not that she'll be without help. We have two daughters, twins actually. And they both have husbands and kids. And Bonnie has lots of friends, lovely friends, but it's not the same, is it, as someone who's there just for you.'

'You're right there,' Jack agreed. 'Take me, for example. I couldn't wait to retire in the end. I had all these plans to do the stuff I hadn't had time for – fishing, walks, cinema, doing up the little Triumph Stag that had been rusting away in my garage for years. And I've done all that and it's good. I'm not complaining. It's just that it would be better with someone to share it with – someone who's just there in the morning to say "do you fancy doing whatever", instead of always having to make plans. Pathetic, really.'

'It's not.' Stan was warming to Jack. He seemed straight up. 'Bonnie likes walking,' he said. He felt a bit like he was offering a crumb to a bird and sure enough, Jack leaned in a little as if to peck it up.

'Does she work?'

'She's an architect.'

'Really? Smart lady, then.'

'Very. Is that a problem?'

'No. Not at all. I dated a physicist for a while. And a university lecturer. And at least two lawyers.'

'I thought you said you hadn't dated much.'

'I'm sixty-eight, Stan – it works out at about one every five years.'

'Of course. Sorry.' He seemed to be apologising a lot. Mind you, so did Jack. It was so easy to get things wrong. 'Would you like to see a photo?' he suggested.

'If that's OK?'

'Course.'

It wasn't really. He felt like a market trader as he drew out his phone and released the screen saver, a photo of Bonnie smiling up at him on an impromptu picnic last year. He forced himself to turn the phone towards Jack and saw him blink appreciatively.

'Wow. She's lovely, Stan.'

'She is.' Stan saw Jack sit up a little straighter and felt vaguely sickened by himself. 'I'm not selling her,' he blurted out.

'I know that. Really. I know that, Stan. It's not the nineteenth century, is it?'

'No. She's a strong woman, is Bonnie. She'll make her own choices. I just want to be sure she *has* choices, that's all. She'll think she can do it alone, you see. She'll think she can be brave and independent, bless her. Us men are much quicker to accept help.'

'And companionship.'

'Exactly.'

Jack nodded keenly.

'I'm good at looking after people. At least, I am now I've got the time. I can cook. I'm tidy. I don't leave the loo seat up.' He gave Stan a sheepish grin. 'I feel like I'm in an interview now.'

'Sorry. I'm not sure we're getting this right.'

Stan fumbled in his pocket and thought he felt Terry quivering with laughter at the stilted conversation. Suddenly he just wanted to escape this strange not-date and chat to his plastic troll instead.

'So,' Jack said awkwardly. 'Where do we go from here?'

'Not sure.'

'Only, if you're serious about all this, I am too. I want someone to care for.'

'That's nice.'

'And she could do worse, I reckon. I've got plenty of money, I'm in OK shape, I'm not thick.'

'Jack, you don't need to . . .'

'I'm white.'

Stan froze.

'What did you say?'

'I said I'm white. Like your Bonnie. It's getting rarer and rarer these days, don't you think?' Stan looked around the pub garden. He picked out one gorgeous little mixed-race girl playing on the swing and a handsome black man watching over her, but everyone else was totally pallid. 'Not here maybe,' Jack said hastily, 'but I see a lot of it. A lot of them.'

'"Them"?'

Stan couldn't quite believe he was hearing this.

'Immigrants.'

Stan rose slowly.

'*You're* an immigrant, Jack.'

'I am not. Lancashire born and bred, I am. My family have been here years and years.'

'Ever since they first arrived from Scandinavia on a Viking ship, no doubt. We're all immigrants here, Jack, save a handful of Celts.'

'Celts?'

'Scots, Welsh. Irish. Or don't you like them either? The natives?'

He emphasised the word far more aggressively than he'd intended and a few people looked over. He could almost hear Terry calling from his pocket, telling him not to make a scene.

'They're not bad at rugby,' Jack said a little desperately. He rose too. 'I didn't mean any offence, mate.'

'No.' Stan stepped out of the bench seat. 'No, I guess you didn't, but let me tell you now, I'd have no problem with Bonnie finding herself a black husband as long as he was kind and warm and caring. Oh, and one other thing . . .'

'What?'

'Not a bigot. Nice to have met you, Jack.' He didn't offer his hand. 'See you around.'

'Stan! Stan, wait. There's been a misunderstanding.'

'There certainly has. I understood you were a decent human being.'

'I am. I like black people. Some of my best colleagues were black people. I just wouldn't want to . . .'

Jack's words trickled out as he noticed people staring. The black dad took a few steps towards him and then, at impressive speed given that his gut wasn't as 'little' as he'd claimed, Jack was gone, ducking past Stan and making for a shiny Land Rover in the corner of the car park.

Stan trudged slowly to his own car and pulled his keys from his pocket. Terry looked inquisitively at him.

'Good beer,' he told the troll. 'Shame about the company.' He started the engine as, behind him, Jack squealed away in an indignant spray of sand and added, 'No more dating, Terry. It was a mad idea.'

Chapter Ten

March 1963

Bonnie looked across the table at her date and could hardly believe she was here, sitting at this fancy table in this fancy restaurant. She'd resisted dating Danny at first, worried she was just doing it to get at Spike, who still crept uninvited into her dreams at dawn, but he had been flatteringly persistent and now she was so glad she'd agreed. Danny was charming and interesting and attentive, and his easy company was a welcome relief after the day she'd had.

'This is so kind of you,' she said, as a smart waiter topped up her wine.

She'd only drunk wine at Christmas before, but Danny had ordered it with such a flourish that she'd not had the heart to ask for something else and, in fact, it had tasted really nice. As had her food.

'My pleasure,' Danny said, sitting back as their plates were cleared away.

He'd had Dover sole with prawns – a very fancy-looking dish. Bonnie had had chicken because it had been the cheapest thing on the intimidating menu but it had been very smart too, wrapped round with some sort of wafer-thin ham and in a rich sauce she'd happily have mopped up with her bread if it hadn't felt like the wrong thing to do.

'Shall we have dessert?' Danny suggested. 'They do a lovely Baked Alaska. Have you had it before? It's warm meringue with sponge and ice cream inside – delicious.'

It did sound nice, especially described in his plummy tones, but he'd already spent a fortune so she shook her head.

'I'm full up, thank you.'

'Oh, go on – my dad gave me some cash so we might as well spend it.'

'Really?'

'Really. He landed a big new customer today so he was feeling flush.'

'What does he do, Danny?'

'Do? Oh, you know, business. Supply and demand and all that. And today he did lots of supplying. So, dessert it is.'

He looked hastily round for the waiter and, though Bonnie was dying to ask more, it seemed only polite just to say thank you.

'I told you – it's my pleasure.'

He smiled at her as he placed their order, relaxed again now, and Bonnie watched him curiously. He wasn't as showy as Spike, but he had a quiet confidence that made her feel safe and right now she needed that. Last night Susie-Ann's brothers had come home with a bag full of Levi's and made her try on a pair. She'd had to heave and pull to get them on and had felt almost naked when she'd edged out of her room with them clinging to every part of her, but seeing the boys' jaws drop had told her they looked good. Buoyed up, she'd let Susie-Ann talk her into wearing them to lectures this morning.

'Those stupid boys on your course won't be able to resist talking to you in these,' her friend had insisted, but Bonnie had barely got through the lecture theatre door when Professor

Sanderson, a thin-faced elderly academic, had called her to the front and demanded to know what she was doing 'showing herself off to all and sundry'.

'But loads of people wear jeans,' she'd objected, pointing as the other students shuffled behind their desks.

'That's different. You're asking for it dressed like that, young lady, and it's just not fair on these poor hot-blooded males.' She'd gaped at him, astounded, but before she could even begin a counterargument he'd pointed imperiously to the door and said, 'I'm going to have to ask you to leave.'

She'd had little choice but to creep away, mortified. She'd longed to call Nancy, who would have soothed her with righteous indignation and wise words, but she was with Astrid in Sweden so Bonnie had just run home and cried into her pillow like a little girl. She'd nearly cancelled tonight's date but she was so glad that she hadn't, because Danny was making her forget all about those idiots at the university. Plus, he looked very handsome.

He was wearing a lovely suit, not his black performance one but a softer, dark brown three-piece that brought out the warm colour of his sandy curls. His eyes looked very blue in the candlelight and they were focused intently on her, as if she were an exotic creature in a cage. She put a hand to her face.

'What is it, Danny? Am I smudged?'

He smiled.

'You're not "smudged", Bonnie Jessop, you're perfect.'

She shifted.

'Hardly.'

'What's not perfect about you, then?'

She giggled at that.

'I dunno. Loads of stuff. My teachers used to say I was impertinent.'

'Did they? Why?'

'It was one teacher in particular, really – Miss Jenkins. She was one of those dull people you think must have been born old. I swear she bought her clothes to blend in with the school walls.'

'What colour were the walls?'

'Beige.'

They pulled a face at each other.

'I know the sort exactly. We had one just like that – Mr Boulder. He taught RE.'

'So did Miss Jenkins! Oh Danny, we should get them together and they could buy a beige house and eat beige food and, and . . .'

'Go to bed under beige covers and have beige sex.'

Bonnie giggled nervously. She'd thought Danny too much of a gentleman to talk like this, but under his lovely manners he was every bit as earthy and funny as the rest of the band. She'd seen them all the other day when Susie-Ann had dragged her along to a rehearsal. It had been horribly awkward with Spike at first but she'd stuck her head up high and tried to pretend she was Nancy, chatting and laughing like an Oscar-winning actress, and then it hadn't been so bad. Plus Lee had been lovely and Sticks even more jokey than usual and Danny had hovered so protectively that in the end she'd been glad she'd gone. At least next time it would be easier.

'What would beige sex even be like?' she giggled now.

'Probably all "would you lift your nightdress, my dear, I won't be long".'

Bonnie laughed so hard that some of the meringue on top of the dessert the waiter was setting before her blew off. And that made her laugh all over again.

'I cannot imagine Miss Jenkins having sex,' she hissed to Danny once the waiter had gone and they'd recovered themselves.

'No? What about you, Bonnie?'

'Sorry?' His voice had gone serious and he was looking at her intently again, making her feel caged. 'What do you mean, Danny?' she asked sharply.

'Nothing. Sorry, nothing. I'm not good with words sometimes. I meant what about you at, you know, school. I bet this Miss Jenkins' problem was just that you were cleverer than her.'

Bonnie considered this; it gave her time to recover from Danny's sudden shift of tone.

'Not cleverer,' she said in the end, 'but maybe a bit sharper. I asked her questions she didn't want to answer, like did she think society would collapse if people stopped going to church.'

'Deep.'

'Impertinent!'

He laughed and all felt comfortable again.

'You must have done OK at school too?' she said.

'Not bad,' he agreed, 'though don't tell the others. I thought about going to university but there's not much point if I'm going to take over from Dad.'

'With his business?'

Danny played with his menu.

'Exactly, yes. Dad's always been desperate for me to take it over as I'm his only son. I hated that for a while. I can't say I'm all that keen to . . . Well, anyway, I told him when I was sixteen that I was going to go and be an apprentice plumber with my uncle, and he almost had a fit. Went on and on about family values. I told him Uncle Mike *was* family, but that just made him madder. He likes to think he's raised himself up a bit, you know – done well in life. He was chuffed to be able to send me and my sister to private school and he's really keen for us to live up to that. In the end it was easier to forget about plumbing, and then I found music anyway.'

'Does he like you playing?'

'He likes it better than me plumbing – though that's not a lot. He likes to keep me close, see.'

'At least he's alive.'

'Sorry?'

'Your dad. My parents died when I was five.'

'Bonnie, no! I didn't know. I'm so sorry. I . . .'

For once Danny's immaculate manners deserted him and he looked lost for words.

'It's fine. My Aunt Nancy brought me up and she's fantastic, but I do sometimes wonder what my parents would have thought of me now. They loved dancing – that's one of the few things I remember about them – and I bet they'd have been thrilled to hear about the Best Boys.'

He beamed.

'I bet they'd be thrilled at how well you're doing too, Bonnie,' he countered. 'Tell me about your studies.'

Bonnie didn't want to change the subject. She was dying to know what Danny's dad did but he'd gone so pink that it didn't seem fair. What could he have done to 'raise himself up' so fast? She thought of the three crates of whisky Susie-Ann's brothers currently had stacked in her room but quickly dismissed the idea. It wasn't fair to jump to conclusions like that.

'My studies are a necessary evil,' she said, after a pause. 'I can't wait to actually work on houses, but if I don't learn how to design them properly I'll be no use to anyone.'

'I guess not. It's a lot of study, though, right?'

'Five years. Feels like ages, especially when no one seems to want me there.'

'What? What did you say, Bonnie?'

He leaned his head towards her. Bonnie knew her voice had dropped but tears were threatening as she remembered the horrible scene in the lecture theatre this morning, and there was no way she wanted to cry on her Baked Alaska.

'Doesn't matter,' she mumbled, reaching for her spoon.

'Of course it does. Of course it matters. Why don't they want you, Bon?'

His big hand closed over hers, warm and dry and confident, and she looked up into his kind eyes and drew in a long breath.

'I'm the only girl on the course.'

'Ah. Right. I guess that is a bit weird but if it's all lads, you'd have thought they'd be panting to welcome you.'

'Well they're not.' She remembered Professor Sanderson telling her she was 'asking for it' and the other students sniggering like schoolboys and bile rose in her throat. 'No one really talks to me. It's the maths bit of it I think – girls aren't meant to be good at maths. That's impertinent, too!'

'Well I say you should be as impertinent as you damn well like, Bonnie.'

'You reckon?'

'Absolutely. And hey, if they give you grief I'll go round and show them what impertinence looks like when it punches them in the face.'

'You, Danny?'

'Don't be deceived by my teddy-bear hair. I played a lot of rugby at school, so I know how to throw my weight about if I have to.'

Bonnie noted the set of his broad shoulders and the considerable muscle in his arms.

'I bet you do, actually – in a good way, I mean.'

'How else d'you think I get the Best Boys gigs?'

'True. You're good at it, Danny.'

Danny shrugged modestly. His hand was still over hers, which meant she couldn't try her dessert but it felt nice all the same.

'And the Best Boys are talented,' she said. 'Very talented. Any manager should be delighted to have them on the bill.'

At that Danny's eyes lit up.

'I haven't told you, have I?' He pulled away to fumble in his pocket and Bonnie seized the chance to grab her spoon. Danny was right – Baked Alaska was delicious.

'Told me what?' she asked, between bites.

His eyes were glowing as he pulled a crumpled letter from his suit pocket and smoothed it out on the table between them. Two white feathers detached themselves and floated across the table to stick to Bonnie's half-eaten meringue. She stared at them.

'What are they?'

Danny flushed and leaned over to pick them off her pudding and shove them under the table.

'They don't matter. Look at this – it's a letter from Bob Wooler. He sent it after I talked to him in the Cavern, remember?'

She did. Danny had been talking to the manager just before she and Spike had broken up.

Before *I* broke up with *him*, she reminded herself fiercely. Not that it mattered. Let Spike go off with silly tarts if he wanted to; she had Danny now.

'Bonnie? Are you listening?'

'Course I am,' she said guiltily. 'You're, er, going to play at the Cavern.'

'No! Better than that – he's offered us the first slot on the next Riverboat Shuffle.'

'Riverboat what?'

'Shuffle. They're music nights on the *Royal Iris* down the Mersey. Wooler does them every summer. The Beatles played two last year – and now us. *Us*, Bonnie!' His eyes were glowing again and he stroked the letter lovingly. 'It's here in black and white. "The management would like to invite the Best Boys to play on the Riverboat Shuffle on Saturday 12 April." And look, Bonnie, look who else is on the bill – The Big Three, The Escorts and Billy J. Kramer. Proper bands, Bonnie! This could be it, this could be our ticket to the big time.'

Bonnie stared at him.

'That's amazing, Danny. Fantastic. Well done!'

She leaped up and, leaning over the remains of the Baked Alaska, grabbed his face and kissed him squarely on the lips.

'Oh,' he said, his eyes even wider than before. And then, 'Oh Bonnie,' and then he was pulling her in for another, longer kiss. It probably wasn't good behaviour in a smart restaurant – it was probably impertinent, even – but it felt so good, and if Danny didn't care, Bonnie didn't care either.

He wasn't as lean as Spike, she thought, but he was every bit as muscly and his aftershave smelled so good. She tasted meringue on his lips and felt them smile against hers and that warmed her heart and, at last, sent a tingle down inside her. Danny was different, yes, but good different, and she was very lucky to have found him.

Chapter Eleven

'There! Up there, in the tree. I see it, I see it!'

Stan watched from the patio as Marleigh hopped up and down, pointing into the branches of the cherry tree in the centre of the back lawn where, nestled amongst the first hints of blossom, sat a foil-wrapped Easter egg.

'That's mine,' Jamie said, swiftly on the scene.

'No it isn't! I saw it first.'

'Yes, but you can't reach it, can you?'

With a triumphant grin Jamie grabbed one of the lower branches and went to swing himself up. Stan saw Marleigh's little face crumple and rose.

'Don't worry, Marleigh,' he called. 'The other one's bigger.'

Jamie faltered, then turned to his little sister.

'Here.' He let go of the branch and held out his cupped hands. Marleigh stared at them. 'For you, to help you up so you can reach it.'

Stan had to admire the lad's ingenuity. Marleigh looked suspicious but was lured, as was the younger sibling's eternal lot, by his apparent kindness and let herself be hoisted into the tree. Her fingers closed around the egg and she came down again, beaming.

'Thanks, Jamie.'

'No problem.'

He gave a manly little shrug then rushed off across the lawn to resume his hunt, sniggering to himself. Stan watched him go, pleased to see he was wearing the new Everton shirt he'd bought him, and perhaps less so to note his big feet trampling the primroses that had sprung up around the edges of the grass. Ah well, they'd recover, and it was so good to be out in the garden at last.

The sun was shining unexpectedly on this Easter Sunday, so they'd grabbed the chance to throw open both sets of French doors and wheel out the barbecue. Stan could hear the soft chopping of a knife against the kitchen board as Bonnie and the girls prepared salads inside, and he'd had his butterflied leg of lamb marinating since first light.

Unveiling the garden furniture from its heavy winter covers had been a joy, and all the more so because his chemo was finished and Dr Mirabi was delighted with his progress. He and Bonnie were going in to get the full results next week and they were both cautiously optimistic.

Stan felt so well that he just could not believe this might be the last spring he ever saw. The other day, he'd ordered a new paddling pool for the kids to play in this summer and only this morning he'd been eyeing up the holiday ads in the paper. He might take Bonnie to the Caribbean, or touring Europe or even swimming with dolphins in Florida. He would definitely take her dancing and to the theatre, and maybe even to an art gallery.

Bonnie had tried to take him round a few exhibitions early in their relationship but he'd never known what to say, and in the end she'd found friends who knew their Turners from their Warhols and spared them both the pain. Surely now, though, he could try again – for her sake. He'd been all for deleting his profile from Cherry Creek after the fiasco with Jack, but Greya had persuaded him to leave it up and he'd not cared enough to argue. He was going to be keeping Bonnie company for a long time to come, he was sure of it, so everyone else would just have to wait.

'Let's see your egg then,' he called to Marleigh, and the girl ran over and perched on the bench at his side.

'It's an Aero Bubbles one. That's my favourite.'

'The Easter Bunny must have known that.'

She giggled.

'Silly Grandpa. There's no such thing as the Easter Bunny. Darcy at school told me it's just a story made up for little kids.'

'No!'

Stan raised his hands in mock horror and Marleigh giggled again.

'Course it is. Think about it, Grandpa – rabbits don't even lay eggs.'

'Silly me. All these years I've fallen for that.'

'Oh Grandpa!'

She rolled her eyes at him, but just then Jamie exploded out of the rhododendron on the far side of the lawn, waving an egg and protesting vehemently.

'It's *not* bigger.'

'Isn't it?' Stan asked mildly. 'I could have sworn it was. My eyes must be playing tricks on me. Ah well, you've found it now. Well done.'

Jamie eyed him suspiciously but when Stan beamed back, the poor lad was left with nothing to do but plonk himself down on the patio at his feet. Stan sat back and watched as Jamie peeled his chocolate egg and, with concentration, struck at the top. The two halves fell apart perfectly and he gave a little grunt of satisfaction.

'Can I have a bit?' Stan asked.

Jamie looked up at him and nodded. He broke a tiny piece off and handed it over.

'That's not much.'

'Isn't it?' came the retort. 'Sorry. I could have sworn it was bigger.'

Stan had to laugh.

'Touché!'

'You what?'

'Oh, nothing.'

Stan sucked on his morsel of chocolate and, after a moment, he felt a nudge at his leg and looked down to see Jamie's hand proffering a far larger chunk. He took it and the three of them sat there, enjoying the perfect sweetness. It was the nicest thing Stan had tasted in ages.

The chemo had nuked his taste buds along with all the nasty little cells it was striking down and until today, everything he'd eaten, from strawberries to steak to soda bread, had tasted of egg-on-the-turn with undertones of rust and chlorine. The chocolate, however, seemed to have the power to cut through the deadly chemicals – either that, or it was Easter Bunny magic after all. Either way, it felt like a gift and Stan embraced it, wallowing in the warmth of the spring sun on his face, the sweetness of the treat on his tongue and the simple grace of a quiet moment with his grandchildren.

'OK there, Dad?'

He looked up to see Rachael stepping out of the kitchen to join them.

'Very well thanks, love. I'm having a nice time with the kids.'

'That's good. They're an all right pair sometimes, aren't they?'

'They're great,' he agreed as the kids squealed in protest. 'You've done a lovely job with them, Rae, you and Andrew both.'

'You reckon?' She sank down next to him. 'I'm an OK mum?'

Stan noticed a wobble in her voice.

'You're tops, Rachael. What's up?'

'Nothing. Nothing's up. I'm just hormonal.'

He grimaced.

'Time of the month, hey?'

'Not exactly. Oh lord, Marleigh, you've got chocolate all over your dress!'

And with that she was up again, tutting and wiping at her daughter with a miraculously produced babywipe. Stan watched her carefully, reminded that the progress of his limited life wasn't the only one of importance, but before he could ask more he heard a cry of 'Happy Easter all!' and Dave marched round the far side of the house with a buxom woman in tow. He waved a twelve-pack of real ales in one hand and an enormous multi-coloured chicken piñata in the other and the kids went bounding over instantly.

Rachael followed, leaving Stan with little choice but to heave himself to his feet and do so too. Lisa, Greya and Bonnie came out of the house and Dave beamed round at his audience as he set his goodies on the table and grabbed a handful of his girlfriend instead.

'Everyone, this is Gail.'

'Gorgeous Gail,' Stan said before he could stop himself and Gail giggled.

'I like you already, Stan.'

She stuck out a hand and Stan took it gladly. Gail was a classic Dave choice – blonde, buxom and dressed to impress in an almost-too-tight orange dress, low on the cleavage and high on the thigh. She was, however, a bit older than Dave's usual women (being closer to his own age than Greya's) and carried herself with confidence instead of just simpering up at him.

'Thanks so much for inviting me along. My kids are both off travelling the world these days, and I do miss being around youngsters.'

'Gail brought the piñata,' Dave said, as proudly as if she'd given birth to it.

'It looks fantastic,' Bonnie said. 'We can hang it from the cherry tree. Hi, I'm Bonnie.'

'Hi Bonnie, Gail. Oh, you know that, don't you? Silly me! I'm a bit nervous.'

'Please, don't be. Come on, let's get you a drink, shall we? G and T?'

'Lovely.'

'Me too, Mum,' Lisa said.

Bonnie hesitated only a moment before smiling her assent. Despite the trial being over, Lisa seemed to have found more work in Manchester and had been around enough for both Bonnie and Stan to have noticed she was drinking quite heavily. Greya had been to see her dad a couple of times over the last weeks but Lisa had refused on the grounds that they'd only be digging soil and had kicked moodily around here instead.

Mind you, she'd seemed a lot happier these last few days. Maybe her outburst at the building site had helped, or the sunshine was making her smile, as it was Stan, or maybe there was more to it. She'd been texting at all hours of the day and he was beginning to wonder if she'd found herself a new man – and if so, how. Maybe she was on a dating app. Imagine if she saw his profile! Still, if Dr Mirabi had good news next week then he'd delete it straight away.

'Drink for you, Rae?' he heard Bonnie asking their second twin.

'No thanks. I'll have tea. Got any herbal, Mum?'

'Yep. Thanks to Greya we have about ten different types. Pick your poison, love!'

'Hardly poison, is it?' Lisa scoffed. 'You're never going to overdose on a rhubarb and ginger zinger. Have a drink, Rae. Enjoy yourself!'

Rachel drew herself up.

'Thanks for your concern, sis, but actually I'm driving.'

'Again?'

'Yes, again. So? We don't all need alcohol to have fun.'

Lisa froze and for a moment the warm spring air shivered with frost but then Gail said, 'Helps, though, doesn't it?' and threw her a wink that broke the tension.

The women stepped inside in search of gin and Stan went to check his barbecue. Inside someone switched the radio on and a tune blared out – 'Yesterday'. He caught the upward lilt of McCartney's voice and then, just as quickly, it was switched off. Bonnie, no doubt. He half turned to go towards her but Dave was waving a bottle under his nose and he was trapped.

'Beer, Stan?'

Inside, the re-tuned radio played an innocuous One Direction song. Stan breathed out and eyed the bottles, but he'd promised.

'Best not. I'm waiting to see what Dr Mirabi says next week.'

'Right. Course. Bound to be top news I'd have thought, though. You look good to me.'

'Thanks Dave. I feel good.'

'Sound.' He turned to Jamie, who'd followed them over. 'What about you then, young man?'

'Can I?' Jamie asked eagerly.

'No!' Stan said.

'Maybe a shandy?' Dave suggested. 'After all, he's doing man's work with us at the barbecue.'

'Sssh,' Stan said. 'Don't let the girls hear you say that. You'll be shot down in feminist flames.'

Dave grimaced.

'It's not discrimination, Stan, just fact. Men are good at cooking meat and women are good at frillying around with leaves. It's why we go so well together.' Jamie looked up at Dave wide-eyed and Dave winked at him. 'It's important you learn these things, lad, along with supporting a proper team. A rugby team ideally, not this shiny football nonsense.'

He tugged on Jamie's precious new Everton shirt but Jamie stood his ground.

'No way. Rugby's for old people.'

Dave blinked, momentarily silenced, but now the women were coming out of the house and Lisa was heading purposefully towards them.

'Shall we string the piñata up, Dave?' she asked, or, rather, ordered, and Dave had little choice but to acquiesce.

Stan watched, amused, as his daughter bossed his poor friend up into the cherry tree to get the perfect position, but suddenly Rachael was at his side, clearing her throat. He spun round and saw that she had dark circles around her eyes again and she was holding a lemonade. He looked to his own lime and soda and felt a sudden curl of dread.

'Rachael?' he rasped.

Her eyes locked on to his and for a terrible moment he thought he saw darkness deep in their centres but then she smiled and light flooded in. And now Andrew was coming up at her shoulder holding a bottle of champagne and he was smiling too, and Stan felt faint with relief.

'Is it the business?' he blurted out.

Rachael laughed.

'No Dad, it's not the business.'

'Is it Andrew's work, then? Has he secured a big commission?'

'No, though he's doing really well. It's something more . . . personal.'

She glanced at Andrew who nodded her on. Everyone else had noticed the bottle and was gathering in and Stan moved over to stand by Bonnie.

'We've got some news.' Rachael paused and blushed. 'It's a bit mad, really. And a bit unexpected, what with me being forty-seven and all, but . . .'

'You're pregnant,' Lisa gasped.

'Lisa!'

'Sorry, but you are, aren't you?'

'I am,' Rachael admitted.

'Pregnant?' Stan repeated. 'Oh my lord, you're pregnant. Of course!'

It all made sense now – the tiredness, the non-drinking, the back pain, Andrew's concern about her working on site. She wasn't ill, quite the reverse. Stan felt joy rise up inside him.

'I'm not sure how,' Rachael was stuttering.

'You're not sure how, love?' Dave chuckled.

Rachael blushed even deeper.

'I just mean that I thought I was, you know, past all that. Conception, that is, Dave, thank you. But it seems not.'

She looked shyly round and then Bonnie darted forward, grabbing her in a huge hug, and Marleigh started chattering about babies and Jamie said it had 'better be a boy to play footie with' and joy swelled inside Stan. If he wasn't careful he was going to blub like a baby himself.

'You OK, Dad?'

Rachael's eyes met his.

'Of course.' The tears were spilling, but so what? This was the best news he'd heard in ages. 'It's wonderful, sweetheart, really. I couldn't be more pleased.'

He folded her in his arms.

'I don't want you to think . . .'

'What? That you're replacing me?'

'Sort of, I guess. Only it's not like that, because obviously the baby was actually here before we found out about, you know, but I just . . .'

'Silly girl. It's fabulous, really, and I fully intend to be here to meet him or her.'

'Him,' Jamie said firmly and everyone laughed.

'Come on,' Stan said. 'Let's bash this piñata, shall we? Bagsy me first!'

And with that, he grabbed the barbecue poker and led the rush on the poor multi-coloured chicken. Let the sweets rain down. Love was in the air and his dear family was expanding and all was going to be well. He just knew it.

Chapter Twelve

'What about this? Or this?'

Bonnie held up two different blouses and Stan stared at them. He hated this sort of question.

'I'm not sure, Bonnie, they're both nice.'

'But which one is more appropriate?'

'How should I know? Does it matter? It's not a date, it's a doctor's appointment.'

'You think I don't know that? I just want to look good, Stan. What if we want to go out afterwards to celebrate?'

She gave a loud sigh and shoved both shirts back into the wardrobe. Stan picked at a stray thread on the end of the duvet and wished he was in Dr Mirabi's surgery so they could get on and find out exactly how effective the chemotherapy had been. He'd been awake half the night imagining the doctor beaming at them and saying he was so pleased to have the one-in-ten-thousand miracle patient in his surgery – and the other half imagining the opposite. Right at this moment, he was wishing he'd stayed grumpy like Terry so the wrong news might hurt less, but Terry was plastic so it was easy for him. And anyway, what was wrong with optimism?

'Wear a dress,' he suggested.

'A *dress*? Why?'

'Because I like you in dresses. Always have, ever since the first night I saw you in that cute little gingham one back in 1963. Proper stunner, you were.'

She rolled her eyes but did at least smile.

'I'm not eighteen any more, Stan. Oh honestly, this is silly. Jeans will do nicely. Now, shoo! Off downstairs and I'll be ready in a minute.'

He escaped gratefully but the house felt hollow and empty as he paced it alone and the clock ticked too loudly on the wall, and he was relieved when he heard her steps on the stairs. He turned to see her coming down in a dress after all – his favourite one, in a sunshine yellow with bold flowers around the hem.

'Stupid to give in to it,' she said as she reached the bottom and he went over to kiss her. 'You wouldn't want me in bloody black, would you?'

He vehemently agreed that he wouldn't. He wasn't sure if they were talking about now or 'after', but decided the answer would be the same anyway. He would specify no black for his funeral if that's what they were facing, but with Bonnie in that lovely sunny dress he could believe that maybe, just maybe, he'd bucked the odds and kicked cancer out for good.

'Oh lord, Stan,' Bonnie whispered, looking round the waiting room an hour later. 'This was so the wrong thing to wear.'

'It was not,' he said stoutly. 'I love you in it and surely that's what counts? Just cause everyone else feels the need to dress like they're already at their funeral doesn't make you wrong. I'm not dead yet!'

'Stan, hush!'

'It's true.'

He took her hand, feeling indescribably proud of his wife. She's with me, he wanted to shout, just as he had every day since she'd first put her hand in his and the future had opened up before him in a glorious shade of sunshine yellow.

He and Bonnie weren't the only ones holding hands in this nasty little antechamber. All around couples clutched tightly to each other as they waited for the big consultant's door to open and let them in to know their fate. Oncology, Stan thought – funny term, as if even the cancer doctors themselves had to hide from the dreaded c-word. He turned to say as much to Bonnie but at that moment the door swung open and every single person in the room looked nervously to it as if the angel of doom herself might come through. Instead, a young woman, not much older than Greya, slid out and said, 'Mr Tillotson?'

To Stan's left, someone gave a little whimper. He looked over to see a woman surely far too stout for such a tiny sound heaving herself to her feet, her husband with her. The man looked to her and she nodded at him, her eyes soft with love beneath a stern grey fringe. Stan saw the man set his shoulders back and knew that behind that look were a hundred night-time conversations, a hundred mopped-up tears and a hundred cuddles in the darkness. They were all the same in here, all looking for one thing – hope.

He watched the couple slide through the door and the young nurse close it behind them as everyone else hunkered back down into the plastic chairs. Stan tried to hold on to all his hard-won positivity but it was tougher here than at home. He picked up the hem of Bonnie's dress and traced his finger round the edge of one of the vibrant flowers, his old scar tickling against the raised threads.

'Do you think Lisa's OK?' he asked her, mainly to distract himself from whatever Dr Mirabi might be saying to Mr Tillotson through the dreaded door.

'About Simon? She seems so. I had a chat to her the other night and she says she's enjoying working in Manchester and she's finding it helpful spending time away from him. Why?'

'She's been texting a lot, have you noticed? And not just work stuff, not unless there's something fun going on in those Manchester offices to make her smile so often.'

Bonnie nodded.

'I have noticed, and I've heard her on the phone late at night too, giggling away. Do you think she's got someone new, Stan?'

'It looks like it to me, but lord knows I'm no expert. If she has, I hope it's someone up here.'

'Why?'

'Because then she might move permanently. It would be nice for you to have her closer, wouldn't it?'

'For *us* to have her closer.'

'Yes. Of course. For us. But if . . .'

'Stan, don't, please.'

The door opened and Mr and Mrs Tillotson came out. Everyone glanced up, then lowered their eyes again at the sight of the wife's red eyes and the husband's bent shoulders. Couples looked to each other and Bonnie grabbed at Stan's hand as if to say *don't even think that will be us*.

Was there a quota of good news for each day, and did the odds of getting it increase each time someone else didn't, like playing the tombola at the end of a fair? Of course not, Stan told himself crossly. Fate wasn't predestined; it was arbitrary, random – and all the crueller for it.

'Mrs Mistry?'

A woman in a dark green sari rose stiffly with another, near-identical, woman at her side. Sisters, Stan guessed and thought again of his own girls.

'It would be nice for Lisa to be near Rachael, right?' he said to Bonnie as the door closed again. 'They get on really, don't they, underneath all the bickering?'

'They certainly do but don't get your hopes up. I don't think

Lisa's staying up here to be near a man, Stan. More to get away from one.'

'Well, she needs to stop answering her phone all the time then. She's more teenage about it than Greya.'

Bonnie smiled.

'True. It was nice that Susie-Ann – sorry, Suzanne – could get Greya those passes to the conference, wasn't it?'

'It really was.' Stan smiled, remembering Greya's beaming face as she loaded the bike, now a pretty aqua-white and re-tuned to the best of Stan's ability, into a van driven by two equally excited lads.

Bonnie had waved them off and then gone on and on about how lovely it was to see Stan and his granddaughter bonding like this, which had been nice, if a bit awkward. Stan was pretty sure she wouldn't be quite so delighted if she knew that his granddaughter had been messaging men on his behalf, but then pushed thoughts of the damned app aside. It wasn't important now and if Dr Mirabi confirmed what they were hoping, he could get Greya to wipe it straight away.

The door opened, everyone looked up and this time a soft ripple of pure happiness passed around the room. Mrs Mistry was openly crying but the tears were spilling over a huge smile and her sister was patting at her hand and babbling over and over about how she 'knew it was going to be OK, just knew it', and suddenly everyone else in the room felt maybe they knew it too.

Stan looked to Bonnie and she gave him a little smile but then the nurse said 'Mr Walker', and for a moment Stan could see nothing at all, not even Bonnie.

'Thank you,' he heard Bonnie say in her best professional voice and then she was getting up and he was following her and suddenly waiting didn't seem so bad. Suddenly he felt he could wait forever. But forever was limited, and he was about to find out by how much.

'Come in, come in.' Dr Mirabi was smiling and Stan's vision cleared a little. He slid into one of the two padded chairs before the big desk, his eyes fixed on the doctor. He was definitely smiling. 'What a lovely dress, Mrs Walker. Such a pretty colour.'

'Thank you.'

Bonnie sat up very straight, leaned in a little.

Dr Mirabi smiled wider then said, 'Good news. The palliative chemotherapy has worked very well. Very well indeed.' If Bonnie sat any further forward, Stan thought, she'd fall off her seat. 'You've responded very well, Stanley. Do you feel well?'

'Very well,' Stan agreed, wondering how many more 'wells' there could be in one conversation and what they meant.

'Good, good.'

There was a pause. Stan looked to Bonnie then they both looked back to Dr Mirabi who shuffled his notes, still smiling.

'So it's worked then?' Bonnie burst out eventually, looking for one moment exactly like the eighteen-year-old of Stan's memory. 'It's killed the cancer?'

For the first time since they'd walked in, Dr Mirabi's smile faltered.

'It's worked as well as we'd expect, Mrs Walker, yes.' Stan looked to Bonnie again. She didn't look back and he was forced to return to the doctor. 'Tests show that around twenty-five per cent of the cancer cells in Stanley's body have been killed.'

'Twenty-five per cent?'

The number thudded into the space between them like a giant lead weight. Stan pictured a room full of ten thousand people with one of them stood apart, beaming. It wasn't him. Of course it wasn't him. He felt a dark, sticky anger begin to bubble inside at his own naivety.

'I'm very pleased,' Dr Mirabi said.

'You are?' Bonnie asked.

'It's above average.'

'Right. Twenty-five per cent. That's good isn't it, Stan?'

Her voice was bravely bright but he heard the dull disappointment beneath and hated it. Bonnie might be the maths star but even he could work this one out: if twenty-five per cent of the cancer cells were dead then seventy-five per cent were still running riot around his bloodstream.

He fumbled for Terry in his pocket as the anger bubbled more furiously inside him. *You were right,* he told the troll in his head. *You were bloody well right, you bugger.* It was no comfort. He didn't want Terry's negativity to win, or his own. He didn't want his house to get a roof without him or his grandchild to be born after his eyes were closed to it or Jamie to become a research doctor, forever haunted by his dead grandfather. He wanted the bloody miracle.

His head sank towards his collarbones. This was not the news they'd hoped for, not the success story they'd written for themselves. Fixing on the bright, pretty, hopeful, ridiculous flowers around Bonnie's beautiful dress, he felt them all fade away to deepest, darkest black and fumbled for her hand but already she was turning back to Dr Mirabi.

'Can he have more? Another course, I mean, to kill the rest?'

Dr Mirabi took a deep, measured breath.

'In a few weeks, perhaps, if we feel it will be beneficial.'

'Of course it will be beneficial,' Bonnie snapped.

It wasn't like her to be rude but having your hope shot out of you hurt, Stan knew, and hurt made people angry. Very angry. He daren't even speak for fear of his own fury bubbling up out of his throat in a tirade on this doctor who was, after all, just doing his job. He'd told them it was 'palliative', had made no promises of a cure, had offered no chance of a miracle. That had been all their own doing.

'How soon can he have it?' Bonnie was asking.

Still pinning her hopes on the damned miracle then.

'Bonnie,' Stan said, 'I don't think . . .'

'How soon?'

Dr Mirabi folded his hands on the table and looked her in the eye.

'That is for Stanley to decide,' he said. 'We wouldn't start anything for at least another month, so there's time to see how you get on.' His expression softened. 'I know this is hard. You'll need to think carefully, decide what's best for you – both of you.'

He turned to Stan as he spoke and Bonnie turned too and as he looked into his wife's violet eyes Stan felt something far, far worse than his own selfish anger. He felt the horrible weight of her endless optimism and the undertow of her inevitable disappointment, and had no idea where on earth to go from here.

Chapter Thirteen

Stan sat up on his haunches and stretched out his back. It ached, but he was used to that now. Everything ached: his gut, his throat, his limbs, his useless, foolish heart. He was a mess. It was pointless him being on the building site, really, but after he'd stewed over the terrible doctor's appointment for days, Dave had given him a stern talking-to and insisted that coming out to do some work would help. So here he was. It wasn't helping, though, and right now he could think of few places he'd less like to be.

Colourful pipe-ducts were sprouting out of the concrete like the blossom on the trees and Stan fixated on them, envying them their newness. Goodness, he really was pathetic. This was meant to be his dream house and somehow he was turning it into a nightmare. He looked around for someone to cheer him up but Rachael was in the office, Dave halfway up a ladder and Bonnie on the phone, talking with the sort of driven determination she had been applying to his cancer until Dr Mirabi had robbed her of that.

She'd been, if possible, even lower than him these last few days, but today the frame of their house was arriving and, despite herself, he could see her getting caught up in the challenge of it. Well, good, so she should – she, at least, would get to live in it.

Stop it, Stan, he told himself crossly. Fitting a timber frame was always exciting and this one would be special so he should at least try and enjoy it. Bonnie had designed their house to be built in a loose, looping S-shape to cut into the natural contours of the site, so the long walls were to be fitted in two matching curves. To make matters even more complicated, the house would rise up from a roomy single storey at the east end to an elegant double storey at the west.

A mezzanine floor inside would extend out to form a three-sided exterior balcony to catch the sun throughout the day and, assuming all went well, the whole tyrannosaurus of a skeleton would be in place before sundown today. Stan knew he was lucky to be here to see that happen; it just didn't feel that way.

He felt a ping from the phone buried deep in his overall pocket and wondered if it was Greya. She was still at the eco conference but had been texting him regularly with updates from the app. It seemed there were lots of lonely people out there, all keen to meet Stan and hear about Bonnie. And a good job too. Finding Bonnie a new husband had been promoted to Plan A as far as Stan and his twenty-five per cent bloody 'success rate' were concerned, and the other day he'd given his granddaughter the go-ahead to arrange a date with whoever she thought sounded best. He couldn't say he was looking forward to it, but then, looking forward wasn't a great idea any more anyway.

Yesterday he'd had to tell Rachael and Lisa that there had been no miracle after all and it had felt as if they were toddlers again listening to him saying Christmas was cancelled, like some mean old Scrooge. They'd been full of care and love, of course, and united at least in ideas to make the most of the time left to him, but he'd seen their faces fall before they'd found the composure to cover it up and hated himself for it. And then, to top it all, Marleigh had weighed in with her own advice.

'Grandpa,' she'd started, in a way that had made him think she was angling for another biscuit. If only she had been. 'Mummy says you're magic at fixing things. Are you?'

'What do you want fixing, Marleigh?'

'Nothing. It's not me. I was just thinking that if you're, you know, so good at fixing things you could maybe fix *your* thing.'

'My thing?'

'Your cancer.'

'Oh. Oh, I see.'

He'd taken Marleigh's hand then, noticing not so much how small it was in his palm, but how dewy-fresh her skin was against the mottled creases of his own. It had looked like a peach in a compost heap, and the stark evidence of his own decomposition had dug at his throat.

'It's tricky,' he'd said carefully.

'Why?'

'I'm good at fixings things you can see – walls and drains and pipes.'

'Livers have pipes. We did it at school. There was a programme on the computer where you had to put the right bits into a man in the right places. I got them all.'

'Well done.'

She'd squeezed his hand.

'It wasn't very hard. I bet you could fix those pipes if you tried.'

Stan had swallowed, not sure if it was her innocence or her trust that tugged at him more.

'I wish I could, sweetheart, but it's a bit trickier in real life than on the computer. There's all the blood, for a start.'

She'd flinched and he wondered if he'd gone too far but then she'd said, 'I could help. I'm good with blood. Miss Carter said so when I cut my knee. I held all the tissues on until it stopped and it did stop. Quite quickly. I could do that for you too.'

It had been the innocence, definitely. Her view of the world was so straightforward, and he hated the fact that it would be ground out of her over the relentless years of growing up.

'I'll have a think about it,' he'd managed, but now here he was thinking about it and the truth was there was nothing to do. He couldn't fix his cancer and neither could the doctors.

Through the fug of his own thoughts, he heard Bonnie calling his name. He looked over to see her waving at him and forced himself to wave back.

'What is it, my love?' he cooed.

She grimaced but chose not to challenge him.

'That was the driver of the timber truck on the phone. He should be here any minute, so we'd better get organised to help him reverse in.' Stan nodded and struggled to his feet. 'Are you OK, Stan? That is . . .'

The question sounded foolish to both of them but now, at least, a huge lorry was lumbering into view, stacked high with the gleaming oak skeleton of their house and she turned to guide the driver in, sparing them both further discussion. Stan saw Dave climb out of the little digger with which he was carving the hole for their septic tank and Rachael emerge from the rickety old caravan office. He squinted at her, trying to make out the bump of the newest member of the family, but she was in a baggy top and there was no telling yet.

Like performers in a well-known dance, the three of them took up positions either side of the track to guide the driver in. Stan, however, stayed rooted to the spot on the stage of the shiny foundation slab as the lorry, with a strident beep, began to back slowly towards him.

The timbers seemed to grow up as the vehicle got steadily closer. Stan could hear Dave and Rachael shouting instructions to keep the truck straight and knew he should be coordinating from the centre, but he was mesmerised. So many times he'd done this and today would be the last. It was both a pain and a joy. He sometimes wished he'd just been hit by a car instead of this slow drip-drip death. Loss was only loss if you were aware of it.

Stan stared at the truck, drawn to the huge wheels. If he stepped forward now he would be in the path of these great wheels. No one would see. He would be in the driver's blind spot and concealed from Dave and Rachael either side and Bonnie up front. One turn of that gleaming tyre and he'd be crushed beneath the weight of all the beautiful wood. He'd be gone, and the waiting would be over for all of them. No chemo, no dates, no conversations or expectations, no false hope.

'Stan! Stan, is he close?'

Dave's cry, so normal, so natural, snapped him out of his thoughts and he looked down.

'Two metres,' he called.

He stepped forward but only to bang decisively on the back of the truck. With a shudder and a hiss of brakes it creaked to a stop, leaving Stan standing in the gap between vehicle and house, alive and well. Or at least, alive.

'Perfect,' Dave said, bouncing towards him, and somehow the dance went on.

Stan watched, frozen, as the driver and his mate climbed out. Hands were shaken then everyone set about unstrapping the oak. The beams shifted as the straps were released from their metal clasps and now a giraffe of a crane was coming up the drive and parking to one side, settling onto its metal haunches and dangling its hook down to the top beam. Bonnie moved next to Stan.

'I love this bit,' she said, almost shyly.

Stan took a deep breath and tried to shake off his melancholy.

'Me too,' he muttered, watching with her as the first pre-fixed rectangle slotted neatly into the bolted-down steel holders to form the frame of the east wall.

'It fits,' Bonnie said on an outbreath, making him realise just how nervous she was. 'Let's just hope we can get the curves right, too.'

Stan nodded and watched silently as the other half of the west wall slid into place. Dave and the two labourers ran ladders up it to bolt on the heavy steels that would lock to the side walls and hold the second-storey frame. Stan heard the familiar rattling whine of the jackhammer and found words at last.

'Bet the Anglo-Saxons would have killed for kit like this.'

'Bet they would,' Bonnie agreed eagerly. 'We should . . .' She stopped. 'We should . . .' she tried again, but now she was the one lost for words.

They had this exchange every time they built a house and she was now meant to say, 'We should do one the old-fashioned way some day,' but she couldn't. 'Some day' wasn't there for them any more, or at least only as a specific – one single day rather than as a blissfully vague one floating on a hazy horizon. Stan fumbled in his pocket for Terry and felt the little troll rattle suggestively against his car keys. Of course!

'We should go on holiday, Bonnie.'

'Holiday? When?'

'Soon. We should get in the car and just go whilst we still can.'

'What about the second batch of chemo?'

'Sod the second bloody batch of chemo.'

'But . . .'

'No, really, Bonnie, forget it. I hate the chemo. It nukes my taste buds and puts me into quarantine and kills at least three days of the week – three days that could be so much better spent doing lovely things together. What's the point?'

He heard her draw in a careful breath. She looked over at the next frame, one of the curved ones, as it lifted high above their heads, and he saw her lips move slightly as she counted to seven.

'The point, Stan, is to eradicate the more aggressive cells to slow down deterioration.'

She spoke the words with control, taking refuge in the medical terms as if they could mask the harsh truth, and he was sick of it. He was sick of all the pussyfooting around. He was sick of cupboards full of spinach and beetroot and other 'superfoods'. As far as he was concerned a bacon sandwich, on white bread, with the fat left on and accompanied by a hearty dollop of brown sauce, was a superfood and he resented being denied it.

'But why use up those days just to gain the same at the end?'

'Because it could gain you so much more. It could be months, years even.'

He ground his teeth.

'It won't be years, Bonnie. How many times does Dr Mirabi have to tell you that before you believe it? We'd gain months at best, and all the time I'd be getting weaker. It's the days we have *now* that we need to seize.'

The beam dropped, inch-perfect, into place but neither of them raised even a small cheer.

'Don't you want to fight it?' Bonnie asked in a small voice.

'Of course I do,' Stan said automatically but he didn't mean it, not any more.

Fighting cancer was hard work. If he won, it would be worth it, of course it would. If by some miracle, beetroot managed to repair his liver and give him ten more precious years with Bonnie he'd eat it every day of his life, for breakfast, lunch and tea. But if beetroot didn't quite manage to fly in the face of years of medical expertise and experience, he didn't want to waste those weeks and months that might still be left to him chained to an endless round of treatment.

'I just don't want fighting cancer to be all I do,' he said.

'It won't be for long.'

'I know!'

The words barked out of him and she jumped.

'I meant the chemo, Stan. The bloody chemo won't be for long, then we can do things.'

'If I'm still here.'

'You will be.'

'I might not.'

'You can't think like that. You've got to be positive.'

Stan felt fury rise and he shook his head violently.

'No, Bon. That's not right. Not any more. What we've got to be is realistic. I spent all Easter being positive. I really began to believe we were going to be the miracle, you know, the one that bucked the odds, but we're not, are we? *I'm* not. You saw how delighted Dr Mirabi was because his damned chemo had killed off twenty-five per cent of my cancer cells – twenty-five per cent. A quarter! There's nothing miraculous about that, is there? And in the meantime every bloody minute I spend strapped to a poison-drip is one I could have spent having fun with you.'

'But it's going to cure you, Stan, I know it is.'

'How?' He grabbed her shoulders, forcing her to turn and look up at him. 'How do you know, Bonnie? What evidence do you have?' She tried to pull away but he held on tight; they'd been avoiding this for far too long. He was aware of Rachael watching anxiously, her hand to her belly, of Dave and the labourers and truck drivers staring, of the beam of their dream home hanging over their heads, but he couldn't bring himself to allow for any of it. She had to understand. 'You were in the surgery with me. You heard Dr Mirabi. It's not going to happen.'

'It *is*, Stan. I know it is. I know it in my heart.'

Stan wanted to howl in frustration.

'That's not knowing, Bonnie, that's hoping.'

'It's believing,' she shouted.

'Is it? Well that's great, Bonnie, but do you know what I believe? I believe I'm dying.' He heard her gasp and felt her go rag-doll limp in his hands. He was aware of Rachael shepherding the workers away but he had eyes only for Bonnie. 'I believe I've only got months left, and I believe I'm wasting them in nasty, sterile hospitals instead of out here breathing real air with real people who I love.' He blinked and looked at Bonnie and saw tears in her eyes. 'Who I love *so much*,' he repeated, softer now. 'I don't want to waste whatever time I've got. Can you see that?' She nodded, still teary-eyed and he reached up and kissed her. 'I certainly don't want to waste it arguing with you, my love.'

'Me neither,' she whispered.

She looked so frail and lost, and his heart ached at this foreshadowing of her grief. He pulled her tightly against him.

'I'm not going anywhere yet, sweetheart. We've got a house to get in place, remember?'

He looked over to his team, hovering at a distance, and gave Dave a determined, slightly desperate nod that his old mate read instantly. Dave strode over to the timber-men and issued orders, and Stan watched as they all snapped back into their places and, with a creak of relief, the second half of the front wall began to lower into place.

'It fits,' he said to Bonnie, still held tight in his arms. 'You got it dead right.'

'Seems I'm better at calculating building plans than medical ones.'

'As you should be.'

She nestled in against him and it felt just the same as when she'd been new in his arms and he'd wanted to hold her there forever. But forever was officially at an end now.

'I'm going to die, Bonnie.'

She looked up at him and he saw her battling to accept the words.

'Not yet?' was all she managed.

'Not yet, my love, and not for as long as I can possibly manage, but I want to do it my own way now. I want to eat what I can and maybe enjoy the odd pint or a glass of wine with my lovely wife. I want to spend every single minute that I can with you and nowhere near a bloody hospital. Can we do that? Can you do that for me? Please?'

He looked into her eyes and saw them harden with determination as he had seen so many, many times before in their lives together. In the past, though, it had always been over house projects or plans for the girls. This would be the biggest challenge of all, he knew, and he hated to ask it of her but he had no choice.

'I can try, Stan.'

'That's all I ask.'

She kissed him long and hard, and then drew back and stood at his side as Dave knocked the beam expertly into place and suddenly their dream house was there before them, curving out and up, swelling with its own promise. Stan looked up at it and felt something approaching peace settle in his bruised heart for the first time since they'd left the doctor's surgery.

'Our own way,' he said quietly. 'From here on in, we do it all our own way.'

Chapter Fourteen

March 1963

'Congratulations, Miss Jessop. Eighty-two per cent. Very impressive.'

Professor Sanderson looked down his thin nose as he handed Bonnie back her mid-term exam paper, his praise laced with icy disapproval. Bonnie took it, head high, trying hard not to care what he thought of her. The result was what counted – that's what would get her the qualification to become an architect. Once she had that, she could get on with the real business of designing beautiful houses and leave this lot wallowing in the murk of their inflated sense of self-worth.

'Thank you, sir.'

She turned to leave the lecture theatre platform but froze as he spoke again.

'No, thank *you*, Miss Jessop. It's a pleasure to nurture such talent, and I'm sure your children will appreciate your expertise with their building blocks.'

Bonnie couldn't stifle her gasp in time. She saw all the male students lounging in the benches before her snigger and nudge each other and suddenly she'd had enough of this. Eighty-two per cent was the highest in the class. She swung back to the professor.

'I have every intention of working as an architect,' she said.

'I'm sure you do, dear, for a year or two.'

'For my entire career.'

'You don't intend to have children?' His white eyebrows shot all the way into his receding hairline, then he added slyly, 'Oh, are you not that way inclined?'

More sniggers. Bonnie felt her cheeks burn and fought to keep her composure. She tried to remember Aunt Nancy when she'd stormed into school to tackle the headmistress about her choice of degree, but feared she lacked her aunt's tank-like determination. The best she could hope for was to escape without tears.

'It is possible to work and have children,' she said as calmly as she could manage.

'Designing Wendy houses, perhaps?'

The professor's chest puffed up with his own pathetic joke and Bonnie gritted her teeth.

'I don't see why I should be limited by being a woman. And neither, sir, do I see what business it is of yours.'

'You don't?' Professor Sanderson drew himself up tall. 'Then let me explain. I put many, many hours into imparting my expertise to my students, Miss Jessop, and I do not like to see it wasted.'

'On building blocks?'

'Exactly so. You, young lady, are taking a place on this course that would be better filled by someone who is actually going to design houses.'

'Like you do?'

The sharp intake of breath from the male students told her she'd gone too far. She'd be disciplined now, probably thrown out. All her hard work would be for nothing. The tears rose and, mortified, she clutched her eighty-two per cent to her chest and fled the lecture theatre for the second time that term.

She ran out of the university and deep into the city, threading her way through the lunchtime crowds and almost reaching the river before she paused for breath. Across the road sat a red phone box and she dived for it, fed coins into the slot and dialled.

'Hello?'

Aunt Nancy's voice almost undid her at just that one simple word.

'It's me,' she managed to squeak.

'Bonnie? What is it? What's wrong?'

'It's them.'

'Who? Deep breaths, lass. Are you in danger?'

'No. That is . . . Oh lord, Nancy, they're going to throw me out. I know they are. They're going to throw me out for insubordination and rudeness and, and for wasting their expertise.'

'What? Bonnie, you're not making any sense. Start at the beginning, girl, or I can't be any use to you.'

The no-nonsense tone was so wonderfully familiar that it calmed Bonnie enough to explain and by the end it was her aunt who was raging.

'Right, that's it. I'm coming down there and I'm going to tell them what's what. You earned that place and you're proving you deserve it, and he had no right to talk to you like that. No right at all, you hear me?'

Bonnie drew in her aunt's support with deep breaths of salty, Liverpool air.

'You're sure?'

'Sure I'm sure. If anyone's being rude here, lass, it's that bloody professor. You had every right to stand up for yourself and I'll damn well tell him so too.'

Nancy's certainty soothed Bonnie but the thought of her turning up scared her too.

'Thanks, Nancy, really, but it's OK. I'll go and see him tomorrow and I'll call again if there's trouble.' She heard Nancy hesitate at the other end of the line and said, 'Was Sweden nice?'

Nancy gave a little sigh of pleasure.

'Lovely, thank you. It's an amazing country, Bonnie. You'd love it. In fact, I'm thinking . . .'

She stopped.

'Thinking what?'

'Nothing. Nothing at all, really. Now look, are you sure I shouldn't come? Astrid could drive me. She's like a bloody rally driver so we could be there within an hour or two.'

'Really, it's OK. I just . . . just wanted to hear your voice.'

'Ah, Sweet Bonnie – hear it loud and clear: you've done nothing wrong. Nothing. OK?'

'OK, Nancy.'

A pause, then Nancy said, 'What are you doing tonight?'

Bonnie looked out of the grimy windows of the phone box. At the end of the street she could see the Mersey and beyond it the soft hills of the far bank.

'I'm meant to be going to a gig at the Tower Pavilion over the river.'

'Meant to be?'

'I'm not sure I'm in the mood now.'

'Of course you are, Bonnie. You have to be. You can't let that old wind-bag rob you of your fun.'

'I can't?'

'Certainly not. A gig sounds like the perfect way to put this arrogant idiot and his antiquated ideas out of your mind.'

'I guess so.' Bonnie twiddled with the phone cord. 'I got eighty-two per cent, Nancy. Best mark in the class.'

'So you should be celebrating!'

'Yes.'

'Oh, Bon.' She sounded sad. 'Say you'll go out, lass, for me.' Bonnie looked out at the city again, pulsing with life. She breathed out onto the glass and drew two little circle eyes. 'Bonnie?'

The phone bipped.

'My money's running out, Nancy.'

'Bonnie – say you'll go. Have fun. Live. Show him he can't get you down. Please.'

'I will.'

'Good. And Bonnie . . .'

But at that, the line went dead and Bonnie was left standing there alone. She closed her eyes for a moment, pressing the phone against her cheek as if it were a kiss from her aunt before replacing it on the cradle.

'Thank you, Nancy,' she murmured, adding a mouth to the face on the glass – a mouth turned up in a smile. If only she could paint it so easily onto her own face too.

Thankfully Susie-Ann's brightest lipstick did a pretty good job and a shot of her brothers' latest acquisition – a full barrel of Jamaican rum – steadied Bonnie's nerves, so it was with something approaching good cheer that she tottered off the bus at the Pier Head two hours later.

The sight of all four Best Boys waiting for them in their performance suits (as instructed by Spike, 'in case Epstein is about'), cheered her further and she sent another little thank you towards her aunt for making her promise to come out. Forget the professor and his bunch of sheep-like acolytes; she was off to dance to Gerry and the Pacemakers and, what's more, Sticks was playing the drums for them. The rising band's drummer was injured and a mate of his was a mate of Sticks and had 'heard he wasn't too bad behind the bongos', so here they were.

'It's the Best Girls!' Sticks cried, grabbing Susie-Ann and swirling her round and Bonnie's spirits rose still further.

It was Lee who'd called them that when they'd all got together to discuss the Riverboat Shuffle, and the term had stuck. He'd said the band needed the two girls for brain power and Bonnie had loved feeling truly part of things and did her best to help wherever she could. She still felt funny when Spike was close, but she'd managed to avoid ever being stuck with him on her own and it was worth putting up with a bit of awkwardness to remain part of the band.

Danny came up at her side and slid an arm around her waist and when she looked up at him she saw his blue eyes gazing down on her with such easy joy that the world seemed instantly more fun.

'Good day?' he asked.

'Not really,' she started but found she didn't want university troubles leaking into this precious time away. 'My professor was pretty mean but, you know, I'm used to it. You?'

'Not the best either. Trouble with a big customer.'

'Oh dear – what?'

He flushed.

'Oh, just stock issues. A delivery was delayed and he wasn't at all happy at having to wait. Got quite violent.'

Bonnie was shocked. What kind of business did Danny's dad run? She'd got used to the Cobdens hiding crates of cheap booze and smuggled records around the place, but this sounded like another level altogether. She should really ask Susie-Ann, but she was a little afraid of the answer.

'Did you say your uncle is a plumber, Dan?'

'Er, yes. Why?'

'Maybe becoming his apprentice *would* be a good idea. You shouldn't have to face violence at work.'

Or prejudice, she thought, but it didn't seem worth saying and now Danny was kissing her.

'That's sweet, Bon, but hey, we dealt with it. And I can handle myself, you know.'

Bonnie remembered his offer to scare the boys on her course and felt rather tempted to take him up on it, but that would surely only make things worse.

'Danny . . .' she started, but he leaned over and silenced her with a soft kiss on the lips.

'Forget it, beautiful. I have. I can't wait for tonight.' He kissed her again. 'God, I really like you, Bonnie Jessop.'

'You do?'

She slid her arms around his neck and felt him run his hands gently down her back before sneaking round and up towards her breasts. She squirmed.

'You like that?' he whispered against her lips.

Did she? She still had no idea, and was relieved when the *Royal Iris* came swinging into the dock and the crowd surged forward, pulling them apart. But now the same movement was pressing Spike up against her and it seemed that she could no longer avoid talking to him.

'All right?' he muttered.

'Yep. You?'

'Yeah.' He twitched at the collar of his suit and nodded his head to Danny. 'You with him now?'

Danny leaned over, placing his arm ostentatiously round Bonnie's shoulders.

'She's with me, yeah.'

'Right. Good. Lovely.' The gates opened and the crowd shifted. A lad on Danny's other side started talking to him about Gerry and the Pacemakers and Spike leaned in close to Bonnie. 'Look, Bon, about that night at the Cavern . . .'

'Forget it, Spike. It was ages ago.'

'I know but you've been avoiding me – and no wonder. I was out of order. I'm sorry. It was just fans, like. A lead singer has to look available.'

'Well, you did that nicely.'

'Yeah. I did, didn't I? It was stupid, though. You're a boss bird, Bonnie, really.'

'Er, thanks.'

Danny had been pulled sideways and there was nothing to shield her from the far-too-tempting touch of Spike's warm body and it was impossible to get away with the crowd so tight around them. 'You sleeping with him?' he shot at her suddenly.

'What?!'

'Nothing. Sorry. Stupid question. You're just so damned pretty, Bonnie. It does things to fellas.'

'And that means I have to have sex with them?'

'No! Course not. That is, only if you want to.'

'Thanks for that.'

'Pleasure. Though if you decide you do, like, wanna go for it, you know where I am.'

'Spike!' His voice was jokey but he brushed her arm and she felt her skin spark dangerously at his touch. 'We shouldn't be talking like this.'

'Can't blame a man for trying and, you know . . .' He looked shiftily around as they all shuffled towards the boat before adding in a hiss, 'I ain't never done it before neither.'

'You? You're a virgin, Spike?'

'Sssh! Don't tell anyone, it'd ruin my image and then I'll never make it big.' He gave a rueful little grimace. 'Bonnie . . .'

He was so close and he was so handsome, and her insides were swirling more than the Mersey but Spike had ditched her without a backward glance and she'd be mad to trust him again. As far as she could see, he was only after one thing and that wasn't enough for her. She shifted uneasily but at last they were stepping onto the boat and she moved gratefully away from Spike as Lee materialised before them.

'Come on,' he urged. 'Let's go and see if the Shuffle poster is up.'

He was jiggling around with anticipation and grabbed Bonnie's arm to tug her forward. She laughed and went gratefully with him. The others crowded behind and together they made for the main saloon of the boat. It was every bit as crushed on board as it had been on the dockside and Danny, biggest and tallest, got through first. Bonnie heard him let out a hilariously girlie squeal and when she finally made it into the saloon, she saw him jumping up and down and pointing to the wall as if he'd seen God himself leaning against it.

There, taped to the metal interior of the boat, was a big poster. *Riverboat Shuffle* it said in bold red at the top and beneath it ran the list of acts, starting with *Billy J. Kramer* then *The Big Three* and *The Escorts* and finally, at the bottom but in lettering every bit as big as the rest – *the Best Boys*.

'It's us!' Lee said. 'Look, lads, it's really, truly us.'

Bonnie and Susie-Ann stood respectfully back as the four band members formed a tight semicircle around the poster, like men at worship.

'It's so exciting,' Bonnie said to Susie-Ann. 'This could be the big break they've been looking for.'

'It could that. And we'll be VIP guests, you and me, Judies of the band.'

Bonnie's heart leaped. Instinctively she glanced at Spike, but he was staring at the poster and didn't notice, thank goodness. She had to stop thinking of herself as his girlfriend. They'd only been together for two weeks, for heaven's sake, and she'd already been seeing Danny for three. She shook herself and tried to focus on the band as a whole, not their tricky individual members.

'You lot look great,' she said. 'I wish there was someone here with a camera.'

The boys preened a little in their performance suits, every inch the pros, though the bright lights of the ferry were less forgiving than the dim world of the Cavern and Bonnie couldn't help noticing the sheen of too many home-cleans on Spike's suit and the neat darns in the elbows of skinny Lee's. Danny's was as immaculate as ever but, to her surprise, Sticks was perhaps the smartest of them all.

'New suit,' he said, twitching at the collar as he saw her looking. 'Me mam said if I were playing with Gerry I wasn't to show her up in scruffy kecks. Da's been moaning about the cost of it all week but I told him I'd pay him back when I gets sent to Hamburg with the other stars.'

Spike looked up, scowling.

'Fat chance,' he scoffed and the drummer's face fell. 'Don't go getting too cocky, mate. I hear Freddie Marsden's all but mended. He's only resting tonight cos it's not an important gig.'

Sticks looked hurt and Lee stepped quickly forward.

'Rubbish, Spike. Freddie's torn a ligament at the base of his index finger. He'll be out for weeks. This is Sticks' big chance and I, for one, wish him all the best.'

'You would.'

'What does that mean?'

'I thought you wanted to make it big, Lee? I thought it was, like, important to you.'

'It is.'

'And here we are with a chance at the Riverboat Shuffle where all sorts of influential fellas might hear us and you're saying you're happy if our drummer legs it to Hamburg?'

He battered his hand against the poster, skewing it slightly, and Danny pulled him away.

'No one's going to whip Sticks off to Hamburg, Spike.'

'And even if they did,' Sticks said, 'I wouldn't go.'

'Course you would,' Spike snapped.

'Not that quick. It'd leave me da in the lurch down the garage, wouldn't it?'

'Like that would bother you. Come on, Sticks – we all want the big break, right? We're all waiting for Epstein to come calling and show Paul bloody McCartney and his gang of frigging insects that we can do it too, so what's the point pretending?'

Spike's fists clenched and he bounced in front of Sticks, who matched him instantly. They made a ridiculous pair, both in their smart suits and both with their hair Brylcreemed into stiff quiffs, like a pair of cockerels, but there was nothing funny about the tension crackling between them. Panicked, Bonnie looked to Susie-Ann for help but she just picked at a nail.

'Let the little boys fight if they want to – like they always have.'

'Always?'

Angular Lee stepped between Spike and Sticks, pushing them gently apart.

'Spike and I were at school together,' he told her. 'And we knew the other two from playing out on the street.'

'I were too thick to go to the poncy grammar,' Sticks said belligerently. 'And Danny went off to his posh-knobs place, but this pair had a fine old time.'

Lee put a calming hand on the red-headed drummer's arm.

'That's not true. I was two years above Spike but I knew who he was. Everyone did. Gobby little shite even then, weren't you, Spike?'

Spike frowned.

'What changed?' Bonnie asked.

'Who said anything changed?' Sticks growled, but Lee still had a hand on his arm and the light touch seemed to be enough to hold him back.

'He got a guitar,' Lee said, with a lopsided grin that lit up his sharp features. 'It made him seem less of a pain in the arse somehow. It was Spike and me started the Best Boys.'

'And then they asked some proper musicians to join them,' Danny said in his smooth voice. 'Right, Sticks?'

'Too right.'

It was an attempt at lightening the mood and Bonnie was glad of it. Spike was bouncing on his toes as if spoiling for a real fight and it made her nervous. He'd been edgy from the moment he'd spoken to her about Danny, and a tiny bit of her dared to think it was because he was jealous – but then she felt bad for rather liking that. She glanced again to Susie-Ann and saw even she was looking worried and her chest tightened further.

'So you and Lee were at the same school?' she asked Spike, fighting for normality.

'The Liverpool Institute, yeah. Same as Paul frigging McCartney.'

Susie-Ann stepped up at Bonnie's side.

'So a breeding ground of talent then,' she said lightly.

'A what?' Spike demanded. 'Lord, Sticks, your Judy speaks posh sometimes.'

Sticks huffed.

'I know. And she's getting worse. It's this university business corrupting her.'

'Corrupting?' Bonnie shrieked.

It came out louder than she'd intended but she was still raw from her encounter with Professor Sanderson and this lot sniping at each other was setting her nerves on edge. She glared around at the so-called Best Boys in their mismatched suits. They looked back at her, stunned, but she didn't care. She couldn't stand any more of this today.

'Just stop it, all of you,' she said. 'This is so stupid. You should be supporting each other, not tearing each other apart. Look, there.' She jabbed a finger at their name on the poster. 'That's your break, the chance you've been looking for, so why the hell are you falling out about it like children? It's ridiculous!'

They all stared at her in silence and she bit her lip. What had got into her today? First the professor and now the Best Boys. She might as well start packing her bags to leave. But then Susie-Ann clapped her long and hard and nudged at Sticks.

The drummer picked at some imaginary fluff on his suit and said, 'You're right. Sorry, Bonnie.'

'It's not me you need to apologise to,' she said stiffly.

'No. Sorry, Susie. It's not your fault you're clever, like.'

It was one of the stranger apologies Bonnie had heard but it at least broke the silence.

'And I'm sorry for being rude to you, Spike,' Lee said. 'You *are* a gobby little shite but you're a damned tuneful one too.'

Spike stared at his old friend for what felt like forever and then gave an exaggerated shrug of his shoulders.

'Yeah, well, you're not so bad yourself, I guess. You neither, Danny.' He looked to the poster and gave a big sigh. 'I just want this to work, you know. Want the Best Boys to be just that – the best.'

'And you will be,' Bonnie said. 'As long as you stick together.'

They all nodded, still cowed, and Bonnie was relieved when the ferry swung onto the far bank and released them from its tight confines. She scrambled off the boat, leaving the others to follow. Susie-Ann came up and took her arm and they strolled ahead of the boys, taking in the evening calm of the resort of New Brighton.

The sun was only just visible above the water but Bonnie could make out children playing in thick duffel coats on the sandy beach further up, where the river rolled out into the Irish Sea. As they strolled towards the big Tower ballroom, the street came alive with slot-machine halls and ice cream stalls and burger bars. Bonnie heard the boys pointing them out to each other and joking around and began to breathe more easily.

'There!' Susie-Ann squealed, clutching Bonnie's arm as they passed under a wrought-iron archway. 'Look at that huge building glowing like the Palace of Versailles – that's the Tower Pavilion.' She spun round to the Best Boys to add, 'And my gorgeous boyfriend is going to play there!'

'Palace of Ver-what?' Sticks asked, crinkling up his pale nose, but Susie-Ann just kissed it.

'Don't matter – you're going to rock tonight, lad. And we're going to rock with you.'

And as Bonnie took Danny's big hand on one side and Lee's slim arm on the other and followed a swaggering Spike up the steps to the Pavilion, she reckoned Susie-Ann had it dead right. She smiled and sent renewed thanks back over the Mersey towards Aunt Nancy for forcing her out. The Best Boys were tight again and their name was up on a poster for all to see, and all she had to do was sort herself out. Tomorrow she would go and see Professor Sanderson and make sure her place on the course was safe, but for now she would have fun. Live. Show him he couldn't get her down.

Following your goals was a tricky business but one worth doing, of that she was sure once more. As she stepped through the magnificent doors of the Pavilion, she looked up at the towering architecture and gave it a firm nod hello. Beautiful buildings were *her* goal and she was going to enjoy this one all night long.

Chapter Fifteen

The alarm buzzed through Stan's whole body as if it were riding rodeo on every one of his poor, hard-working blood cells. He banged it off and crawled down under the covers. Five minutes later it cracked the whip again, muffled by the duvet but increasingly insistent. Stan stuck an arm out, fumbled for it and knocked it to the floor. There was a small crack and then the sound of the batteries making an escape for freedom across the floorboards.

'That's shut it up at least,' Bonnie said, burrowing across the bed to find him.

Stan opened his arms to let her crawl into them but feared opening his eyes would be another level of difficulty. He was so tired. Getting up to an alarm had always been difficult. He'd never been one of those ping-and-I'm-up-and-ready-to-go people. The early years with the twins, when one or other had seemed to be shouting for attention every hour, had been hell.

Back then, though, his body had at least functioned even whilst his brain had stayed nestled in sleep as he changed nappies and heated milk. Since the cancer had started to take hold, though, his body was every bit as fuggy as his mind. With every morning that passed, his limbs seemed to become more like stroppy teenagers, headphones clamped on, music up high, refusing to listen to anything he asked of them and, even if he got through, obeying only with reluctance.

'I don't want to get up,' he murmured to Bonnie.

'Then don't.'

'What?'

'Stay in a bed a bit longer – a *lot* longer.'

Now he was awake.

'No. No way. I'm not letting this bloody thing turn me into a bed-bound invalid.'

He tried to throw back the covers but she had her arms wrapped around him and he was too weak to resist.

'Stop overreacting, Stan. There's a wealth of difference between a lie-in and a "bed-bound invalid" and besides, I'm not proposing chicken broth and an audiobook.' She wriggled closer. 'D'you know, Aunt Nancy once told me that she'd done all her best learning in bed. I was tucked up with a load of books swotting for my A-levels at the time and didn't think anything of it, but looking back I'm sure Nancy had an altogether different sort of learning in mind.'

Stan opened his eyes.

'Your aunt was – *is* – a wise lady. Maybe we should invite her over. It would be lovely to see her again before, you know . . .'

'Before she gets too frail to travel?' Bonnie said, a little too loudly.

'Before that,' Stan agreed, because it was easier. 'Anyway, what can I learn in bed all on my own?'

'You won't be on your own. I'll be here with you.'

Stan stared suspiciously at her.

'You? You don't do lie-ins, Bonnie.'

Bonnie *was* one of those ping-and-I'm-up-and-ready-to-go people. If he was honest, *that's* how they'd survived the first two years of the twins.

'I do lie-ins if they're with you. Remember how long we used to stay in bed when we were first married?'

Stan did remember and the thought of it hummed pleasurably through his body. With him working as an apprentice plumber and Bonnie still studying architecture, money had been tight. They'd lived in a grotty house with a tiny bedroom and a rickety old bed. He'd hate it now, he was sure, but back then they'd spent many happy hours breakfasting on toast and jam and, if he remembered correctly, each other.

'I'm not sure I'm up to those sorts of lie-ins any more,' he said sadly.

'Maybe a little bit?'

He grinned.

'Well, maybe a little bit, yes.'

Stan ran his hand down Bonnie's back. The doctor had warned him that chemo might drain away his sex drive but thankfully Stan's body – or maybe Bonnie's – had defied that particular symptom.

'Excellent,' she purred. 'The brick delivery isn't until midday so I reckon they can cope on site without us til then.'

She reached out to kiss him but something inside Stan had frozen. Maybe it was the memory of those big timber-truck tyres bearing down on him, but the thought of another delivery felt almost too much to bear.

'Can't they cope without us all day?' he said lightly.

'What?'

'Then we could just stay here. Together.'

She pulled away.

'You don't want to see the bricks?' she asked sharply.

'I didn't say that. But they won't change, will they? They'll look the same tomorrow, or the next day. That's kind of the point of bricks.'

Bonnie frowned.

'But by then they'll be part of a wall and it'll be too late to change if we don't like them.'

'They're bloody bricks, Bonnie,' he snapped. 'What's not to like?'

He saw her confusion and hated himself for causing it but a few tiny aberrations in brick colour didn't feel like the top of his list of concerns right now. Truth be known, he wasn't sure he really wanted to be on site anyway. He reached for her hand and she let him take it but her fingers were stiff within his grasp. He sighed.

'I'm sorry. Of course you can go if you want to but I'm sure Rachael could do it just as well. She's bouncing around now she's felt the baby kicking – can't keep her still, bless her.'

He attempted a smile. It wasn't returned.

'You don't want to go to the site, do you?' she said.

Damn – she knew him too well. He swallowed.

'I just thought we could have a day off today, that's all. Go out for lunch or something. That would be nice, wouldn't it?'

'Why don't you want to go?'

'Bonnie, please.'

'Don't you like the house? Is that it? Is it too "designery" for you? Too modern?'

'No! It's a beautiful house, Bonnie. I just fancy a day off, that's all. The lie-in was your idea, remember?'

'The lie-in, yes, but not, not . . . giving up.'

He sucked in his breath.

'That's what you think? That I'm giving up? Is this because of the chemo? It is, isn't it? You didn't really mean it when you said you'd do it my way.'

'I did!' She jumped out of bed and stood before him, gloriously naked, not that he could let that distract him now. 'I *did* mean it, Stanley Walker, and I *am* trying but I didn't know your way meant avoiding everything we usually love to do.'

She put her hands over her face and he scrabbled out of the bed and pulled her close in against him.

'This is ridiculous, Bon. Come back to bed, please. We'll have that lie-in and then some nice jammy toast, just like the old days, and then we'll go and check the bricks. '

He tried to tug her towards the bed but she stood her ground.

'No, Stan. Lie-in, yes. Jammy toast, yes. But no bricks. If you want to go out for lunch that's what we should do.'

'Because I'm dying?'

'Well, yes. I suppose so. Isn't that what this is all about? Isn't "your way" some sort of bucket list? Well, fine. I can build the house after, after . . .'

She covered her face again and Stan felt helpless before her distress. How had this morning gone so wrong so quickly? He didn't even want to go to lunch now, or to the building site, or any bloody where. He just wanted to reset the alarm and start the whole damned day again.

'I'm sorry, Bonnie. I want to build the house, really I do. It's all we've been working up to.'

'All *I've* been working up to, you mean.'

She was shivering now and he tried to tug her back to bed, but she stood her ground.

'What are you saying, Bonnie?'

'You wanted to play music.'

'What?' Lord, this whole conversation was spiralling out of control. 'When?'

'Back then. Back when we met. Back when you were with the Best Boys.'

'That was years ago, Bonnie. And the Best Boys were crap anyway.'

She winced.

'They weren't crap, Stan.'

'They were that night – on Bad Friday.'

166

'Maybe we overreacted.'

'What?' Stan couldn't believe he was hearing this. 'No way, Bonnie. Why are you saying this now? Would you change what happened?'

'Maybe.'

Stan felt his chest tighten. He'd known it. All along he'd known it.

'But I thought . . . I mean, we're happy, aren't we? We've been happy?'

Her eyes widened in horror.

'Lord, yes. I wouldn't change *you*, Stan. Is that what you thought? Fifty-four years of marriage and you can still think that?'

'Everyone wanted you back then, Bonnie.'

'And I wanted *you*. Oh come on, idiot.'

She tumbled back into bed, dragging him with her, but once there they sat awkwardly on either side, like a medieval bride and groom put together for the first time.

'I didn't mean I'd change things for me,' she said eventually. 'I meant for you.'

'But I got exactly what I wanted. I've had a great life – *have* a great life. We've built some wonderful houses, haven't we? That's better than a few tunes. And our next one is going to be the most wonderful of all, isn't it? Isn't it, Bonnie?'

He could hear his voice rising, becoming shrill.

'Of course it is,' she agreed hastily, but her voice was dull and they both lapsed into silence.

'Toast?' Bonnie said, after a long pause.

'Please,' Stan agreed, but it didn't sound as enticing as it had before and they both sat there unmoving, a crumpled duvet and a whole heap of tangled emotions wedged between them.

He was just trying to work out what the right thing was to do when a door crashed open downstairs and a voice cried,

'Helloo! Anyone home?' Greya came bounding up the stairs and there was no time to do anything more than pull the duvet higher.

'Well, hello there,' she said, bounding in. 'Having fun?' Bonnie looked to Stan, embarrassed, but Greya didn't seem to need an answer. She perched herself on the end of the bed. 'I've had such a great time at the conference, Granny. Thank you so much for setting it up for me. I met your mate, Suzanne, and she's so cool. She really liked our bike, and she knows loads of important people and she says she's going to talk to someone about us taking it to this big renewable energy expo in Paris in a few weeks. Paris! Imagine.'

'I'm so glad,' Bonnie said, reaching for her dressing gown.

'And you, Gramps, you're quite the hero. Jonty – that's one of the lads that picked me up – says he's been working on the bike for months and he's never got anywhere near as high a performance out of it as you. He wants to meet you.'

'*Now?*'

'Oh no, not now. Later, maybe. When we go to get the cogs.'

'Cogs?'

'Yes, Grandpa, cogs – for the bike. Remember?'

She gave him a huge wink, which Bonnie was thankfully too busy pulling on her dressing gown to notice, and suddenly Stan did remember. They *had* planned to go and buy new cogs today but the proposed trip was also a cover for his second date.

Lawrence was a retired solicitor and his picture showed a good-looking man – perhaps too good-looking if Stan was honest, but he supposed that's what he got for putting a teenage girl in charge of his choices. Still, his profile said he was 'keen to find someone to care for' so that, at least, met Stan's demands and he'd agreed to meet him in some bar in Birkenhead. He'd been nervous about it all week, so how could he have forgotten?

'I'm not sure today is a good idea for that, Grey,' he said, looking at Bonnie, but she was making for the door.

'Why not?' Bonnie asked over her shoulder. 'I'll be busy with the brick delivery so you might as well get on with it.'

He felt the sting of her words but had no idea how to find a balm with Greya sat on the bed.

'See, Grandpa,' the teenager said happily. 'Don't worry, I'll drive if you're tired.'

'That's very kind, Greya,' Bonnie said from the doorway. 'Isn't that kind, Stan?'

And with that she swept from the room, leaving Stan all alone in their now chilly bed. Well, fine, let her go and see her damned bricks if she was so keen; he'd be busy finding someone to live within the walls they'd create. The thought twisted him up inside and he nearly went after her but she was gone and it felt too late somehow.

Chapter Sixteen

Several hours later, Stan stood outside the door of the bar and tried to calm the crazed butterflies in his stomach. He'd dragged out the cog-shopping for as long as possible, treated Greya to lunch and even allowed himself to be led around Topshop for what had felt like forever, but there was no putting it off any longer.

'Go on, Grandpa – he'll be waiting.'

Greya nodded him towards the door.

'I don't think this is a good idea, Grey.'

She tossed her silvery hair.

'Don't worry, I'll be here waiting for you and I'll drive you home and we can stop at that pub you like on the road back.'

He had to laugh at that. Here was his granddaughter bribing him as if he were the child and she the adult.

'Don't go far,' he said.

'I'll be right here, Gramps. Now go on! Have fun.'

Stan thought that highly unlikely but he couldn't put this off any longer, so he pushed on the door and headed inside.

He hated the place straight away. It was a shiny wine bar, all funky orange tables and chrome stools. The relentless gloss made him feel giddy barely four steps in.

'What am I doing here?' he mumbled to Terry, but Terry didn't seem any more impressed than he was and just hunkered deeper into his pocket.

Stan sighed and scanned the tables. It was just gone 5 p.m. so the bar was empty of all but a handful of after-work suits and a gaggle of young women drinking cocktails beneath a 'Birthday Girl' balloon. Lawrence wasn't hard to spot, sat alone in a giant booth looking very smart, though his bald patch was caught in the big mirror behind, as if the glass was maliciously giving away his secrets. He was looking straight at Stan and now he gave a half-wave and rose to meet him.

Stan swallowed. Lawrence was a good-looking man, no doubt about it. If anything, his profile picture hadn't done him justice. He was taller than Stan and still in good trim. His hair was a distinguished silver and his cheekbones as pronounced as the movie stars the girls used to pin to their walls and drool loudly over. Stan glanced to the comforting bald spot, still caught in the mirror, and moved forward.

'Lawrence?'

'That's me. Good to meet you, Stan. What are you drinking? I'm on wine.'

'Figures,' Stan said, glancing at the floor-to-ceiling racks behind the fancy bar.

'But they have some decent beers too if you don't mind them bottled.'

Stan did mind. He could have bottles at home. In drinkeries he expected a tap.

'To be honest, I'm not really drinking at the moment,' he said.

'Ah no. Course not. Sorry. Efie, my wife, she couldn't drink after her brain tumour was diagnosed so I should have realised. Insensitive of me.'

'It's fine, really. And I'm so sorry – about your wife, I mean.'

Lawrence just gave a sad little smile and Stan looked awkwardly around for a waiter to order a lime and soda.

Lawrence refilled his own glass.

'All this for me then, hey? Good job it's a nice vintage.'

Stan noted that the bottle was already half-empty.

'Have you been here long?' he asked, glancing at his watch.

'Only about ten minutes. Oh, this?' Lawrence held up the bottle and gave a funny little laugh. 'Dutch courage and all that. Though why Dutch, do you think? They're not known as great drinkers, are they?'

Stan knew this one.

'No. It's an English thing – of course. It's from the Thirty Years War back in the seventeenth century. English soldiers drank Dutch gin before battle to keep their spirits up.'

'Ah right. Very impressive, Stan.'

'My wife, Bonnie, likes gin so I got her a book on its history a while back.'

'Ah, Bonnie, yes.'

Neither of them knew what to say next. The waiter returned with Stan's lime, covering their awkwardness for a few moments.

'So,' Lawrence said when he'd retreated. 'Have you done this a lot, Stan? I mean, met a lot of men?'

He took a big drink of his wine. Clearly he was still nervous and that gave Stan a perverse courage.

'Only one so far – until now.'

'Right. And?'

'No good. Nice enough bloke but, well, let's just say his social views didn't meet with mine. Or Bonnie's.'

'In what way?'

'He was a racist.'

'Ah. Crap. Can't believe they still exist in this day and age.'

'Me neither.'

Lawrence leaned forward.

'Most of my work as a solicitor was in social care. You know, fighting for people's rights in some terrible circumstances. I saw awful prejudice and I hated it. It makes animals of us all.'

He was speaking with real passion suddenly and Stan liked it.

'It just seems so ignorant to object to someone on the basis of their skin colour – so, so inherently stupid,' he replied.

'Absolutely. Efie was mixed-race. Her dad was Ghanaian and her Mum Welsh. It was quite a combination, I can tell you. She ran faster than me and sang like an angel.'

He stopped suddenly and gulped at his wine. Stan wasn't sure how he knew it was a nice vintage – it was barely touching the sides.

'You must miss her?'

'I do. Every day since the tumour took her. And every night even more so. Not so much the . . . you know, just the warmth of her beside me. It's so cold when you're alone in a double bed. So very, very cold.'

He stared into what was left of his wine and Stan looked away to give him a moment to compose himself. He was reminded of the people posting on the Golden Years app about the blessings of finding companionship and everything about this poor, lonely man made him sure it must be true. It was as if the mirror was showing him the bald patch on Lawrence's heart as well as on the back of his head.

'I'm so sorry,' he said.

Lawrence put a hand to his own chin to physically lift it.

'No, Stan, *I'm* sorry. You didn't come here for this. You've got your own problems, clearly. Don't pay any attention to me. Tell me a bit about yourself.'

Stan appreciated his effort and did his best. He talked of Bonnie and the twins and their kids. He showed Lawrence Bonnie's picture and he stared at it for ages as Stan talked about Foundation Stone and of the houses they'd built and the

173

one they were building now and tried not to think of Bonnie on site without him.

'Do you have children?' he asked Lawrence eventually.

'No. No, it never happened for us. We didn't mind. We were happy just with each other. And we got very close to many of the young people we worked with.'

'Efie was a lawyer too?'

'A social worker. She had a very big heart, did my Efie. Very big. I miss her every day.'

'You said.'

'Sorry. I'm boring, aren't I? My friends tell me I am all the time. I've got to move on, find new interests. That's why I responded to your profile, Stan. It spoke to me – called to me even. I can be the support your Bonnie's going to need, I know I can.'

'That's nice. She –'

'Because I'll know what she's going through, you see. I won't expect her to forget you, Stan – you needn't fret about that.'

'I wasn't, I –'

'I will nurture her love for you.'

'Nurture? I'm not sure that –'

'I will let her grieve, as I grieve. We can help each other.'

He was smiling but to Stan it looked like the grin of a vampire, tinged with Chianti and a dark lust for sorrow. He felt a shiver run down his spine as Lawrence looked at Bonnie's photo and ran a finger her cheek. He tugged his phone away.

'Lawrence, wait a minute . . .'

The birthday girls were up and dancing around the suits who, unable to believe their luck, were ordering Prosecco. Two corks popped and the girls cheered and Stan longed to ditch this painful conversation and go and join their carefree fun, but Lawrence was on a roll.

'We can cherish each other through it, Bonnie and me. I know grief, Stan. I've lived grief for three long years.'

'Lawrence . . .'

'I'm an expert at it.'

'Enough!'

Stan slammed his glass down on the chrome table. It rattled between them and Lawrence at last fell silent.

'You've spilled your drink,' he said.

'It doesn't matter,' Stan said crossly. 'You need to listen. I'm not looking for someone to "nurture" Bonnie's grief. I'm looking for someone to lift her out of it, to show her that life is still worth living.'

Lawrence gave a dry laugh.

'It's not that easy, mate.'

Stan looked at Lawrence and saw lines of deep sadness in his handsome face, saw how his hand shook on the stem of his wine glass, saw the glaze of deep-seated melancholy across his eyes.

'Lawrence,' he said more gently, 'do you actually want to move on from Efie?'

Lawrence looked indignantly at Stan.

'Of course I do.'

'Because your friends have told you that you need to?'

'And my therapist.'

'I see. But you – what do you think?'

Lawrence frowned a little then straightened his shoulders.

'I think I'd be perfect for your Bonnie.'

'Because?'

'Because we can be sad together.'

'No!' Lawrence flinched and even the birthday girls paused in their dancing and looked over. Stan took a deep breath. 'That's not what I want for Bonnie.'

'You don't want her to be sad?'

'No! Why would I want that? I've spent my whole adult life working to make her happy – why should that change now?'

Lawrence gaped at him, his wine-stained teeth a slack curve.

'But you must want her to miss you? I told Efie how much I'd miss her. I told her as she lay dying in my arms.'

'So, what, you owe it to her to do so?'

Lawrence's frown deepened. Stan sighed and stood up.

'I know Bonnie will miss me, Lawrence. I don't need her to do it in some big melancholy way just to prove it. I'm sorry you're still sad and I suspect Bonnie would make you happier because she's a wonderful woman, but I do not think you will ever make her happier and that's no use. I want Bonnie to smile and laugh when I'm gone. I want her to go places and see things and live. I don't want her to be chained to sadness like, well, like you are.'

Lawrence had shrunk in on himself.

'I don't think your marriage can be as happy as mine was,' he mumbled into his glass.

Stan's fingers twitched, but he'd only ever hit a man once in his life before and he'd vowed never to do it again.

'Nice to meet you, Lawrence, but I don't think this is going to work out. It says on my profile that I'm looking for someone kind and warm and caring and I don't think that's you, not yet anyway.'

Lawrence looked up, panicked now.

'Don't go. I'm sorry. You're right. Everyone's right. I need to pick myself up. I can. I will. I'd like to meet your Bonnie, I'd like to care for her.'

'Best not, Lawrence.'

'I need her.'

The words were raw, desperate. They chilled Stan and he stepped away.

'But she doesn't need you. Please get help, Lawrence.'

And with that, he turned his back on the poor man with his bald head and his bald heart and his bald grief and made for the door. Stan tumbled out, gasping at the fresh air as if he'd been breathing in poison for the last half hour. No way was he subjecting Bonnie to this sorrow vampire. She'd laugh him out of town.

He felt a sudden, fierce longing to tell his wife all about Lawrence but he couldn't, could he? He reached into his pocket for Terry but then angrily pulled his hand out again. Look at him – a plastic toy had become his primary confidant! Was this whole thing a madness?

'Grandpa?' Greya leaped up from the pavement where she'd apparently been sitting like a faithful dog and Stan's heart rose. Of course, Greya was here! He could talk to Greya. 'It didn't go well?' she guessed.

'You could say that.'

Stan glanced back at the shiny wine bar and shook his head, then turned back to his granddaughter. She was stood there, all concern, her bag of bike cogs hanging from her young hand and reminding him of all the positives in life. What was he doing leaving Bonnie on her own whilst he wasted precious minutes with strange men? Gently, he took the bike-shop bag from his granddaughter.

'At least we got the cogs,' he said. 'Come on, sweetheart, take me home, will you? I need to see Bonnie, make sure the bricks are all right. We don't want to build the wrong walls after all, do we?'

Lawrence, like Jack, was definitely not a good brick. Ah well, perhaps it would be third time lucky.

Chapter Seventeen

March 1963

'Sticks won't play!'

Susie-Ann accosted Bonnie outside her lecture hall, drawing the eyes of her fellow architecture students, and Bonnie quickly tugged her aside. Professor Sanderson had condescended to forgive her 'emotional outburst' on the basis that it simply proved him right about women, so her battle to justify her place amongst his students continued.

Several times, she'd thought about giving up on the whole damned idea but she loved the work too much to do that. And then Danny had suggested he walk her to lectures and his big frame and smart clothes had put paid to some of the worst of the comments. She felt a little pathetic relying on him, but he seemed to love taking on the protector role and Aunt Nancy had always told her to make the most of the resources to hand, so why not? The last thing she needed, however, was more drama in front of the lecture rooms.

'When won't he play?' she asked when she'd got Susie-Ann further away.

'At the Riverboat Shuffle.'

'What? Why on earth not? That's the Best Boys' big break!'

'I know, Bonnie, but Sticks doesn't seem to care any more. Gerry and his bloody Pacemakers want him to do a gig out at Aintree and he says that's more important.'

Bonnie stared at her friend, stunned.

'He can't do that to the others.'

'That's what I said but he said he had to "consider my own career now" – all hoity-toity, just like that. Prick. I even told him if he didn't do the Shuffle I'd never sleep with him again and d'you know what he said?'

'No,' Bonnie squeaked, though she suspected she did.

'He said "all right then", just like that. "All right then", after two whole years together. Bastard. It's over.'

'Over?' Bonnie gasped. 'But. . .'

'Over. I've packed him in. I don't have to put up with that crap, right?'

'Right,' Bonnie agreed hastily.

Susie-Ann looked as if she might break down right there in front of everyone and Bonnie threw an arm around her shoulders and guided her further off campus.

'And that wasn't all,' Susie-Ann went on, her voice getting shriller and shriller. 'He said I was too buried in my "stuffy old history" to get what this might mean for his future.'

She gave a loud wail and when Bonnie reached out to give her a hug Susie-Ann collapsed against her. Bonnie shifted her books to the other side and patted her friend's back, feeling Susie-Ann's tears soak into her blouse.

'I'm so sorry, Susie. That was a horrible thing to say.'

Susie-Ann sniffed loudly.

'Yeah, well, I'm used to it, aren't I? My family said the same sort of stuff when I first said I wanted to go to university.'

'Really? I thought they were proud of you?'

'They are. That is, they know they should be but they don't

really see the point. I'm not earning, see, not bringing any money into the house. Except you, sorta.'

She grimaced at Bonnie who stared back, feeling stupid. She'd been living with Susie-Ann for weeks and she'd never noticed. She knew her friend's family joked about her being a 'smart arse' but had assumed it was loving teasing. Now she thought about it more carefully, she could see the hidden sting in their words.

'Don't listen to them, Susie. They're like the boys on my course – scared of someone doing something different. You're doing really well, you get As all the time. You have to stick at it, and when you get a fancy graduate job earning more money than the rest of them put together, they'll see the point all right.'

Susie-Ann smiled through her tears.

'That prof still giving you a hard time?'

'Not hard enough to stop me. I'm here to get a degree and I'm going to do that whatever they try to put in my way – and so are you.'

Susie-Ann looked her up and down.

'Hark at you, all fierce these days! You're right, though, I know you are. Thanks, Bon. You're the best.' She scrubbed at her face with her sleeve and then added, 'The Best Boys still don't have a drummer, though.'

Bonnie considered.

'They must be able to get a stand-in. Lee knows people, doesn't he, from the Cavern?'

'Well, yeah, he did say he'd got a contact. But even so, they've got nowhere to rehearse.'

'Why?'

'Cos they do it in the back of Sticks' auld fella's garage, don't they? Sticks says they can still use it but the others won't have that and I don't blame 'em. Bastard.'

'But if they need the room . . .'

Susie-Ann gave another sniff.

'Danny reckons his dad's got a storeroom of some sort they can use.'

'Storeroom?'

'Well, he said cold room but it's got to be similar, right?'

Bonnie felt a shiver run down her spine but Danny's family couldn't be dealing in anything that bad, surely?

'When did you decide all this?' she asked crossly.

'Earlier. Down the Jac. Emergency meeting. Danny found me – said they needed the Best Girls for brain power but we couldn't find you in time, sorry.'

'I was in the library.'

'There you are then.'

'You could have come and fetched me,' she said, annoyed at having been left out at a key moment for the band.

'Me? How would I get in?'

'With your card?'

'I don't have a card.'

'Why not?'

'Dunno. I'm just not a library sort of a person, all right?'

'Not a . . .? Susie-Ann, libraries were made for people like you. And, besides, if you'd had a card you could have come and found me.'

Susie-Ann folded her arms mutinously.

'Yeah, well, I'm here now, aren't I, and I reckon they still need our support, so you coming or what?'

'Where?'

'Danny's da's place. And quick. Apparently this storeroom hasn't got much in the way of lights so they've got to get a shift on before the sun goes down.'

Now it was Bonnie's turn to stare.

'What on earth does this man do?' she demanded, but Susie-Ann was gone and she had no choice but to scurry after her.

'Here we are.'

Bonnie stared up at the sign over the shop front. *Top Chops' Butchers*, she read. *All meat freshly slaughtered on the premises.* She looked at Susie-Ann.

'Danny's dad is a butcher?'

'Yeah. Didn't you know?'

Bonnie shook her head, though it all made sense now – the rubber gloves in his pocket at the Cavern, the feathers at the restaurant, the cold room. It was so much more ordinary than she'd been imagining.

'He wouldn't tell me what they did.'

'Are you surprised? Dead cows aren't very glamorous, are they?'

Bonnie looked back to the shop. It was neat and bright but not very big.

'This is how his family makes all that money?'

'Not just this. They've got five of these across Liverpool and three more on the Wirral. His family have been butchers since bloody Henry the Eighth was on the throne and his dad is determined he'll continue the tradition. Now, come on, Danny said they'd be round the back.'

'But . . .' Bonnie looked again to the sign. *All meat freshly slaughtered on the premises.* 'Are there animals?'

Susie-Ann pulled a face.

'Course there are, stupid, but they're not alive. Come on.'

She led her round the side of the shop and down a narrow alleyway to a thin gate on which she knocked loudly. Bonnie felt like she was in a spy film as Danny's dark head appeared over the gate, which then clicked open. Susie-Ann shot past and Bonnie faced her boyfriend who looked shy, scared even.

'Hi, Bon,' he said, not quite meeting her eyes. 'Susie-Ann found you then?'

'Eventually. Said something about Sticks.'

'Bastard.'

'Yeah. Still, sounds like you've got someone new.'

She peered past him into the yard. There was an outhouse beyond, from which came the sounds of a cymbal. Danny nodded.

'Lad from the Cavern – Tony. He's not very good but it's early days yet.'

He looked pale and tired. The Riverboat Shuffle was only a week away and Bonnie knew how much it meant to him – to all of the boys – and felt petty for being cross over coming late to the scene. She stepped up and wrapped her arms around his neck.

'It'll be good, I know it. A few rehearsals and you'll be fine.'

He kissed her nose.

'I hope so. Thanks, Bon. I knew I was right to call in the Best Girls.' She smiled up at him and he added, 'You, er, coming in then?'

'Love to.'

He ushered her sheepishly into the yard and she looked around, taking in the scrubbed cobbles, the crisply painted back entrance and the large outhouse from which came strained sounds of tuning-up.

'Nice place,' she said. He looked at her sharply. 'I mean it, Danny.'

'Thanks. Sorry I didn't tell you about, you know, the meat thing.'

'I wish you had. I was imagining all sorts.'

'Like what?'

Bonnie shuffled her feet.

'I don't know. Like, gangster stuff.' Danny burst out laughing and she crossed her arms defensively. 'Well, you didn't have to make such a secret of it, did you?'

'Sorry. It's just . . . You're such a nice girl, Bonnie, and you're at the university and, well, wellies and whites aren't exactly high-powered, are they?'

She groaned at his strange logic but relief was flooding through her that her boyfriend wasn't a petty criminal and she could afford a smile.

'I'm just a village girl from Cheshire, Danny – you don't have to impress me. I like you just as you are.'

'You do?' He ran a finger down her cheek. 'That's good. Come on in. Oh, but have you got a coat?'

She frowned.

'This *is* a coat,' she said, fingering her new jacket.

She'd bought it with some money Nancy had sent inside a letter telling her she was going to Sweden again. She'd promised to be back for when Bonnie came home for Easter but she'd sounded so excited that Bonnie had a horrible feeling there was more to this than just the odd tourist trip. It had shaken her more than she liked to admit and she'd gone straight out and bought the coat in a burst of extravagance. It was a bold purple, just like the one she'd seen in the cloakroom at the Cavern, and she was proud of her daring.

'It looks great,' Danny said. 'It's very nice, really – very now. Just not very warm.'

Bonnie suddenly realised that he was wearing a massive jacket, and a hat and scarf besides.

'But aren't we going inside?' she asked.

Danny gave a funny little grimace.

'We are, yes – inside the refrigerator.'

Bonnie blinked but Danny had ducked through the door to the outhouse and she had little choice but to follow. The cold hit her instantly and she pulled her flimsy jacket close, trying to take in the sight before her. The Best Boys, all wearing the same sort of heavy padding as Danny, were standing flanked by two half-pigs suspended from the ceiling. Behind them, plucked chickens sat on scrubbed shelves, heads still attached and glassy eyes fixed ghoulishly on their unexpected entertainment.

Various other joints were ranged around in neat compartments, and right in the middle were huge coils of sausages. A meaty odour pervaded the cold air, reminding Bonnie disconcertingly of school changing rooms, and the whole place was muted by the thick walls, like a wardrobe or maybe a coffin. Not that the strange peace lasted long. Someone, presumably Lee, had connected the guitars and amps to an extension cable leading out of one of the thin windows high up in the walls. As Spike struck a chord, the whole cold room seemed to vibrate, sending the pigs swaying gently on their hooks.

'Hey Bonnie,' he said into the microphone on a stand before him and her name echoed off all four walls. 'Welcome to the new Cavern! Think it'll catch on?'

She laughed.

'It's cleaner than the real one,' she said, edging round the left-hand pig to find a space to stand next to Susie-Ann. Danny caught her eye and smiled at her. 'And it's good you've got somewhere to rehearse.'

'We certainly need it,' Lee said. 'You ready, Dan?'

Danny nodded and grabbed his guitar.

'"Twistin' the Night Away"?'

'Let's do it!'

The sound was deafening in the small space. The electric guitars screamed and when the boys sang, the music came out of their mouths in great clouds and wreathed around the pig carcasses like a Hammer horror film. The drums, played by a chubby lad who looked about twelve, pounded through it all – loud and insistent and, if Bonnie wasn't mistaken, out of time. She saw Lee wince and Danny's jaw tighten. Spike wasn't so restrained.

'It's in three-four time,' he roared as the drummer missed the beat yet again.

'You do it differently to my guys.'

'It's still three-four time. It's not rocket science.'

Tony stood up.

'Well if you don't like it, I'll go. I'm bloody frozen in here anyway.'

Lee rushed over.

'It's fine, Tone. We're getting there, honest. Spike's just nervous cos the Riverboat Shuffle's a big deal, yeah? Could be a great platform for us – *all* of us.' Tony grunted then shuffled back behind the drums. 'Great. Let's just take it from the top, shall we?'

The chickens seemed almost to nod their agreement, and the substitute drummer sank back onto his stool as they tried again. It was a little better this time but as they hit the chorus, the first chords rang out harsh and sharp. Bonnie put her hands to her ears and Spike spun round again, furious.

'That was me,' Lee said. 'Sorry. I'm sorry. It's just my fingers – I've got no feeling in the ends.'

'Oh, this is hopeless!' Spike swung his guitar off his back and let it clatter to the concrete floor. 'The Shuffle's in a week, we've got a drummer who can't keep time and a guitarist with frostbite, and unless we're very lucky we'll all have bloody pneumonia before the boat sails.'

'Spike . . .' Danny started but Spike was shoving his guitar into its case and heading for the door.

'Forget it. We might as well cancel the damned gig – at least that way we won't make twats of ourselves. Cheers and all, Dan, but I've got better things to do than perform to dead chickens. See ya.'

And with that, he was gone. Bonnie looked after him, intrigued. One minute Spike seemed to act the 'knob' Susie-Ann fondly claimed he was, but the next Bonnie would see true passion driving him and feel dangerously drawn in. There was a shocked pause and then Tony stood up too.

'Guessing you won't be needing me then, Lee lad?'

'We will,' Lee said. 'We really will, Tone, but give us a day or two to find somewhere else to rehearse, hey?'

Tony's only answer was another grunt and then he was off after Spike. Danny and Lee stood amongst the debris of their gear looking less like the Best Boys and more like toddlers left at playschool for the first time. Danny gave a big sigh that puffed out into the room in a long, mournful cloud.

'Don't suppose either of you two sing?' he asked Bonnie and Susie-Ann.

They shook their heads and Danny looked back to Lee and then patted the solid rump of the nearest pig.

'Looks like it's this pair's big break then,' he said and, with their nerves shredded as far as they would go, there was little else to do but burst into laughter.

Chapter Eighteen

'Aunt Nancy!'

Bonnie jumped up from the table as the twins ushered her beloved aunt into the kitchen. She'd taken up Stan's idea of inviting her aunt over from Sweden and, seeing his wife's joy as she hugged her, Stan was so pleased she had. Dr Mirabi had been in touch to ask about more chemo and the subject was simmering darkly between them. He was desperately hoping that some other company would ease the strain.

Nancy usually came back to Britain every six months or so but somehow this last year had flown past without a visit, and Stan hadn't realised just how much they'd missed her. She and Astrid filled the kitchen with an easy joy that was just what they needed.

'Nancy – welcome,' he said, stepping towards her.

Nancy detached herself from Bonnie and hugged him.

'Oh Stanley, you're wasting away, laddo.'

She spoke in a Cheshire accent with an endearing Scandinavian lilt. If you were to write it down, Stan thought, it would be as if someone had taken all the soft Cheshire Os and put two little Swedish dots above them – *laddö*.

'I am,' Stan agreed, and then she was hugging him again and for a few moments she seemed to have more than enough flesh for both of them. 'I'm so glad you could come.'

'Of course we could come. It has been too long.'

Löng, he thought; it made him smile. He ushered Nancy into a chair, noticing as she passed him that she seemed to have shrunk below even the minimal five foot height she'd always claimed and had widened commensurately. She walked with a stick and her swollen ankles were tightly bound in compression socks, but both socks and stick were neon pink and, with their aid, there was still a spring in Nancy's step.

He turned to Astrid, her 'toy girl', who had turned eighty-five last year. Once a Scandinavian Amazon, even she was a little stooped now and her beautiful mane of blonde hair was ice white. It suited her. He hugged Astrid too and her muscular arms tightened around him with the assertive care of family. Stan relished it. He'd vowed to make the most of whatever time he had, and what better way than with these lovely guests.

'Let's get the kettle on, shall we?' he suggested and Nancy gave a sigh of pleasure.

'Get the kettle on – what wonderful, British words.'

Bonnie went to make the tea as Lisa and Rachael sat down at the table with Nancy and Astrid. Rachael's belly was tight and round now that she was into her fifth month of pregnancy, and Nancy was asking how she was getting on when Greya burst through the back door.

'Look what I've found in the garage!' she cried, waving a stiff-looking piece of paper, then she noticed the new arrivals and flushed. 'Oh, sorry – I didn't realise we had guests.'

'Guests?' Nancy exclaimed. 'We're not guests, we're *family*. You must be Greya. When did you grow into such a beautiful young woman?'

Greya gave a self-conscious grin and flicked back her purple hair as Lisa rose and drew her forward.

'Greya is off to university next year to study law.'

'Eco Studies, actually.'

Lisa's eyes narrowed but she said nothing. The argument had bubbled on in the rare evenings when both Greya and Lisa were in the house but neither of them seemed prepared to back down. At the end of the day, though, Greya was an adult now and free to make her own decisions, so Stan supposed it was credit to their relationship, however strained, that she was still bothering to try and talk her mother into it at all.

'Eco Studies?' Astrid asked. 'How wonderful. You will have all our futures in your hands.'

'Exactly!'

Greya beamed and Lisa rolled her eyes but still kept her peace. Stan was impressed. Lisa's texts and phone calls had continued and whilst he was a little worried what it meant, they were clearly improving her mood.

'Greya has been working on a prototype power-bike to generate electricity in the home,' he said as Bonnie brought a pot of tea to the table. 'She's shown it to the Minister for Energy, who's very impressed.'

'Heavens, how enterprising. How did you manage that?'

'Granny knows her,' Greya said. 'She went to uni with her.'

Nancy turned with a raised eyebrow to Bonnie, who slid into a seat at her side.

'Susie-Ann – remember her?'

Nancy laughed.

'How could I forget? That little minx transformed you.'

'Did she?' Rachael and Lisa asked as one.

'She did,' Nancy confirmed. 'Jazzed up her wardrobe and introduced her to make-up and took her off to all the most happening venues in Liverpool. Goodness, without Susie-Ann she'd never have met the Best Boys.'

'The who?' Lisa and Rachael demanded.

Nancy squinted at them.

'The Best Boys – your dad's band. Surely you know about them? They played all the big gigs, didn't they, Bonnie?'

'They were very good,' Bonnie agreed, her voice sharp.

Stan looked nervously her way but the girls were crowding in with more questions.

'God, yes – you said something about that the other week, but we didn't realise you were, like, a proper band.'

'They really were,' Greya said, bouncing forward with her piece of paper to reveal the red and white Riverboat Shuffle poster.

The others gasped but Stan hardly heard them as he stared at it, seeing that same poster on the wall of the *Royal Iris* as clearly as if he had stepped back in time.

'The Best Boys,' Rachael was saying, jabbing at the name at the bottom of the list. 'Is that you, Dad? Really? Up there with Billy J. Kramer and The Escorts? I've heard of them – they made records.'

'They did,' he agreed.

'Did you?'

'No. No, we split up before we got that far.'

'What a shame! Why haven't you said anything before? No wonder Marleigh's been begging to play the guitar – it's in her frigging genes. Her grandpa was an actual rock star.'

'Well now . . .'

'Don't be modest. You were – the poster proves it. Tell us more, Dad. Please.'

'Oh no, I don't think . . .'

'Yes, Stan, tell them more.'

It was Bonnie again – and it sounded more like a challenge than an invitation. Stan glanced to her but she'd turned away to refill the teapot. Well fine, let her be mardy if she wanted.

'We were just four local lads making music at a time when it was the cool thing to do. It was fun whilst it lasted but we were never going to make it really big.'

'So what happened to everyone else?'

'A couple of them stayed in the business. One of them played with all sorts of bands, even Depeche Mode once or twice, though I've not heard anything of him for years. The other became a producer with a small indie label. It had some hits in the nineties and still has a bit of a name for itself.'

'And you were part of a real life band with them? And Mum was, like, your groupie?'

Bonnie put the teapot down with a clatter as everyone looked to her.

'I suppose I was. Susie-Ann was going out with the drummer and she introduced me to the band.'

'And that's when you met Dad?'

'Yep.'

'How cool is that? Was it love at first sight?'

'It was for me,' Stan agreed, 'but your Mum had all the boys after her.'

'Stan!' Bonnie objected. 'You're making me sound like a right slapper, and I wasn't that at all. I was a serious architecture student.'

'She was,' Nancy agreed. 'She worked very hard – just played hard too. And there's nothing wrong with that. No one had heard anything like the Merseybeat before. It was exciting, right Bon?'

'Did you meet the Beatles?' Lisa asked eagerly, but Bonnie just gave a little shrug.

Rachael frowned at her sister.

'Mum doesn't like the Beatles. She always turns them off.'

'We all have our own preferences,' Stan said quickly. 'And luckily we didn't distract your mother too much from her studies – she got a first, after all.'

'Top of the year,' Nancy agreed. 'You should have seen the faces on all the boys who thought girls shouldn't study architecture – sour as lemons they were, the lot of them. It was great!'

She cackled with laughter.

'Was it hard studying architecture then?' Greya asked Bonnie.

'It was unusual for a girl, so yes, it wasn't that easy at times.'

'You had a lot of opposition?'

'I did.'

'But you stuck at it anyway? Because it was your passion?'

'That's right,' Bonnie agreed, but a little more uneasily now. Everyone looked to Lisa, who threw her hands in the air.

'Not subtle, Grey!' She turned to Nancy and Astrid. 'Greya and I don't agree about what she should study.'

'I know that feeling well,' Nancy said. 'I was so worried about Bonnie taking architecture.'

'You were?' Bonnie asked. 'You never said!'

'Not to you, no, but it used to keep me awake at nights. Oh, the midnight cups of tea Astrid and I had over that one, especially after that stupid professor started getting at you. Poor Astrid hadn't been with me long and she got dragged into the whole thing.'

'I did,' Astrid said. 'Good job Nancy looked so cute when she was worried.' Nancy blew a kiss fondly at her wife who added, 'In all seriousness, though, Nancy was scared about how hard you'd have to fight to survive at it, Bonnie, and she was right to be, wasn't she?'

'She was, but I managed.'

'Eventually.' Nancy looked sad for a moment then shook herself. 'I mean, you did. You did brilliantly, and I've never been prouder than when we finally got to your graduation. You were right, Bonnie, to take the subject you loved. Having a passion is a gift and should be embraced.' She caught sight of Lisa's face and grimaced. 'Sorry, Lisa, but it's true. I bet you were dead set on law, weren't you?'

'Wasn't she just!' Stan said.

'And besides, if Greya's made a stupid choice she'll have to come crawling back saying you were right, and what could be more satisfying than that?'

Lisa gave a rueful laugh.

'I guess you're right, Nancy.'

Greya looked at her.

'You mean . . .?'

'I mean you can study your eco-whatsit stuff if that's what you really want – and with my blessing.'

'Really? Oh, Mum, thank you! Thank you so much!'

Greya flung herself into Lisa's arms, and her mother hugged her tightly. Stan was delighted to see them at peace and delighted, too, to spot the Riverboat poster fall to the floor. He'd retrieve it later and put it back out of sight where it belonged. It was easier that way.

'So,' he said, looking round at the others. 'What are we going to do whilst you pair are over here?'

'Shopping,' Nancy said promptly. 'Clothes are shockingly expensive in Sweden. And drinking, now I come to think of it – that's shockingly expensive over there too.'

'That's easy. What about . . .'

'Midsummer,' Astrid said.

Stan looked at her, confused.

'Sorry?'

'It's Midsummer next week.'

'Is it?' She seemed to expect more from him, so he added, 'That's nice.'

Nice?

Astrid's reply dripped with scorn and Stan looked to Nancy for help.

'Midsummer is a big deal in Sweden,' she explained. 'It's almost as important as Christmas.'

'*More* important,' Astrid said firmly. 'And a lot more fun.'

'Sounds great,' Greya said, disentangling herself from Lisa. 'What do we do?'

Astrid shook her white head.

'I'd forgotten you foolish Brits don't do Midsummer. Have we never had you over for it? How very remiss of us. Really, you don't know what you're missing. You get together with family. You eat, you dance, you sing.'

'I'm sure we could manage that,' Bonnie muttered, but Nancy gave a little cough.

'It's quite specific, Bonnie. You eat herring and potatoes and strawberries.'

Bonnie's head went up and Stan recognised the familiar flint in her eye as she spotted a challenge.

'We can find them, Nancy.'

'And you sing Swedish drinking songs.'

'We can learn.'

'And you dance the *Små Grodorna* – the "Little Frogs".'

'Right. Is it complicated?'

At last Astrid laughed.

'No. No, it's not complicated at all. There are a few small moves but mainly you just hop around the maypole.'

'Maypole?' Stan asked. 'We need a maypole?'

'You don't have a *maypole*?'

Astrid looked at them as if Stan had said they didn't have a washing machine.

'Well no, there's not much call for them here.'

Astrid tossed her hair.

'I can see there is much to do,' she said. 'We must treat you to a proper Swedish Midsummer. Right, Nancy?'

'Right,' Nancy agreed. She looked to Rachael. 'The kids will love it, honestly, and it's the perfect way to get everyone together.'

No one seemed to be objecting, so Astrid stood up decisively.

'But not without a maypole. We must make one.' Her eyes drilled in on Stan. 'We will need a pole, wire, rope, vines.'

'Vines?' he asked. Astrid's eyes narrowed. 'Vines! Right. Of course. Now?'

'No time like the present. Unless you need us for something, Bonnie?'

'No, no,' Bonnie said. 'I'll be getting on with dinner, so you've got plenty of time. Why not take them to your garage, Stan, and see what you can find?'

Stan narrowed his eyes at her but she just gave him a sweet smile and, relieved to see her looking happy again, he pushed himself to his feet.

'I'll help,' Greya said, joining him.

Astrid beamed at her.

'Thank you. And you too, Nancy. Come along.'

Nancy giggled.

'I love it when she's assertive,' she said and slotted her hand into Astrid's like an obedient child.

There was little left for Stan to do but follow.

'How big a pole?' he asked, but Astrid was already heading for the garage and he wasn't sure if he'd heard her right when she called back, 'Ten feet at least.' He feared he had.

Chapter Nineteen

It was Midsummer and, though the sun was still high in the sky, Astrid was in a frenzy of preparations. Stan had found himself getting rather caught up in her plans and so for this, his first – and probably last – Swedish Midsummer, he had impetuously booked a house overlooking the beach at Red Rocks. Astrid had been delighted at being able to create the apparently 'vital' waterfront feel and although they'd only arrived a few minutes ago, she was now rushing about finding the perfect spot for her maypole.

Jamie and Marleigh had made a dash for the house to bagsy the best bedrooms, Andrew hot on their tails and Rachael following more slowly behind. Stan had spotted Marleigh lugging in a shiny new guitar and had been curiously moved by the sight, but there was too much to do to follow her right now.

The others were milling around outside, admiring the beach and the eponymous red rocks stretching out into the Irish sea beyond. Only Lisa wasn't here, as she'd gone somewhere 'with a friend'. Bonnie and Stan suspected this was the reason she'd been in a notably better mood recently but hadn't dared to ask more, so last weekend over a drink, they'd invited Dave and Gail to take the last bedroom. Gail had snatched at the invitation.

'Oooh, super! We'd love a chance to get away together, wouldn't we, Dave?'

Dave had looked less enthusiastic but had hardly been able to say no.

'Is that OK?' Stan had asked later when the men had gone to the bar. 'Have we put you on the spot?'

'Not really, mate. It's fine. I have a bit of a rule not to take them away, that's all.'

'"Them"?'

'Women. Makes them think things are, you know, serious. But I can make an exception for you.'

'You're too kind, Dave. Is "serious" such a bad thing?'

'Yes,' Dave had said, so emphatically that Stan had left it at that and just been glad his friend was coming along.

Now, however, he opened the boot of his car to find it unexpectedly rammed with beer.

'Dave!' he cried, but for once Dave looked genuinely innocent.

'It was me,' Astrid said, returning to the car. 'I just wanted to make a little contribution.'

'Little?!'

Stan's eyes roamed across the boot. There had to be at least seventy-two cans of beer in here and that was on top of his own twenty-four pale ales. The time had, amazingly, come round for his home brew to be drunk and he'd pottered about loading the bottles into the car two at a time, tearfully glad that he was still here to do so.

It was almost four months since his diagnosis now, and Dr Mirabi seemed convinced he'd have at least four more. It wasn't a lot, but he'd take it, and he'd been looking forward to the grand tasting. Now, though, his ales seemed to cower in the shadow of Astrid's bully-boy cans and their escort of four large vodka bottles.

Even the maypole, strapped carefully to the roof rack, seemed to loom over him. Astrid had been persuaded to go for a mere six feet in height, but had not been prepared to compromise on the triangular top section or the endless vines wrapped all around it, which were now flapping loosely after the exertions of the half-hour trip to the seaside.

Stan felt tears rise and turned away to mask them. This was happening at lot. One minute he'd be fine, working on something at the house, or cooking dinner, or even just doing the crossword and the next there they'd be – tears. They'd come out of nowhere and melt him into a little pool. He hated it, and now he scrubbed furiously at his face as he strode across the lawn in the hope of convincing everyone he just wanted a look at the sea beyond.

He left an uneasy silence in his wake, broken only by Bonnie's footsteps. He felt her hand in the small of his back and stiffened.

'Nice view,' he said, clearing his throat gruffly.

'Isn't it?' she agreed, but the pressure of her hand increased against him and he leaned into it.

With Nancy and Astrid in the house, things had definitely been easier between them but the chemo issue still niggled. Every time he tried to talk to Bonnie about it, he just seemed to make things worse. He was starting to think he should have the damned treatment just to make her happy but that rankled too, and, at this moment, he was pleased just to feel her support.

'I can't carry it, Bonnie,' he admitted.

'What?'

'The beer. I can't carry all that beer. I'm too . . . too weak.'

She rubbed gently at his back and he luxuriated in her touch, no longer caring that she would see the tears rolling down his face.

'Good job you invited Gorilla Dave then, hey? We don't want him sitting around uselessly enjoying himself, do we?'

Stan had to smile. The movement cut up the flow of his tears, sending them off the edge of his chin.

'Good point.' He looked over his shoulder and saw the others stood there in a forlorn semicircle. 'Hey, Dave, shift that lot inside, will you?' he called, his voice firmer.

'Sure will, boss. Got to be an easier job than erecting that blinking maypole.'

'I will sort the maypole,' Astrid said imperiously, 'and Nancy will help me.'

She marched up to the car but the minute Dave had made for the house with the first crate, she walked over to where Stan was standing on the lawn.

'I apologise, Stanley. I should have asked your permission.'

'Of course you shouldn't. It's fine. It's lovely of you to provide so much. Ignore me. I'm just a little tired.'

'I'm not surprised. You, Stanley are fighting a vicious enemy with every beat of your heart and I admire your strength in doing so with such grace.'

Stan blinked, stunned.

'Er, thank you.'

'You're welcome. Take a seat a minute.'

Stan looked back to the car where Bonnie, Nancy and Greya were untying the maypole, watched by a truculent Terry hanging, forgotten, in the ignition. He smiled and perched gratefully on one of the boulders positioned around the edge of the lawn. It was a beautiful afternoon and he let the scene absorb him, thankful Astrid was content to rest in silence too. There was barely a wrinkle in the water to separate it from the sky. The sun sat dead centre, resting on wisps of cloud like a courtesan awaiting her lover, and beneath it a flock of gulls sat on the water like crumbs from her table.

'I'm dying too.'

'What?'

At first Stan didn't think he'd heard Astrid correctly but as he twisted to face her, she nodded calmly.

'Cancer for me as well. Breast. They found it two years ago and killed it or, as it turns out, nearly killed it. A little bit escaped, it seems, and rode off down my blood to create chaos in my . . . my nodes?'

'Lymph nodes? Yes. I'm so sorry. How . . .?'

'How long?' He nodded. How stupid that he of all people couldn't just ask outright. 'How long is a piece of rope?' Astrid said.

'String.'

'Pardon?'

'It doesn't matter. What does Nancy say?'

He glanced to Bonnie's aunt, still untying the maypole, but Astrid put a hand on his arm.

'She doesn't know.'

'What? Astrid, you can't – '

'I can. She thinks I am in recovery – remission? And you won't tell her otherwise, will you? It is my dying wish.'

It sounded so stark in her guttural accent, and Stan groaned.

'But why, Astrid? Why not tell her?'

'It is not necessary. It will become all we talk of. It will colour all we do.'

That much, Stan knew, was true.

'But it could be in a positive way.'

'It would not. I saw her last time. It is better this way. I know I am dying in here . . .' She hit her hand suddenly to her heart. 'But I do not wish to give it any space in my life.'

Stan looked out to sea.

'You're dying and still you came here to see me?'

'Of course. Nancy wanted to come and, besides, I was curious. I wanted to see how someone else was doing it.'

'Doing dying? And? How am I getting on?'

'Very well. Better than me, I think. Nancy will be very angry with me when I'm gone.'

Stan exhaled.

'Bonnie is angry with me already.'

'Surely not?'

'Oh, she is. Because I don't want any more chemo. She thinks it means I'm not fighting as hard as I should.'

Astrid nodded sadly.

'See, Stanley – that is why I cannot tell Nancy. I can manage my own upset but hers would undo me.'

Stan knew exactly what she meant. He was beginning to wish he'd kept shtum himself. He placed a hand gently on Astrid's shoulder.

'You won't tell her?' she asked urgently.

'Not if you don't want me to.'

'I don't.'

'But . . .'

'Or Bonnie – for all the reasons you just said. Promise, Stan? It is a pact – a pact between dying people.'

It sounded so fierce, so frighteningly absolute. Stan did not want to be part of a dying person's pact but it seemed he had little choice.

'I promise,' he agreed, then something else occurred to him. 'Oh, but Astrid, it might be your last Midsummer and you're spending it here, on the Wirral, where no one understands it properly.'

She patted his leg.

'Nonsense. Midsummer is about friendship and community and love and I think you understand that every bit as well as us – though your maypole is definitely too short.'

He had to laugh, and now Nancy was waving and shouting that she'd got it free and the moment for confidences was gone.

'Come on then, Astrid, let's get this damned thing up and maybe then you'll be happy.'

'I will,' she agreed. 'I will be happy. Everyone will be happy, for it is Midsummer, time of happiness, and we must make the most of it.'

And with that there was no arguing.

They all assembled on the lawn to kick off with the official tasting of Stan's home brew. He felt ridiculously nervous as he prised the cap off the first bottle. If this batch was bad, he might never get to improve on it. *Slowly does it*, he told himself, letting a gentle stream curve round the edge of a bulbous glass and pool in a clear, honeyed liquid at the bottom.

'Looks decent, mate,' Dave said. 'Might taste like piss yet, mind you, like that rancid lot last year.'

Stan winced at the memory but confined himself to a calm, 'I'll leave you to decide.'

Everyone watched as Dave smelled it.

'Bloody hell,' he said, looking round at his audience. 'I feel like I'm on some talent show or something.'

He took a tentative sip and Stan saw his eyebrows rise in something that looked promisingly like admiration before he drank again.

'OK?' he asked eventually.

'Nah, mate. That's not OK.'

'No? Too thin?'

Stan's heart fell.

'No, you idiot. I mean it's not just OK, it's bloody delicious. Get yourself one whilst it lasts, folks – the boy's a genius!'

Everyone cheered and Stan felt a rush of relief and joy. If this beer was to be his last hop-based mark on planet earth then at least it was a good one. He popped more lids, poured, smiled.

'*Skål*!' Astrid cried. 'Cheers! To your very good health.'

If there was an irony there, no one dwelled on it. The beer was too good and so were the spiced vodka chasers Nancy handed round and it was in a fine mood that they all sat down to dinner.

Jamie screwed up his nose at his herring and then, after his first taste, pronounced it 'Well nice.' Marleigh was less sure of the fish but wolfed down endless potatoes and was in raptures over Nancy's strawberry cake – a gooey concoction of fruit, cream and whipped-up sugar. Stan, not normally a man for a fancy pudding (by which he meant pretty much anything that wasn't a crumble), had to agree with Marleigh that the strawberry cake tasted 'divine'. He felt a bit like that cake right now – whipped up into a bigger, sweeter version of his usual self and, despite having confined himself to just one delicious beer, he threw himself into learning one of Astrid's endless run of drinking songs.

At last, she dried up and stared out across the now burning horizon.

'On Midsummer in Sweden,' she said, 'the sun does not go down.'

Everyone looked shamefaced at the sun which hunkered further towards the line of the Irish Sea as the clock nudged past ten.

'It never gets dark at all?' Marleigh asked.

'No. Not for one minute. Your days here are shockingly limited.'

The little girl blinked up at her.

'Had I better get on with my music then?' she asked.

'You have music? Wonderful!'

'Music might be pushing it,' Andrew said, earning himself a shove from Rachael, but luckily Marleigh was running off and didn't hear.

She returned clutching the little guitar Stan had noticed earlier and with her tongue out in concentration, played a halting but recognisable version of 'Smoke on the Water' that had everyone clapping madly.

'That was great, Marleigh,' Dave said, 'Magnificent! I salute you.'

He raised his glass to the little girl, who beamed and gave a self-conscious curtsey.

'It wasn't bad actually,' Andrew said, grabbing his protesting daughter in a big hug that turned rapidly into a tickle.

'Maybe she gets it from her grandpa,' Rachael said, putting a protective hand over her belly as Marleigh's feet kicked dangerously close, 'what with him having been in a band and all!'

'A band?' Jamie asked, his eyes wide. 'Have I heard of you?'

'No, lad, though you might find a trace of the Best Boys on Google I suppose. And you'd certainly be able to track Justin James and John Dalston – they went on to do stuff in the industry. In fact, give me your phone and . . .'

'No, Gramps,' Greya interrupted, 'I've got a far better idea. Why doesn't our own Best Boy give us a tune?'

Stan put his hands up.

'No. No way. I'm nowhere near as good as Marleigh.'

But Marleigh was already pushing the guitar into his lap and everyone was looking expectantly at him and as he picked it up, it felt so good in his hands. He stroked it gently and looked to Bonnie.

He thought he saw the last of the light flicker across uncertainly across her eyes but she said, 'Go on. It would be nice to hear you play.'

'It would?'

Her eyes met his for what felt like the first time in weeks.

'It really would. Please Stan.'

He looked down at the instrument but all he could think of were Beatles songs and he wasn't going to play one of them, no way. And then it came to him. Corny, sure, but fun.

'My Bonnie lies over the ocean . . .'

Everyone whooped in delight.

'My Bonnie lies over the sea . . .'

Behind them the sea seemed to lap in appreciation.

'My Bonnie lies over the ocean, oh bring back my Bonnie to me.'

Everyone joined in the chorus and Stan felt the music creep into the very heart of him and swell up, filling him with quiet joy. He looked to Bonnie and sang the song straight to her and she blushed and clapped and returned his gaze and it felt wonderful. Why hadn't he done this before?

He knew why of course – it all went back to that night at the Cavern – so maybe the question was actually why was he doing it now? Was it something about his imminent death that had made it OK to look back into his youth again? What with Greya finding that poster and everyone asking about the Best Boys, it was as if the past was creeping up on the present. It was a little strange but right at this moment, it felt fantastic. He struck the last chord, to rapturous applause.

'Thank you,' he said, feeling suddenly shy, and handed the guitar back to Marleigh.

'Oh don't stop Grandpa, that was ace.'

'It was,' Dave agreed. 'Quite the hidden talent you've got there, mate.'

'Nonsense. Come on, what's next in Swedish Midsummer?'

Stan looked round, keen for the attention to move on. Bonnie had fallen silent and he was glad when Nancy, perhaps sensing his unease, leaped up and called, '*Små Grodorna*!' In a flash Astrid was up too and the guitar, thank the lord, was forgotten.

They all headed for the maypole, erected where the lawn met the sand and looking magnificent now that the light was low enough to mask its imperfections. Under Astrid's enthusiastic tuition they all tucked their hands into the smalls of their backs, bent their knees and hopped like demented and rather unsteady frogs around the maypole. Stan felt ridiculous at first but within about two hops that changed to a sense of freedom.

Marleigh and Greya were bobbing energetically before him in the low light and Nancy was wobbling in their wake. Bonnie was neat, Andrew had a strange sideways gait and Rachael moved with her hands curved beneath her belly, tentative but determined. Dave and Gail seemed more interested in jumping on each other and Stan could hear the steady thuds as Jamie's young feet hit the ground behind him. And there, in the middle of them all, hopping like her legs were elasticised with some vestiges of her long-gone youth, was Astrid.

Watching her through a gentle fog of unaccustomed alcohol, she seemed to Stan almost a figure of legend. Her big body was tensed with concentrated movement; her dress, long and flowing in swirls of reds and oranges, rippled like a wild sunset and her white hair flowed around her as he imagined a unicorn's mane might.

Her head was turned up to the sky, her eyes closed and he wondered if she was leaping through every midnight sun she'd ever known and maybe from there into the darkness of her eternal night. It was important in life, he knew, to look to the future rather than to dwell in the past, but watching Astrid now, he knew that there also came a time to dwell and that maybe that time was now.

He glanced over to Marleigh's little guitar, resting in the shadows, and thought he saw in it the shape of another life, though not one he regretted not living. Life was too short for regrets, that much he knew more than ever, and as he hopped round the maypole with his beautiful family, he decided that he would, like Astrid, try and glory in every last moment he had left to him. But first, he had to talk to Bonnie – and soon.

Chapter Twenty

It was dark but someone must have polished the curve of the moon for it was reflecting more than enough mercury glow for the family to still see each other. Andrew had shepherded a sleepy-eyed Rachael and two half-heartedly protesting kids off to bed at midnight and Greya, looking round the remaining three couples, had said she'd leave the three couples to their Noah's ark and retreated too. The others had considered following but then Dave had found a fire pit in the shed and they'd huddled round it.

They'd all pulled on jumpers, but after a run of fine days, the earth was holding its warmth and it felt almost continental looking out over the placid Irish Sea in the soft arms of night. A tipsy Gail had crawled into Dave's lap and Astrid had her arm round Nancy. Bonnie was at Stan's side but the wide arms of her camping chair kept her separate from him, and he felt the absence of her touch like an ache.

'Let's stay up all the way to sunrise!' Gail cried.

'Perhaps not that far,' Stan said, but as he peered into the silvery sky he sensed a strange magic in the midsummer air. 'But it does feel like tonight is elastic. Like it could stretch out into all our futures.'

Bonnie flinched, but Nancy chuckled.

'Wise words, Stan, but then, you always did have a nice turn of phrase. Elastic night – that'd make a good song, hey?'

Stan shifted.

'I don't write songs.'

'Well no, but you . . .'

Bonnie was looking as tense as an overwound g-string and he couldn't bear it.

'"All You Need Is Love",' he blurted. 'That's a good song.'

He saw Bonnie flinch and cursed his choice but Nancy, at least, took the bait.

'It is indeed, laddo. I consider myself very blessed to have found love. Not that life wasn't good before, but when Astrid came along it all just seemed so much brighter.'

Astrid grabbed at Nancy's hand, looking suddenly ageless in the moonlight as she smiled at her partner.

'It was the same for me, *Älskling*.'

Stan watched them fondly. Nancy was ninety and look at her, still revelling in life. If Bonnie had her genes then she, too, could have at least twenty years more and she couldn't spend them alone. More than ever he knew that he was right to keep looking for someone to cherish her as these determined old women cherished each other.

He hated that it wouldn't be him at his wife's side as she rolled into her nineties, hated it with a red-hot passion, but there was nothing he could do but put it to one side for Bonnie's good. He glanced back to the house where Greya was no doubt even now tapping away on her phone in bed, maybe even exchanging messages with the man that would take his place. But now Dave was leaning forward with a curious expression and Stan was diverted from his own worries.

'So you've only ever had each other?'

Nancy looked at him.

'Sexually, you mean? Lord, no! I did the rounds when I was young – and every which way I could too.'

'Men?' Stan gasped.

'Of course men, dear. I spent my early years in the navy. Not many women about back then, though one commandant had a very accommodating wife, as I recall.'

'Did you know about this?' Bonnie spluttered to Astrid.

'Oh yes. Nancy is a very sensual woman.'

Stan snuck a glance at the ninety-year-old. Nancy might be a little wizened these days but her eyes still sparkled with a life that drew you towards her. He could easily believe she'd never been short of company, of either sex.

'Do you still . . .?' Bonnie dared to half ask.

'Oh no! Not with men.' Nancy said the word with withering scorn. 'They were just on hand at the time. And they could be entertaining, if in a rather limited way.'

'Limited?' Dave choked out.

'Yep. It's all about one thing with men, isn't it? And one not especially clever thing either. Not that it didn't take me a while to realise, but the minute Astrid walked into that cocktail party everything seemed to just fall into place. I knew I had to make her mine.'

'And you did,' Astrid said fondly.

'Too right. Though you were a stubborn *mula* for far too long.'

'I was married, Nancy!'

Bonnie and Stan gasped again.

'I never knew that,' Bonnie stuttered.

'Well, no,' Astrid agreed. 'It wasn't the sort of thing you shouted about back then. Poor man was the Swedish ambassador and it would have embarrassed him terribly. I just slipped quietly back to Sweden, leaving him to his work.'

'And taking me with you,' Nancy said smugly. Stan raised his eyebrows and Nancy laughed. 'Told you we weren't all innocent back then. You sixties lot didn't invent free love, you know. You just made more noise about it than us.'

'Clearly,' Stan stuttered.

'But once Astrid came along it was her and only her. It was as if all I'd been doing before that was waiting for her to arrive.'

Stan understood that; he'd been exactly the same with Bonnie. He'd thought he'd been going about his life, making plans, having dreams, but really he'd just been waiting. He stared deep into the fire. If Bonnie had never bounced into his life, would he still be waiting? He rather thought he would. The idea sent shivers down his spine and he looked to his wife, dying to get her alone, to talk to her properly, but now Nancy had scrambled to her feet and was looking wickedly round at them all.

'If I'm not very much mistaken, folks, there is one Swedish tradition we've not done yet.'

She turned her eyes to the sea and now Astrid's eyes glowed too.

'What?' Stan asked, uneasily.

'*Nakebad*!' Nancy cried. 'Skinny-dipping.'

'Oh no,' Stan said. 'No way.'

'Yes way. Come on. The sea's right there, Stanley. And look at the moon shining so beautifully on it, beckoning us in. Live a little!'

The moon was, indeed, casting a perfect silver path all the way up to the frothing edge of the water. And now Dave was getting up too.

'Sounds fun to me. I haven't been skinny-dipping in ages. Gail?'

Gail looked round a little uncertainly but both Nancy and Astrid were casting off their clothes and, with a giggle, she said, 'Why not?' and yanked off her dress.

Stan looked to Bonnie. She'd stood up and was looking longingly at the sea but he felt her hesitation and knew it was mirrored in his own.

'Shall we?' he said, reaching out a hand to her.

'In a minute.'

The others were all running down the sand now, white bottoms flashing as they fanned out on the beach. Maybe the silver moon was pulling them in by some magical force but, if so, they were more than happy to be pulled. Stan was twitching to run free with them but Bonnie had taken his hand and he turned towards her.

For a long, long moment – way longer than her usual count of seven – she just looked up at him, then she licked her lips nervously and spoke. 'I'm scared, Stan.'

He squeezed her hand.

'Me too, my love. I don't want to leave you.'

'It's not that. Well, it is that. But . . . Oh Stan, when I heard you playing earlier it was so beautiful.'

He looked down at her, confused.

'That silly song?'

'Not the song. You. You looked so, so alive – so exactly as you should be. And I'm scared, Stan, scared that I robbed you of that.'

'What?'

'I know you don't want to come to the new house, and I know why. It's because it's *my* dream, isn't it? Because it's not fair on you that I get to have my dream and you never did. Never. Because of me.'

Her voice broke on the final words and Stan tried to pull her against him but she resisted.

'Oh, Bonnie! My dear, sweet, beautiful Bonnie, that is such total twaddle.' It wasn't his most eloquent line ever but it was one of the truest. 'The Best Boys was a goal, an ambition – not a dream. And the house, Bonnie, it's the same. I know we call it our dream house but it's not really your "dream", is it? It's the pinnacle of your career, yes, but not your "dream".

212

The dream is *us*, Bonnie – us and the girls and the grandkids and all the wonderful people we've been blessed to live our lives with. I don't give a shit about the rest.'

'Stan!'

'Well it's true.'

'Are you sure? I thought maybe with, you know, the cancer, you'd been looking back and wishing you'd done things differently.'

'No! I have no regrets, Bonnie, none. I was thinking that just now as we hopped around Astrid's damned maypole. Actually that's not true – my only regret was that you and I weren't talking like we usually do. Why would you think I'd be bothered about the bloody Best Boys, my love? What have I said to make you feel that way? Is it because of the chemo?'

She sighed.

'No! Or at least, I did wonder if maybe you didn't want to do it cos you were fed up of pretending to like houses.'

Stan felt laughter building up inside him like the swell of a wave. He heard Astrid cry out as she reached the line of the surf and turned to see her splash into the water. She took several big strides into the sea, sending droplets flying up either side of her, shimmering like a thousand mini moons, before she dived in fully and came up whooping.

Nancy reached the water and barrelled fearlessly in after Astrid. Gail hesitated at the first sting of the cold but Dave scooped her up and carried her in deeper, kicking and laughing, before dropping her with a hearty splash and a joyous scream that seemed to echo through Stan's very skin.

'Oh, Bonnie.' He turned back and clutched her against him, refusing to let her resist this time. 'You are an idiot of the highest degree! I have never "pretended to like houses". Houses are great but mainly because I get to build them with you. And I do not regret walking out on the Best Boys one bit because we were a bunch of tossers and even if it hadn't been for Bad Friday I doubt we'd have made it. And, yes, I'm scared I'm going to die but not because any of my life so far has been wrong, just because I want more of it. I want more of *you*. So much more. But if I can't have that, then I want what's left to us to be the best it possibly can be. Can you see that, Bonnie?'

She pulled back, looked up at him for a long moment and then smiled, wide and true, and said, 'Idiot of the highest degree?'

'Yep.'

She grimaced.

'I'm sorry.'

He shook his head.

'Don't apologise, my love. Please. Let's not waste any more time.'

'No. Let's not.' Her eyes were shining now as she stepped firmly back, grabbed the hem of her dress and lifted it straight over her head. 'Race you!'

Within seconds she'd lost her underwear too and was off down the beach after the others, glancing tantalisingly back as he scrambled to follow her lead. The sand gave way beneath his bare feet as he ran to catch up and he could feel every grain, every tiny crushed shell, every bit of seaweed and stone urging him on. The air was cool against his skin and salty in his lungs and he felt his balls knock against his legs and laughed with the freedom of it.

'Come on, Stan!'

Bonnie was near the edge but stopped and turned to hold out a hand to him. Her body shone in the moonlight, and without hesitation he seized her fingers and together they ran in.

'Don't stop!' she cried. 'We mustn't stop!'

The cold water snapped at his toes but he ignored its sting. It hit his calves, his knees, his thighs and then the resistance was too great and he was falling, taking Bonnie with him, and the water was rushing all around like a greedy lover, sucking his breath away and replacing it with a swirl of sensations, as if his emotions and his physical self were one, ice-bright unity. He surfaced, choking and laughing and shouting all in one shaky breath.

'It's so cold,' Bonnie gasped, and he pulled her through the water towards him.

'It's not that bad!'

He bent his knees to submerge to his shoulders and pinged himself out of the water, feeling his body explode into the night air.

'I'm a little frog!'

'*Små grodorna,*' Nancy agreed, delighted. 'I am too!'

And now she was leaping and Astrid was leaping and even Bonnie was leaping.

'We must look crazy,' she cried.

'Happy,' Nancy corrected, her ample bosom bouncing off the water's dark surface. 'We look happy.'

Stan certainly felt happy. His body might be turning on him, but for now it felt perfect in the rush of water on bare skin. Gail cried out and pointed to the horizon and Stan turned to see tendrils of pink linking hands to form a sharp band of colour across the sky, pastel at the moment but growing brighter all the time.

'Sunrise,' he gasped. 'We made it.'

'And it's beautiful,' Bonnie breathed.

Stan snuck a sideways look at his wife as the new day lit up her dear face.

'It is,' he agreed, and pulled her tightly against him, feeling her warmth permeate the cold and spread all across his body and deep into his heart. 'It's the most beautiful thing I've ever seen.'

Chapter Twenty-One

April 1963

'Oh lordy, Bonnie, it's Billy J! He's looking over, I swear it.' Susie-Ann nudged Bonnie and pointed across to the door of the *Royal Iris*'s front saloon. A handsome young man in a dark brown suit came out and looked around the mid-deck where they were hovering. 'He is! He proper is. He's signed to Epstein, you know. Smile, Bonnie lass, look cute.'

'Cute?'

'Yes! He might ask you out if you play up to him.'

'I'm with Danny, Susie!'

'Well, yeah, but this is *Billy J*! And he's looking at you, Bon, I swear it. Oh, this is all so amazing!'

Bonnie couldn't agree more. The *Royal Iris* was done up in bunting and snatches of music were drifting out of the saloon windows as the bands warmed up. All the people on their everyday commute were, she was sure, looking enviously over and even the air was warm at last, as if winter was finally loosening its grip on Liverpool. It felt like a night full of possibility, and despite not having touched a drop of alcohol, Bonnie felt tipsy.

'He's coming over,' Susie-Ann hissed on a giddy inrush of breath.

'Hey girls.'

Billy J. Kramer had swagger, but as he drew closer Bonnie could see that his hair was styled more lightly than most of the boys around and that he had freckles dusting his nose. For a disorientating moment, he looked exactly as Bonnie remembered her dad, and she couldn't take her eyes off him.

'Hey Billy,' Susie-Ann cooed and he gave her a nod but he'd picked up Bonnie's stare and met it with an intense one of his own.

She tried to think of something to say but the pounding of her heart was drowning out any coherent thought and she could only smile coyly and hope he read it as cool.

'You with the Best Boys?' Billy asked eventually in a slow drawl that did little to disguise his natural Scouse accent.

'That's right.'

'Can't wait to hear them play. I've heard they're good.'

'Very good,' Bonnie agreed, finally finding her tongue. 'They're going to be big.'

'Aren't we all?' he agreed with a wink. 'I'm looking for a new backing band, actually, so who knows . . . Maybe see you later, girls?'

And with that he was gone, back into the saloon where all the artists were doing their sound checks, leaving Bonnie and Susie-Ann gaping.

'Did he say he needed a band?'

'He did! We have to tell the boys.'

'Have to tell the boys what?' someone asked, and they turned to see Danny strolling out of the saloon.

'Danny!' Bonnie cried, rushing up to him. 'We just spoke to Billy J. Kramer and he says he's looking for a new band.'

Danny's eyes widened.

'I'd heard that too. The Coasters don't want to turn pro, lord knows why. What divvies would turn that sort of chance down?'

'Not you lot,' Bonnie suggested. 'Billy J. Kramer and the Best Boys – it sounds good, Danny.'

'It sounds boss. Oh lord, wait til I tell the others.' He spun back to the saloon door, then paused. 'You two coming in?'

'Can we?'

As they weren't technically part of the band, they were meant to stay on the mid-deck til the doors opened to punters but everyone looked too busy to care.

'Don't see why not,' Danny said. 'Come on, quick.'

Bonnie grabbed Susie-Ann's arm and they slid inside to find a hive of activity around the stage. Lee was kneeling before the right-hand amp, frowning over the connector into his precious guitar, but he rose as Danny beckoned him and Spike in. Bonnie watched them huddled together and it struck her forcibly that tonight was the Best Boys' big chance to take the next step.

Her stomach fluttered with nerves for them and she looked around for Tony, the stand-in drummer. Danny's uncle had got them rehearsal space in a plumbing warehouse last week, and the pipes and valves had proved a more appreciative audience than dead chickens – and a warmer one. Danny said that things had been going a bit better but now Tony looked pale and was clutching at the walls as if he feared the boat might be going down at any minute. Bonnie nudged Susie-Ann.

'What's up with Tony?'

'Dunno. He doesn't look very well, does he? Come on.' She strode over. 'Tony?' No answer. She shook his arm. 'Tony, what's up?'

Tony turned but his eyes were glassy and he seemed to only half see her.

'Feel sick.'

'Oh, lord!' Susie-Ann turned to Bonnie. 'Sea sickness and we've not even pushed off yet. What do we do now?'

Bonnie grabbed Tony's flabby arm.

'Deep breaths,' she urged. 'You'll be fine. You can do this. You *have* to do this. Billy J. Kramer's here.'

'So?'

'So all his management will be watching. The Best Boys have to impress them – it's your big chance.'

'I'm not a Best Boy though, am I, not really. I'm not good enough and everyone knows it and besides, I really do feel . . . Oh God!'

He pushed past them, dashing for the mid-deck. The girls both watched in horror as he puked over the side. The others turned at the sound and Bonnie saw all their hopes heaved over into the water with the contents of Tony's stomach.

'What do we do?' Lee whispered, as white as his crisp new shirt.

'Maybe The Escorts will lend us their drummer,' Danny said.

'But we won't have rehearsed, not even once.'

'It'd be better than nothing. And the set is all well-known songs. It's not like we're doing an original.'

'It's not like you *have* an original,' Susie-Ann said.

'That's not true, actually,' Spike snapped back.

'What?'

He drew himself up tall.

'We have originals. I wrote one the other day.'

'You did?' Bonnie asked.

Was this the real, passion-driven Spike emerging again? She pictured him sitting in his bedroom strumming on his guitar, a pen between his lips as he conjured pretty words and felt an ache of desire. Did he write love songs? And if so, who were they about?

'Don't sound so surprised,' he said, breaking into her reverie. 'I'm not just a pretty face, you know.'

'You're not even a pretty face,' Susie-Ann shot back automatically, but curiosity got the better of her and she added, 'What's it called then, this song?'

'This is hardly the time, Susie,' Danny protested. 'We need a drummer.'

'So go and find one. Look, The Escorts are over there – try them.' Danny glared at her but, as no one else moved, he shuffled reluctantly over. Susie-Ann turned back to Spike. 'So this song of yours, Spike?'

Spike looked embarrassed and Bonnie grabbed Susie-Ann's arm.

'Stop interrogating him, Susie. Danny's right, it's not the time, and . . .'

'"My One True Love".'

'What?'

Spike was staring straight at Bonnie, she was sure he was. She looked nervously around but the others seemed to have frozen. For an agonisingly long time, no one spoke. Bonnie heard the soft *plish* of the Mersey against the sides of the boat, the chatter of the punters gathering on the dock, the hum of the techies and, above it all, the heavy, awkward silence between their little group.

'It's just something I'm playing about with,' Spike said eventually. 'Seemed like it might be popular. Lads might buy it for their Judies, like. And at least I'm trying.'

'That's true,' Danny said, rushing back and throwing an arm around Bonnie's shoulders to block Spike out. 'Trying too hard if you ask me, especially that creepy one you were singing with Lee the other day. "Stalking Her", or summat.'

'"Watching Her",' Lee corrected him, shooting Spike a quick grin. 'And it's not creepy. I think it could be a hit, actually.'

Again Bonnie pictured Spike songwriting. 'Watching Her'? It was a great title but who was he watching? And why should she care, anyway? She was Danny's girlfriend and Danny did not deserve her disloyalty.

'How did you get on, Danny?' she asked, wrapping an arm around his waist.

Danny closed his big hand over hers but shook his head at the others.

'Nothing. Reckon they've heard about Billy J. being on the hunt for a band and are quite happy to have us look rubbish. We'll have to play without a drummer.'

'We can't do that!' Spike said. 'It'll sound dreadful.'

Bonnie looked to the window but Tony was still retching into the Mersey. Beyond him, a gaggle of people were chattering and laughing and pushing at the barrier. Any minute now, they would be released onto the boat to hear the Best Boys play and they were down a man.

'It's all going wrong,' Lee wailed and Bonnie felt his pain cut through her.

The barriers were lifted and the boat rocked as people started to flow onto it. The saloon door was still shut but the captain was clapping his hands and calling, 'Best Boys on in thirty minutes.'

Time was running out.

'It can't be,' Bonnie said, grabbing instinctively at Lee's hand. 'There must be something we can do?'

He looked at her as if she might have the answer but she had nothing to offer until, like some sort of divine intervention, she heard a loud shout from the bank and turned to see someone elbowing his way through the crowds.

'Make way! Make way for the band!'

'Is that . . .?'

Bonnie's hand was still in Lee's and she felt him squeeze it tight for a moment before he ran forward.

'Sticks! You came back! You're here!'

The lad drew his eponymous sticks from behind his back and waved them calmly.

'Of course I'm here. Wouldn't miss it for the world.'

They all crushed round him, talking at once.

'Gerry drop you, did he?' Spike asked after the babble had died down a little.

Sticks shook his head.

'Nah, lad, I dropped him. I was all set to go out to Aintree, like, but then when I was getting ready, I had a moment. Like an, an . . .'

'Epiphany?' Susie-Ann suggested sharply.

He looked at her and flushed.

'If you say so, Susie. Any which way, it felt all wrong and I knew, I just knew that I wanted to be here with the Best Boys and so I grabbed my sticks and I ran and here I am.'

'And thank God for that,' Danny said. 'Come on, lads, let's get set up.'

The rest of the band nodded and made for the stage area, where Lee produced a bit of paper and began running them through the set list. They only had time to do five songs, so it was vital they nailed them all. Even Spike seemed focused now and Bonnie turned to Susie-Ann, who was looking a little shaken.

'You OK?'

'Course.' Her friend tore her eyes away from the newly returned drummer. 'Course I am. Good, isn't it, that he's back for them?'

'Very good,' Bonnie agreed cautiously, wondering if it was good for Susie-Ann.

She had maintained a frosty silence about her split from the red-haired drummer she now only referred to as 'bastard', but sometimes at night Bonnie had been sure she'd heard weeping in the room below and had lain awake, uncertain whether to go and comfort her spiky friend. Now Susie-Ann looked worryingly wild-eyed, but the crowds were cramming into the saloon and The Best Boys' first big-time gig was about to begin and, for a little while at least, the music had to be all that mattered.

Bonnie could swear the lads were standing taller for having Sticks back and now Spike eyed the crowd, paused dramatically and then gave a huge grin that wrenched her heart.

'Hey there all you gorgeous people, welcome on board the *Royal Iris*. Lovely to see you with us tonight. Who's ready to shuffle?'

The crowd roared and a gaggle of girls at the front squealed. Sticks struck a flamboyant beat, Danny and Lee lifted their guitars and, with a wink at the girls, Spike launched into 'Ain't She Sweet'. It was their favourite opener and a great choice – by the time they hit the chorus people were starting to dance. It was more or less the Cavern Stomp as space on the boat was tight, and everyone loved it.

Bonnie glanced to the doors of the saloon, wedged open to let the sound out to the more sedate cruisers on deck, and saw heads turning and people moving over to be closer to the band. No doubt many were here to see Billy J. Kramer and had thought to enjoy the space on deck for a while first, but the driving sound of the Best Boys was pulling them in. It was a great sign.

'People are loving it,' she said excitedly to Susie-Ann.

'They are,' she agreed, eyes welded to the band. 'Course they are. They're good.'

And they were. Spike was working the crowd like a pro and Danny and Lee were backing him with great harmonies. Sticks looked as if he'd never been away and they were killing it. For the first time, Bonnie felt that all the talk of hit singles and huge gigs for the Best Boys might actually come true, and as the song wound to a finish, she screamed with the rest in a cry of utter happiness.

'What's next?' she gasped to Susie-Ann, praying it was something just as good, but the answer came with the first rocking chords of 'Runaround Sue' and the crowd were off again.

Space was getting tight as more and more people pressed in. Girls were squirming to the front and Spike was loving it. He was owning the stage, his lithe body prowling before the screaming front row like a panther, his dark eyes fixing on every girl as if he was singing straight to them. But Danny, too, was holding his bass guitar with new assurance across his strong chest and singing throatily into his mic. A blond curl had escaped from his quiff and was flopping across his blue eyes in a way that made Bonnie's stomach turn over deliciously.

Even Lee was looking confident, moving his slim hips with a fluidity Bonnie hadn't seen before and looking down into the crowd so the low stage lights caught the clear lines of his face and made him look like a film star. And then, at the back, there was Sticks, bossing the drums with new energy, his ginger hair on fire and his hands flying as if he were a music-demon incarnate.

The Best Boys moved into their third song and then their fourth. It was going too fast. Part of Bonnie wanted to slow it all right down to savour, but another part wanted it to be over without mishap and she squealed in a confused mix of delight and sorrow as they moved seamlessly into 'Long Tall Sally' to finish. The whole boat seemed to be dancing and Bonnie was sure she would be bruised all over tomorrow from all the shoulders that had clashed with her own and all the feet that had trampled her, but she didn't care. This was surely the start of something.

But all too soon, it was also the end. The Best Boys crooned their final harmony, wiped sweat from their foreheads and said goodnight to cries of approval and entreaties for more. The rules were strict, though – the Riverboat Shuffle ran to a tight schedule and already The Escorts were stepping onto the stage to claim their turn, looking more than a little disgruntled at the boys' success.

Bonnie tried to push forward to reach Danny and the others but they were surrounded and she couldn't get close. She felt a rush of jealousy but then Danny was reaching out and pulling her through to him and laughing and gasping out how much fun it had been. And Spike was hugging her and even Lee was kissing her cheek and saying he was glad she was here. And she was glad too. So glad!

She thought back to last term when she'd been stuck in halls with only dry books to keep her company, and couldn't wait to tell Nancy how different life was now. Her feet hurt, there was a ladder in her tights and her hair was thick with sweat and no doubt all over the place but she didn't care about any of it because she was alive and dancing and she just wanted it to go on and on.

And now a portly middle-aged man was stepping up and looking intently at them.

'The Best Boys?' he asked in a deep voice. The boys nodded, dumbstruck. 'Who's your manager?'

Danny drew himself up tall and pulled back his shoulders.

'That'll be me, sir.'

The man shook his hand.

'Good, good. Can we talk?'

'Of course.'

Danny followed him to the relative quiet of the top deck but at the door he looked back and gave the rest of them a wild-eyed, wide-smiled thumbs up.

'He said, "Can we talk?"' Bonnie squealed once they'd gone. 'That has to be good, right?'

'Right,' Lee agreed. 'Come on, let's dance!'

The Escorts were calling their hellos and striking up their first song and to Bonnie's astonishment, Lee grabbed her and seized the opportunity afforded by the relatively clear area to fling her round in a lively and very neat jive. His fingers were

slim around her own but his grasp was firm and his move-
ments slick and strong, and the others clapped as he spun
her out across the floor and back in against his chest. His
usually earnest face was glowing and she looked at him closely,
loving his clear joy, until he noticed her eyes on him and self-
consciously let her go.

'Sorry, Bonnie – got carried away.'

'Don't apologise, Lee. It was great fun.'

But already people were crowding back into the saloon and
there'd be no more space for jiving. Bonnie followed the others
out to the main area just as Danny returned and they crushed
around him to hear the news.

'That man,' he said, drawing out the moment, 'is a booker for
Silver Blades. It's an ice rink in town,' he explained as Bonnie
looked at him blankly. 'People go to skate but to listen to bands
too, and he wants us to play there next Saturday night. He
says people will love us. And if they do it could be a regular
slot. Paid. One pound a night.'

The boys whistled. One pound was decent money, even split
between four. More than that, it was a chance to get heard,
and if the booker liked them, he might get them other gigs
too. Who knew where this could lead?

'Well done, Danny,' Lee said, pumping his hand. He was like
a different man tonight, as if already stepping into his longed-
for future self as a professional musician. 'This is all down to
you talking Wooler into giving us this chance. You're the best
manager – the best. And not a bad old guitarist, either. Oh,
I'm gonna write a song about this, I really am.'

Bonnie looked at him, entranced.

'*You* are?'

'Why not? We should all be writing stuff if we wanna be
the next Beatles, right?'

'Absolutely. What'll you call it, Lee?'

'Flying high? Over the moon? Top of the world?' I dunno – something like that. This is honestly the best night of my life so far. This'll show my folks I can do it.'

'Better than their business, hey?' Bonnie said, but at that Lee sobered a little.

'Not better, Bonnie – just more what I wanna do with my life.'

Bonnie thought of Danny's dad's butcher's shop and of Sticks' dad's garage and Spike's dad down the docks and saw, anew, how hard the Best Boys were having to work to get away from all that was conventionally expected of them.

'What d'your folks do?' she asked Lee.

'Plumbing and household repairs.'

'Right.'

'It's not a bad business, like. A good one, even. If this don't work out, I'll be fine doing bathrooms – once I've swallowed my pride and legged it back to Dad! But I'd rather not.'

He grinned but it was a little wobbly round the edges and, to Bonnie's surprise, Spike gave him a friendly punch on the arm.

'It'll work out, mate, and tell you what, if it don't we'll be plumbers together.'

'You and me, Spike?'

'Why not? It's bloody cold doing the pipework down the docks, so I reckon bathrooms'd be a doddle.'

'And I could apprentice with Uncle Mike and come along too,' Danny said.

'But what about your dad's shops?' Bonnie protested.

'What about them? My sister's desperate to take over, and why shouldn't she? If you're going to be an architect, Bonnie, she could be a butcher, surely?'

'Absolutely,' Bonnie agreed. 'Right, Susie-Ann?'

But Susie-Ann was hanging back, and for the first time Bonnie realised that she'd barely seen her friend in the heady hour since the set.

'Hey,' Sticks said, 'we could all train up and do pipework in the day and gigs at night. And we could rename ourselves The Plumbers.'

They looked at each other.

'Sounds quite good, actually,' Spike said. 'Spikey Boy and The Plumbers.'

'No way. You're not getting star billing, lad!'

They fell on him, laughing. Bonnie laughed too but she couldn't help noticing Susie-Ann standing coldly to one side with her nose in the air and her arms folded.

'You back for good then, Mickey Cobden?' she demanded.

Everyone took a small step back from the drummer, who looked nervously at his one-time girlfriend.

'If I'm allowed?'

'Course you're allowed,' Spike said. 'You're a bit of a tosser, like, but . . .'

But now even he noticed that Sticks was looking straight at Susie-Ann and he coughed and buried himself in his beer. Everyone tried to ease away but it was too crowded and they were stuck there as Susie-Ann put her hands on her hips and stepped up to Sticks.

'You back for me too, then?'

Sticks swallowed.

'If I'm allowed,' he repeated. 'I've missed you, Susie baby.'

Bonnie could see her friend start to soften, but Susie-Ann was made of stern stuff.

'So you're cool with me going to university?'

'Sure,' he muttered.

'Say it proper.'

Sticks looked around the pulsing ferry.

'Here?'

'Yes, here. Now.'

'But I'm only just back, like. Can't we talk about it, baby?'

'Do we need to? It's simple, isn't it? Do you approve of university?'

'I guess, for some people.'

Susie-Ann's eyes narrowed.

'For men?' she asked icily.

'Birds too.'

'Just not *your* bird, right?'

He shifted from one foot to the other and shoved his hands in his pockets.

'I didn't say that. It's just, well, it would be a bit weird, wouldn't it, if you had a better job than me?'

'"A bit *weird*"?' Susie-Ann stamped her foot and turned to Bonnie. 'D'you hear that, Bon? This is what I have to deal with. This is the bloody ignorance I battle day after bloody day. Well forget it, Mickey bloody Mouse. The band might be happy to take you back no questions asked, but that's not good enough for me. *You're* not good enough for me. I've moved on. I can get better fellas than you.'

And with that she spun round, reached out and grabbed the nearest man – Spike. He looked down at her, confused.

'All right, Susie-Ann?'

'Over the moon. Let's do it, shall we, Spike – let's do it again.'

And with that she drew his head down to hers and kissed him passionately. Spike responded automatically, oblivious to the red-faced Sticks who stormed off, shoving people roughly out of the way as he went. Bonnie watched him go, then looked back to Susie-Ann and Spike, who'd already pulled apart. Spike was looking stunned and Susie-Ann frankly dangerous. Bonnie felt all her giddy happiness rush out of her as if someone had pulled the plug.

'Again?' she choked out.

When had they done it before? When they were younger? Whilst Susie-Ann had been with Sticks? Last week? Her stomach churned with jealousy and anger and bitter betrayal. She remembered Spike talking about his song earlier this evening. 'My One True Love' he'd called it, and she could have sworn he'd been looking at her but Susie-Ann had been right at her side.

'Tart,' she muttered furiously.

You shouldn't kiss your friend's exes, should you? Everyone knew that. Or was that not true any more? Not even when you know they still liked them.

Used to like them, Bonnie corrected herself firmly. With horrible clarity she saw how foolish she'd been these last weeks, carrying on with Danny whilst all the time holding a torch for Spike – and why? Just because he'd been the first to draw her into the magic of the Merseybeat scene. Just because he had the darkest eyes, and the most fluid hips, and the most carefully cultivated hint of the Buddy Hollys and Eddie Cochrans she'd mooned over in her bedroom. Well, enough!

She looked frantically round for Danny and was hugely relieved to see him still there, his big frame so solid and safe in the milling crowd and his smile so fond as he caught her eye.

'Danny!' she cried, flinging her arms around his neck and blocking out the sight of Susie-Ann and Spike still stood together in the middle of the crowd. 'Thank God I've got you to myself at last. You were so amazing!'

And with that she grabbed his collar, pulling him down to her and kissing him long and hard. Danny was a good man, a kind man – *her* man. Forget Spike. He was as much of a tart as blinking Susie-Ann and she was far, far better off without him.

Chapter Twenty-Two

'Grandpa? Grandpa, wake up!'

Stan heard Greya's voice through a fug of half-sleep and shifted in his armchair. He'd been tired ever since they'd come back from Red Rocks two weeks ago. At first he'd thought it was just the effect of the party weekend slowing him down and had gone to bed at eight o'clock two nights in a row without much thought. By the third night, however, the excuse had worn a bit thin and by the fourth it had run out altogether. It wasn't partying grinding the edges off his energy, but cancer.

Dr Mirabi had confirmed it last week after another run of scans had peered into his innards and found them wanting. As always the doctor had refused to be drawn on exact timescales, but had conceded that Stan was unlikely to celebrate another New Year. He'd offered chemo again but warned that the rate of regrowth made it unlikely to be effective and that there was a risk it might sap his strength to dangerous levels. Stan had said no. Bonnie had backed him up.

'Grandpa?'

Greya's voice was scared now and he forced himself to sit up in his armchair and retrieve the newspaper from where it had fallen into his lap. It wasn't even nine o'clock yet but a summer storm was rolling in and the sky was gloweringly dark.

'I'm fine. Just having a little snooze.'

'Right. You awake now?'

'I am.'

'Good, cos look what I've found.' She'd obviously been rootling in the back of the garage again and Stan woke up fully as she lifted up a black and white photo. 'Is this your band, Gramps? Is this the Best Boys?'

Lisa looked up from her laptop and the endless click of keys halted. That was some relief at least. His eldest daughter had returned from the weekend away with her 'friend' in a dark mood and seemed to have been clattering crossly about the house in the time since. She hadn't been back to London once and, as Greya had reported that the house there was filling up with seedlings and tools and even a small dog, it didn't seem likely she ever would. Now she came over and peered at the photo and Stan saw something that might even have been a smile cross her face.

'That's us,' he agreed reluctantly. 'Where did you find it?'

'In an old box in the garage. A wooden one – dead pretty.'

Stan frowned. He owned no such box.

'It's mine,' Bonnie said from the window where she was peering out on to their little street like some sort of neighbourhood-watch-obsessive.

'Yours?'

Stan put his hands on his chair to rise and go to her but his arms seemed to rebel at the idea and he sank back onto the cushions. Outside he caught a low rumble of thunder.

'Mine,' Bonnie agreed. 'I thought we should keep a few bits from, you know, then.'

'I didn't realise.'

'No.'

She gave him a shy smile but then turned back to the window as the rain started battering against it.

'Which one's you?' Greya demanded, and Stan forced himself to pull his gaze away from his wife and study the photo.

It was grainy and faded with age but the faces of the four Best Boys still stared brightly out at him, looking so young and smart and so very, very hopeful.

'That one,' he said, pointing.

Lisa and Greya moved into the light to look at his old self more closely.

'Ooh, you're handsome, Grandpa,' Greya said. 'Look at all that gorgeous hair. No wonder you fancied him, Granny. Granny?'

Bonnie, however, was still staring out of the window.

'Mum?' Lisa prompted, and at that she turned.

'What? Oh sorry, love. I wasn't listening. It's just that he's out there again.'

'Who is?'

'This weird man. I saw him yesterday and he's back, lurking.'

'Lurking? In Brecksby? Are you sure?'

'Yes, I'm sure. Come and see.'

Lisa and Greya tumbled over, abandoning the photo on the coffee table and crowding in next to Bonnie. Stan heard them agreeing that there was, indeed, a man out there and eyed the gap between his chair and the window. It wasn't far – twelve paces maybe – but right now that felt at least eleven too many.

'It's probably just someone waiting to be picked up,' Greya said.

'In this weather? He's been there half an hour.'

A sudden flash of lightning lit up her face, pale and anxious, and Stan suddenly realised how serious she was. He pushed himself up out of his chair but noticing the effort it cost him, she darted across instead.

'Oh lord, Stan, I'm sorry. It doesn't matter. Someone's probably fallen out with their boyfriend or something. He

233

doesn't look menacing, not really, and we've got good locks, haven't we?'

He heard the undertone of fear beneath her cobbled-together assurances and felt a fierce, lion-like urge to rush out, claws bared, to protect her from this bloke preying on her peace of mind. But these days he'd be more kitten than lion.

'Let me see.'

He strode, or, at least, shuffled with as much purpose as possible, to the window. Greya and Lisa stepped back and he saw the man instantly, or rather the outline of him. He was standing in the edge of the trees outside number twenty-nine opposite, clearly facing in their direction. The rain was lashing down now, pulling heavy clouds across the last of the sun, but the man just hunkered deep into his coat and showed no signs of leaving.

'I'll go and talk to him.'

'No. No don't, Stan. I'm sure you're right. It's nothing.'

Bonnie took his arm and tried to pull him back towards his armchair but he stood his ground.

'No, Bonnie, if this bloke's upsetting you I want to know what he's up to. It won't take a minute.'

'I don't want you to go out there. It's raining.'

Beyond the window, as if backing her up, a second dagger of lightning lit up the sky.

'It's the Wirral, Bonnie,' Stan snapped. 'It's always raining. I'm used to it.'

'But I don't want you catching a chill.'

'A chill? This isn't the twenties.' He stared at her. 'Oh you mean because I'm weak – because I'm dying.'

The thunder came now, like a growling echo of his words.

'Stan, please. Don't. I wish I hadn't mentioned it. I wish I hadn't said. I wish, I wish . . .'

She crumpled and, horrified, he clamped her against him. She was shaking.

'See, Bonnie, you *are* scared. I need to . . .'

'You stupid bugger.' Her hands thumped softly against his chest. 'Can't you see – I'm far more scared of losing you than I am of him, whoever the hell he is.'

Stan drew in a ragged breath but now Lisa was pushing past them and yanking the door open, her eyes flashing with fury. Before they could stop her, she was striding across the street shouting, 'Oi, you!' The man stiffened and started to move away, but it was too late. 'What are you doing here?'

They were too far away to hear the lurker's reply but it clearly didn't satisfy Lisa, who put her hands on her hips. She was wearing a thin work blouse and already the rain was soaking through it but she didn't even seem to notice.

'Think you can just hang around on street corners scaring people, do you? You're all the same, you men – you only think of yourselves. Well, let me tell you now, if you've got the hots for someone in this street then you should ring their doorbell and tell them so like a proper human being instead of hanging around like a bloody ghost satisfying nothing but your own pathetic little need for drama.'

Huddled in the hallway, Bonnie raised her eyebrows at Stan but there was no stopping Lisa now. A third lightning strike came, seeming to stab down beneath the two figures as they faced each other across the street and right with it the thunder – matched only in volume by Lisa's next outburst.

'I don't know if you think this is a relationship you're having here, mate. I don't know if you're getting off on snooping around some poor girl – or boy – but let me tell you now that you're a creep and a coward and the best you can hope to get out of this is a smack in the gob. Most likely from me.'

'Go, Mum!' Greya said in awe.

They all watched as Lisa lifted a clenched fist high but the man, whoever he was, wasn't hanging around to see if she meant what she said. He picked up his feet and ran, water splashing around his feet as he scrambled up the street and was gone. Lisa stood watching him then turned back to the house, sheepish now. Greya gave her a hearty clap.

'You told him, Mum!' she called.

Lisa grimaced.

'I did rather, didn't I? Sorry, Mum. Hope it doesn't turn out to be anyone you know. I think I went a bit over the top.'

'Not at all,' Bonnie said. 'I rather enjoyed it. Did he say anything in reply?'

'I'm not sure I gave him the chance.'

Lisa came through the door, her hair dripping and her expensive blouse clinging to her body. She was shivering now that her anger had drained away, and Bonnie sent Greya running for towels.

'Thank you for that, sweetheart,' she said, towelling Lisa's hair.

Lisa sniffed.

'If I'm honest, Mum, I don't think I did it entirely for you.'

'It sounded as if there were a few things there you'd been bottling up.'

'You could say that.' There was another flash of lightning but paler now, further away and with the thunder more of a grumble than a growl. Lisa gave a big sigh and looked up at her mother. 'You know the other weekend?'

'When you went away with your, er, friend?'

'That's right. It wasn't a friend, not really.'

'No, we . . .'

'It was Simon.' Bonnie gasped and looked to Stan. They hadn't expected that. Lisa grinned. 'You thought I was off with some hot new man, didn't you?'

'No, we . . . Well, we did wonder. Why didn't you say, sweetheart?'

236

'I'm not sure. He'd been texting me a lot and we'd been talking and it was nice. Romantic. It was like he was wooing me all over again and I began to hope that maybe I'd been wrong, maybe we still had something together.' Lisa looked over to Greya. 'Is it OK, talking like this?'

'It's fine, Mum. I'm eighteen.'

'It's not so old, sweetie, but I'm afraid you've been rather caught up in it all, so you need to know. I'm sure you'd rather we were together and we tried, we really did. Both of us tried, but it was clear it wasn't right any more. It's easy when you're apart, isn't it? You can do all the mushy stuff and it feels exciting and fun and full of possibility, but once we were actually in the same room we just started arguing again.'

She reached out and took Greya's hand.

'We do still sort of love each other, especially as we share you, but what we want out of life has changed. Your dad's mad for his blinking allotment and now he's muttering about a caravan and I'm just not ready for that. I don't want to be old before my time. I'm sorry.'

'It's OK, Mum,' Greya said, 'really it is. I'm not stupid, you know. I can see the problems. It's primal, you know, a caveman type thing . . .'

Stan remembered Greya's rather lively summary of her parents' problems when she and Lisa had first arrived, and gave a low cough. Greya glanced over and pulled a face at him but she clearly got the message.

'It's OK,' she said again. 'I'd rather see you both happy than have you together arguing all the time.' She gave her mother a brave smile and then straightened her shoulders and added, 'And this way I get to hang out on Dad's allotment and then come and do cocktails in the city with you.'

'Cocktails!'

'Why not? I'm eighteen now, remember?'

Lisa shook her head fondly.

'How could I forget?'

Then she was hugging Greya and Greya was hugging her back, and Stan was suddenly glad that the damned lurker had turned up because if this is what it took to get Lisa's problems out in the air then it was worth a bit of trauma. Already his older daughter looked more relaxed, happier in her own still slightly shivering skin, and after all these tense weeks that was wonderful to see. He just hoped Greya was as fine with it as she claimed to be.

'Greya?'

He found her in the garage, carefully painting a yin and yang onto the cog-protector on the power bike, accompanied by the sound of the rain hammering down on the corrugated roof. On a shelf above her head he noticed a carved wooden box. It must be the one that Bonnie had kept for him all these years. He longed to open it up and see what was inside, but it wasn't important right now.

'Hey Gramps,' Greya answered. 'Isn't it past your bedtime?'

'Probably,' he agreed, 'but I just wanted to see what you were up to. Nice design.'

'Thanks. I got a letter from Granny's mate, Suzanne, this morning, with four tickets to the Renewable Energy Expo in Paris. Can you believe it? Mum's already said she'll pay for my ticket on the Eurotunnel. She really seems to be getting behind me. Mind you, that's probably just cos she's feeling guilty about her and Dad splitting up.'

'How d'you feel about that, Grey?'

'Getting a Eurotunnel ticket to the biggest eco expo in Europe?' Stan raised an eyebrow at her. 'OK, OK. I'm fine, really. I mean, of course I'd like it if they stayed together and worked things out, but I'm off to uni in a few months so it really won't matter that much to me, will it?'

'If you say so, but you know you can talk to me about anything if you need to, right? Or Granny if I'm not, you know, here any more.'

She stood up and came across to fling her arms around him.

'You being ill makes me much sadder than Mum and Dad splitting up, Gramps.'

Stan swallowed. It seemed so tragic that he was finally getting to know Greya properly and it could only last a little longer.

'I'm sorry. I've loved having you here. And I'd so like to see your bikes go global and you make speeches at fancy conferences and win awards. Cos you will, I'm sure of it, and I'd be so proud. I . . . I . . .'

Tears clogged his words and as Greya's arms tightened around him he could only hold on tight and wait for them to pass.

'I'm sorry too, Gramps,' she said, stroking his head as if he were the child. 'And if I ever do win an award I'll dedicate it to you, really I will, cos you've been an inspiration to me these last months. Truly. And we've fitted a lot in, haven't we?'

Stan wiped his eyes.

'We have, Grey. We really have. I feel very blessed, but it's just so frustrating. This bloody cancer is taking me over and however hard I try there's nothing I can do about it. Everything else that's ever happened to me before has been solvable with hard work and dedication but this . . . I can't even see it, let alone fight it.'

Greya pulled back a little but still held tightly onto him.

'But you *are* fighting it, Grandpa. I bet lesser men would have been dead already, and look at you . . .'

'Yeah, look at me – falling asleep in my armchair and shuffling around in slippers whilst my daughter sorts out lurkers for me.'

'And what's wrong with that? Equality, Gramps. It's got to have its plus sides for men as well as women, surely?'

He looked at her, her eyes staring earnestly up at him from beneath her sparkly hair.

'You're right. Of course you are. You're very wise, Greya – wiser even than Terry.'

'Who's Terry?'

Stan flushed.

'Oh, just the funny little troll on my key ring. I, er, talk to him sometimes. He was the first one to know . . . about the cancer. He's very wise.'

'I bet. I talk to my scratty old stuffed cat.'

'You do?'

Stan looked askance at his cool granddaughter and she laughed.

'You bet. He knows more about Mum and Dad being twats than anyone, I can tell you, and he's delighted to hear they're going to do their own thing – really. He's deffo coming to uni with me. We all need someone to listen to us, don't we?'

Stan imagined Terry nodding, enthusiastic for once, and smiled.

'We do. Maybe I should give Terry to Bonnie for once I'm, you know, gone. Maybe he'd be a better idea than a new man.'

'Maybe,' Greya agreed, 'though you've had some more interest in your profile, and I don't think you should give up on it just yet. It takes a really big man to do what you're doing, Gramps.'

'Nonsense. It's a crazy idea and it's been a disaster.'

'So far, but you've only had two dates, for heaven's sake. You've got to be patient.'

Stan grimaced. He'd sworn to give up the dating after Lawrence, but seeing Bonnie looking so scared at the window tonight had shaken him. She wasn't good alone. He'd known that when he first came up with the idea of looking for a new husband for her and he'd let just two bad experiences put him off. That was hardly hard work and dedication, was it?

'Does anyone look any good?' he asked.

Greya drew out her phone.

'Yes, actually. I tweaked your profile after the last idiot as I felt we were projecting the wrong image.'

Stan hadn't been aware he was projecting any image, but if he was, he certainly wanted the right one.

'So now?'

'So now you are looking for an "upbeat, positive companion to make happy times".'

'I am? I liked "kind, warm and caring" more. This sounds a bit icky to me.'

'Maybe, but people are loving it. You've had loads of responses. This man looks good, I think. See.'

She flashed him a picture of a dark-skinned man with a wave in his lightly greying hair and a twinkle in his eye.

'Why are they always good-looking, Grey?'

'Are they? Sorry.'

'It's OK, but this one looks quite young too.'

'So? At least he'll outlast her.' Stan almost choked at her honesty and she had the grace to look a little sheepish. 'I didn't mean to say that out loud, sorry. He's not that young, anyway – nearly fifty. He's called Adi and he's an electrician.'

'Really? We need an electrician on site.'

'I know. Two birds with one stone, hey?'

Stan looked at her and had to laugh.

'Economical.'

'Yep. And he's local. He says he's free Friday afternoon. Will you go, Gramps? Will you meet him?'

Stan listened to the rain drumming on the roof and pictured Bonnie twitching the curtains and his heart twisted. Fifty was surely too young but on the other hand, Bonnie looked pretty young herself and at least he'd have some energy about him. And they did need a sparkie, right? He suspected he was kidding himself with that but he was kidding himself about a lot of things these days, so what was one more? He nodded decisively.

'I'll go, Greya – let's just hope it's worth it this time.'

Chapter Twenty-Three

Adi had suggested the meeting place – a café called The Flowerpot that sounded to Stan suspiciously like one of those Dutch places and looked even more so as he shakily approached. His legs were getting weaker and weaker and Bonnie had bought him a stick. He hated having to use it but today he felt grateful for its support as he gazed up at the location of his third date.

The café had a hand-painted orange façade covered with a mural of vines in bloom. Did vines bloom, Stan wondered? These ones certainly did and in all sorts of vibrant colours Stan was pretty sure would never be found on the same plant. They looked very pretty in the August sunshine, mind you, and surely their cheeriness was more important than their verisimilitude. What's more, the sign on the door urged him to 'Step inside and take the weight off for a while', which appealed. Stan felt as if his weary bones were carrying more and more weight these days, despite the bathroom scales and his loose waistbands confirming otherwise.

Once inside, The Flowerpot felt even more welcoming. The tablecloths were a soft green and in the middle of each one sat a pot of creamy daisies, as if each table was your own personal lawn. An assortment of wooden chairs had all been painted the same orange as the façade, making a bold contrast with the bleached white floorboards. The result was fresh and natural and almost as inviting as the rich scent of coffee. Stan breathed in deeply and edged across to the nearest table.

'Can I help you?'

An attractive lady with a neat orange apron and a welcoming smile came across as he took a seat.

'I'm, er, meeting someone.' Stan glanced around the café but could see no one likely to be Adi. Two girls were giggling over milkshakes at one table, a group of mothers and babies were nattering at another and a smart young man was listening to a girl sat on a high stool singing softly to an acoustic guitar. 'He's not here yet.'

'I'll come back shortly then, shall I?'

Stan smiled his thanks and looked around for somewhere to stash the wretched stick. People were forever falling over it and it would hardly do to trip this Adi bloke up when he arrived. He glanced to the door. No one. The young man in the corner glanced curiously at him and Stan did his best to look like the sort of person who met people in cafés all the time, but it didn't come naturally.

He wished he had Terry to keep him company but he'd come on the bus – Bonnie didn't like him driving alone these days – so hadn't needed his car keys. The troll had not looked best pleased at being left behind but Stan reassured himself that he wouldn't have liked all this light and prettiness anyway and buried himself in the menu until the door opened and a man of about his own age walked in.

He didn't look as Stan had remembered from the app but Greya had warned him that profile pictures could be very misleading, so he pushed himself to his feet to say hello. Just then, though, one of the milkshake girls called, 'Grandpa, over here!' and, blushing like a strawberry, Stan sank back down.

'Stan?'

He looked up again to see the young man from the corner standing before him.

'That's right,' he confirmed nervously.

'Great. I'm Adi. Pleased to meet you.'

'And you,' Stan managed, shaking the outstretched hand for far longer than normal as he strove to equate the person in front of him with the information on his app.

Surely profile pictures weren't *this* misleading? Adi appeared to be more like twenty-five than nearing fifty. He wasn't especially tall but was very toned and his neatly muscular shoulders gave him an air of natural authority. He was wearing black jeans tight enough to make it clear his arms weren't the only toned part of him and a dark red T-shirt that showed off his brown skin to perfection. He had fine, clear features and dark eyes and was definitely not the sort of man Stan would have expected to be answering ads about other people's wives.

'You had grey hair,' he stuttered.

Adi put a self-conscious hand to his dark locks.

'*Had*,' he agreed. 'I dye it. Vain, hey?'

'Effective,' Stan said, liking his honesty. 'Would you like to sit down?'

He nudged at the chair opposite with his foot and his stick clattered to the floor. He cringed but Adi just bent down, picked it up and laid it neatly against the wall behind him.

'It's always easier with a nice coffee, I find. And Sylvie – that's the owner here – does really nice coffee. Or tea, if you prefer. She has all sorts of fantastic herbals – fresh ones, not out of a bag. She makes them herself.'

Was this code? Stan wondered. With the bright colours and the girl singing in the corner it all felt very relaxed and loose – definitely Dutch. He and Bonnie had gone to Amsterdam when the twins had been two years old. They'd left them for three whole days with his parents and been giddy on forgotten freedom from the moment they'd got off the plane.

They'd been too early to check into their hotel so had stopped at a coffee shop for some light lunch, and very light it had turned out to be – floaty even. They'd known what they were doing. It had been the seventies by then, after all. The Beatles had long since made *Sergeant Pepper* – not that they'd listened to it – and everyone knew what space cake was. What they hadn't known, however, was how long it would take to have an effect. Long enough, as it turned out, for them to decide it wasn't working and order a second slice. Lord, but they'd been giggly.

Now, though, too many years on and sitting opposite a handsome young man who seemed, for some unknown reason, to be after Stan's seventy-three-year-old wife, he was unsure of the etiquette. Pot wasn't legal, that much he knew, but doubtless the youngsters had some clever code to get around that. Sometimes Greya spoke in runs of words that all sounded like gibberish to Stan or that, at least, seemed to have had their meanings turned upside down.

'Herbal?' he asked.

'Yes, you know – camomile, blueberry and elderflower, sweet thyme, that sort of thing.'

Adi pointed to a hand-written menu on the wall behind and Stan studied it. They looked like the sort of teas Greya had stuffed their kitchen cupboard with and that Lisa was always moaning about, so presumably they were straight up but at the bottom in jaunty script it said, 'For a natural boost', which sounded rather coy.

'What sort of a natural boost?'

Adi squinted at him.

'What sorts are there?' He looked at Stan, confused, and then grinned suddenly. 'Oh, you think . . .! No, no, no. It's not like that. Sorry.'

'Don't be – sorry, I mean. Blueberries sound fine to me. I just wasn't sure, you know. I'm old and uncool.'

Adi laughed.

'You seem pretty cool to me, Stan. Let's get Sylvie over and see what cakes she's got on, hey?'

'Great.'

Adi waved at the woman Stan had spoken to earlier and ordered blueberry tea and slices of carrot cake for them both. As he watched the waitress flirt with Adi, Stan wondered again what this stylish young man, who could surely have his pick of half the girls in the North-West, wanted with him – or rather, with Bonnie.

The girl on the guitar struck up a quiet version of 'Love Me Do' and the song tugged at his mind. His fingers had been twitching at ghost-strings ever since he'd played Marleigh's guitar at Midsummer, and now this. Yesterday he'd seen an ad on Facebook for a new band he liked called the Jetsetters. They were playing at the reopened Cavern and Stan had felt a fierce longing to go and see them. He hadn't dared ask Bonnie if she'd go back there, but hearing the girl playing this haunting Beatles' song sharpened his own desire to do so. It was all very confusing, and he turned back to Adi.

'Do you, er, date a lot?' he ventured.

Adi smiled and sat back in his chair so his muscles strained gently at his T-shirt. Stan tried not to stare.

'I do, "er date" a lot,' he agreed, totally unabashed. 'Though usually I deal direct.'

'Sorry?'

'With the women directly.'

'Oh I see. Yes, of course. Me too. That is, I would date women if I was single, but I'm not. I've got Bonnie, as you know.'

Adi smiled again. He smiled a lot.

'Have you been married a long time, Stan?'

'Fifty-four years.'

Adi's chiselled jaw dropped and Stan was pleased he'd surprised this suave young man.

'Fifty-four years? That's phenomenal. That's got to be some sort of record.'

'Oh no. Way off. The record is eighty-six years. An American couple. They married in 1924 and made it all the way to 2011 before she died aged 103.'

'Right. Wow. That's very specific, Stan.'

'Bonnie and I looked it up on our fiftieth anniversary. We wanted to see how long we had to go. We were full of confidence back then, but I'm afraid we won't even make fifty-five years now.'

Stan's heart tugged but for the first time he felt the stirrings of acceptance at the new parameters of his life. He was tired, that was the problem, so very tired.

'I'm sorry.'

Adi said it naturally, without any of the twitches or dropped eyes that afflicted most people as soon as the subject of his imminent death was raised, and it soothed Stan.

'Thank you,' he said. 'So am I.'

'And you're looking for someone to make her happy once you're gone?'

'That was the idea, but you seem very young.'

'I'm forty-seven.'

'Really!' Stan took in Adi's sharp body, clear skin and bright eyes. 'Perhaps I should drink herbal tea more often.'

Adi laughed again.

'I lead an active life. It helps. And I have good genes – my mother is very youthful.'

'How old is she?'

'Seventy-two.'

'Younger than I am. Younger than Bonnie, just. Adi, you're about the same age as my daughters.'

'So?'

'So what on earth makes you think you'd be a good husband for my seventy-three-year-old wife?'

Unfortunately the waitress picked that exact moment to arrive with their drinks. Stan had no idea where to put himself, but she didn't seem fazed at all. Adi calmly made space on the table and helped the woman unload the cups and then two slices of truly delicious-looking cake.

'Thank you, Sylvie,' he said with a dazzling smile and, with one of her own in return, she was gone.

'I'm so sorry,' Stan said, but Adi waved his embarrassment away.

'Don't be. Sylvie's French. She won't bat an eyelid. But I do have to correct you on one thing before we go any further – I don't want to be anyone's husband.'

'You don't? Partner, then?'

'Not that either, save in the transitory sense.'

'Transitory?'

Now Stan was confused again. The herbal teas were as they seemed but Adi was throwing young people's upside-down language at him anyway.

'Cake?' he squeaked. He reached to the nearest slice but to his surprise and horror Adi took his hand in his own. 'What are you doing?' Stan demanded, trying to pull away.

Adi let him but leaned in.

'Perhaps we should be straight here, Stan. What I am offering for your dear wife are my services – my sexual services.'

Stan felt his eyes widen like a cartoon character.

'Oh,' he said, the word all drawn out and hollow-sounding. Then, 'Oh, I see.'

'I am what you might call an escort. I'm employed to make women happy. That's what your ad said, wasn't it?' Stan nodded. He felt a laugh bubbling up inside him. Here he'd been fretting about Adi's use of language and all along it had been his – or rather Greya's – that had held hidden meaning. He looked at Adi and saw to his relief that the handsome young man was smiling too. 'I take it that's not what you were after, Stan?'

'No. I'm so sorry. The profile used to say "kind, warm and caring" but I let my granddaughter persuade me to change it. I should have stuck to my guns.'

'But then I wouldn't have got to meet you. Don't apologise, please. The fault is all mine.'

'Not really. I feel a bit of a fool. I should probably go.'

'Not at all. We have our cake to eat yet and the music is good and I'd love to hear about your wife.'

'Even if I'm not going to pay you to, to . . .'

'To make sweet, sweet love to her?' Adi asked with a cocked eyebrow and now the laugh was bursting out of Stan and Adi was laughing too and it felt so silly and so foolish and so very, very funny. There might as well have been a certain natural boost in his tea, for he seemed to be as helpless with mirth as he had been that time in Amsterdam.

'I'm no laughing matter, I'll have you know,' Adi said, but he was still chuckling and Stan felt a giddy rush of affection for this total stranger who had made him feel so at ease in the most ridiculous of situations.

'I bet you're good at your job,' he said, recovering himself a little.

'I get decent reviews,' Adi agreed, with a wink.

'Five-star, hey?'

'Ten.'

'Isn't it a bit exhausting?'

'I'm not at it all the time. Maybe twice a week on average.'

'And you live off that? You *must* be good at it.'

'No! Lord, no. I make my living as an electrician. The night work is just a bit of a bonus.'

'You really are a sparkie then?'

'I am, yes.'

'Are you good at that too?'

'I get decent reviews. Why, do you need work doing?'

249

'Always. I'm a builder. Well, I was a plumber originally but Bonnie is an architect and for years now we've run Foundation Stone, a design-and-build business. We're always on the lookout for good tradesmen.'

'See,' Adi said, 'this meeting was fate. What are you working on at the moment?'

'A house on the outskirts of Brecksby,' Stan said, choosing to omit the fact that he wasn't personally working on it at all.

But Adi's face had lit up.

'No way! The new build? The one with the curves? I love that house. It's going to be gorgeous.'

Stan flushed.

'Bonnie designed it.'

'Your wife? She's very talented.'

'She is. It's for us. At least, it was meant to be, though I may not make it over the threshold now.'

Stan heard the words choke in his throat and felt suddenly swamped by all that empty, wasted future. He looked down, fighting tears, but Adi just placed his hand over Stan's again and this time Stan let him. Adi made no attempt to offer platitudes or advice but just sat there calmly, letting the young guitarist's melodies fill the space between them until Stan had recovered himself.

'Thank you,' he said as soon as he felt able. 'Most people fumble for words.'

'I don't do fumbling,' Adi said, and again there was the wink and Stan felt instantly better.

'Would you like to come and see round the house?' he heard himself asking.

'I'd love to.'

'Great. Our sparkie's not very good to be honest so Dave, that's my business partner, is looking for a new one if you're interested?'

'Totally. How about tomorrow? I'll bring cake.'

'You make cake too?'

'Nah. I'll buy it off Sylvie. Everyone's got to stick to their own talents, don't you think?'

'I do.'

'What's your talent, Stan?'

He thought about it.

'Making Bonnie happy. At least, I don't know if it's a talent as such. Someone else might do it much better – you for a start – but it's the thing I'm best at. It's the thing I do. That's why it's so hard knowing I won't be able to do it for much longer.'

'And you think that finding her someone else will help?'

'It might.'

Adi chewed on a bit of cake – he managed to make even that look sensuous, Stan thought – before swallowing and leaning forward.

'I suspect, Stan, that if you're so good at making Bonnie happy – and I'm absolutely certain you are – all that happiness you've given her will last a few years, even once you're gone.'

'What? How?'

'Happiness builds, I think, like warmth. Take this summer. It's been nice, right? The odd rainy day, the odd nippy morning, but basically nice.'

'Yes,' Stan agreed, confused.

'And as a result everywhere stays warm even when the sun's gone down. The warmth is stored in the earth.'

Stan thought of Midsummer Night, when they'd sat up to see the dawn in with little more than blankets over their sea-stung skin.

'That's true,' he agreed.

'Well, I'd say that happiness is the same. You and your Bonnie have built up so much together that it will be stored inside your marriage even once you're gone.'

Stan stared at him, charmed.

'That's a lovely thought.'

Adi shrugged.

'I'm no expert. I'm rarely in the same bed twice in a week, but I watch people and some couples just have that solidity about them, that warmth. It won't die with you, Stan.'

Stan felt a tear gather in the corner of his eye and for once he didn't brush it away. It formed, then fell quietly onto the carrot cake, making a tiny dent in the creamy icing.

'I'm glad you contacted me, Adi,' he said.

'Me too, Stan.'

'I envy you your job.'

'That's very kind, but I can see it's not true – and therefore I envy you your wife.'

'You should,' Stan agreed. 'She's the best. The absolute best. And now I think, if you don't mind, I'll head home to her and maybe take the rest of this cake with me. Carrot is her favourite.'

'Let me get you a fresh slice.'

Stan looked at the cake, half-eaten and tear-stained.

'Nah. This bit is good, thanks.'

'OK. Here.' Adi offered him a daisy-patterned napkin to wrap it in. 'Can I offer you a lift home?'

Stan knew he should say no but he was so tired and the thought of having to catch a crowded, jolting bus felt almost too much to bear.

'Would you?'

'Of course. Let's go.'

'The bill . . .'

'Oh, don't worry. I have an account.' Stan raised an eyebrow at him and Adi gave him a wicked grin. 'You're not the first person I've met at The Flowerpot, Stan – though to be fair you are the first man.'

Stan smiled.

'Nice to know I can still be someone's first,' he said and reached for his stick.

Chapter Twenty-Four

Adi's car was a flashy little Porsche Boxster in electric blue. Its interior was cream leather and its dashboard polished to a high shine. There wasn't a sweet wrapper or a tissue or a stray bit of pipe in sight, and Stan sank blissfully into the plush seat as Adi roared away.

'Not bad for an electrician.'

'As I said, the night work is for bonuses and this girl is the main one. By day I drive a beat-up van.'

'Do you feel like two different people?'

'A bit, I suppose. The escort job is a role and it suits me for now. Brecksby, right?'

'Please.'

Stan wondered if he was being naive again, letting this charming young man know where he lived, but his eyes were closing and it was hard to care. Adi's car was warm and comfortable, his music was soft, his driving impeccable. This would be a lovely car to go away in, Stan thought. He'd never booked that holiday for Bonnie, so perhaps he should hire one tomorrow, before it was too late. Just go. Head for the hills and if he died, so what?

But then the thought of Bonnie stuck in some strange place all alone invaded his sleepy mind and he cried out and jerked awake.

'You OK?' Adi asked.

'Yes. Sorry, yes. Just dropped off. Lovely car.'

'Thank you. Look, nearly home. That's your new place, right?'

They were approaching the building site and Stan forced himself to look over. Despite all he had said to Bonnie about loving the house, he still found himself avoiding it. It wasn't the poor house itself, or the dear people working on it, just the stark way it seemed to represent the future he would never see.

He glanced around the site. Dave's digger sat to one side and he could see his friend locking it up and checking his watch, doubtless wondering if The Crown would be open. Such a simple worry. But then, Dave was a simple man. The other day he'd asked Stan to go to some local football game with him in a couple of weeks.

'Why?' Stan had asked him, uncertain if he wanted to waste even an hour of the time left to him on one of his friend's whims.

'Why not?' had been the easy reply, and Stan supposed that if you weren't measuring out the droplets of your life as they ran through every single day, it was a fair question.

His eyes moved across the site and he saw Rachael come out of the battered office and stretch her back, her belly looking even more swollen than usual in such clear profile. She was due in just over two months and Bonnie was certain Stan would get to see his fourth grandchild into the world, but he knew his body was getting weaker with every day, as if accelerating towards the grave, and feared she was wrong. He drew in a painful breath as he watched Rachael and Dave chat for a moment before heading for their cars, and he envied them the simple interaction.

That was his building site, the one that had welcomed him to work in various guises over the last forty years, but it welcomed him no more. He turned his face away and directed Adi to his old street, his safe, comfortable old street, but even here things seemed spoiled. For the man from the other week was standing against the trees outside number twenty-nine again and he was staring across the road at Stan's house – at Bonnie.

'Bastard,' Stan spat. Adi jumped and the car jerked a little. 'Sorry. Not you. I didn't mean you. I meant him – over there. I don't know who he is but he's been hanging around scaring my wife.'

'Well, we can't have that.'

Adi pulled onto the drive, flung open his door and leaped out. In four strong strides he was across the road shouting, 'Oi you!' just as Lisa had the other day.

The man twitched but stood his ground. He wore sunglasses and had the collar of his light jacket pulled up high like some 1920s spy but in daylight something about him looked very familiar. Stan stared and suddenly he knew what it was – that bald patch.

'Lawrence?' He tapped over with his stick to join Adi. 'Lawrence, what on earth are you doing here?'

Lawrence shuffled back but didn't move away.

'I wanted to see her,' he said, his voice thin. 'I wanted to see Bonnie. I wanted her to know I was here.'

'She knows that all right. You've been frightening the life out of her.'

'She doesn't need to be frightened of grief.'

'She's not frightened of grief, she's frightened of *you*.'

Lawrence did not seem to even hear him and Stan grabbed at the lapel of his coat, desperate to make him see how very wrong this was. Lawrence's eyes, though, were locked on the house, opaque with the film of his delusion and he didn't even look at Stan when he shook him.

'Grief has its own comforts, its own charms. I can help Bonnie see that, Stan, when you're gone.'

'No, Lawrence. I told you – that's not want I want for Bonnie.'

'But it might be what Bonnie wants. Bonnie might embrace her grief like . . .'

'No!'

He had to shut this man up, had to get him away before he told Bonnie that, like an idiot, he'd sought him out as her next husband. A terrible guilt was creeping up through his whole body that in his ill-thought-out quest he'd actually put his dear wife in danger. He heard the front door open and looked back to see, to his horror, Bonnie herself stepping out.

'I'd like you to leave,' he hissed urgently at Lawrence.

'Why? I'm not doing anything wrong, Stan. I'm just watching her.'

It was those two words that did it. *Watching her.* He'd watched Bonnie once, too, but not like this, surely not like this.

'Get away from me, Lawrence,' he shouted. 'Get away from us. You don't belong here.'

Lawrence's red-rimmed eyes narrowed and he looked over to Bonnie, who was coming across the street, Lisa in tow. A nasty smile crossed his face and Stan feared all his silly lies were about to be exposed but he hadn't factored in Adi. The younger man stepped quietly forward, his muscles bulging.

'This is a private road, sir, and you are trespassing. You have been asked to leave and I suggest you do so – now.'

Lawrence looked from Stan to Adi to Bonnie.

'You're a fool, Stanley Walker. I'm offering your wife . . .' But at that moment Lisa stepped out of Bonnie's shadow and he paled. 'Fine. Have it your own way. No one appreciates me. No one sees what I have to offer, not now Efie is gone. No one . . .'

'You again?' Lisa said menacingly.

She glanced curiously at Adi but stepped up at his side and folded her arms. It was all too much for Lawrence who, thank the lord, pulled down his sunglasses and strode off, head held high and bald patch glinting in the sun. Stan felt relief flood through his guilt-ridden body and almost collapsed with the tide of it.

'Who on earth is that man?' Bonnie asked.

'More to the point, who is *this* man?' Lisa said, looking to Adi.

Stan seized on the question.

'This is Adi, Lise. I met him because, because . . .'

He searched desperately for an excuse, looking from Bonnie to Lisa.

'Because I'm a sparkie,' Adi said smoothly, 'and I'd love the chance to work with you. You must be Bonnie Walker? I've heard a lot about you – and about the new house. It's such an amazing project.'

He held out a hand to Bonnie, who took it.

'Thank you,' she said. 'You're very kind. And thank you for your help here. It saved Lisa a job.'

Adi looked to Lisa, who gave him a wry smile.

'I chased the wretched man off the other day,' she told him. 'I'm impressed.'

'Oh, I can be pretty scary when I want to be.'

'I don't doubt it.'

Lisa pushed her hair out of her eyes and looked coyly up at him.

'You were pretty scary yourself.'

Stan saw Bonnie roll her eyes before she stepped up to her elder daughter.

'Should we call the police, Lisa?' she asked.

Lisa blinked and turned from Adi with evident reluctance.

'I suppose we should, really. If you want to prove harassment you need to log your concerns from the start.'

'Harassment?' Stan echoed. What on earth had he done? 'I don't think it was that serious, was it? The poor man just seemed a bit, well . . .'

'Sad,' Bonnie filled in and Stan felt a rush of love for her tender heart. 'I agree. He doesn't seem a threat, does he? We'll call if he appears again, but let's leave it for now. Can we offer you a cup of tea, Adi?'

'That would be lovely,' he agreed. 'Do you have any herbal?'

Bonnie opened her mouth to reply but before she could form the words Lisa had slid past.

'Of course. All sorts. I'm a big fan. Do come in, Adi, and see what you fancy.'

She took his arm and led him indoors without a backward glance. Stan stared after her in astonishment. Adi truly *was* talented if he could soften his prickly daughter that quickly.

'Maybe,' he said to Bonnie as he took her arm to follow the younger pair into the house, 'there's more to be said for a rhubarb and ginger zinger than any of us have ever credited.'

And then they were both laughing and Lisa was looking back indignantly and that only set them off more. Stan clutched at Bonnie and felt blessed that he was still here to feel the glorious ache of mirth for a little time yet.

Chapter Twenty-Five

April 1963

'Gis a kiss!'

Danny came flailing towards Bonnie, the blades of his skates flashing in the lights as he struggled to keep upright.

'You'll have to catch me first,' she cried lightly, shooting out into the centre of the rink.

Aunt Nancy had taken her skating quite a bit at the Ice Palace in Manchester when she was little, and the technique had come flooding back to her within just a few turns of the Silver Blades rink. She wondered if Nancy was even now skating with Astrid in Sweden, maybe on some lake somewhere with clean air and beautiful scenery and a cosy log cabin. She tried to feel glad for her dear aunt, but it had been just the two of them for so long that she felt sad it was coming to an end, however much fun she was having in Liverpool. Not that it had been much fun so far tonight.

She drove herself faster, trying to at least enjoy the skating. Silver Blades was a striking 1920s building with art deco chandeliers high up in the curved ceiling and an elegant balcony running around three sides where people could meet and chat and watch the skaters. There was even a restaurant overlooking the ice, but Bonnie was enjoying skating again too much to waste time in there. Danny, however, had barely been out of it since the Best Boys had played earlier.

'Not fair,' she heard him call now, his voice sounding slurred. 'You're sooo quick, Bonnie-Bon.'

'True,' she agreed but didn't slow down.

There was something manic about Danny tonight and she didn't like it. Then again, there was something manic about every one of the band. Danny had told her that rehearsals for this gig had been fraught, with Sticks refusing to even speak to Spike and Spike retaliating with ever-more exaggerated tales of the girls who'd stopped him in the street since the Shuffle. It was only the possibility of being spotted that had kept them in the same room and, to be fair to them, they'd somehow shoved their differences aside for their set, but it had been disappointing all the same.

They'd been given the five til six o'clock slot when it was really just little kids on the ice and there hadn't been the adoring audiences or, more to the point, potential managers they'd been hoping for. No one had heard from Billy J. Kramer about his hunt for a band, and now this. It was all a bit of a let-down.

'We played our hearts out,' Lee had said as they'd packed away, the mood dark, 'but there wasn't anyone to hear.'

'This time,' Bonnie had consoled, 'if the rink manager liked it, he'll invite you back again and put you on later. It takes time, that's all.'

'Time! Great. I'll be drawing my damned pension before we make it if it takes this long – and that's if the others don't bloody well kill each other first.'

He'd gestured to Sticks stomping off with his drum cases in one direction and Spike with an amp in the other, and Bonnie had feared the truth of Lee's words. Sadly, however, none of them had gone home, as if they all wanted to carry on needling at each other to rub salt into the hurt of the empty gig. Danny had met up with some school friends, newly returned from various universities and brandishing wallets as fat as his own, and had been keen for Bonnie to meet them. After polite introductions, however, they'd been too busy catching up with each other and she'd gladly left them to their own devices and taken to the ice.

The only issue was the wretched pair snogging ostentatiously on the sidelines.

'Why Spike?' she'd demanded furiously of Susie-Ann as they'd headed for home after the Riverboat Shuffle.

'Why not Spike? Is he too good for me, is that it?'

'Of course not, Susie. It's just, you know, he and I . . .'

'He and you what? Dated for about a week? So?'

It had been hard to fault the logic, and Susie-Ann had been sparking for a row so Bonnie had let the subject drop, but it had not been so easy to drop it from her mind. Every night this week she'd lain awake, straining to hear if anyone was climbing up to Susie-Ann's room and torturing herself with thoughts of Spike down there doing lord knows what with her one-time friend.

What really hurt was that it had all been going so well. The Shuffle had been such a wonderful night right up until the very last bit, and that made it worse somehow. The contrast between the warm joy of the performance on the boat and the emptiness of tonight's icy gig could not be more pronounced, and Bonnie wasn't surprised everyone was in such a bad mood.

She stopped dead as Danny came up behind her again, warbling along to the second band's terrible version of 'Love Me Tender', and then went flailing helplessly past. She shook her head.

'You OK there, Bonnie?'

She turned to see Lee.

'I'm OK, yes. I'm not so sure about Danny, though. Do you think he's been drinking, Lee?'

Lee gave a low laugh.

'More than that, I'd say. Looks like he's been at the LSD.'

'LS-what?'

'LSD – lysergic acid something or other. It's what all the cool people are taking.'

'It's a drug?'

'Yeah.'

'Oh.' Bonnie kicked her skates against the side. Nancy had warned her many times about the dangers of drugs, and her heart lurched at the thought of her own boyfriend getting caught up in them. 'Why would he do that?'

'I dunno. For fun, I guess. I haven't got the money for that sort of caper but people down the Cavern rave about it. And it looks to be doing Danny good – he's the only one of us not moping.'

'Spike's not moping,' Bonnie shot back, indicating the lead singer, wrapped around Susie-Ann.

'You reckon?' Lee said dryly.

Certainly the pair of them made kissing look more like a challenge than a pleasure, but perhaps they liked it that way. Spike obviously hadn't been keen on her own shy approach, so who was she to tell when he was happy? But now Danny was shooting towards her and Lee again and this time he came clattering to a stop against the barrier.

'Good news,' he cried. 'Manager loves us. Luurrvves us. Really. Says we're cool, like, or fab or good or, well, something like that. And we can have six til seven next week – replace this lot of crooners.' He jerked a thumb towards the current band. 'Good, hey? How clever am I? Clever Danny, that's me, right Bon? Clever, clever Danny. The Best Boys are on the way up!'

'Slowly,' Lee said, but a small smile crept onto his lips and he added, 'That's great, Danny. Well done.'

Danny just beamed and executed a ponderous spin, staring at the ice beneath his feet as if his eyes were attached to the patterns his blades were making. Bonnie watched him, horrified.

Suddenly he looked up and fixed Lee with an over-bright stare.

'We can do originals, too. Originals, Lee-boy. What about the creepy one you were helping Spike with? You reckoned that could be a hit, right?'

He rammed a finger in Lee's direction so hard that he toppled himself over onto the ice but he was up again in an instant, waving to his friends and laughing. They seemed to find it hilarious, but Bonnie saw the sheen of sweat on his brow and felt the tension coming off him in palpable waves. She edged behind Lee, who seemed reassuringly unmoved by his bandmate's antics.

'I'm not sure, Danny. I'd say it needs work yet. I'd have to talk to Spike.'

'So talk. Tell him that if he thinks he's so clever he needs to get on and prove it. Like me. I'm clever at . . . What am I clever at? Bonnie?' He looked round but failed to spot her behind Lee and instead jabbed a finger at him again, announcing, 'We're doing "Watching Her" next week. Move over John Lennon. Anything he can do we can do better, right? Right, Lee?'

'Right,' Lee agreed and Danny gave him an approving nod.

'Good. We have to seize this chance. It's our time, I'm sure of it, but for now, the night is young and so are we.' He flung his arms wide. 'Let's skate, my friend.'

Lee shook his head.

'Nah. I might try and find Spike. I'll catch you later.'

He loped off, hands in pockets, head down, already deep in thought. Danny pulled a face at his back.

'So bloody serious!' he said, making a lewd gesture that had his crass mates cheering from the sidelines.

Bonnie watched Lee's lips moving silently as he tried to remember Spike's song.

'The band means a lot to him.'

Danny jumped as if he'd only just spotted her, revealed from behind Lee's thin frame.

'So? Means a lot to me too. To all of us. We just don't make such a song and dance about it.'

He cackled at his own joke and attempted a dance step on the ice. Bonnie felt her temper rising.

'That's not very fair, Dan,' she said as calmly as she could.

'No?' He stopped dancing and stared at her, his pupils moving in and out as he tried to focus on her face. 'Come on, Bon. So what if Lee works? We all bloody work! I lug bloody frozen bloody cows around all day and manage to turn up to rehearsals without sighing all over the bloody place.'

'He's worried.'

'He's no bloody fun.'

Bonnie looked at her boyfriend in disgust. Danny was pouring with sweat and his eyes were wild and unfocused.

'Life can't be all fun, Danny.'

'You're telling me,' he agreed, nodding vigorously. 'A month we've been going out, Bonnie-Bon, and we've barely had any bloody "fun" at all.'

Bonnie froze.

'What do you mean?'

'You know what I mean. Reckon I'd get further with a bloody nun.'

Bonnie's skin burned with mortification. Two of Danny's friends had come up and he was clearly playing to his crowd, but that only made it worse. All this time he'd seemed such a gentleman, charming her like a prince and protecting her like a knight, but in the end had it just been for this, for sex? He was every bit as bad as Spike.

If you fancy it, why not? Nancy had told her back when all this was just a film-reel dream, but it turned out the films were just a pack of big fat lies. Sure, her parents had danced like Rogers and Astaire but look what had happened to them. There was no such thing as love and no such thing as care; it was all just jealousy and one-upmanship and bloody trouble.

'Fine,' she said, 'if it's such a chore for you, I won't trouble you to keep me company any further. You're free to go and look for someone more obliging, Danny – though I wouldn't recommend a nun.'

'Free?' His eyes narrowed as he tried to focus on her. 'What do you mean, free?'

'What do you think I mean? I thought you were clever, Danny.'

'I am. Look, Bon, I didn't . . .'

'Have a nice night,' she said and shot off before any of them could see her shaking.

Danny still looked stunned but Bonnie didn't care – she just wanted to get away from him. From them all. She picked up speed, anger driving her on faster and faster. Ahead of her, against the barrier, Susie-Ann was still locked onto Spike, but as she got closer she saw her so-called friend's eyes were wide open and fixed behind Spike. Sure enough, Sticks was skating past, dragging along a pretty little brunette, and the sight of it made Bonnie rage. She was sick of this, all of it. It was time to talk.

She shot up to the pair, pulling Susie-Ann roughly away from Spike.

'Oi!' she said, but her heart wasn't in it.

'Come to the loo with me.' Susie-Ann frowned, but Bonnie had had enough. 'Now!' she snapped and with a look of shock, Susie-Ann obeyed.

They clumped off the ice, walking across the rubber floor in their skates, and pushed their way through the double doors. There were girls crowded all around the mirrors and Bonnie pulled Susie-Ann into the first cubicle.

'I want to talk to you.'

'Here?'

'Yep. Here.'

Susie-Ann folded her arms.

'What about?'

'Spike.'

'What about him?'

'Do you like him?'

'He's all right.'

'All right? Is that the best you can do now?'

Susie-Ann glared.

'Yeah, well, we can't all be as pretty as you, can we? We can't all have every boy in the place mooning after us so, yes, "all right" will do me, ta.'

Bonnie's stomach tightened and she stared in horror at her one-time friend.

'Is that how you really see me?' she asked, her voice breaking.

Had all those times getting ready with Susie-Ann been a chore for her? Had all those happy nights in front of the little TV with the Cobdens been a lie? Was she kidding herself, thinking they'd welcomed her into their family? Lord, she'd have been better off staying in the cold halls – at least she'd known where she stood there.

She pushed on the cubicle door but then the other girl flung her arms around her, clinging on for all she was worth.

'Of course it's not how I see you, Bonnie! I love you to bits, you stupid queen. You're, like, the best friend a girl could have, and now I've made you miserable.'

'Not miserable, Susie . . .'

'I have. I know it. You like Spike still, I can tell.'

'I don't, I . . .'

'Course you do. You have right from the start, and I just steam-rollered over that to have my revenge on Mickey. I only picked Spike cos he was there when I was mad, Bon, nothing more.'

'Nothing more?' Bonnie wasn't having that. 'What about all that stuff about having sex, Susie – having sex *again*?'

The other girl gave a thin laugh.

'Made up on the spot. To hurt Mick.'

'And me.'

'I didn't really think that. Oh lord, I'm sorry Bonnie. Really. I'm so, so sorry. I'm such a tart. I know I am. Can you ever forgive me?'

Bonnie's heart melted instantly, but Nancy always said she was too soft-hearted. She had to think about this.

'And since? Have you had sex with him since?'

'Spike? No! Course not. I couldn't. It wouldn't feel right with anyone but, but . . .'

'Sticks?'

She nodded glumly.

'I've been an idiot, haven't I?'

Bonnie stroked her hair back from her face and drew in a deep breath.

'Not totally. You were right that Sticks has to accept you as you are. You just maybe didn't talk it through as fully as you might have done.'

'Understatement of the year,' Susie-Ann groaned. 'Oh lord, this is all wrong and it needs to stop. I should give up getting a stupid history degree and marry him and it'll all be boss again.'

Bonnie recoiled in shock.

'No! That's not what I meant.'

'But that's how it is. You've seen my place, my folks. That's the sort we are – get up, work all week, collect your payslip and go down the pub with it. And why not? It's norra bad way to be, is it?'

'Course not, but you can be more – that is, different. You'd get bored doing that, you know you would.'

'Better bored than lonely. What's the point of pursuing a bloody dream, Bon, if you end up doing it on your tod?'

'It doesn't have to be that way, not for you. You've got a great mind, Susie-Ann. You can do anything – research, law, politics.'

'Politics?'

'You could be the first woman Prime Minister.'

'Bollocks!' she said, but Bonnie caught a glimmer of a smile and snatched at it.

'I bet you could, Susie, if you wanted to. You can't give up your degree.'

'Then I can't have Sticks.'

They stared at each other, pondering the impossibility of the situation.

'He has to see how important it is to you,' Bonnie said eventually. 'And how good it could be for you both. Talk to him, Susie – talk to him properly. What have you got to lose?'

Susie-Ann wiped a half-formed tear from her eyelid and nodded slowly. Then she opened her bag, rummaged inside and pulled out a gold bullet of a lipstick.

'You're right, Bonnie. Talk, good plan. If I'm so bloody brainy I must be able to make him see we can make things work, right?'

'Absolutely.'

Susie-Ann rose and flung open the cubicle door, sending a startled girl skittering aside. She strode across to the mirrors, elbowing her way to the centre spot, and applied bright red to her lips.

'Wish me luck then,' she said into the mirror.

'You're going to talk now?'

'No time like the present, right? Watch out.'

And with that she pushed the loo door and strode out. Bonnie ran after her. What had she done?

'Susie-Ann!' she called but her friend was gone, stomping off in her skates towards the café where Bonnie could see Sticks' poor, unsuspecting date accepting a milkshake. Sticks looked up as Susie-Ann marched towards him and Bonnie saw joy brim in his eyes, swiftly drowned by naked fear. He moved forward but at that moment Spike stepped into Bonnie's line of sight.

'What's she about, Bon?' he asked, jerking his head towards Susie-Ann.

'I'm not certain. It could be explosive.'

'That'd be right. She's scary, Bonnie. I don't know what I was doing with her. Sorry.'

'You don't need to apologise to me.'

'Don't I?' He looked almost shyly at her, then added, 'What's your Danny up to?'

He pointed to where Danny was back on the ice with his mates and seemed to be attempting a pirouette. Bonnie watched as he made one, then two, very wobbly spins before plonking down on the ice with a broad grin. She shook her head grimly.

'He's not my Danny.'

'What?'

'We've split up.'

'Really?' His eyes looked suddenly, wonderfully bright and as his fingers found hers, she felt the touch of him thrill through her and it was as if she was back at the beginning again, back in a hushed stairwell in the Jacaranda club with this boy standing before her and the future still a giddy possibility. 'So you're free, right? And I'm free. Might you then, maybe . . .'

But his words were cut off by a strange roar, so loud it stopped the band mid-chorus. Bonnie whipped round and saw Danny sprawled on the ice, bellowing in agony. Blood poured from his right hand, spreading out across the ice in manic red veins.

'Oh God, no!' Spike cried, looking far more concerned than Bonnie would ever have expected, before adding, 'That's his strumming hand!'

Of course! Was the band really all these boys truly cared about? Spike shot onto the ice and hesitantly she followed but the moment Danny saw her, he babbled her name. Seeing the real fear in his eyes, she flung herself guiltily down at his side. She shouldn't have finished with him when he was like this. And she shouldn't have skated off and left him when he was clearly unstable.

'It's OK, Danny,' she said. 'I'm here. I'll look after you. It'll all be all right.'

But he was screaming blue murder and shaking and she was relieved when a man with a red cross on his jacket skidded up.

'Stand back,' he commanded the crowd. 'Go on – clear the ice. And you,' he said to Danny, 'stop screaming. You're not helping yourself.' Danny clamped his mouth shut. The man reached for his hand and Bonnie winced as his index finger was revealed, the tip hanging limply to one side. Behind her Spike gave a groan and staggered backward. 'Nasty,' the medic said, 'this is going to need stitches.' He looked at Danny, muttering to himself, and frowned. 'Has he taken something?'

'I'm not sure,' Bonnie stuttered, not wanting to get him into trouble.

'Well try and be sure. It could be vital when he gets to the hospital.'

'Right. OK. Someone said something about, er, about LSD, sir.'

The medic groaned.

'Not again. Bloody drugs, nothing but trouble. Right then, hold his wrist.' Bonnie did so, swallowing back tears as the medic pulled a long bandage from his bag and bound it tightly around the flapping finger. 'What's his name?'

'Danny.'

'Are you here with him, miss?'

'No. That is, I was but . . .'

'Because someone needs to go to the hospital with him. Can you do that?' Bonnie swallowed. Danny was as pale as the ice he was lying on but still dripping with sweat and she longed to get away from him but that would hardly be kind. 'Can you do that, miss?'

She drew in a deep breath.

'Of course I can,' she said.

For a moment, she thought she saw Danny shoot Spike a triumphant look but with the state he was in that couldn't possibly be right. She looked at Spike herself. What had he been going to say to her before this mess? 'You still like him, I can tell,' Susie-Ann had said and she did, she really did.

'Would you come too?' she asked him but he was visibly shaking and was almost as pale as Danny.

'To the hospital? Oh no, Bon, I couldn't. I'm rubbish with blood. You'll be much better without me, really you will.'

He was backing away now and Bonnie cast around for Susie-Ann but her friend was at the edge of the rink, tonsil-deep in Sticks and oblivious to the drama on the ice. That was a comfort at least, and there was no way Bonnie was going to interrupt their reunion, even if Danny's fingers were like a claw in her shoulder as she rose to help lead him off the ice.

But then a low voice said, 'I'll come,' and she turned to see Lee stepping up at her side.

'Oh, Lee, thank you. Thank you so much.'

'Anything to help, Bonnie.'

'You're a star. I'm so grateful.'

She grabbed for his hand and for a moment they stood there together before Danny tugged on her shoulder and Lee blushed and looked away.

'It's the Best Boys, see,' he said. 'He'll need that finger mended if we're playing here again next week, so we better make sure they sew it on properly, right?'

'Right,' Bonnie agreed weakly, stepping back.

For a moment then, she'd thought he was worried about her – fool. These lads were here to get themselves a record deal; the rest was incidental. And she got that, didn't she? She understood about goals more than most.

'Anything for the Best Boys,' she said fiercely, but it sounded hollow even to her.

Chapter Twenty-Six

Stan leaned heavily on his stick and looked out across the busy playing fields on the edge of Brecksby. On the horizon he could see his and Bonnie's new house rising up over the hedge. The bricks were laid, the timber cladding was glowing in the August sun and the roof was in place. Dave had taken Adi on as sparkie and now, if Stan ever went past in the darkening evenings, he could see lights glowing from the windows. Bonnie's grand project was looking less and less like a skeleton and more like an actual home, and Stan knew he should go and see it.

The problem was, the longer he stayed away the harder it got. Dave and Rachael kept assuring him that they were less than a month from completion, as if this might somehow convince his liver to hang in there, but the problem was less with his liver and more with his heart.

Dr Mirabi insisted he would see every last leaf fall off the trees and he was trying hard to believe it, but even so he couldn't quite bear to see the house he might never get to live in. With a sigh, he forced his eyes away from the looming shape of his non-future on the horizon and back to the young boys running around on the grass immediately in front of him.

'Tell me again, Dave, what I'm doing here?'

Dave rolled his eyes.

'Watching football – obviously.'

Stan groaned.

'OK, mate, ten out of ten for stating the obvious, but you never mentioned it was a kids' match.'

'What's wrong with kids?'

Stan gaped at him.

'Nothing, Dave. They're great. OK, let me try again then – *why* am I here?'

'Because I asked you to come.'

'Dave . . .'

'OK, OK. I'm thinking Foundation Stone should maybe sponsor this little lot, Brecksby Rovers. It's good publicity. You know, supporting the local community and all that – looks great on Facebook.'

'Fair point. And Jamie plays for the older lads so that would be good. But why football? You hate football, Dave.'

Dave gave a horrified look along the touchline, checking no one had heard. About twenty parents were gathered to watch two teams of eight-year-olds line up against each other and Dave seemed strangely keen to impress them.

'I do not,' he insisted loudly. 'Great game, football.'

Stan dropped his voice. 'But you're always teasing poor Jamie about it. The kits are too shiny, the wages too high and the hairstyles ridiculous, right?'

'Premiership, yes, right. Grassroots isn't like that, though. Look around you – lovely atmosphere, isn't there?'

He nodded companionably at the nearest parents and Stan looked along the line, confused. The sponsorship *was* a good idea but there had to be more to it to have piqued Dave's interest. He couldn't see any single women yet, but that was surely the only logical explanation.

'Did someone approach you about this sponsorship, Dave?'

He flushed.

'Maybe.'

'A woman? Have you met someone new?'

'No,' his friend said, a little too quickly.

'You have! Why have you ditched Gail? She was nice.'

'I've not ditched her, we're just keeping it casual.'

'Why, Dave?'

'Oh, I dunno. It's just easier, right? If you become "a couple" they expect things of you and not fun things like sex in the middle of the night, but dull things like unloading the dishwasher and watching chick flicks and meeting their friends.'

'I quite like chick flicks,' Stan said.

'Boring, the lot of them. They all peddle the same happy-ever-after-unload-the-dishwasher way of life. It's so narrow-minded.'

Dave spoke with unusual vehemence. Stan looked up to the house on the horizon, wondering if Adi had installed a dishwasher in his kitchen yet. From there it was only a short hop to wondering if he'd ever get to unload it, and he forced his eyes away. The boys were skipping keenly about as the ref blew his whistle to start the match but still no woman appeared at Dave's side to justify his new interest.

'But Dave, if you live alone surely you have to unload the dishwasher anyway?'

'Course I do. I'm not a boor. But I do it when I want and how I want without anyone telling me I shouldn't put the bloody knives in blades up.'

'Ah.'

'Don't be like that. Anyway, what's wrong with footie? There's a nice positive atmosphere, don't you think?'

They both winced as a man a little further up shouted, 'Kick him, Benny!'

'It,' Dave said quickly. 'He said, "Kick *it*" – the ball.'

'Right.'

They watched in silence for a minute or two as the boys all chased after the ball whilst their coaches shouted in vain from the far touchline about positional play. Then suddenly one of the lads broke free, making a run up the wing.

'Yes!' Dave shouted, leaning forward. 'Go on!'

Stan watched as the lad cut inside and struck for goal. The ball hovered in the air for an agonisingly long time before the keeper dived and caught it firmly in both hands. Dave groaned and Stan looked at him askance.

'Who's that, Dave?'

'Their star striker. Lad called Charlie. Scores loads. Gets in the papers a lot. It'd look good, wouldn't it, if he had Foundation Stone Builders across his chest?'

'It would, yes. But come on, Dave, who's the real interest here?'

Dave scuffed at the edge of the touchline.

'You know I told you an old girlfriend had been in touch?'

'The naked star jumps one?'

'Ssshh!' Dave leaned closer to him. 'Emma, yes. I met up with her a while back.'

'You don't hang around, do you, mate?'

'Not like *that*. She got married recently. Nice bloke.'

'He came for the drink too?'

'No.' Dave looked even shiftier. 'I went to their house, OK, to say hello.'

'To "say hello", Dave? Rubbish. What aren't you telling me?' His eyes widened. 'Are you having a threesome?'

Dave grinned at him.

'I wish!'

But now the little striker had the ball again and Dave was instantly focused back on the game. Stan looked harder at the lad as he made another run up the wing right past them and suddenly saw exactly what was going on.

'He looks just like you.'

Dave didn't respond, so intent was he on the play. Charlie made a nice looping cross into the box and another boy ran up to boot it into the net – and missed.

'No way!' Dave groaned. The dad next to them looked crossly over and Dave quickly called out, 'Unlucky, lad. Next time, hey?'

'Dave,' Stan said, 'why does that Charlie lad look just like you?'

Dave rolled his head, cracking the muscles in his neck, then rubbed self-consciously at them.

'OK, OK. Emma met me to tell me that she has a son – a son who turns out to be mine, too. Charlie.' He waved to the boy on the pitch. 'I didn't know, Stan. She didn't tell me. We'd split up by the time she found out she was pregnant. She went off to work in France, remember? Wanted me to go too but I said no way was I going to live in Frogland.'

'I remember,' Stan said. 'Very enlightened of you, Dave.'

'Yeah, well, we didn't part on the best of terms because of it so she didn't tell me about him – Charlie.'

His voice swelled with pride and Stan looked again to the pitch. Charlie was running past them, calling for the ball and now Stan could see even more of his mate in the determined set of the child's shoulders and his insistent shout.

'So why has she told you now?' he asked.

Dave didn't take his eyes off Charlie for a moment.

'It was her new hubby's idea. He told her it'd be best for Charlie to get to know me and it seems she listened. Guess I owe him one. Go on, Charlie!'

The ball had come the lad's way and he controlled it beautifully and was off. Dave jumped up and down like a child himself and Stan watched, touched and amused. Was this really the man who'd always said kids were millstones around their parents' necks?

'Go!' Dave urged. 'Go, Charlie!'

He clutched at Stan's sleeve as Charlie dribbled past a defender, side-stepped and then, with a look of utmost concentration on his little face, shot. The ball hit the side post, ricocheted off the poor keeper's head and pinged into the back of the net. The team went wild, Dave with them.

'Isn't he good?' he said eventually, eyes glowing with pride. 'Great hand-to-eye coordination. He gets that from me.'

'You've never played footie in your life.'

'That's not true. I was in the school team.'

'Only til you got old enough to play rugby.'

Dave frowned at him.

'Come on, Stan, you're the one always telling me what a great game football is, so why the downer now?'

Stan shook himself.

'Sorry. I'm sorry, mate. It's great. And obviously Foundation Stone would be pleased to sponsor the team. Is Charlie pleased to, you know, have you about?'

'He is. He really is. Emma had told him she didn't know who I was so he thinks I've been magicked up in some way. I thought he'd hate me for not being there before but he just seems dead chuffed to hang out with me every so often and I can do that, I think. For now. Maybe more in a bit if it goes well for everyone. We'll see. Day at a time, you know, but it's going OK.'

As if to prove it, Charlie looked over and gave Dave a shy wave. Dave returned it with a thumbs up and the boy beamed.

'I bought him a phone,' he told Stan as the lads ran back to the centre spot to kick off again. 'It's just an old thing. I'm not trying to buy his affection or anything, but I thought it would mean we could keep in touch a bit. He texts me loads and we've got something called Snapchat so he can send me pictures. It's great. He tells me bits about school and his mates and footie stuff. Transfer news and that.'

Stan looked to the pitch where the team seemed to be back to all chasing the ball around the midfield.

'This lot have transfer news?'

Dave flushed even deeper.

'Everton,' he muttered.

'Sorry, Dave?'

'He supports Everton, OK? Not surprising really, is it, living around here?'

This one, however, Stan could not let his old friend get away with. He recalled Dave taking the piss out of Jamie's shirt back at Easter and rubbed his hands. Revenge was going to be sweet.

'I see, Dave. How nice. You'll be taking him to a match then, will you?'

'I might.'

'You'll look lovely in blue. I think I've got an old Toffees top I could dig out for you if you'd like – show Charlie how long you've been a fan, hey?'

Dave held his hands up in surrender.

'OK, OK, you can take the piss out of me all you like. I deserve it, I know. But he loves it, Stan, and it's something we can talk about and you know what, that's worth more than my pride.'

Stan stared at him in awe.

'Dave Roberts, I didn't think I'd ever say this but I believe you may finally have grown up.'

'God no, not that. Anything but that!'

Stan smiled.

'Seriously though, mate, I'm pleased for you. Ooh, is that half-time already?'

With relief he watched the boys run off to their coach and reached back for the stool Bonnie had insisted he bring. He'd felt a prat sitting on it whilst the match was in progress, but his legs were tired and surely it was OK at half-time. He sank onto it and Dave crouched at his side.

'I'm glad you came, Stan. I'm a bit of a sore thumb at the moment, as you can imagine.'

He gestured to the other mums and dads. A couple of them nodded hello.

'You'll be fine. Looks like you'll soon have all sorts of new friends,' Stan said lightly, though the thought of it tore at his gut.

This time next year, were these the men Dave would be drinking with instead of him? Well, good – he didn't want his mate to be any lonelier than his wife. But somehow, the thought of them all living on without him made him feel more tired than ever. He looked to the horizon once more. The sun was high in the sky now and it glinted suddenly in the newly installed windows, as if the house was winking at him. Stan looked straight at it and took a deep breath.

'Dave,' he said, 'when the game is over, would you take me on site?'

Dave glanced at him, started to say something and then stopped himself.

'Course I will, mate. It'd be my pleasure.'

Chapter Twenty-Seven

Stan sank into the passenger seat of Dave's car feeling jittery. Bonnie would be at home and he couldn't wait to tell her about Charlie, but first, the house. Now he'd made a decision, he was dying to see it and he fidgeted like a toddler as Dave drove them the few minutes round the village and onto the site.

He hated being chauffeured around, but he was finding driving increasingly tiring and Bonnie didn't like him doing it unless he really had to. Poor Terry was left at home more and more these days and was every bit as grumpy about it as Stan, but hey, he didn't have a liver to give up on him so he could just stop complaining.

'What did you think of Charlie, then?' Dave asked him.

Stan had said a brief hello to the lad at the end of the match but he'd been heading off to a mate's to play and had had little time for an old man with a stick. Stan hadn't blamed him.

'He seems great, Dave. It's good to see you happy, mate.'

'Me? I'm always happy.'

'Content then – properly content, not just high on booze or sex.'

'Oi, don't go knocking booze and sex! But you're right – I am content. Weird, hey?'

'Good. And Rachael and Andrew seem happy with the new baby on the way, and Greya had an amazing time in Paris. Some firm are interested in sponsoring their bike project and she's buzzing with it. Everyone seems to have so much stuff to look forward to. Except me, of course – and Bonnie.'

Dave drove in silence for a minute, then said, 'She'll be OK, you know, Stan. We'll look after her, I promise.'

'You can't look after anyone, Dave Roberts.'

'I'm learning.'

Stan sighed.

'You are. Sorry.'

They turned up the rough driveway onto the site and reversed up beside a battered old van.

'Is someone here?' Stan asked, feeling shy. He didn't want strangers around for this moment.

'That's Adi's van. He must be putting in a few extra hours. I told him I wanted this finishing fast.'

'Because I'm dying?'

'No, Stan. Because I want you to live in it.'

Stan drew in a deep breath.

'Thanks, Dave.'

'Pleasure, mate. Now, look!'

He pointed out of the windscreen and Stan sat forward, craning to see. With all the walls now finished, the S-shaped curve was coming to life before his eyes, snaking round the land and rising up from east to west as if it were stretching luxuriously beneath the arc of the sun. Stan stared, taking it all in.

'It's beautiful.'

Dave gave a modest shrug.

'It's coming on. Shall we go and have a look around?'

Stan nodded and climbed slowly out of the car. His back ached and he fumbled for his stick but a childlike excitement pushed him on. Wait until he told Bonnie he'd been to see it. She'd be so pleased. She and Greya were forever gabbling on about the build, though they almost always stopped themselves when he came into the room. What had he been playing at, doing that to them? This beautiful building shouldn't be a secret, and if Bonnie was going to enjoy it once he was gone, he shouldn't taint it with memories of his reluctance.

'Has Lisa been to see it?' he asked Dave as they progressed across the rough ground towards the door.

'Lisa? Not for ages. She'd be welcome any time she wants, though. She's still living up here, right?'

'Right. In fact, she's talking about moving up permanently now that she and Simon are definitely splitting up. The Manchester office seem keen to take her on and she's been looking at flats. I've got my fingers crossed, but it's up to her.'

'This anything to do with her dirty weekend at Midsummer?'

Stan shook his head.

'No. That didn't work out, I'm afraid.'

'So she's single?'

'Don't you dare, Dave!'

'What?'

Stan paused just outside the porch and looked at his old friend.

'I know how you "help" women.'

Dave winked, still in high spirits.

'She's a good-looking girl, mate. And I could be a son to you. To Bonnie, too.'

'No way. That's foul, even by your standards. Hands off!'

'Joke, mate, joke!' He stepped up to the door and drew out a key but was apparently unable to resist a last tease. 'Lisa can get her hot loving elsewhere, I'm sure.'

Stan put his hands over his ears.

'Not listening, Dave. So not listening.'

Dave laughed again then slotted the key into the lock and turned it with a flourish.

'Shall we go in?'

Stan took a deep breath, looked down at the mark of his and Bonnie's hands clear in the concrete, and stepped firmly over it and into the building. The house was still a shell but all the internal walls were in place and he could see the individual rooms forming. In the kitchen area the units and appliances were marked on the floor in bold green pen and in the big double-height living room, the bi-folding doors had been fitted. What would be their day-to-day view was perfectly framed and just waiting to be enjoyed.

Stan looked around him, absorbing it all with rising wonder. For the first time he could see himself living here and it renewed his determination to survive long enough to do so.

'I love it, Dave,' he said, pacing the open space with something like a spring in his step for the first time in ages. 'You're all doing an amazing job.'

'Of course we are. Foundation Stone are the best.'

Stan smiled.

'I like the lights,' he said, pointing his stick to the beautiful curving glass fixtures on the walls.

'Good, aren't they. Adi sourced them for us. He certainly seems to know his stuff.'

Stan looked around.

'Where is he?'

'Not sure. He must be upstairs. I think he's working on yours and Bonnie's bedroom.'

'Mine and . . .'

It sounded wonderful, and Stan followed Dave to the rough temporary steps upwards, his stick tapping across the floor as fast as his heart rate. His and Bonnie's bedroom! Why oh why had he kept himself away for so long? He headed slowly up the temporary staircase and looked around.

'Wow!'

Dave straightened his shoulders proudly.

'Not bad, hey?'

They were on the three-sided balcony running around the living room below. Stan looked over the makeshift barriers and saw the elegant line of the curved walls twist enticingly below him.

'It's amazing.'

'Wait til you see your room. This way.'

Dave moved up the balcony towards the higher west end of the house. A beautiful deep-arched doorway stood before them, the curved oak door already in place, and Dave reached for it, then froze. There were sounds coming from the other side and they weren't sounds of drilling or hammering or any of the usual noises of a sparkie's trade. A low moan snaked under the closed door and then a series of high-pitched gasps. Dave looked at Stan and then back at the door.

'The cheeky bloody git!'

He flung the door back and right there before them, elegantly crescent-shaped with taut muscle, was Adi's bare backside.

'How dare you?' Dave cried.

Adi looked back, horrified, and grabbed at the trousers around his ankles whilst trying manfully to shield the woman from them as she made herself decent. Stan moved to the window to give them a little time, then had to duck back to grab Dave, too. Stan was finding it all quite funny but Dave seemed furious, perhaps because for the first time in his life someone else was up to naughtier tricks than him. He waited until the sparkie had restored his clothing, then turned on him.

'I employed you on trust, Adi. How dare you betray that by bringing strange women onto our building site and . . .'

He was interrupted by a delicate cough from the woman in question as she stepped out from behind her lover.

'Not so strange if you don't mind, Dave,' she said, facing them.

'Lisa!'

Stan's daughter gave him a funny little wave. Her usually immaculate hair was all over the place and her cheeks were flushed scarlet with embarrassment.

'Hi, Dad. So sorry. We didn't know anyone else was here.'

'Clearly,' Stan said dryly. He glanced over at Dave, who was gaping at the scene, and burst out laughing, enjoying the way it shook through his tired body. 'You did say she'd find her own hot loving, Dave,' he choked out.

Dave still looked puce with anger, but now Adi was putting a sheepish arm around Lisa and apologising over and over.

'It was my fault, Dad,' Lisa assured him. 'I asked him to show me round and then I shamelessly seduced him.'

'Are you sure? Lisa, are you paying . . .?' Adi shook his head violently at Stan. 'Paying enough attention to what you really want?' he finished lamely.

'What? Weird thing to say. Course I am, Dad.'

Lisa edged towards the door.

'Me too,' Adi put in, following her. 'I mean, we've been seeing quite a bit of each other, sir. I mean, Stan. We've been dating. Properly. And I like her a lot. I . . . I . . . I should go.'

'That might be best,' Dave agreed, still stern.

Stan just smiled but on her way past he grabbed Lisa and gave her a big hug.

'You're happy, Lise?'

'Very happy.'

'Then that's all that matters.'

She kissed his cheek.

'Thanks, Dad. Will you, er, will you tell Mum?'

Stan looked down at her.

'What do you think, sweetheart?'

She pulled a resigned face.

'You will, won't you?'

'Absolutely. And as soon as I possibly can.'

'That's brilliant, Stan. Absolutely brilliant.'

Stan hadn't seen Bonnie laugh this much in ages, and it was glorious. She'd been delighted that he'd gone to the house at last and chattered away about every last aspect of the build, filling him in on the details of all the work that had been done and all that was left to come. Part of him had felt terrible for not going sooner but he'd vowed not to have any regrets, so he told that part to sod off and just got on with enjoying her evident delight. Plus, of course, he'd been keeping the secret of Lisa's liaison with Adi for an opportune moment.

'In *our* room?' Bonnie said. 'The cheeky mare. I wanted to christen that with you.'

'Possibly optimistic,' he dared to say.

She shrugged.

'You've got to allow me optimism about something, Stan.'

'Fair point.'

'Mind you, I can't fault her taste. He's a good-looking man, isn't he?'

'He does have a certain something,' Stan agreed. 'And I've seen more of him than most.'

Bonnie laughed again.

'Oh Stan, this has done me so much good. I still can't believe Lisa did that.'

'Did what?' asked a young voice, and they both spun round to see Greya standing in the living room doorframe.

Bonnie froze and looked to Stan, but he was no better at lying than her. He groped around for a believable answer but came up blank.

'Doesn't matter,' was all he managed.

Greya looked from one to the other and rolled her eyes.

'Is this to do with that hot electrician Mum's been seeing so much of?'

Now it was Stan who grimaced.

'You, young lady, notice far too much,' he told her and she smirked.

'Brought up to be observant, you see. But never mind about Mum, look what I've got.' She pulled a letter out of her bag. 'It's from that firm we met at the expo. They're interested in sponsoring us – how great is that? And, even better, two of the other lads on the project are at Sheffield uni, so we're going to make that the base. I'm going to be at the heart of it all, Gramps! I can get into my accommodation in two weeks and I cannot wait!'

'That's fantastic! Well done, sweetheart.'

He grabbed her in a big hug. Bonnie bounded over too and they stood there, all locked together for a long, cosy moment before she pulled back and cried, 'Champagne!'

'Good idea,' Stan agreed. 'It feels like there's a lot to celebrate today.' To be honest, he could feel himself rapidly tiring and wanted little more than a mug of tea and maybe a kip, but that wouldn't be very supportive, would it? 'Sorry Bon, could you get it?' he asked.

'Course. Absolutely. You've had a busy day. You have a sitdown and tell Greya all about the house. Well, not *all* about it, but you know what I mean.'

He could hear the laughter in her voice again and was glad of it. He hated having to send her to the kitchen like a maid, but his legs had gone on strike and he could do little more than sink into his armchair. Bonnie made for the kitchen and Greya came scuttling over to kneel down at his feet.

'Glad I caught you, actually, Gramps,' she said in a whisper, whipping out her phone and flicking the now familiar Cherry

Creek logo to life. 'I changed your profile back to the original kind, warm and caring thing like you said and we've had another very promising-looking response.'

Both of them glanced to the door but they could hear Bonnie through in the back of the house, finding glasses. Greya shoved a picture under Stan's nose and he looked at a kind-eyed man with a shy smile. Not quite as good-looking as Greya's previous choices, and definitely the sort of bloke Stan would strike up a conversation with at a bar. He looked interesting and intelligent and fun. Best of all, he looked healthy. Stan felt a bitter twinge of jealousy at all this man might have before him, especially if it included his Bonnie.

'He's called Martin,' Greya went on as Stan struggled to control his emotions. 'He's been widowed two years but he does lots with himself, not like weirdo Lawrence. He's a retired lawyer with his own house not far from here and he claims to like walking, wine and art. Sounds good, right?'

'Art?' Stan repeated, his jealousy ranking up another notch. This man, this Martin, would know his Turners from his Warhols so he might suit Bonnie more than Stan. Not that that would surprise him. He'd always known there must be someone better out there and just clung on to his luck at keeping her all these years. But why stand in the way now?

He glanced to the door again. He could hear Bonnie singing 'You Sexy Thing' to herself and the fridge opening and closing. She'd be finding nibbles to make an occasion of it – and to be sure the wine didn't go to his tired head – so they had a minute or two yet.

'Does he want to meet?'

'He does, Gramps, and here's the best bit – he says there's a band called the Jetsetters that he likes playing in town. I said that I – that's you – like them too and he suggested you meet at the gig, and guess where it is?'

Stan swallowed.

'I know where it is.'

But Greya wasn't really listening.

'It's at the Cavern, Gramps! You know, where you used to . . .'

'I know about the Cavern, thank you, Grey. I'm just not sure about meeting someone there. I . . .'

'Stan?' Bonnie's voice called. 'Do you know where the hummus is?'

'Oops,' Greya called back. 'Sorry, Granny, I ate it.'

'No problem. I'll find something else. Could you help me carry, Grey?'

Greya looked apologetically at Stan.

'Go!' he said, nodding her to the door.

He watched as she leaped up, her legs like springs. He'd been like that once, running up and down the Cavern steps helping bands with their equipment. He closed his eyes and pictured the old place. Saw the low ceilings and the smoke-fugged air, smelled the rotten veg and the sweat and heard the raw, exciting sound of the Merseybeat kicking into gear.

'I want to go,' he said.

'Sorry, Grandpa?'

He opened his eyes to see Greya standing before him bearing a tray of nibbles and Bonnie at her shoulder, champagne bottle in one hand, three glasses in the other. Both were staring down at him.

'Want to go where, Stan?' Bonnie asked gently.

'To the Cavern. I want to go back to the Cavern.' He looked to Greya. 'This band you were talking about, Grey . . .?'

'The Jetsetters?'

'That's them. Could you, er, sort it out?' She nodded and Stan looked to Bonnie. 'Greya and I are going to see a band together.'

'How lovely. And at the Cavern, too?'

'Yep.' Out of the corner of his eye he could already see Greya tapping away on her phone and he felt a surge of panic. 'Would you like to come?'

Greya paused, fingers hovering over the screen as Bonnie set the bottle and glasses carefully on the table and considered. Stan leaned over and placed a hand on one of hers.

'You don't have to, sweetheart. I've got Greya to take me, remember?'

Bonnie looked to Greya who gave her most cherubic smile, then back to Stan.

'I think, if you're sure, I'd rather not.'

'Quite sure.' Stan said, pulling her close as, over her shoulder, Greya began tapping away again. 'Probably best if you don't. You said on that night that you'd never go back, and why change that?'

'What night?' Greya asked, looking up, but this time there was no hesitation from either of them.

'Doesn't matter,' Bonnie and Stan said as one.

And it didn't, not any more.

Chapter Twenty-Eight

Good Friday 1963

'And he said . . .' Susie-Ann paused dramatically, mascara wand halfway to her lashes, and eyed Bonnie in the big mirror propped up against the wall of Bonnie's little attic room. 'He said, "Susie-Ann, will you marry me?" '

'No way! What did you say?'

Susie-Ann grinned and slicked on mascara.

'I said, "Don't be a soft lad, Mickey, we've only just got back together. Ask me in a year and then we'll see."'

'No! Was he upset?'

'More relieved, actually. I think he only asked me cos he thought it was what I wanted, lord love him.'

She switched the mascara wand to the other eye but not before dabbing at both with a tissue. Bonnie smiled to herself.

'How did you resolve the university issue?'

'I pointed out that if I graduate I could earn, like, five hundred pounds a year, and he said in that case he could probably put up with a smart-arse and would I buy him his own garage.'

Bonnie laughed.

'He meant it,' Susie-Ann added.

'Good. He'll do well with it – if he's not a pop star, of course! I'm so glad you've sorted things out, Susie.'

'Yeah, me too. Thanks, Bon for, you know, pointing me in the right direction.' She threw herself on Bonnie in a sudden, sharp hug, then swung away again, embarrassed. 'And guess what – they've got some fancy car at his auld fella's place at the moment and he's letting Sticks borrow it this evening so we're off to the Cavern in style. Give it toes, Bonnie Jessop, or we'll be leaving without you.'

Bonnie smiled and grabbed her top. It felt strange to be getting ready to go out with the sun high in the sky but tonight was the Cavern's Good Friday R&B Marathon, featuring not just the Beatles but seven other local acts and it started at four, so they had to get a move on.

'Which skirt?' she asked, holding up two – both with several inches of hemline removed by Susie-Ann.

'The red one.'

'Isn't it a bit tarty?'

'Yes it is – that's why I chose it. You're only young once, lass, so make the most of it. Besides, we're picking Spike up on the way and he'll love it.'

Bonnie flushed. She'd gone over and over that moment at the ice rink with Spike, wondering what he'd been going to say. It had sounded very much as if he'd been asking her out again and she already knew that if he did she'd say yes. He'd been nothing but sweet to her since they'd split up, and she couldn't deny the jump in her heart every time he was close.

If you fancy it, why not? Nancy had told her and she fancied it with Spike, she was sure she did. Besides, Nancy was off doing who knows what with Astrid and it was time she got on and did the same. She imagined bringing gorgeous Spike home to meet her aunt and smiled at how surprised and delighted she'd be to see this evidence of her cool new life with the Best

Boys. Problem was, she'd only seen Spike briefly since Silver Blades, when he'd come to visit Danny in hospital. She'd been sat at his beside and Spike had nodded at her but honed in on the patient.

'When will you be able to play again, Dan? Will it be in time for Good Friday? Cos there might be a chance, you know. Epstein is going to be there and if there is – a chance, I mean – we need to be ready to seize it.'

Danny had looked a little dazed and Bonnie had excused herself and lurked about the corridor hoping to catch Spike on the way out. When he'd emerged, however, he'd already been late for work and had spun past her shouting apologies. He had at least run backward to blow her a kiss and had almost fallen through the doors as he did so and she'd laughed and put up a hand to catch it but he'd already been gone.

She'd not, therefore, been able to explain that she was not back with Danny but tonight she might get another chance, especially if they were picking Spike up first. She rushed to the mirror. Oh lordy, her hair was all over the place and her mascara was smudged and . . .

'Ooh, listen – is that Sticks?'

Susie-Ann scrambled for the window as a car horn tooted. She shoved it open and leaned so far out Bonnie had to grab at her ankles for fear of her falling.

'Who's making all this racket in our street?' she shouted down.

Bonnie joined her in time to see Sticks pull up in a fancy new Ford Anglia and jump out just below them. He flung his arms wide.

''Tis I, your knight in shining armour, bringing your carriage to take you to the ball – well, the Cavern.'

'Even better,' Susie-Ann giggled and blew him a kiss before slamming down the window and making for the door. 'Come on, Bon – let's shoot.'

'But my hair . . .'

'We can sort it in the car. Come on!'

'OK, OK.'

Bonnie grabbed her bag and let Susie-Ann pull her down-stairs and out to where Sticks was proudly showing off his car to her brothers.

'Stand aside,' Susie-Ann commanded, shoving them apart and kissing her reinstated boyfriend full on the lips. 'Hey gorgeous.'

'Hey gorgeous yourself.'

Sticks pulled her in for another, longer kiss, to loud protests from Susie-Ann's brothers. Sticks finally prised himself away and opened the passenger door for her before doing the same for Bonnie at the rear. She slid onto the smart leather seats feeling very important and sat back as Sticks took the wheel and they pulled away.

'What does this do, Mickey?' Susie-Ann was asking, tapping on a dial. 'And this? And this?'

Bonnie listened to Sticks answering and felt as if she were a kid again, sat in the back of Aunt Nancy's old Morris Minor with her and her current 'friend' chattering as they drove to work or the shops or occasionally to the seaside. She'd loved staring out of the window at the world passing by, feeling the thrill of going somewhere special, and tonight was no different.

It was Easter Weekend. Nancy had written to say she was back from Sweden with all sorts of goodies for Bonnie to try. Tomorrow she was going home to her, safe in the knowledge that she'd survived two terms at uni, enjoyed them even. After the upset at the ice rink, everything seemed to be settling again, and now they were going back to the Cavern and the Beatles would be there. It was going to be a wonderful night, she was sure of it.

'There's Spike!' Susie-Ann called into her reverie and Bonnie snapped to attention to see Spike as he waved them into the pavement.

He looked very handsome in a new suit and she tugged nervously at her hair, but it was too late to do anything about it now. She would just have to rely on her smile, and luckily Spike seemed in a very good mood as he bounced in next to her.

'Evening, beautiful,' he said, grabbing her hand and kissing it loudly.

'Evening yourself,' she managed, flushing. 'Nice suit.'

'Thank you kindly. Fit for a star, d'you reckon?'

'Totally.'

'It was me da's, can you believe. Me mam found it up in the loft and took it in a bit, well a lot actually – Da's a fat git – but she's done a boss job, I reckon.'

'You look dead good.'

He preened.

'Thanks. I thought I ought to make an effort.' He gave her a sideways smile and her heart fluttered as if there was a nest of birds inside it; he was making an effort for *her*. It would all be OK. But then he went on, 'Epstein'll be there tonight and he might be looking out for the next hot property to come out of Liverpool.'

Her heart-birds had their wings instantly clipped, but he had a fair point.

'I've been rehearsing all our songs just in case,' he went on. 'What we need is for one of the bands to have an accident or sommat, and then . . .'

'Spike! You can't wish that on people.'

'Just a little one, Bon, not fatal, like. Just enough to keep them from getting to the Cavern on time and then we can step in and save the day.'

'And grab a recording contract whilst you're at it?'

'Exactly! It's all about being in the right place at the right time. Epstein's the key, I'm sure of it and tonight just might be the night. I hear the Roadrunners' singer had flu last week so who knows – they might want a stand-in.'

'They wouldn't need a whole band, though.'

'Well, no. Good job with Danny still all bandaged up but *I* should be prepared, right? Drink?'

He took a flask from the inner pocket of his new jacket and offered it to Bonnie.

'What is it?'

'Rum. Found it in here. How lucky is that?'

Bonnie eyed the flask nervously.

'When did your dad last wear the suit, Spike?'

'Me uncle's wedding – 1951.'

'That's twelve years ago!'

'So? Rum don't go off, does it? Tastes fine. And I needed a bit of courage before I saw you. Bonnie, I . . .'

But just then Sticks turned into Matthew Street and pulled up just past the Cavern and anything Spike might have been going to say was drowned out by the sound of five hundred excited fans waiting to get inside for the biggest night of the year so far.

'You lot get out,' Sticks said. 'I'll go and ditch the motor. I won't be long.'

'I'll come with you,' Susie-Ann told him.

'But it's four o'clock,' Bonnie said, pointing to the Cavern doors as they creaked open.

'We won't be long.'

'Not long at all,' Sticks agreed, a catch in his throat.

Bonnie rolled her eyes and climbed out.

'Suit yourselves.'

'Oh, we will,' Susie-Ann assured her wickedly and then they were gone, leaving Bonnie and Spike to head for the queue shuffling down the stone steps into the best of cellars.

Bonnie glanced at Spike, hoping he might take her hand as he'd done at the ice rink last week, but he was looking at the Cavern entrance, oblivious to anything around him.

'Susie and Sticks seem very happy to be back together,' she said, looking up at him through her eyelashes. He turned to her.

'Yeah. They're good.' He paused and the birds in her heart started up their fluttering again. 'And you, Bonnie – what's happening with you and Dan?'

'Nothing, Spike. That is, we're friends and I was worried about him, you know, but there's nothing more between us now.'

'Right. So you're single, like.'

'I am.'

He was going to say something, she was sure he was, but now someone in the crowd called out and he turned to see what was going on. Those at the front were pointing at them and nudging each other and Spike's hands went straight to his hair. He stepped away from Bonnie as his walk bounced into a swagger.

'All right, ladies,' he said, but no one paid him any attention.

All eyes were fixed over his shoulders and, as the screaming began, Bonnie turned to see John, Paul, George and Ringo sauntering towards them. The bouncers leaped into action, hustling everyone back as the boys headed for the door but the crowd were wild for their home-grown stars and broke free of the cord to mob them. Bonnie found herself crushed up against Spike, but he was staring furiously over her head at the fab four.

'Dunno what all the fuss is about,' he grumbled. 'Paul's just a blert from the year above, like, and the rest the same. They're not superhuman.'

Bonnie looked at him, surprised.

'Well, no, but you've got to admit they're pretty famous.'

'Maybe I will be too, one day.'

'I hope you are.'

'Then you can say you knew me.'

'*Knew* you, Spike – past tense?'

'What?'

He looked at her, confused, but just then she heard someone else calling her name and turned to see Danny loping awkwardly towards them, his hand in a bandage. Her heart dropped. Danny was nothing to her now. It felt as if last weekend on the ice he'd revealed his true self and she didn't like it one bit. She'd done her best to be civil to him, with him being injured and so upset about it, but she'd been desperately hoping he'd feel too ill to come tonight.

'You made it,' she said awkwardly.

'Wouldn't miss it for the world. I don't reckon the Beatles'll be playing little venues like this much longer, so it's good to catch them now.'

'They're just local lads,' Spike repeated.

'Well, yes, but they're local lads who've made it big, right? How cool is that?'

Spike grunted and Bonnie felt her world shift slightly.

'We were just saying that it could be the Best Boys like that in a year or so,' she said brightly.

'Well actually . . .' Danny started, but Spike interrupted him.

'Not with a drummer who keeps buggering off and a guitarist with no finger,' he snapped and marched forward a few steps leaving Bonnie and Danny stood in his wake.

'What's got into him?' Danny asked.

Bonnie shrugged, her spirits plunging. This was not how she'd imagined her reunion with Spike.

'He thinks tonight might be the night to get Epstein's attention but I'm not sure how he means to do it. How's your hand?'

'Doing well, thanks. Doc says I'll probably have a scar for life that but I was lucky not to lose it. Thank you so much, Bonnie, for looking after me. You don't know how much it means to have you care.' He leaned in. 'You do care? I mean, I know I was a bit of an idiot.'

'Idiot?'

'OK, a cruel, miserable bastard. I've been trying so hard to be gentlemanly, Bonnie, because you deserve it, you really do, but I guess I'm just a crass butcher's son after all.'

'There's nothing wrong with being a butcher's son, Danny – that's not an excuse.'

'No. No, you're right. I just fancy you so much, Bon, and with the drugs and that I got carried away. I'm sorry. You just shouldn't be so beautiful.'

'So it's my fault?'

'No. No, of course not. Oh God, I'm not doing this right. But I've got some good news, really. Please just give me another chance.'

'I don't think so, Danny. Look, we're going in.'

The people ahead of them had plunged inside and she turned to follow as quickly as she could. The stone steps led downwards, and she looked out over a sea of Brylcreemed quiffs and set bobs. The first band were calling out a welcome somewhere below the arches. She could see Spike's slicked-back hair just two steps ahead and as she stepped through the doorway he looked back and suddenly, unexpectedly, gave her a big wink.

She smiled at him but then Danny's plaintive voice called her name from behind and Spike turned away again. The mixed smell of damp, veg and sweat swarmed up the steps and for a moment she hesitated, but she told herself not to be so stupid and moved determinedly out of the sunshine and into the bowels of Matthew Street. Never mind about the boys, any of them. It was Good Friday, the Merseybeat was going to rock until midnight and she was a part of it – what could be better?

It was completely crushed inside, with hundreds of fans dancing and chatting and roaring encouragement at the

Roadrunners who had taken the stage with, much to Spike's disappointment, their lead singer in fine form.

'He's off-key,' he grumbled, turning to Bonnie as they made it into the main part of the little club. 'Isn't he, Bonnie? Isn't he off-key?'

He sounded fine to Bonnie, but she was so glad Spike was speaking to her again that she didn't want to say so and was relieved when they reached the cloakroom and she could turn away to hand her coat to Lee.

'Hey Bonnie, good to see you.'

His smile was so genuine that she felt instantly better.

'Good to be here. Busy, isn't it?'

'Madness. Cilla and I are run off our webs and she's full of cold, lord love her.'

'Need a hand?'

'No. No, we'll manage. You enjoy yourself.'

'I liked being in the cloakroom, it was fun.'

'And I liked you being in the cloakroom too, but the management are on proper high-alert tonight, so best not. You might be a superfan trying to get to the Beatles.'

'A superfan?'

'Crazy people who'd do anything to get close. Management found a girl crammed into the cupboard in the dressing room earlier. She'd been there since last night. Poor bird was so stiff they had to carry her out. Imagine if she'd actually stayed there til the Beatles arrived – she'd have literally fallen at their feet.'

Bonnie laughed and a little of the tension of her arrival drained out of her.

'The Beatles came in at the same time as us. It was madness.'

'I bet. Here, touch me and maybe some of their fame'll rub off.'

He held out his hand and on impulse Bonnie took it and kissed it.

'I hope it does,' she said but he just stood there, staring at the lipstick imprint on his skin. 'Oops, sorry.'

She reached out to wipe the pink stain off but he snatched his hand back.

'It's fine. I'd best get on or Wooler'll go mad.'

'Too right,' Cilla agreed, her voice sounding more nasal than usual and her poor nose red with cold. 'Hey, girl – you helping out?'

'She can't tonight,' Lee snapped and Cilla raised her eyebrows.

'Someone's touchy.'

'Someone's been running the cloakroom single-handed whilst someone else sucks up to Epstein.'

'Oh sack it, Lee, I've gorra try all I can.' Cilla turned to Bonnie. 'He might sign me, you know. I might make a record.'

'Epstein might?' Spike demanded over Bonnie's shoulder.

Cilla fixed her sharp eyes on him.

'That's right. What's it to you?'

'Is he here?'

'Course he is, stupid. He . . .'

But Spike was gone, plunging into the crowd. Bonnie gave Cilla an apologetic smile.

'That's fantastic news, Cilla,' she said.

'It is,' Lee agreed, softening enough to give his co-worker a friendly nudge. 'But until then there's coats need hanging up.'

Cilla rolled her eyes.

'Cracks the whip, this one – though he's a softie inside, all right. You heard his song – "Watching Her"?'

'Lee's song?' She turned to him. 'I thought Spike wrote "Watching Her"?'

'Spike?' Cilla laughed. 'No way. He's just a chancer with an eye for a hit. It's all Lee's, and proper fantastic it is too.'

Bonnie longed to hear more but the queue was getting impatient and she had little choice but to let the pair get to

302

work and head after Spike. But Danny was still at her shoulder and now he grabbed her arm.

'What?' she demanded, trying to shake him off, but he was pointing into the crowd and she saw Spike talking animatedly to a tall slim older man.

'Who's that?'

'It's Brian Epstein! Lord, what's Spike saying to him?'

Bonnie pressed closer and heard Spike say something about the Best Boys. She caught the words 'Riverboat Shuffle' and 'rapturous reception' and had to admire his guts, but Epstein did not seem impressed.

'I'm not looking for a new group right now,' she heard the legendary manager say.

'You want solos?' Spike asked.

'Yes, but I have . . .'

'I can go solo.'

Bonnie stared at Spike, shocked, but his eyes were fixed on the Beatles' manager, who was looking round for an escape. Danny had heard too, though, and barged forward, waving his bandaged hand furiously in Spike's face.

'You can go solo?' he demanded. 'Well thanks, Spike. Sack off the rest of us, why don't you?'

'Because you're in a real fit state to play, right?'

'Someone nearly sliced my finger off.'

'Only because you were lying on the damn ice off your face on LSD. That's hardly commitment is it?'

'We'd finished playing.'

'And now you're finished playing for weeks. I need more than that.'

'Because you're the star?'

'Exactly.'

'The star who'd step away from his band without a moment's hesitation?'

Bonnie saw Epstein starting to edge away and tried to catch Spike's attention but he was locked on to Danny.

'Oh, and you wouldn't?'

'No! We're the Best Boys. We're a group. Groups stay together.'

'Sticks didn't.'

'Sticks came back.'

'Yeah, well, drummers can't go solo, can they? Who'd listen to that? What Mr Epstein here needs is singers with charisma and style and . . . Oh.' Finally he looked around but Brian Epstein had slid away into the protection of the crowd. 'Damn you, Danny – I had him there.'

Danny shook his head.

'No you didn't, Spike. But listen.' He made a visible effort to control himself. 'It's OK. It's all going to be OK. I've been trying to tell you – I had a call yesterday.'

'From who?'

Danny smiled secretively.

'From who, Danny?' pressed Spike.

'I'm not sure I should tell you if you wanna go solo.'

Spike rolled his eyes.

'Don't be a baby, Dan. All I said was that I could if I had to, like. Call from who?'

Reluctantly Danny relented.

'Billy J. Kramer. Turns out he was at Silver Blades last Saturday. Wanted to hear us play a full set.'

'And . . .?'

'And he'd like to join us when we play there tomorrow – see how we fit.'

'As his backing group?' Danny nodded. 'Great.'

Spike's voice was flat and Bonnie saw Danny's disappointment written clear across his face and stepped in between them.

'It's a start, Spike,' she said.

'I guess.' He looked mournfully after Epstein, just in time to see him sliding through the stage door at the back of the Cavern. He frowned again and turned back to Danny. 'But how on earth are we going to play with you looking like a bloody mummy?'

'I've arranged a stand-in.'

'A stand-in? Oh goodie! Cos they go really well, don't they? Will we get to rehearse with the dead pigs again, Dan, like real pros? And where will this one be sick – on the ice? Maybe they won't have cleared your blood up yet and it can be like some sort of body fluid art.'

Danny stared furiously at him, then spun on his heel and pushed away through the crowd. Bonnie was relieved to see him go, but not this way.

'Spike!' she said. 'Don't be horrible.'

His shoulders sank.

'Sorry, Bon, but really, the Best Boys are a joke at the moment.'

'That's not true! Billy J. Kramer's a big deal, and he wants you lot to play with him.'

Spike sighed and, apparently without thinking, reached for her hand. She felt his fingers warm around her own and held her breath as he stood there, lost in thought whilst everyone else in the heaving cellar seemed to fade into a low hum.

'Billy J. Kramer and the Best Boys?' he said eventually.

'It sounds good.'

'It does, but Bonnie – he'd be the star.'

She nodded. She could see that would be hard for Spike.

'It'd be experience, though. And you'd play big gigs, meet people.'

'You're right.' His head went up and he looked straight at her. 'You're always right, Bonnie. And besides, the Beatles are last on so Epstein's here all night. I might yet get to show him what I can do.'

'You might, Spike.'

He stepped closer.

'You're a proper stunner, Bon. Did I mention that before?'

'Once, I think.'

She remembered the first time he'd kissed her, in the stairwell at the Jacaranda, and moved a little closer. He looked intently down into her eyes and the birds in her heart began fluttering once more. This was the real Spike again at last – the honest local lad from down the docks with a passion for a music and a burning desire to make the most of himself and he was so, so gorgeous.

'I've missed you, lass. I know we weren't together long but I was really happy with you and I messed it up, I know I did. Like Sticks did with Susie-Ann. We're stupid, us lads, can't see what's good for us sometimes. But you, Bonnie Jessop, you are so good for me and I really like you.'

His face was so close to hers now that she could feel his breath against her lips and longed for more.

'I like you too, Spike.'

'You do? Will you go out with me again, then? Please.'

There was only one answer.

'Yes,' she said. 'Oh yes.' And then his lips were on hers and the birds in her heart were singing fit to burst as the Cavern sprang back to life around them.

Chapter Twenty-Nine

Bonnie thought she'd never been happier. The Cavern was alive with dancing and she was right at the heart of it. She could barely stomp for Spike's arms tight around her waist but she didn't care. He felt so good against her, his lips brushing her neck, his voice husky in her ear telling her how wonderful she was.

'You'll be at my side all the way to the top, won't you?' he whispered as they paused for breath.

She giggled and spun round in his arms to face him.

'Course I will. You and all the Best Boys. I wouldn't miss that mansion for the world, Spike.'

He kissed her.

'I can see you now, lying by the pool in a bikini when we have parties for all the fancy folk. We'll invite Elvis and Bob Dylan. And the Beatles'll beg to come too, right?'

'They'll be the Best Boys' best mates, Spike.'

'God, yes.' He grinned wickedly but then someone bumped into him, sending him sideways and he blinked and looked almost crossly around. 'But we're not going to do it as a bloody backing group. We've gotta get that contract. Where's Epstein gone?'

He peered into the crowd but Brian Epstein was nowhere to be seen.

'He'll still be in the dressing room with the Beatles,' Bonnie said, nodding to the little door to the far right of the heaving Cavern.

Spike looked at it longingly but then gave a resigned sigh. 'True enough. Come on, queen, let's dance again.'

She didn't need asking twice. Sticks and Susie-Ann were with them, happily locked together, and Bonnie felt as bubbly with joy as she had that night in the Jac when Susie-Ann had first introduced her to the Best Boys and this crazy Merseybeat world had opened up to her. The only difference was that Lee was stuck in the cloakroom and Danny was standing against the wall, watching her and Spike, his eyes glazed over.

'Is Danny on something?' she asked Spike.

He looked over.

'Nah. Well, only rum. I gave him my hipflask. Seemed only fair as I'd got you.'

He leaned in to nuzzle at her neck but Bonnie ducked away, uneasy at his casual tone.

'I'm not some commodity to be bartered, Spike.'

'Hey?'

'I make my own choices, I'll have you know.'

'I do know, and you chose me.' He flashed her a cheeky grin. 'And I'm made up about it. Danny just looked like he needed a little consolation, that's all.'

It sounded a bit better that way and if Bonnie doubted the wisdom of Danny's "consolation", it was hardly her place to say so. And anyway, there was dancing to get on with. She threw her hands in the air and stomped as wildly as everyone else as the penultimate band rocked out their final number. The Beatles were up next and the very walls of the Cavern buzzed with anticipation. Bonnie felt her heart beat faster as the song wound to a close.

'This'll be a night to tell the grandkids about, hey?' she called to Spike.

He stiffened a little and she feared she'd scared him but it was apparently not the prospect of family life that had jarred.

'Not as good as the Shuffle.'

'Er, no.'

'Or our next big gig, or our first recording session, or . . .'

'Not as good as any of those, Spike.'

She kissed him and though he resisted at first, he soon gave way.

'I just want to get you that mansion, Bon.'

'I'll design it for you.'

'You? Oh yes, the architecture thing. Great. A dream house!'

'Exactly. Spike . . .'

But Spike was looking to the stage. The band had finished and techies were rushing on with the Beatles' extra-big amps. People rushed to the front, girls pulling rollers from their hair and reapplying lippie as they fought to get into the sightline of a Beatle, and Spike watched it all with longing so raw that Bonnie could almost smell it. What would he do to succeed, and could she keep pace with that?

Judy Tyler to his Elvis, she reminded herself and put her head up as Nancy had always taught her. She needed to stop changing her mind and just embrace life – and what a life it was right now. The calls of the fans grew, bouncing back off the low ceilings so that the best of cellars reverberated with anticipation, but still the dressing room door stayed shut. The techies were fiddling with wires and frowning and Bonnie spotted Bob Wooler mopping his brow and pacing in the tiny space between the cloakroom and the stage.

'This is going to take a while,' Susie-Ann said into Bonnie's ear. 'We're heading to the loo.'

'Now?'

'Yes, now. It'll be deserted. Perfect!'

She gave Bonnie a huge wink.

'You're going to . . .?'

'You bet. Sex in the Cavern – one for the tick list.'

Bonnie looked at her incredulously.

'But the Beatles . . .'

'Will be ages yet. We'll find you again, don't you worry. And you've got Spike, anyway. He'll keep you amused.' She lowered her voice. 'Glad that's all sorted for you, by the way. Told you you still liked him, didn't I?'

Bonnie laughed and hugged her friend.

'You're so wise, Susie! Go on – get off with you. But hurry back.'

'We will,' she promised and then they were gone, wriggling through the crowd towards the gents.

'Where are they going?' Danny demanded, stepping up next to her.

'Where d'you think?'

'Lucky gits.' He took out Spike's hipflask, put it to his lips, then took it away again and upended it. 'Empty. Bugger.'

'Maybe you've had enough.'

'Maybe I've had nothing at all.'

His eyes were red-rimmed and bloodshot and seemed to drill into her in the low light and she wished again that he'd stayed at home, and was grateful when Spike peeled himself away from the Beatles' amps to tug on her arm.

'What's Wooler up to?' Bonnie looked across and saw the Cavern manager speaking urgently with Cilla. The redhead was shaking her head and spreading her hands wide. 'Looks like he wants her to sing.'

'She can't, though. She's got a sore throat.'

'Oh. Right. Bet she's proper cross – big crowd like this.' Spike's eyes lit up. 'Tell you what – I'll do it.'

He pushed through the girls at the front, heading for Wooler, but now Cilla was climbing onto the stage after all and dragging someone behind her.

'Lee!' Bonnie gasped.

Lee looked stunned but Wooler was grasping the one mic still wired for sound.

'Just a little delay, folks, but we'll soon be getting the Beatles out for you.' Screams greeted this and Wooler waited for them to die down before saying, 'But in the meantime here's a treat from our very own cloakroom boy, Lee, singing an original song – "Watching Her".'

'No!' Spike cried. He looked desperately at Bonnie as the huge crowd in the Cavern turned their faces expectantly up to Lee. Cilla shoved a guitar into Lee's hand and nudged him forward to the mic and something like silence fell. 'No,' Spike said again. 'Not Lee, not with Epstein here.' He looked around frantically. 'It should be me. He needs *me*.'

He made a move towards the stage but Danny put a big hand on his shoulder.

'Leave it, Spike.'

Spike glared at him.

'Why? What's he doing up there without us?'

'Maybe he's going solo,' Danny sneered.

'No! No way. This is a Best Boys song. You may be bitter cos you've lost your finger – not to mention your bloody girl-friend – but I don't see why I have to lose out too.'

'Spike!' Bonnie said, horrified, but Spike wasn't listening.

He was glaring at Lee as the older lad cleared his throat and the sound echoed round the Cavern. He looked more like a rabbit in the headlights than a pop star in the making and Bonnie's breath caught in her throat.

'Can he do it?' she croaked.

'Course not,' Spike said. 'He's a backing singer, norra front man. He's frozen – look.'

Sure enough Lee seemed fixed on stage, his fingers twitching nervously at his guitar as all eyes stared up at him. The crowd started to murmur. Someone called, 'Get on with it then!' and Cilla nudged Lee frantically. He looked blankly at her and she smiled and nodded him on, though Bonnie saw even her ever-ready confidence slipping.

'See,' Spike said. 'I'll have to do it. I know the song and I'm better at it anyway.'

He pushed forward and people turned, spotted his swagger and parted before him. Bonnie followed in his wake, unsure what to do for the best. On the one hand, Lee did seem to be struggling, and if Epstein was here then it was stupid not to make the most of the moment. On the other hand, it was Lee's song. She looked up at the earnest older lad on the stage and saw his aquiline profile caught in the lights, sharp and handsome.

'Don't, Spike,' Bonnie called. 'Not yet. Let him try.'

But Spike barely even glanced back as he said, 'He's had his chance. It's my turn now.'

And with that he stepped onto the stage and offered Lee his most charming smile.

'I'm here for you, mate. I can do this now.'

His voice was low but forceful and it rippled across the near-silent crowd as they pushed in towards the two young men facing each other on the stage. Everyone in the Cavern watched, transfixed, as Spike held out his hand for the guitar and Lee looked down at it.

Sing, Lee, Bonnie willed him. She knew she should be loyal to Spike but right at this moment her gorgeous boyfriend looked ugly in the stark glare of his own ambition and she didn't like it. 'Watching Her' was Lee's song. This was Lee's moment.

'He's scared,' Danny drawled into her ear, standing closely up against her.

Bonnie tried to wriggle away but the crowd were crushed in and there was nowhere left to go. And now they were chanting 'Sing, sing, sing' at poor Lee, driving him further to the back of the stage with every word. Spike held out a hand to his old friend and then, in one slick movement, seized the microphone and, without a single chord to accompany him, began to sing,

She doesn't know, she doesn't see,
She doesn't feel a thing for me . . .

His voice was a little husky but as the crowd stilled and he picked up the lilting melody, it grew in strength. He turned his back on Lee and stepped to the front of the stage, feeding off the girls who held out their hands to him. Bonnie saw him glance to the left where the stage door was opening and Brian Epstein was sliding out. Instantly his chest puffed out and he turned up the power. Bonnie didn't know whether to be proud or sickened. She willed Spike to meet her eyes, to sing to her, to prove that she'd been right to get back with him, but he didn't even glance her way.

Behind him, Lee seemed to come to a decision. Quietly he lifted his guitar and picked out the melody for Spike.

She doesn't sense my poor heart stir,
She doesn't know I'm watching her.

With the guitar, the song came to life and Bonnie saw Lee's head lift as if sensing it and now he was singing too. The crowd leaned in intently but the second voice threw Spike and he stumbled over the lines and flushed dark red.

Bonnie heard Danny give a nasty little laugh as Lee stepped forward and into the song, carrying it on into the chorus alone. His voice wasn't as strident as Spike's but it had a soft sweetness that seemed to ooze amongst the five hundred people crushed into the Cavern and charm them into utter hush.

I'm watching her,
But she can't see,
How much I wish,

She was watching me.

Lee's eyes seemed to find Bonnie homing in on her through the crowd and singing straight to her. She stared back, transfixed, but then Danny gave a low growl behind her.

'Not him too,' he snarled. 'It's everyone but me, isn't it, Bonnie Jessop? Everyone but bloody me. Well I'm not having it, not any more. I was good to you and you owe me.'

'*Owe* you, Danny?'

She dragged her eyes from the stage and, as if with that one small movement she'd released his cage door, Danny dived. His lips fixed onto hers and instantly his hands were roaming all over her body, probing at the hem of her wretched tarty skirt as if he might rip it off right there in front of everyone. She tried to fight him off but he was as strong as he'd always assured her he was and held her tight.

'No!' she screamed, the moment he came up for breath.

She feared the cry would be swallowed up by the crowd but then the girl next to her looked over and as their eyes met she must have seen the panic in Bonnie's.

'Oi, lad!' she shouted shrilly. 'What the buggery do you think you're doing to her?'

Danny, lost in his own dark desires, only tightened his grip but now others were turning and, in a crash of strings, both boys on stage stopped singing.

'It's OK, she wants it,' Danny rasped, pushing his hand higher under her skirt and Bonnie felt the sharp twist of humiliation and closed her eyes against the horror of it.

She heard the crowds shift as someone fought towards her and, even whilst she longed for him, she feared Spike would be no match for her powerful assailant. But then came a cry of fury and she opened her eyes in time to see a fist swing straight into Danny's face. His hands flew to his nose as blood spurted and he staggered backward.

'She said no!' a furious voice roared, and Bonnie looked weakly up at her saviour and gasped.

'Lee!'

'Are you OK, Bonnie? Did he hurt you?'

He leaned in and she tried to reply but she couldn't get enough of the thick, stinky air in the Cavern to breathe.

'Come on.' He put a gentle arm around her shoulders. 'Let's get you out of here.'

'But your song . . .' she choked out.

'Is in good hands.'

Lee gestured back to Spike, still stood on stage, holding the microphone. Bonnie looked up at her supposed boyfriend but his eyes slid away from hers to where Epstein was still standing by the stage door and he reached, instead, for Lee's abandoned guitar.

'You can't let him have it,' she gasped, but Lee just laughed.

'Of course I can. It's just a song, Bonnie, and I wrote it for you anyway. Let's go.'

His arm tightened around her and she leaned gratefully into it and let him lead her through the staring crowd. Her legs were shaking and the fight to the door seemed to be taking forever. But then, out of the corner of her eye, she saw Epstein turn and pull open the stage door, releasing the Beatles into the tense atmosphere.

For a millisecond Bonnie seemed to be the only one who had noticed but then those closest spotted them too and the Cavern went insane. As the crowd surged to the front, a welcome sliver of space opened at the back and Bonnie gulped in the clearer air as Lee guided her to the stairs.

'Lee!' A voice stopped them, loud and distressed even over the screams of Beatlemania. They looked back to see Wooler fighting his way after them. 'Lee, where are you going?'

'Out of here,' Lee said, his voice clear and certain. 'Don't expect me back.'

'But you can make something of yourself, Lee. I know you can.'

Lee just shrugged.

'I've had enough, Bob. This isn't the place for me.'

His arm tightened around Bonnie and he began propelling her forward again as, on stage, Spike was thrust aside and the first chords of 'Love Me Do' bounced off the ceiling to cries of rapture. It had been Bonnie's favourite song for so long but now it sounded mocking and she closed her ears to it.

'Lee!' Wooler called, desperately. 'Don't go, Lee. Stanley!'

But they'd reached the narrow stairs and, without a moment's hesitation, began to climb up and away, leaving the music world behind them in a tangle of broken strings at the foot of the Cavern stage.

Chapter Thirty

The Cavern Club the sign said, just as it always had. Stan stared up at it, lost for a moment in some strange gap in time. He'd left here back in 1963 on a tide of anger and fierce, desperate protectiveness and had never been back. He'd been glad when they'd pulled the damned place down in the seventies but here it was, resurrected, and here he was too, and it felt . . . He fumbled around in his fading heart to see how it felt but there was only one real answer – it felt good.

The Cavern Club he read again and despite everything, the three simple words put an instant bounce into his tired old legs. He put an automatic hand to his head to slick back his quiff but got only the last wisps of the hair that time and chemotherapy had left to him. He sighed and looked around.

'OK, Stan?'

He jumped. For a moment he'd forgotten Bonnie was here. Not that she was meant to be, but at breakfast this morning she'd sprung a surprise on him.

'I've been thinking about the Cavern, Stan,' she'd said, all coy as she poured him more tea.

'You have?' he'd asked.

'I have. A lot. And, well, I think I was wrong.'

'About what?'

'About not wanting to come with you. After all, you didn't want to go to the house, did you, but you still did it. For me. So why shouldn't I come to the Cavern for you?'

'Oh Bonnie, you don't have . . .'

'And for me too. I was eighteen when I ran away from that place, Stan. I've had fifty-five years to get past that stupid night – it really ought to be enough.'

Then she'd reached up and kissed him and he'd felt unendingly blessed – as well as really rather stupid. Here she was, making a big romantic gesture whilst he snuck around dating other people behind her back. He'd pictured her meeting Martin and his heart had quailed.

'What about tickets?' he'd stuttered, but she'd just smiled and said she'd called them and there were several left.

How could he have said no? All that had been left to do had been to send an urgent message to Martin asking him not to come, or at least not to talk to him. He just hoped it had got through.

'The Cavern Club,' Greya read out loud now, bouncing up behind him. 'Cool. And you played here, Grandpa?'

'Once or twice. Mainly I worked in the cloakroom.' He peered up at the brightly lit entrance. 'It's in the wrong place.'

'What is?'

'The door.'

'It looks OK to me,' Greya said, squinting up at it.

'It is, but this isn't the original. That was a bit further down the street, right Bonnie?'

'If you say so,' she agreed, taking his arm.

He'd known it would be. The project to restore the closed-down Cavern Club had been set up in the wake of John Lennon's tragic death at the start of the eighties, but structural problems had meant it had to be reconstructed a little further down Matthew Street. Still, word had it that they'd done a good job and the fact that it was skewed sideways felt right somehow.

He was glad, now, that he'd made the effort to come and glad, too, that Bonnie was with him. She'd been such an important part of it, after all, and it was far better to have her here than some random man off an app. He just hoped Martin stayed away.

'And you played here, Grandpa?' Greya was asking. 'You really played here?'

He looked back to her.

'I did, Grey, with the Best Boys.'

'That's so cool. Did you know the Beatles then?'

Stan waited for Bonnie to freeze, but it didn't happen.

'A bit,' he admitted. 'I went to school with Paul.'

'Paul McCartney?'

'That's the one.'

'That's so cool, Grandpa. He's, like, an icon of pop culture.'

Stan smiled.

'That's true, but there were hundreds of bands in Liverpool in the early sixties, Greya. I mean literally hundreds. Everyone was at it, and most of us played here. It was obvious fairly quickly that the Beatles had something special about them but no one knew they'd be such megastars. They were just Liverpool lads, you see. Liverpool lads didn't get famous.'

'It could have been you.'

'Well, now . . .'

'Maybe if Epstein had signed the Best Boys instead of the Beatles, it would have been you off touring America and making crazy albums and becoming icons.'

Stan smiled.

'It was close,' he admitted. 'Things were starting to happen for us, so we could maybe have done more.'

'Why didn't you?'

Now Stan did feel Bonnie stiffen. He thought back – back to that night when the Beatles, without anyone knowing it at the time, had sung their penultimate gig at the Cavern and Spike had stolen Stan's mic and Danny had turned nasty and Stan had thrown his beloved guitar aside and taken Bonnie into his arms instead. He smiled.

'I had more important things to do, didn't I, Bonnie?'

She gave him a tight smile back.

'Shall we go in?'

Greya stood back to let them go first. Stan eyed the steep stairs down into the 'best of cellars' with a mixture of nostalgia, joy and physical fear. At least the stairs were wider than they used to be and had a handrail. He clutched it firmly and began to descend, memories clouding around him.

They'd been such happy days, exciting ones too, but as he doddered down the steps he knew that, even with cancer eating at his gut, he was happier now. Life had been so worrying then. The future had still been his to write, and whilst that had been thrilling, it had also been a huge responsibility. He'd been so desperate to get it right, but he'd not really had any idea what he was doing until that night when he'd put his arm around Bonnie and walked her up these steps and away from it all and never, ever looked back. Until today.

They'd reached the bottom at last and here was the desk, just as it had always been, only now with a smart little laptop replacing the laborious card system for checking membership. He found the tickets and handed them over to the young man behind the desk.

'Thank you, sir. Have you been to the Cavern before?'

Stan looked sideways for Bonnie but Greya came forward, all enthusiasm.

'Sure he has. Grandpa used to play here in the sixties.'

'Really, sir?'

'The Best Boys,' Stan admitted. 'It wasn't often. We weren't that big.'

'The Best Boys? Rings a bell. Hang on a minute.' He turned to a wall of black and white photos behind him, searched for a moment and then all of a sudden reached out a smooth young finger and pointed. 'There. That you, sir?'

Stan leaned in and saw the exact same photo that Greya had pulled out of Bonnie's special box a few weeks ago. He'd been a little embarrassed then but here, in the Cavern, it felt right. And, after all, it *was* him. Him and Sticks and Danny and Spike: the supposed Best Boys.

'That's us,' he said wonderingly. 'I had no idea we were on the wall.'

'Of course you are. We've got every band who ever played here. You're part of our history, sir.'

Stan stared at the wall, a glorious black and white patchwork of faces, all young, all hopeful. He honed in again on his own photo and there was Sticks beaming from behind his drums. He'd married Susie-Ann the minute she'd finished her degree and happily became a house husband to their four children as her political career rocketed.

His eyes moved sideways to Danny, tall and confident. He'd played with so many bands after the Best Boys collapsed that Stan had lost count. They hadn't spoken since that night, but Stan had kept discreet tabs on him through the music press and, later, Google. At some point around backing Oasis, Danny had switched to his real name, Justin, and at some point after that, the drugs had done for him and he'd sunk without a trace. His sister, mind you, still ran one of the biggest chains of butchers in the UK.

He clutched tightly at Bonnie's hand as his eyes moved to Spike, posing in the front, all 'look-at-me'. Once he'd finally dropped 'Spike' and gone back to being solid old John, he'd become a decent producer. He'd sent them a wedding present, the odd Christmas card and even, once, a sorry letter, and Stan had been glad to see him having some quiet success. He'd never married, mind, but he had golden discs instead of a ring and he seemed content.

'There's you, my love,' Bonnie said, pointing.

And indeed, there was him, 'Lee', looking shy but a little bit fierce – so determined to make it in a world that hadn't really suited him at all.

'You look like a film star, Grandpa, with those gorgeous cheekbones,' Greya said.

'I always thought that too,' Bonnie cried. 'I used to think a photographer would die to do a portrait of him.'

'When?' Stan asked, looking at her askance.

'Pretty much the first time I saw you.'

Stan flushed like a teen and kissed her, delighted now to see the Best Boys up there with Cilla, his old cloakroom mate, and the Beatles and Gerry and the Pacemakers and all the others who'd turned the music scene on its head from this damp, stinking cellar beneath the grimy Liverpool streets. But Greya wasn't done yet.

She had her phone out and was demanding selfies of them all by Stan's picture, and the lad on the desk rang for the manager, who bobbed up and insisted on shaking Stan's hand and offering him VIP seats, and all those in the thankfully modest queue were staring and pointing and some of them were taking pictures too.

'We weren't that big,' Stan said again, but no one was listening and Greya looked so pleased with it all that he just relaxed and smiled for the cameras and even waved a little and for a fraction of time he was it – the musician he'd so wanted to be right up until the day he'd found something better. He turned to Bonnie.

'You OK?'

She slapped at his arm.

'Will you stop asking me that, Stanley Walker. I'm more than OK. It's wonderful to see. Sometimes it's felt as if that whole part of our lives was an illusion, and I feel guilty now that we let that happen.'

'Guilty? Not the dream thing again, Bon?'

'No, not that. But they were amazing days, Stan, however they ended, and we shouldn't have let them fade as we have.'

'They just didn't really matter any more once we were making a business and a family and . . .'

'But they did, Stan.' He flinched at the vehemence in her voice. 'Sorry. I'm sorry, but this was a big part of you and you shouldn't have had to forget it.'

'I didn't, Bon,' he assured her. 'I just moved on.'

'And let it go, which was wrong. I knew that, really. That's why I kept the box of memorabilia, but what use was it in the back of the garage? We should have had it on the mantelpiece, should have had the Best Boys picture on the wall like they do here. I'm so sorry, Stan.'

She looked tearful and he hated it.

'Please don't apologise. If I'd wanted that I could have done it myself, couldn't I? It really didn't matter to me, sweetheart, though it's kind of fun to be back now.'

'It is.' She smiled at him and, thankfully, blinked away her tears before they fell. 'But Stan, what if Greya's right – what if Epstein *had* signed the Best Boys?'

He laughed.

'But he didn't. And that's fine. We've had a wonderful life, Bonnie.'

'We have, but the band was your dream, as the house was mine, and it doesn't seem fair that we've nearly got the house but you'll never, ever get the band.'

He laughed again.

'The band wasn't the dream I'd thought. It's fine, Bonnie, really. The Best Boys found me my best girl, and that was all I needed.'

Bonnie still looked uncertain, but Greya was sighing and declaring him a 'true romantic' and now they were being shown to a table by the stage and brought beers on the house and Stan could hardly believe he was back here in the Cavern after all these years. He knew the past had been creeping up on him these last few months, and now it seemed to have finally found him. But, wonderfully, it had found him with Bonnie still at his side.

He reached across the table for her hand but then a tentative voice said, 'Stan Walker?' and he turned to see a bloke stood nervously before him.

'Martin?' he stuttered, praying it wasn't.

'That's me. Nice to meet you.'

He reached out a hand and Stan had little choice but to heave himself out of his VIP chair and greet his supposed date.

'You didn't get my message?' he hissed.

'No. Sorry. Left my phone at home. Stupid of me. Was it important?'

'No. That is, er . . .'

He glanced nervously to Greya, who came up at his side.

'Hi, Martin. I'm Greya, Stan's granddaughter, and this is Bonnie, his *wife*.'

Martin looked at Bonnie, a little surprised, but stuck out his hand.

'Lovely to meet you. I'm Martin.'

'A friend of Grandpa's,' Greya said quickly. 'They've been chatting about this band online, haven't you, Gramps? Very up to date.'

Stan nodded dumbly, but Bonnie seemed satisfied.

'How lovely. Do come and join us, Martin.'

She drew out the remaining seat and as Martin slid into it Stan reluctantly considered him. Martin was about his own height and build with more hair (not that that was hard) and less of a stoop (not hard either) and kind, smiley eyes.

'Great table,' he said, glancing at the stage, barely two metres away.

'We've got VIP seats because Stan used to play here back in the day,' Bonnie told him.

Martin turned to Stan.

'Wow. You really played here?'

'A few times. Most people did.'

'I didn't. Tone-deaf. I worked the bar for a while, though. I bet I saw you play. What was your band?'

'The Best Boys,' Greya said proudly and Martin nodded.

'I remember.'

'You don't,' Stan said.

'I do. You had a proper poser of a front man. Mike? No, not a real name. Stripe?'

'Spike,' Stan said, impressed. 'You *do* remember.'

'Yep. He was always hassling me for pens to sign autographs. No idea why he didn't just think to bring his own.'

Bonnie leaned in.

'That was you? God, I remember Spike begging pens. He did it the night I first split up with him. Should have kept it that way.'

She laughed, and now Stan looked more closely at Martin and thought he detected something of the fresh-faced barman he'd half known back then.

'You must have been young to be working?'

'I lied about my age,' he admitted with a grin. 'I'm seventy-two now.' Almost Bonnie's age, Stan noted, glancing at her. Martin glanced too and Stan felt a growl of jealousy in his treacherous gut and put his hand to his stomach. 'I loved that place,' Martin went on. 'I'd do anything to get in there. I was fourteen the first time I saw the Beatles. It was in a school lunchtime, but we were allowed out back then, weren't we? Weren't all locked up safe like they are now, poor kids.'

'Not so poor,' Greya objected. 'We have the internet.'

'It's an amazing thing, I'll give you that, but I'd take the Cavern over it any day, even if it was a bit dark and damp and stank of rotten veg.'

'Yuck!' Greya said.

'It was,' Bonnie confirmed.

Martin grinned at her and she grinned back. Stan told himself that was a good thing, though his grumbling gut didn't seem to agree. Suddenly he remembered all too vividly being stuck in the cloakroom watching Bonnie out here, dancing with Spike and Danny; Danny and Spike. He'd thought she'd never notice him and of course she hadn't, not until he'd stuck his arm round her and walked her out of there and into his life. But had he, that night, been trying to control her every bit as much as either of the others?

'We didn't really notice,' Martin was saying to Greya, 'cos there was rock and roll to dance to and other kids to dance with and we were giddy with it all, weren't we?'

'We were,' Bonnie agreed, but Stan could only stare at her and remember his younger self telling her earnestly how the Cavern smelled of promise. She'd looked unconvinced and she'd been right. In the end, all it had smelled of was raw ambition and that was an altogether sourer scent.

'Martin could have been there on the same nights as us,' Bonnie was saying to him and he nodded and smiled and tried to make his mind come back to the here and now, but it was rebelling.

He looked around the revamped Cavern picturing all those long-ago nights. Martin must have stood next to him in the loos, helped him with equipment, served him Cokes at the bar. If any one part of any one evening there had turned a different way, Martin might have got talking to Bonnie, might have asked her out. She might even have gone. Everything could have been different. And now here they were, back again, as if their paths had meandered out from the Cavern and were finally converging again, moving in – in on Bonnie.

'Are you married, Martin?' Bonnie asked him, and Stan felt his throat constrict a little.

'I *was*, yes, for many years. My wife, Rose, died two years ago – cancer.'

Bonnie's eyes melted.

'I'm so sorry. Stan has cancer too, did you know?'

Martin looked confused.

'I did know, yes. He told me when . . . '

'When you were chatting about the Jetsetters?' Greya interjected.

Martin frowned at her but then blinked and nodded.

'That's right,' he agreed slowly. 'The Jetsetters, yes. I'm sorry. He looks well, though.'

'An illusion, I'm afraid,' Stan said. 'I'm not the man I was.'

An awkward silence fell. Stan saw Bonnie look to Martin for help and his head spun. It was happening. His plan was happening here, now, right in front of him, and in the Cavern too. Was that right, or all too wrong? He had no idea, but the low ceilings seemed to be looming in and the heat was rising uncomfortably and now the band were coming out of the dressing room door – the *same* dressing room door – and the quiet applause felt like the screams of five hundred giddy fans.

'What do you do to keep busy?' Stan heard Greya ask Martin, and half heard the answer through the heavy pounding of his heart.

'Rose and I had a campervan and I nearly sold it after she died. It didn't feel the same without her, but then I told myself it would have made her sad to think of me giving it up like that so instead I rolled my sleeves up, gave the van a good clean and went on a bit of a tour. I saw new places and old friends, and it was good. Not as good as it would have been with her, but good all the same.'

He looked a little sad until Bonnie leaned in and said, 'I think it's great you're still doing things, Martin,' and he recovered himself.

'Yes, well, life is precious. Rose losing hers taught me that, and it seems to me that I owe it to her to keep on living as best I can. But I'm lonely sometimes. It's harder work on your own. It would be nice to share stuff, even just sometimes. That's why . . .'

He stopped and fumbled for his drink. Greya stepped in again, babbling about how cool campervans were and Bonnie agreed, seeking to put their guest at his ease without even knowing why he was uncomfortable.

Stan snuck a sideways look at Martin as the band warmed up in front of them. The guy seemed straight. Better than that, he seemed kind and warm and caring – everything he'd asked for. Here, then, was a man he could actually, tentatively picture Bonnie with. Indeed, here he was with her already. That was good, wasn't it? After all, Stan hadn't got long now. His body was giving up. He had neither the time nor the energy to 'date' again, so it was a good job he wouldn't have to. Well done, Stan. Nice work.

So why, then, did it feel as if his heart was being torn from his ribcage? Where was the satisfaction he'd always gained from a job well done? The band were striking up, the lights dimming and Stan looked at Bonnie, noting the oh-so-familiar tilt of her head, the way she leaned in slightly to the music, to life. And here, at her side, was this man, this Martin. And he need only reach out a still-strong arm to pull her against him and it would look right. It would look all too right, as if Stan could simply be rubbed out of the picture and this man inserted quietly into his place. And suddenly Stan didn't want to be erased. He didn't want to slide out of Bonnie's life. He didn't want to be replaced. Damn it – he didn't want to die.

'Grandpa?' He saw Greya turn, saw the panic in her eyes. 'Grandpa, are you OK?' He nodded, gave her a thumbs up, but she was a sharp little thing. 'You're not. I can see you're not. Does it hurt?'

It did hurt. It hurt so much.

He shook his head. But now Martin was looking too and he saw concern wash across his kind eyes and with it something else – a memory, perhaps. Martin had seen this before. He knew, better even than Stan, what was happening.

'We should go.'

'No,' Stan protested, but now Bonnie was jumping up, her chair clattering to the floor as she darted to his side. He stood up too and grabbed for her hands. 'I found Martin. I found him for you.'

'Don't, Grandpa,' Greya gasped, tugging on his arm. He saw tears in her eyes and tried to focus. 'Sssh,' she was saying. 'Sssh now. You're not well, you're . . .'

'I'm not well, no. I'm dying. That's why I did it. That's why I dated.'

'You did what?' Bonnie stuttered.

'Ask Greya. Ask her about Cherry Creek.'

'About what? Stan, you're not making any sense.'

'I am. Greya, tell her. I dated men just like I once dated . . . Actually, I never did date you, did I Bonnie? Why was that? Why did I never take you on a date? Bonnie, I want to take you, to take you . . .'

Where did he want to take her? What was he saying? His head was spinning and his chest felt tight and his legs were wobbling beneath him and he let go of Bonnie and sank to his knees, clasping at his gut to somehow hold his treacherous liver together. The band stopped playing as if the past was truly coming round full circle. No doubt everyone was staring, but he had no energy to care. He had energy only to breathe.

'Stan!' It came out of Bonnie as a scream and she dropped down at his side.

'I'm OK,' he gasped but he couldn't make himself heard and now she was pulling him against her and saying his name over and over. 'Stan. Don't go. Don't go, Stan.'

He desperately shook his head. He wasn't going, not yet, not before he explained. He curled in on himself and concentrated on drawing air into his lungs. He felt Bonnie's tears against his face and tried to pat at her shoulder to tell her just to give him a moment but his hand wasn't working properly.

Breathe. That's what it came down to. He just had to breathe through this and it would be OK. In and out. He focused on his lungs, on his stomach and his treacherous liver. *You're not having me*, he told the cancer lurking in there like a malevolent dragon, *not yet*.

'Stan,' she said again, 'my Stan,' and he clutched at that like a raft as everything else seemed to rush up over his head like a dark, cold wave, swamping Greya and Martin and the shadow of the Best Boys and the whole of the Cavern. 'My Stan,' he heard over and over like a musical beat against his heart until his head spun and he toppled sideways onto the Cavern floor and heard no more.

Chapter Thirty-One

'Stan? My Stan?'

She was still there.

'Bonnie?'

'Stan!'

'Bonnie.'

This was ridiculous. Stan opened his eyes with an effort. He was in hospital. He'd known it, had half heard the beeps and whirrs of artificial life but hadn't wanted to credit them.

'Hate hospitals,' he said gruffly.

'Everyone hates hospitals, darling.'

'Except doctors, presumably.'

'Except doctors, yes. Oh God, this is no time for jokes. I can't believe you're awake. Well, I can. That is, I refused to believe you wouldn't be but still, here you are.'

'Here I am.'

'And a good job too, Stanley Walker, cos you've got some explaining to do.'

He winced.

'Maybe I'll just die after all.'

'You better not.' She softened. 'Really – how are you? You must be exhausted.'

'Hardly. I've just been lying here for . . . for how long, Bon?'

She glanced at her watch.

'Pretty much twelve hours. It's the middle of the night.'

Stan looked to the window and saw blank blackness beyond the sickly hospital lights. He was in a single room – he must be bad – and an ugly cannula was biting into his left hand. He frowned at it.

'Is that thing keeping me alive?'

'Nope. Just giving you a bit of food.'

'I'd rather have one of your roasts.'

'Stan! Be serious.'

'I am!'

'Ok, fine, but we're stuck til morning at the very least, so I intend to make the most of it and find out exactly what you've been up to.'

Stan shifted uncomfortably beneath the sheets.

'You have me at a disadvantage, lass.'

'And will use that mercilessly.' She sighed. 'Greya explained everything, Stan. Showed me the Cherry Creek app, told me that's how you met Adi – and the lurker.' Stan grimaced. 'She was very apologetic, poor girl.'

'It wasn't her fault.'

'I know that. She was just the organ grinder's monkey.' Stan attempted a smile but Bonnie wasn't letting him off that easily. 'You, Stan, my Stan – were the organ grinder.' He grimaced and she leaned in. 'Are you OK?'

'What, with being told off by my wife?'

She huffed.

'It's very hard telling you off when it might send you into relapse at any moment. No fun at all.'

'Sorry.'

'Not your fault, my love – though advertising for another husband for me very much is. Why, Stan? Why did you do it? Why did you think I'd want another husband?'

'To look after you.'

She stared at him, astonished.

'You've said that before, but I don't get it. I don't need looking after, I'm an independent modern woman.'

'I know. I do know that. I just . . . just couldn't bear the thought of you having no one there for you. I remember, Bonnie. I was there. I can still picture you shaking in the middle of the Cavern with Danny trying to feast on you like a bloody vampire. You were so vulnerable.'

'I was eighteen, Stan.'

'So alone. I hated it. I was stuck up on the stage and I hated it. I didn't ever want you to feel alone. And I still don't. Looking after you, Bonnie – it's what I do.'

She shuffled her chair a little closer to the bed.

'That again. I don't get it, Stan. I don't get why you see it that way.'

'Well how do you see it?'

'I see it as you loving me.'

'Oh, it is. I do. Of course I do, always have from the first moment you came down the steps at the Jac. But looking after you – that's what I have to offer.'

'What?'

'It's how I won you.'

'What! Stan, you're talking shit! Oops.' She put a hand over her mouth as a nurse walked past the door. 'Sorry, but you are. That's not how you "won" me, whatever that means. I wasn't some goldfish in a bag to be taken home by the Best Boy with the biggest hook.'

'I didn't mean that.'

'Then what *did* you mean?'

He shifted again. God, he hated hospitals.

'Can I at least get out of bed?'

'No. I don't want you dying on me til you explain yourself.'

333

Her eyes flashed at him and it did funny things to his wonky insides.

'God, you're gorgeous when you're angry.'

'Stan! Stop it. Explain.'

He pushed himself up a little on his pillows.

'There isn't much to explain, Bonnie. It's all pretty clear.'

'To you maybe.'

'OK, OK, let's take it right back. You arrived in Liverpool fresh and pretty and clever and somehow, thank God, you fell in with us lot – a bunch of local lads with dreams bigger than their talents.'

'That's not true, Stan.'

'It's how I see it, Bonnie, and that's what you asked for.' She subsided and he fumbled for her hand. 'You were wonderful, Bon, really – so full of life and joy. You were the one we all wanted and I was the one who got you, and I did that by being there to care for you.'

'Bullshit.'

'Bonnie!'

'Well it is. You think I married you cos you "cared for me"?'

She looked angry again, furious even, and Stan wasn't quite sure why. He looked to the window but it reflected him mercilessly back – pale and wizened and dying.

'Didn't you?'

'Oh, Stan!' Her anger seemed to rush out of her on a huge breath. 'Oh, Stan, please tell me you haven't thought that for the last fifty-four bloody years?'

'Why else would it be? I was the quiet one, the serious one. I wasn't suave like Danny or flash like Spike.'

'And look where that got them.'

'Well, yes, but even so. I was kind of the booby prize. The one left over when the others proved themselves more useless than me.'

334

She stood up.

'You're the booby prize and I'm the goldfish? What a pair.' She took his hands, both the free one and the one with the damned cannula chaining him to the bulbous drip between them. 'Listen to me, Stanley Walker, and listen well. I married you because I loved you. No, more – I married you because I was head over heels in love with you. I loved you from the moment you put your arm round me and led me out of the Cavern. No, from before.'

'Before?' he said, his voice stupidly squeaky.

'Yes, before – I just didn't realise it. When I look back on the crazy, wonderful days when I was rushing around with Spike and Danny, the moments that stand out were the ones with you – because with you I didn't have to pretend. With you, I could just be my natural self and I was mad not to see it sooner.

'I loved you, Stan-*Lee* Walker, from when I hung up coats with you in the cloakroom and you told me about your dreams. I loved you from when you thought people were mad to tell a girl she couldn't do architecture. I loved you from when you came to the hospital with me when Danny cut his finger off on the ice and I loved you from when you jived with me at the Shuffle and then blushed and apologised. Bloody apologised – for being the most honest, most open, most kind man there. I loved you for *you*, Stan, not for anything you did for me.'

Stan stared at her, all those wonderful moments flashing before his eyes clear as day.

'But I took you away,' he said.

'You took *me* away? I'm the one who robbed you, Stan. If it wasn't for me you'd have been a musician. Epstein would have signed you for "Watching Her" and you'd have been famous. I'm the one who took *you* away. I robbed you of it.'

'That's not true. I never would have written "Watching Her" if it hadn't been for you.'

'But you'd have written other stuff. You had talent and you gave it up for me and I didn't even . . . I didn't even let you play the Beatles ever again. I didn't even give you that kindness. I just took, took, took.'

'No! All I wanted was you.'

'And that, at least, I gave freely and wholeheartedly.'

'Truly?'

'Truly, Stan.' She sighed. 'Maybe we should have spoken about this before. Maybe we shouldn't have locked our Merseybeat days up in a stupid box and refused to revisit them.'

'Maybe. But it was just how we did things back then.'

'More fools us.'

Stan lay back against his pillows and thought about what she was saying. It was true that they had buried those heady days from the moment they had stepped out of the Cavern and turned their backs on its glittering door. It had been easier not to speak about it, and besides, she'd gone home for Easter and he – he'd packed his bags and gone cap-in-hand to his father, who had been kinder than he could ever have imagined.

The family had moved out to the Wirral by then and Stan had joined them, relieved to be clear of Liverpool with its clubs and music and endless tangle of memories, and thrown himself into plumbing with every ounce of his frustrated energy. He and Bonnie had written, though, and when she'd returned to Liverpool he'd been at the railway station to welcome her back.

That term had been a struggle. She'd battled through it, pale and tight-lipped, and there'd seemed no point in revisiting the events of Bad Friday. Then in the summer she'd come to see him on the Wirral and he'd plucked up the courage to kiss her and everything had fallen into place. He'd proposed two weeks later and it had seemed only natural for her to continue her degree from over the Mersey.

'D'you remember,' he said now, 'how you used to catch that ferry into Liverpool every day?'

'And come back every night. Of course I do. I'd all but run onto the boat to escape home to you. And every night you'd be there waiting for me.'

'Terrified that you'd have changed your mind and stayed in the city.'

'Why, Stan? Why would you feel like that? What did I do to make you feel that way?'

'Nothing. Really. I just felt that I was, you know, second best, and that one day you'd work that out.'

'Second best? To vain Spike, or violent Danny? Good God, man, that's ridiculous. All they ever truly cared about was success, whereas you, who deserved it more than any of them, were the one prepared to give it up. And for me. That was amazing. And besides, why would I marry second best?'

'Common sense? Like being a plumber, not a musician – not as glamorous or exciting, but ultimately far more reliable?'

Bonnie narrowed her eyes.

'I'm going to get really angry with you in a minute, Stan.'

'What were you before?'

'Mildly frustrated.'

'Lord help me, then.'

'Exactly. For such a talented and gorgeous man you can be very stupid. I loved the way you cared for me, yes, but only because I couldn't believe my luck that someone so magical might feel that way about little me, not because it was some need you fulfilled, like taking out the bins or making the tea. I loved *you*, Stan – every single bloody fibre of you. And I still do, so, so much. Every day spent without you feels like a day wasted because you, Stanley – musician, plumber, husband, father, best, *best* friend - are all I ever wanted. Without you, I may well fall apart but there is nothing whatsoever you can do about that, save giving me even more lovely memories to keep me glued together. Is that clear?'

Stan nodded dumbly, but inside his heart was soaring for joy.

'First best?' he whispered.

'First best,' she agreed with a smile. 'Always. Now, budge up – we've not had a night apart in years, and I don't want that to change now.'

She edged him across the bed and, adjusting the cannula, he eagerly complied. She crawled on and fitted in against him perfectly, slotting into the grooves that had been worn deeper by years together but that had, in fact, been there from the start – he could see that now.

Stan put his arm around Bonnie and breathed in the scent of her and felt the artificial world of the damned hospital fade away to take him back to rotten-veg cellars and pavilions and riverboats; to Brylcreem and mascaras; to cloakrooms and rehearsal warehouses and stages. And to him watching her, and her, as she'd told him back then, if only he'd been listening properly, watching him too.

Chapter Thirty-Two

'Your car, sir.'

Dave held open the door for Stan, doffing the chauffeur's hat he'd miraculously produced when they'd left The Crown after a quiet drink together. Stan looked him up and down.

'I know I asked for a lift, mate, but you didn't need to go that far.'

'Oh I did. All the stops for this one, Stan-boy. And besides, I tried it on Gail last night and, let me tell you, she loved it. Apparently she's always had this fantasy where . . .'

'Enough, Dave!' Stan looked into the car. 'Not . . . not in here?' Dave just smirked at him and Stan groaned. 'Did I need to know that?'

'Auspicious signs for your date, lad.'

'Only you would think like that,' he groaned, but he climbed into the car anyway. Tonight was too important to delay. 'Gail still around, then?' he added lightly as Dave got into the driver's seat in front of him.

'Still around,' Dave confirmed, starting the engine. 'She's all right, you know.'

'Praise indeed.'

'OK, OK, I like her. She's caring and interesting and fun and I'm not going to run away from that this time.'

'Delighted to hear it.'

Dave pulled away and looked back at Stan in the rear-view mirror.

'Is it really your first date with Bonnie?'

'Technically, yes. I've never picked her up like this before.'

'Never? What about at first?'

'At first?' Stan smiled. 'We pretty much moved in together from the moment she came to my home.'

'No way? You old devil!'

'It wasn't like that.'

'What was it like, then?'

'Slow. Nice and slow. Like your driving, frankly. Are we nearly there?'

Dave rolled his eyes.

'You know this isn't actually a first date don't you, mate?'

Stan just shrugged. It felt like a first date, only a million times better because he already knew how it was going to turn out, so he could enjoy the nerves and the anticipation and the giddy joy of being together.

'I'm just excited to see her,' he told Dave as they turned up the road to the house.

Dave shook his head.

'You've got it bad, mate.'

'Yep,' Stan agreed happily. 'And it's wonderful – you should try it.'

'Maybe. I'm picking Gail up again once I've dropped you off, which makes two nights in a row so perhaps I'm getting there.'

'That's why you're wearing the hat?'

Dave winked in the mirror but his voice was more serious.

'Not tonight, actually. Tonight we're going somewhere special.'

'Where?'

'McDonald's.'

'McDonald's?'

'Yep. We're picking Charlie up and we're going to McDonald's. The three of us, together.'

Stan smiled.

'That's great, Dave, really great. Perhaps not tell Charlie the chauffeur story, though?'

Dave pulled up outside the house and looked back at him.

'I thought being a father was all about passing on your wisdom?'

'A bit at a time, hey?'

Dave laughed.

'That's what I'm doing. Or trying to, at least.' He coughed. 'I've got you to thank for this, you know Stan.'

'For Charlie? Nah, that was all your own work, and to be honest it's a miracle there aren't more Charlies out there.'

Dave stared, his neck twisted round to try and see Stan sitting in the back.

'D'you think there might be? God, I could have more sons. Or a little girl. I might have a little girl. How would I find out?'

The thought of Dave contacting his long list of exes to see if any of them had, by any chance, provided him with a child was momentarily diverting.

'A Facebook campaign?' Stan suggested, but Dave wasn't to be put off.

'Forget it. Look, I mean it, mate. I hate that you've got, you know, ill.' He still couldn't say the c-word. 'I hate what it's doing to you, but if you're looking for a silver lining, here I am. Not much consolation to you, I know, but it was thinking about time running out, about us not going on forever, that made me open to meeting Charlie when his stepdad suggested it. And I'm so glad I did.'

'I'm glad too, Dave. Hey, what is it?'

Dave was coughing again and fidgeting about in his seat.

'Lord, Stan,' he burst out suddenly. 'What will I do without you to talk to?'

Stan felt his insides shift like wet concrete.

'I'm sorry, Dave.'

'No. No, don't be stupid. Not that you are. It's me being stupid. It's me . . . Oh lord!' He dragged his sleeve across his face. 'I just want you to know, that's all. I just want you to know that you've been a great mate, OK? *OK*?'

He was so fierce that Stan cowered back a little.

'OK. You too Dave, really.' Stan looked around the car and an idea suddenly came to him. 'I know what you need.'

'Sectioning?'

'No. Terry.'

'Terry? Your ugly key ring thing?'

'He can't help being ugly, he's a troll. Bonnie says he looks like me on a bad morning.'

Dave let out a welcome laugh.

'He does a bit.'

'And he's a grumpy sod. But he's a very good listener.'

'A good listener, you say? Yeah. Yeah, I'd like that. Cheers.'

'Pleasure.'

Neither of them knew what to do with themselves from there and it was with relief that Dave called, 'Oh look – I believe that's your date.'

Stan turned and, sure enough, there was Bonnie, standing in the doorway of their house and his heart turned over as if this truly were a first date. Lord, but she looked lovely. She was wearing a new dress in a rich, dark red that clung to her still glorious figure and ended at the knees to show off her elegant legs. She'd had her silvery hair cut in a sharp bob and around her slim shoulders she clutched a soft scarf in red and white gingham, just like the dress he'd first seen her in so many years ago. His eyes misted and he flung open the car door and leaped – well, creaked – out to go to her.

'It's like I'm in 1963 again,' he said, offering her his arm.

'Except for all the wrinkles.'

'They're not wrinkles, they're laughter lines.'

She smiled.

'Well, if so, then you put them there. Are you going to kiss me?'

'I hardly dare.'

'Then I'll have to make the first move.'

She stood on tiptoe, placed a hand round the back of his neck and pulled him down to press her lips to his. He moved into the kiss, sliding his arms around her back and losing himself in her. Or rather, finding himself.

'Bonnie,' he breathed.

'Stan. I love you so much.'

'And I you. Now, shall we go? I believe you've booked a very fine venue?'

'The finest on the Wirral.'

'Which is the finest place on earth. Let's go.'

He led her to the car and Dave got out to open the door.

'Nice hat, Dave,' Bonnie commented.

'Thanks. It's very . . . effective. I might let Stan borrow it if you're lucky.'

Bonnie raised a questioning eyebrow at Stan.

'Don't ask,' he said. 'No hats needed, thanks Dave. Keep it for Gail.'

'Your loss,' Dave said with a shrug and slid into the driver's seat to start up the engine.

Bonnie looked over her shoulder at their old house as it receded in the back windscreen.

'It's been a lovely home.'

'The best, but we're moving on now.'

'We are.' She took his hand, squeezed. 'I'm so glad you're here.'

She didn't add 'for now', though they both knew it was there. Stan was fading, his energy dropping away like the leaves on the trees. Some days he could barely get out of bed, but they'd learned just to take what they could get and tonight was special. He'd been asleep half the day to be alert for it and he could sleep all tomorrow too, all eternity if he had to. But tonight – tonight was theirs.

'I can't wait to see it,' he said. 'Your dream house.'

'*Our* dream house, Stan. Oh God, look – we're almost there.'

Stan sat forward. He hadn't been to the building site since the day they'd walked in on Adi and Lisa almost a month ago when the house had still been a shell, all blank walls and exposed pipes.

'I feel like Kevin McWotsit on *Grand Designs* when they cut to the final shot.'

'This isn't the final shot,' Bonnie said quickly, and then caught herself. 'But I know what you mean. Take a deep breath, Stan. I hope you like it.'

'Of course I will.'

She thought he was being kind, but he wasn't. He knew he'd like it because she did. He didn't actually know that much about houses despite having spent most of his life building them. He knew what went into putting them together but design, that was Bonnie's business. She'd poured her soul into how this would look because it was a vision she'd had embedded in her from those very first days as an architecture student in Liverpool.

It was a vision that had helped her complete her studies and a vision that had shaped her career. This was the pinnacle of Bonnie the architect, and he was so pleased that he'd get to see that. For him, though, he'd love the house best reflected in her eyes, for it would shine there far brighter than with any fancy LED lighting. Oh, but . . .

They'd turned into the drive and there it was, and Stan had to admit that even without Bonnie the new house would have been a stunning sight. The October sun was going down, casting a soft pink glow over the lower east wall like a projector shining up the rising length of the curved cream building. Soft lights glowed behind the many long windows and spilled out of the curving porch, dead centre. Stan's hand went to his mouth as it fell open in an O of disbelief and he crushed forward between the front seats, drinking it in.

'Bonnie, it's beautiful. Stunning. Magnificent. It's, it's . . .'

'Ours, Stan.'

He could only nod. Dave pulled up outside, right where Stan had stared into the heavy wheels of the delivery truck back in May and considered throwing himself into the mud beneath them. He stepped out onto the perfect asphalt and looked around for Bonnie as she joined him before their new home.

'You like it, then?'

He looked at her, and now he did see the house through her shining eyes. He drank it in and then he kissed her.

'I love it, Bonnie lass. Can we go inside?'

'Of course.' She indicated the porch but the sight of it gave him a stab of pain and he hesitated.

'I can't carry you over, Bonnie.'

She tutted.

'And I don't want you to. Come on, Stan – hasn't all this damned talking we've done shown you that I don't need carrying? We'll walk over side by side, like we've always done.'

She held out her hand and, with a rueful grin, he took it in his own. She was right. He'd been looking after her, of course he had, but she'd been looking after him, too, every bit as much. It was the best way. Together they stepped up onto the smooth paving around the house and made for the door, but there Stan paused.

'A glass doorstep, Bonnie? Are you mad? How will we ever keep it clean?'

'We won't,' she said, 'and that will be fine. But if we want to, we can.'

'But why?'

In answer, she pointed down and he looked to see, clearly embedded under the pretty blue-green glass, the mark of their two hands, fingers entwined.

'All it will take is a little soap and water and whatever of life's dirt has covered us up, we'll be there again, clear for all to see. For me to see.'

Her voice wobbled and Stan saw a stark picture of her crouched alone over the step, rubbing it clear to see this imprint of their love. It cut like a knife and when he looked at her both their eyes filled.

'No tears,' Bonnie said fiercely. She reached up and ran a finger along the rims of his eyes, catching his sorrow. Swallowing, he did the same for her, seeing the old scar where he'd lost a fight with a jigsaw magnified for a moment in the droplets. 'I like it, Stan. It will be a comfort, really it will.'

He nodded, fought to stop more tears and, failing, pulled her tight against him. They clung to each other for a moment, then a moment more, and then they forced themselves apart.

'You going to show me round this joint then?' Stan managed, and with a watery smile Bonnie nodded and reached for the door handle. But someone beat her to it from the other side.

'Welcome.'

Stan peered in to see Rachael stood there, bulging with her third child, and with Andrew, Jamie and Marleigh at her back, all beaming at Bonnie and Stan and chasing away any lingering sadness. They hustled them inside and Stan stepped from the porch into the body of the house proper and gasped with wonder yet again. The main room was wide and light, dominated by their much-loved dining table stretching the length of the glass doors beyond. The last of the sunlight was rolling across the horizon behind the trees at the bottom of their new garden, and rose-tinted lights in the patio drew it all the way up the house like a modest blush.

'Isn't it cool?' Marleigh spoke first, bouncing up and down on her tiptoes. 'Do you like it, Grandpa? I like it. I've bagsied which bedroom I'm going to have when I stay, and Jamie has too. And we're going to stay often cos this is way nicer than our house, isn't it Jamie?'

'It is pretty smart,' Jamie agreed gruffly. 'Granny says I can have a sleepover here for my birthday if I want and I do want. Is that OK with you?'

'Erm, of course. Sounds great, Jamie.'

'That's good, cos I've told my friends already. I mean . . .' He looked a bit sheepish, then said, 'Look, Grandpa – I lit the fancy fire for you.'

'Fancy?'

Stan turned and saw, at the far end of the long room, just past their own squashy cream sofas, a log-burner like none he'd ever seen before. It had glass panels on all sides so that the flames seemed to dance out into the big marble fireplace, making it feel more like a campfire than a hearth.

'It looks amazing,' Stan said. 'Thank you, Jamie.'

'No problem, but hang on. It's not done yet.'

He ran to the fire and, carefully putting on the heat glove, opened the door and threw in a handful of something.

'Jamie . . .' Stan warned but Bonnie shushed him.

'Watch.'

The fire crackled and then gave a series of giggling little pops, and glowed blue and green and purple.

'It's magic,' Marleigh said.

'It's copper salts, silly,' her brother corrected her.

347

'But magic all the same,' Stan said softly.

'I think it's like Midsummer,' the little girl said. 'And look, Grandpa – look what I did for you.'

She pointed above the fireplace where he saw a picture, blown up on a canvas like a true piece of modern art, showing a maypole, exuberantly crooked against a purple sky with silhouettes dancing below it.

'It's us,' Marleigh said, bouncing up and down again. 'All of us. I painted it! There's you and Granny, and Mum and Dad, and Jamie and me, and Greya, and Dave and Gail, and Nancy and Astrid. See!'

Stan peered at the figures and saw them all, in their various shapes and sizes, from little Marleigh to Amazonian Astrid. He smiled to see it. Nancy was talking of doing Midsummer in Sweden next year. No one said that Stan wouldn't be there, but they knew it to be true. What Nancy still didn't seem to know was that Astrid most likely wouldn't be there either. Clearly her wife was still keeping her illness a secret. Stan wished her well with that but was glad he'd gone his own way. It was painful at times, but it gave him a chance to say goodbye properly and that was worth all the pain.

'It's beautiful, Marleigh,' he told his granddaughter. 'You have your daddy's talent as an artist.'

Marleigh beamed.

'Thanks, Gramps. And yours as a musician – aren't I lucky?'

'Very,' he agreed with a smile.

'And look,' she said, pointing, 'I added Auntie Lisa too, because she was sort of there, wasn't she?'

'She definitely sort of was,' someone said, and Stan turned to see Lisa coming out of the kitchen at the far end of the house.

'Lisa! You're here too.'

Lisa had moved into a flat this side of Manchester a few weeks back but she seemed to be in Brecksby a great deal. She'd cut down to a three-day week as she settled into her new office and often came to have lunch with Bonnie and Stan, chatting to them in a way Stan couldn't remember her doing since she'd been about five. She was always off at the end of the working day, though, and not, they were sure, back to her flat.

'I'm here,' she agreed happily now. 'Someone had to cook you a decent meal, Dad, and I, er, invited someone along to power the cooker.'

'To do *what*?'

In reply, Lisa tugged him over so he could see through the alcove into the kitchen, where a bright, aqua-white bike had pride of place in the middle of the slate tiles. Sitting on it, pedalling fit to burst, was Adi.

'Nice to see you with your clothes on,' Stan said.

Adi flushed and Lisa came across and gave him a protective kiss. Stan had grabbed a quiet word with Adi once it had become apparent things were getting serious between the pair, and been assured that he'd dropped his 'night work' and was very keen on Lisa.

'What about your lovely car?' Stan had asked him.

'It's not as lovely as your daughter,' had been the response, and Stan had recognised a little bit of his sixties self in the answer and prayed that it would work out for the pair.

'But this is Greya's power-bike,' he said now, going over to check it out as Adi climbed gratefully off.

'She gave it to me when I went to see her at uni the other day,' Lisa said. 'Right pain to get in the car it was, but she wanted you to have it and she seemed so happy I hadn't the heart to say no. Now the project has secured their grant they've been able to make two newer prototypes, but this one is the first of its kind in the UK and Greya says it's all down to you.'

'Which is a nonsense,' Stan said gruffly. 'It was far more her work.'

Even so, he felt his throat swelling to see what might be an invention of the future sat in his brand new kitchen. Although . . .

'You don't really have to use it to work the cooker, do you?' he asked.

Lisa laughed.

'Nah. But it's fun to make Adi try.'

'Slave-driver,' he said, kissing her again, and Stan was warmed to see the clear connection between the pair.

It was sad that things hadn't worked out with Simon, but if they were both happier this way then maybe it was for the best. It was certainly good to see his little girl smiling so much again.

'I wanted Rae do it,' Lisa said, nudging her sister, 'but she'd probably topple off the damned thing with this huge bump.'

Rachael snorted in disbelief and nudged back.

'That huge bump is your nephew, Lisa.'

'Nephew?' Stan asked, turning back to his younger daughter. 'It's a boy?'

Rachael nodded and looked for Andrew, who came up and slid an arm around what was left of her waist.

'It's a boy, Dad,' she told him. 'They confirmed it at the scan the other day. It's a boy, and we're calling him Stanley. Everyone agrees.'

Jamie and Marleigh nodded eagerly, their little faces turned up to Stan, but he had no idea what to say. Stanley – a tiny new Stanley to take his place in the world.

'Dad?' It was Rachael again. Her voice was hesitant, scared. 'Dad, is that OK?'

He looked for her and grabbed her in a big hug.

'Is it OK? It's fantastic, amazing, wonderful. I'm flattered. Delighted.'

'Really?'

'Of course. Stanley – Stan?'

'Or Lee,' Bonnie said softly, and he looked to her. For so long he'd turned his back on Lee, but it had been Lee who had found Bonnie and it was time to let him breathe again.

'Whatever the lad wants,' he said. 'He should be whatever he wants. You all should.'

Rachael kissed him.

'Thanks, Dad. Look, we're going to go now. We've crashed your date long enough, and anyway, I'm knackered. Stanley Junior is a restless little bugger . . .'

'Mummy!'

'Well he is, and I need all the sleep I can get. We'll leave you two to it.' She kissed him and then Bonnie. 'Have fun. Oh, and I hope Lisa's food isn't too burned.'

'Cheeky moo!'

Lisa chased her twin, laughing, from the house, the rest of her family in tow, and Stan watched them go with a fond smile.

'We'll leave you to it, too,' Lisa said when she returned. 'This is your date, after all – we're just the hired help. Come on, Adi – these starters won't make themselves.'

With a grin they were gone, through the alcove to the kitchen beyond, and Bonnie and Stan were alone again.

'Fancy the tour?'

Stan looked up. Above him, he could see doors leading off from the rising mezzanine on three sides of the room. They looked enticing but his body was tiring already and his heart felt achingly full of his family's welcome bounce. He remembered labouring his way up the chipboard steps when he'd snuck in with Dave, and was glad he was still here to climb the beautiful cherry wood staircase, but the finish would make little difference to the effort required.

'Are there a lot of steps?'

'A few. And a lift.'

'A lift? For me?'

'And me. I'm not getting any younger either, you know, and I swear I'm never moving into a bungalow, so lift it is. See.' She pointed and Stan did see – a glass-fronted platform discreetly tucked at the far end of the room. 'Shall we?'

They stepped on board and, with a smooth whir, the funky platform lifted them above the soft sofas and the fancy fire and the family table and onto the balcony above.

'Not quite a stairlift.'

'Never. Now, come and see.'

They headed for the master bedroom first, the curved archway now filled with cleverly shelved books.

'I call it "hint of library",' Bonnie said with a self-conscious wave as she led him through.

'I call it enchanting,' Stan told her, but now they were in their bedroom and he'd run out of superlatives.

The room, at the highest end of the house, was tall and airy and dominated by an oak four-poster bed hung with diaphanous duck-egg drapes and piled up with the softest-looking duvet Stan had ever seen.

'Four-poster, hey? Is that for the wild sex?'

'It certainly is. And this . . .' She indicated the French doors leading out onto their section of the balcony and flanked by padded duck-egg armchairs. A little table was set with tall glasses and an ice bucket holding a glistening bottle of champagne. 'This is for sharing.'

'I like it.'

Stan sank into the left-hand chair as Bonnie lifted the bottle. He'd have liked to open it, have liked to fire the cork out of the doors into the night sky beyond and pour the frothing liquid into their glasses, but Bonnie did it just as well and he was content to watch. He took the glass she proffered and raised it to hers.

'Cheers, my darling. To us.'

'To us.'

They drank and the bubbles chased through Stan's weakened body like over-excited children. He welcomed them in. They hadn't felt much like celebrating recently but, really, that was silly, wasn't it? There was always something to celebrate.

'Remember us getting planning permission for this place, Bonnie?'

'At the start of the year, yes. And here it is – built.'

'Everyone's worked so hard to get me here.'

'Because they love you.'

He swallowed sorrow, chasing it down with champagne.

'I'm a lucky man.' He looked to the bed, so big and sure of itself. 'You know, Bonnie, it might have been a crazy idea me dating husbands for you . . .'

'It *was* a crazy idea.'

'Maybe. But the point is, it's not necessarily a crazy idea for you to do it. If you want to.'

'I don't.'

'Not now. But later. If you wanted to.'

'I won't.'

He looked at her.

'You can be very stubborn, Bonnie.'

'Yep.'

'But I just want you to know that if you ever did, you'd have my blessing. I know I had a bit of a funny turn with Martin, but he's a good bloke. His number's on my phone if . . .'

'Delete it.'

'I just want you to be happy.'

'I know, Stan, and I thank you for it, but I think being with anyone else would just make me miss you more because it could never, ever be what we have together. I'd rather cuddle my memories, thank you – they'll be enough for me.'

Stan looked into his glass and watched the bubbles chasing each other up the glass.

'D'you know what Adi said when I first met him in this funny little café in . . .'

'Wait – Adi was one of your dates?'

''Fraid so. Good job for Lisa, hey?' She pulled a face at him and he grinned. 'Anyway, Adi said he thought you could store love and that if there was enough of it, it would last on after one of you was gone. Like the sun stays in the earth on a warm day.'

'Or like solar panels?'

'I guess so. Love solar panels. Do you think that's true, Bonnie? Do you think . . . do you think you'll be able to hold on to us? Have I done enough to keep you warm?'

'Oh Stan.' Bonnie put her glass down but her eyes were on him and she missed the table. It cracked against, polished wood but neither of them even noticed as she tumbled into his arms. 'You've given me so much that my love solar panels are going to be glowing red forever more. Even when they put me in my grave, they'll light up the sky like an eternal sunset and everyone will look at them and wonder at what joy I had to be so blessed.'

Stan held her tight against his wasted body and took in the picture of his wife in a rosy glow of his care and tried to hold on to that too. It wasn't enough, it would never be enough, but that was a blessing in itself.

'Bonnie,' he whispered.

'Stan,' she said back, tipping her face up to his and, with a smile, he kissed her tears away.

Acknowledgements

It has been a joy to write this book. After years immersed in historical fiction, having the chance to write a contemporary novel has been very exciting and I am hugely grateful to everyone who made that possible for me. First among those must be my fabulous editor, Sam Eades, who came up with the core idea for what eventually became *Bonnie and Stan* and took a chance on me writing it. I am also, as ever, massively indebted to my wonderful agent, Kate Shaw, who spoke to Sam about that idea and was trusting enough to bring it to me. I was stunned at the time as it was so different to the last three books we'd been working on but it was similar to work of mine Kate had seen a long time ago and it was all down to her foresight and belief that I found the guts to give this novel a go. Thanks heavens I did, so bless you Kate. And thank you Sam and all the wonderful team at Trapeze who have been so welcoming and such a joy to work with.

I want to thank my parents, not just for all the usual giving birth to me, keeping me alive into adulthood, being endlessly supportive stuff (though thanks for that too!) but also for being such vibrant, fun people. It was thinking about you both and the way you both attack life with such vigour that really helped me to get my head around creating Bonnie and Stan as products of the Sixties and part of a generation that were perhaps the first to really demand more of the world – good on you!

A big shout out has to go to my trusty research assistant, Brenda – although I have to say that accompanying me on a tour of Liverpool's pubs and clubs is perhaps not the hardest of trips she's ever had to make! Even so, singing Yellow Submarine in public at the top of our voices in the middle of the afternoon was perhaps above and beyond the call of duty, so thank you Brenda.

There are hundreds of people who have been kind enough to be interested, helpful and encouraging but listing them all would take forever so I hope they know who they are and I can thank them more effectively in the pub! I will simply end, therefore, on a huge thank you to all my family and especially to Stuart, Hannah and Alec who put up with the daily ups and downs of living with a writer so wonderfully. I love you all.

Playlist

Love me Do	The Beatles
The Hippy Hippy Shake	The Swinging Blue Jeans
Some Other Guy	The Searchers
Jailhouse Rock	Elvis Presley
Save the Last Dance for Me	The Drifters
Yesterday	The Beatles
My Bonnie	Tony Sheridan
All You Need is Love	The Beatles
Ain't She Sweet	The Beatles
Runaround Sue	The Overtones
Long Tall Sally	Little Richard
Love me Tender	Elvis Presley
Ferry Cross the Mersey	Gerry and the Pacemakers
Please, Please Me	The Beatles
Dizzy Miss Lizzy	The Beatles
Yakety Yak	The Coasters
That'll be the Day	Buddy Holly
Summertime Blues	Eddie Cochran
Anyone Who Had a Heart	Cilla Black
Do You Want to Know a Secret	Billy J Kramer

Plus, for a touch of Midsummer:

Sma Grodorna (Little Frogs)	Hej Tomtegubbar
Smoke on the Water	Deep Purple

Author Q & A

What was the initial jumping off point for *Bonnie and Stan*?
I cannot claim the honour of coming up with the initial idea. It came from my fab editor, Sam Eades, who spotted a very moving piece in the *New York Times* in which a dying woman was advertising for a new wife for her husband. The idea of someone being loving and realistic enough to want a new happy-ever-after for their partner after they'd gone really appealed to her, and I was the author lucky enough to take the idea on.

It was also Sam's idea to turn it round and have a man trying to find a new husband for his wife, and that the characters would be in their seventies. I was a little surprised by that at first but the more I thought about it the more intrigued I was by the question: when are we old enough to just accept a terminal diagnosis? The answer, I felt sure, was never and certainly not in our seventies when many people are still enjoying very full lives, and so Bonnie and Stan and the history of their long and happy marriage were born.

What came first, character or plot?
Definitely character. The plot hook of dating on your partner's behalf was there to spark off the book, but as I took that and started developing the concept it was all about getting to know

Bonnie and Stan and letting them lead how their story should be told. I knew early on, for example, that I wanted Bonnie to be an architect and from that grew the idea of them building their dream house, around which so much of the present day action revolves. With Stan, it was important to me that he was 'dating' on Bonnie's behalf not out of some boorish or even chivalrous motivation but from a deep-rooted belief that he'd been put on this earth to look after her. From that came the events of the past and the rather sudden and even difficult way he actually won her.

For me the characters are the main point of this novel. It was originally going to be called 'First Last Dates' to explore the dating theme, but once I'd written the first draft everyone at Trapeze just kept calling it 'Bonnie and Stan' and in the end we decided that had to be the title.

I've been writing historical fiction for some years (as Joanna Courtney) so it was a new experience for me being able to just make up my characters, and I had so much fun with it. I fell in love with both Bonnie and Stan but I also really enjoyed getting to know the side characters. Stan's mate Dave and his granddaughter Greya both grew as the novel went on, and so I gave them more and more space in the narrative. I perhaps especially enjoyed exploring the relationship between grandfather and granddaughter as I think it can be wonderful, free of some of the shackles of the parent-child one, so it was lovely when Greya emerged as Stan's dating partner-in-crime.

What was it about Liverpool and the Cavern Club that inspired you as a setting?

I can, at least, take credit for choosing the Liverpool setting for the novel and, in particular for the sixties sections. My editor, Sam, wanted to play with the idea of juxtaposing Stan's dates in the present day with the dates he and Bonnie went on when they first met, so I did the historical maths and worked out that today's seventy-somethings are a product of the sixties. That seemed to me a crucial difference from previous generations of 'older people' who grew out of the wartime and the fairly traditional culture of the 1950s.

Today's grannies and grandpas were the rebels in the miniskirts and quiffs who shook up popular culture as we know it, so it's no wonder that they're still pretty cool now. I wanted to explore that and there seemed no better place to set a sixties narrative than in the Beatles' heartland. Plus, the research trip was fantastic!!

What role does the theme of music play in shaping the narrative?

For me it's less about music per se and more about how important the creative side of people can be, in whatever way it finds expression. Stan suppresses his musical side after what happens at the Good Friday gig and when it starts to come out again that creates some tensions – although not, perhaps, in the way that Bonnie thinks. I enjoyed the fact that they both see the results of that night differently and that, in over fifty years together, they haven't really sorted it out.

Bonnie has an underlying guilt that she deprived Stan of something he really loved when he left the band but Stan, as a pragmatic sort, just feels that he gave it up for something even better. His worry is more that Bonnie 'settled for him' as a safe second best. Despite them knowing each other really well, they still have insecurities about each other's feelings and to me that's rather romantic.

Why did you decide to include the scene of Swedish Midsummer? Have you experienced it yourself? How would you say that scene illustrates the central themes of the book?

I confess that I haven't experienced Swedish Midsummer, though I have a friend who has and it sounds wonderful. I decided to include it because for some reason when I created Nancy, her life partner Astrid just presented herself almost fully formed and very much Swedish. I researched Swedish culture to develop her a little further and Midsummer came out as a critical day. The more I read about it the more I loved the sound of it, and I'm definitely going to try and make it to some celebrations sometime soon.

For me the midsummer scene sits right at the heart of the book. It's a moment of intense happiness for them all before things start to go downhill with Stan's health, and I really wanted to use it to draw out the importance of family, of being close to other people and being open with them. It's the point where Bonnie and Stan actually begin to talk about what happened 'that night', sparked by Stan picking up Marleigh's guitar and playing again for the first time in so many years. It's therefore the point where the present day strand and the past day strand merge.

But it's not just critical for Bonnie and Stan. Midsummer is also important for Dave because, for the first time, he allows himself to go away with a woman and we get a sense that he might be ready for a tiny bit more commitment. It's also where Astrid confesses to Stan that she, too, has cancer so it draws out the idea of how different people deal with terminal diagnoses and how much of that can be shared with your nearest and dearest.

I love the skinny dipping moment. I'm a big fan of a skinny dip myself and I felt that the raw, visceral joy of it was just right for this point in the novel where they are all stripped back and open to their other halves. Plus, it's a bit of fun, and being able to just have fun is also an important point in the novel.

What is it you love most about Bonnie and Stan's relationship?
I love that they are so natural with each other – that they are friends as well as lovers and that they know each other's foibles

and can tease whilst still being secure in each other's love. On the flip side of that, however, I like that there is still this point in their lives where everything changed for them that they've never really talked about. I'm sure most of us have private parts of ourselves that we don't share – whether consciously or not – with our other halves and I hope this novel can get people thinking about that.

I loved being able to write a romance about a happily married couple as I think there are so many of them in the world and they are often under-represented in literature. A long marriage is a wonderful thing and I hope that this novel celebrates that.

What is the main message you'd like readers to take away from *Bonnie and Stan*?

I love the idea of storing up warmth in your relationship and am sure that, in the busy times in which we live, it's something we could all do with thinking about. Being with someone for a long time isn't going to be plain sailing all the way, but if we can be kind to each other and explore life together and make happy memories then I think we've achieved a lot.